MARIANO'S CROSSING

A Novel

David M. Jessup

www.pronghornpress.org.

Joy's trick is to supply
Dry lips with what can cool and slake,
Leaving them dumbstruck also with an ache
Nothing can satisfy.

—Richard Wilbur
from *Hamlen Brook*

Acknowledgments

This book couldn't have been written without the insights and encouragement of people in several critique groups, aspiring writers all, including Sandy Deng, Ellen Bartlett, Deb Kotz, Connie Wiedell, Heidi Kerr Schlaefer, and especially Suzanna Banwell, whose tough approach to both my and her own writing proved most helpful.

My profound thanks go to Laura Pritchett, author of one of my favorite books, Hell's Bottom, Colorado, who provided valuable feedback and kept me plugging away with her belief in my book and her willingness to extend herself to promote it in countless ways.

I'm also indebted to Page Lambert, author and connector of writers with nature, for her sage advice and suggestions for revisions, Liane Norman, poet, literature professor and super sister-in-law, for her meticulous word-smithing and for helping me better understand the meaning of "show not tell," Gray Wolf and Kathi Willkomm (Shines) for their input regarding the history, culture and customs of Native Americans, Mike and Sharon Guli for their deep knowledge of period clothing, fashions and styles, Bill Meirath, historical preservation activist, for his knowledge about the Medina family and his efforts to preserve the Medina cemetery in Loveland, Colorado, and Kim Johnson, a rediscovered high school friend, who turned out to have a wonderful gift for ferreting out typos and inconsistencies in my copy.

I seem to write best in coffee shops, and I thank Loveland's Anthology Book Company and Coffee Tree lounge for putting up with many hours of me occupying one of their coffee tables.

For the history of the Medina family and early Loveland, Colorado, we are all indebted to the late Zethyl Gates, Loveland's historian, author of *Mariano Medina, Colorado Mountain Man.* Other works on which I relied for local history include Harold Dunning's *Over Hill and Dale*, and Ansel Watrous' *History of Larimer County*.

Finally, my thanks to Linda Jessup, my beloved wife since 1966, whose enthusiasm, support, critical feedback, excellent suggestions and gift for vivid imagery contributed much to the writing of this book.

PART 1

NOW

July 12, 1872

1

Takansy

Takansy tightens her grip on the soft doeskin shroud holding her daughter's body. The lightning is closer now, and she readies herself for a silent count of five. She prays her sleeping husband will not hear the sound she is about to make.

Despite herself, she jumps as a spasm of blue-white light lances through the window and illuminates her husband's Hawken rifle hanging on the wall beside her. It flickers lethally for a moment before the room goes black again.

Tensing, she begins. One, two, three, four. On five, the thunderclap vibrates through the soles of her moccasins and rattles a china cup against its shelf-mate. Its roar masks the whisper of leather against wood as she drags the bundle a few steps closer to the cabin door.

She pauses as the rumble rolls away into the blackness. Was it only last night, a lifetime ago, she had dragged Lena's lifeless body from the river, stared at her death-white skin, slightly open mouth, and reddish patches marring her neck and face?

Her throat still burns from the sounds she had made, strange animal noises, as she pulled the dress over her daughter's stiffening limbs, combed her hair for the last time, tried to close her resisting eyelids, then wrapped her in the doeskin shroud. Keening claws at her throat again, but she chokes it back. The wailing time must wait. Now her heart must be stone.

A stirring from Medina's bed propels her hand to the haft of her skinning knife. Would she actually use it against her husband of twenty-eight snows? She has no plan, no talking way, to explain her actions should he awake and confront her. A week ago, knifing him would have been unthinkable. Now, everything has changed.

When no further sound comes from the bed, her hand relaxes. Another flash pierces the room. She counts four beats this time. Another crash, another stealthy drag, and she is at the door. Her hand finds the cast iron latch and rests there.

The thunder is so loud she worries the sound of the storm, rather than the click of the latch, will rouse him. When the next thunderclap comes, she eases the door open and wrestles the corpse over the threshold. The rusty hinges, greased the day before with lard, do not betray her. Her shoulders relax. The storm's cool wind stirs the sweaty roots of her hair.

The wind! Like scouts for an advancing army, chill drafts slip past her, lift the corner of the oilcloth on the eating table, and chase the cabin's tobacco-pipe air into the next room across Medina's inert form. The storm had answered her prayer to cover the sounds of her escape, but she failed to consider its whispering outriders.

The door swings closed, *whumps* against the door jam. The latch falls into place with a metallic chunk.

"God be damned!"

The curse shocks her as much as the noise. She clutches for her rosary, then remembers. The black beads dot the floor where she flung them the night before. Glistening reminders of Jésu's betrayal.

She presses her ear against the keyhole and hears...what? The straining creak of bed ropes in their sideboard moorings? A footfall on the squeaky floorboard under the Hawken rifle?

Stifling a grunt, Takansy hefts the bundle and staggers off the porch. Her hip joints creak under the weight of Lena's fifteen-year-old body as she lurches toward the barn. A fat raindrop splatters on her cheek and runs into her mouth. It tastes of salt. She bites her tongue to make herself stop crying.

The smell of trampled horse droppings and sweaty leather overpower the scent of rain as she opens the barn door. She eases the leather bundle to the packed earth floor, grabs a handful of grain from the tack room and runs through a side door into the corral. Storm-spooked horses mill about, tails aloft, necks arched.

With the grain, she coaxes her daughter's horse into the barn.

"Shy Bird, you will carry Lena one last time." She slips a rawhide chin rope into the tall mare's mouth, slings the single rein over her neck and urges her toward the front door where Lena lies.

Scenting the body, the black mare snorts and sidesteps, eyes rimming white.

"Do not be afraid," Takansy says, to herself as much as to the horse. She strokes the animal's quivering shoulder and croons a sleep song from her childhood, the same song that had quieted Lena when she was a baby. With her other hand she reaches into her waist pouch to touch the beaded leather bag she had removed from her daughter's neck the day before, the otter pouch amulet she had given to Lena to bind their spirits together.

She pins the mare's chin rope against the ground with her foot and wrestles Lena's body up and over the horse's tall withers. Tying a rope on the shroud's ends, she pulls down hard to bend it in the middle and snub it down. Its ghastly stiffness unnerves her. She bites her hand to quell the swelling in her throat.

From the tack room she grabs two large blankets she had rolled up the day before and leads Shy Bird out of the barn. In the next lightning flash, the cabin jumps out from the blackness, its dark logs and white chinking momentarily reduced to a uniform, silvery gray. Nothing moves in the shadowy doorway.

She leads the horse beside the corral fence, climbs onto the first rail and hoists her right leg over the mare's back. She settles stiffly into place behind her daughter's body. It is the first time she has been on a horse since her vow to Jésu, taken in the long ago in atonement for her sins, a vow to never ride again. The vow no longer matters.

With her knees she urges the big mare forward toward the wooden toll bridge on the north side of the compound. Two more drops splat on her rein-holding hand. There is still no sign of life inside their house. Maybe she will make it. Then Medina can rave at her all he wants, beat her, even. He will never find Lena's body. She will make sure of it.

In the early fur-trapping days, when Medina slept on the edge of consciousness, he would have heard the soft brush of leather against floor, heard the door closing. At the Crossing he had grown less cautious, and at sixty-three snows, less keen of ear. Last night, shocked by Lena's death, he had drunk several cups of Taos Lightning. A grim smile pulls at her mouth. Two kinds of lightning are helping her this night.

At the bridge she reins in, waiting for the next roll of thunder. When it comes, she digs in her heels, and the mare clatters across in a burst of storm-sparked energy. They pass the fort, square and squat, its whitewashed stone walls slotted with black gun holes. Built by her husband after a Ute raid years ago, the fort was never used for its intended purpose. Just like the fancy schooling Medina had tried to cram into Lena. Bitter bile rises in Takansy's throat.

Takansy lopes upstream along the river trail directly into the storm. The splatters of rain are now laced with tiny needles of ice that sting her face, hail on the way, formed in the tumult of the thunderhead that blots out the night sky. Windy gusts snarl through low willows, chasing the dank scent of moss-coated river rocks away from the onrushing rain. Ahead, the rain forms a wall so dense that nothing can be seen beyond it, its growing roar overpowering the river's steady rush. The rain swallows them, drenching them in seconds, blotting out all other sound.

They arrive at a small stream entering from the south. Dry Creek, the settlers call it, but wet tonight, like her eyes. Her plan had been to follow this rivulet a while before returning to the main channel across a rocky sandstone ridge, a maneuver to slow her husband's pursuit. But the storm makes this bit of cunning unnecessary. Shy Bird's hoofprints have melted away without a trace.

The mare slows, picking her way through liquid mud, steam rising from her back. Warmth seeps into Takansy's legs. Despite her long absence from the back of a horse, she molds herself to Shy Bird's rocking rhythm, marveling at the body's recall of things past. Like when she was Lena's age, long hair blowing, face alight with smile, lithe body glued to a mare's back.

After an hour, the rain dribbles to a stop. A nearly full moon emerges under the cloud's western edge, bathing the landscape in startlingly bright silver light. Cottonwoods stretch dripping arms skyward. Pine needles glisten in the fresh washed breeze. A dismal beauty, considering what is now revealed in the river trail behind her: Shy Bird's hoofprints, stark as signposts, outlined in moonshadow. Hair prickles on her neck. She glances over her shoulder and urges Shy Bird into a trot.

Not far ahead is the hidden valley atop the sandstone ridge that stretches up to meet the moon. It was to have been their escape route, hers and Lena's trail to the north land, far from the reach of Medina and Lena's young suitor, John Alexander. Now, it would become her daughter's final resting place.

Lena. Why didn't I act sooner? But Medina had insisted their daughter attend the nuns' school, kept her there despite her unhappiness, despite the advances of that Castillo youth with his red top and haughty air. And worse, she had gone along with her husband because she had thought young John, the poor lumberman's son, to be the greater danger.

At the spot where the river flows around the ridge's base, she urges Shy Bird a few steps into the water next to a flat sandstone slab. She dismounts and unrolls the blankets next to each other over the stone. With a tug on the chin rope, she coaxes Shy Bird onto the first blanket, then the second, then retrieves the first and places it in front of the horse, urging it forward once again. Blanket by blanket, they leave the river trail without a trace. Behind a bush, she remounts and rides toward the saddle in the rimrock that forms the gateway to the hidden valley. From its summit she looks back. A cloak of white covers the ground around their house, extending out onto the plains. Hail, fallen there, but not here. Awed, she murmurs gratitude for the storm's gift.

Lena's corpse begins to slip. She pulls it back into place, recoiling at its coldness, then turns from the rimrock and crosses the valley to the higher crest on the west. She rides north, parallel to the cliff edge, through juniper trees and stunted pines rising darkly among a wild jumble of sandstone rock formations. Her eyes cast about for the one she is seeking. The rock spirits whisper around her. She feels lost.

At last she sees the entrance to the hideaway. Two huge sandstone slabs leaning together to form a tipi-shaped cave screened from view by a thick juniper bush. Lena's resting place. The secret spot revealed to her by Otter Woman, coming to her in the form of a gray jay. Its purpose had only come to her yesterday as she keened Lena's death song. In this cave she will do for Lena in death what she failed to do in life—wrest her from her husband's control.

To the east, the storm sparks and crashes over the vast plains beyond their house. She imagines Medina sleeping there, and bitterness seizes her heart. If only he had not sent their daughter back to that accursed school, Lena would be alive today.

Yet, as she dismounts and leans against the leather shroud, feeling the shape of Lena's stiff legs, there spreads in her a guilt so profound she must grab Shy Bird's mane to keep from falling to the rocky ground.

2

Medina

Medina pulls the buffalo robe over his ears to shut out the roaring. The small window next to his bed shakes from the force of the wind. The eaves groan. Then hail hits the roof with the clatter of a Gatling gun and chases away any hope of slumber.

Lena's image looms through the fog in his mind. Death-pale with reddish blotches on her face and neck, lips swollen and cracked, hair matted with river mud.

He pulls himself to the edge of his bed. His stomach revolts. Before he can reach the chamber pot, a slug of acidy vomit erupts onto the floor between his bare legs. He drops to his hands and knees, his back arching at the sour smell of last night's whiskey. When the spasms fade, he rises and lights a candle with a phosphor stick. Even before its flame forces the blackness into flickering retreat, he senses that he is alone.

"Woman!"

He peers through the door at Takansy's empty sleeping pad. Her moccasins are gone. Her leather bag that usually hangs from a nail above her sleeping robe—gone. *Where is she? Out in this storm?* The howl of wind and clatter of hail make it hard to think.

He kicks at her sleeping robe and nearly falls, accidentally snuffing the candle. Cursing, he rekindles the wick and gropes his way toward the table where Takansy had laid his daughter's corpse.

A prickle suddenly runs up his neck. He lurches forward and thrusts the candle toward the table. The shroud is gone! The ribbons and prizes from Lena's riding competitions are scattered about. The silver cross he had placed on Lena's chest lies broken in the corner, its shadow dancing crazily against the wall. On the floor, a scattering of black rosary beads wink at him, insect-like. He thrusts the candle toward the cast iron stove, the cupboard with fine china, the altar where Takansy's crucifix used to sit. Nothing.

He sways as if kicked by a mule. His low moan grows into a hoarse bellow. *Even in death she takes my daughter from me?* He hurls the candle against his wife's altar. In the sudden darkness he finds a chair and smashes it into the table. A flying chunk of wood grazes his head. His next blow strikes the dish cupboard. Glass shards fly in all directions. He retreats toward the fireplace and sweeps the mantle clear with a chair leg. He gasps as his toe stubs the leg of another chair, but the affront only increases his blind thrashing. He destroys a wall painting and demolishes his wife's basket of beadwork.

Panting, he lights an oil lamp, slumps into a chair and pulls moccasins over his bleeding feet. He will track her down. He will force her to tell him where she has hidden Lena. *I will bring my Lena back home. Give her last rites, bury her in the family cemetery.*

He pulls on his clothes, cinches on his belt and tomahawk, lifts Old Lady Hawken from its wall perch and lets himself out the door. Hail covers the ground. As the storm cloud slides past the moon, he sees the open barn door. He runs to the corral and counts horses. Shy Bird is missing.

"*Mierda!*" He pounds his fist into a corral rail. *Which way?*

He saddles his big roan and tries to remember what Takansy told him about Flathead Indian burials. Not like the barbaric Cheyenne and

Arapaho who leave corpses on tree branches to be ravaged by crows. His wife's people bury their dead in shallow graves with things they will need in the next world—knives, clothes, cooking pots. Then they pile on stones to keep scavengers away. Most of her tribe, staunchly Catholic since the days of the Blackrobes, also give last rites. But he suspects that despite her long devotion to Jésu, Takansy has something else in mind. Something primitive, something from before the time of the Blackrobes. He grinds his teeth at the thought of it.

Stones. He rides across the toll bridge and turns upstream along the river trail, west toward the sandstone hogbacks. Somewhere up there, he thinks, on the ridges that flank the great mountains. *Plenty of stones.*

In less than a mile he reaches the edge of the hail blanket. The river trail is again visible, but no prints have survived. At the fork of Dry Creek, he studies the ground, then chooses to follow the main stem of the river, a hunch. Perhaps the rainfall will have been lighter to the west, and he will pick up the trail, if this is the way she has gone. He kicks the roan into a trot.

Two years ago on that first school day, on the steps of St. Mary's academy, Lena had stood next to the daughters of Denver's wealthiest businessmen, black hair framing her face, more beautiful than any of them. He had sacrificed much to give her the education and social acceptance denied to him. He had protected her from that young pig, Castillo, and steered her away from her decent, but poor, suitor, John Alexander. *Now she is dead. Takansy's doing.* If only his wife had not lured Lena away from the school. *Damn her!*

He catches himself grinding his teeth. His jaws hurt. Anger, he reminds himself, often makes things worse. And with that notion comes another that nips at the edges of his mind. The blame for Lena's death may spread beyond where he wishes it to go.

3

John Alexander

John Alexander paces in circles beside Boulder Creek, where he has been waiting since midnight. The water swirls and gurgles beside him. His nerves feel as though they might snap at the next lightning flash. The slightest sound freezes him in place. A rustle of leaves. A clink of his horse's bit. The moan of the wind. *Lena should have been here by now.*

Dark thoughts assail him. Maybe Lena's pa got wind of their plan. Mariano Medina's anger is not something John Alexander wants to think about. And what about Lena's mama? She's quiet, but Indian watchful. Those strange, gray eyes don't miss much. If she found out, she'd go right to her husband, despite their quarrels over Lena.

He swallows hard at his betrayal of the Medinas, then hardens himself to the course he has chosen. *They deserve to lose their daughter, those two. Lena must be rescued!*

Then a more troublesome notion pushes in: What if Lena has changed her mind? He recalls her indecision, bending to the will of first one parent, then the other. *Worse, what if Lena has gone off with Richard Castillo?*

An image of his rival's aristocratic nose, sneering smile and lock of dark red hair flits into his mind. His gut turns a somersault.

Dawn brightens his line of sight, even as it darkens his hopes. He throws stones into the creek, fusses with his tack and gear, straightens his shirt and tightens his belt. He hunkers, stands, hunkers.

Finally, as the sun breaks around the edge of the receding thunderhead, he mounts up and lopes downstream a mile to Tim and Jennie Goodale's place. *Perhaps they will know something.* A thin plume of smoke rises out of their tipi's smoke hole. Tim Goodale stands just outside the dripping lodge flap, stretching, snapping his suspenders. His eyebrows knit into a bristly frown as John approaches.

"You looking for Lena, too?"

John pulls up short. "What do you mean? Who else was here?"

"A man from that Catholic school. Caretaker, he claimed. Said the nuns sent him looking for her. Came a-riding in last night, woke us up."

"When did Lena leave the school?"

"Two nights ago."

"But that's the wrong..." John catches himself, almost saying it was the wrong day, a day too early. He tries to sound casual. "She run away again?"

"That's the queer thing," Goodale says. "The man, a Mr. Oliver, said Lena was sick. Bad fever. In bed with it. No shape to travel. Even a little out of her head at times. That's why they's worried. They was giving her poultices and the like, trying to get her better. Then they tucks her in Wednesday night, and the next morning she's plumb gone. Disappeared."

"Wednesday." John Alexander fights to keep his chest from exploding. "When did she get sick?"

"She come dragging in a week before, the man said, dress all tore up, scratches on her arms, told them she'd taken a fall off a horse, although that's hard to believe for a rider such as the likes of her."

Goodale's Shoshone wife steps out of the tipi carrying a steaming black pot.

"Light on down here and have yourself some coffee," she says.

Then she recognizes him. "You have seen Lena? We are big worried. She is sick, and gone from…"

John cuts her off.

"Which way'd he go? The school man?"

Goodale answers, "Boulder City, to ask around. I told him I'd head to the Crossing to let Mariano know. That's why we's up so early."

John wheels his horse around. "I'm going to look for her."

Goodale shouts something back, but John Alexander doesn't hear. A dark suspicion grows in his mind. A week ago, Lena had an "accident," dress torn, arms scratched. *No horse did that.*

He turns south toward Denver City and pushes his pinto into a ground-eating lope. He will find Richard Castillo. He will force that red-topped bastard to tell what he knows, where Lena has gone, why she left a day early. His hands, holding the reins, ball into fists.

PART 2

THEN

Ten Years Earlier
July 1862

David M. Jessup

4

John Alexander
July 1862

"John Alexander! Where are ye, boy? Is it another whupping ye'll be wanting, then?"

Pa's voice came rolling down the timbered hill from the sawmill to the hollowed out oak tree where Johnnie sat reading a forbidden book. Johnnie let the call roll past. He was good at shutting out the world.

Mama was always nagging at him to pay attention. "Don't be a fencepost, Johnnie," she'd say. "Shake a leg or your Pa'll get out the razor strap." She was always trying to protect him from the razor strap.

"John! Get up here!"

Insistent now, Pa's voice caused Johnnie to sigh. He was wrapped up in the story of *Malaeska, Indian Wife of the White Hunter*. Pa didn't allow any books in their house except the Bible and *Pilgrim's*

Progress, so the dime novel had to be kept hidden in the hollow of a tree.

It had been slipped to him last November, right before his eighth birthday by his Uncle Blackie. This morning, instead of joining his father in the sawmill, Johnnie had snuck away to the book's hiding place and begun to read. Danforth, the book's hero, was about to be tortured and killed. It took two more shouts from Pa, each angrier than the last, for Johnnie to poke the book back into the tree hole and hurry up the wagon track toward the sawmill.

It was one of those damp, hot days in early July when people in Illinois broke out in a sweat just standing still. Bugs were everywhere. Gnats swarmed around Johnnie's face and snuck into the corners of his eyes. Thumb-sized locusts, black with big red eyes, crawled up tree trunks and thrummed their deafening drone. He mostly liked bugs. Not the pesky gnats, but the others—fireflies, locusts, 'hoppers, and especially praying mantises. His bug collection, pinned to a large shingle and displayed on a shelf in the corner of their shared bedroom, fascinated his younger sister Mattie, disgusted his older sister Jennie, annoyed his father, and worried his mother, who fretted whenever his father was annoyed.

As he neared the sawmill, Johnnie's spirits sank into a sour mix of guilt and trepidation. As the oldest boy, he should be more willing to help his struggling family. But the sawmill boiler unnerved him. Looming ten feet tall at the back of the shed, its fiery maw demanded wood. Its open grate smiled crazily, a row of grinning orange teeth. Smoke puffed from three seams near its top, dragon nostrils in a black, sightless face.

Panting, Johnnie pushed through the sawmill door. Smoke seared his lungs. The boiler's roar assaulted his ears, darkness his eyes. The sawmill had no windows, just an opening in one side for the logs. The only other light came in between the slats of the wall boards, casting tiger stripes on the boards stacked along the sides of the shed to protect them from the southern Illinois rains. Two rats, big as squirrels, scuttled up the boards, turned their glittery eyes on him, then dove into an opening between the boards. Johnnie hated rats.

"It's about time." Pa stood by the boiler holding a chunk of wood. Streams of sweat ran down his face.

He opened the boiler door and tossed the wood in. His hair and beard were red, and in the firelight they were even redder. His eyes sparked orange.

"Get your lazy self over here. Ye know I can't manage this all by myself."

Johnnie cringed. He should be used to the whip of his father's voice, the constant chastisement. But it always stung, because Johnnie knew Pa was right. His job—*his family duty*—was to stoke that boiler, and here he was, late again.

Pa picked up another piece of wood and tossed it Johnnie's way. Johnnie tried to catch it, but it smacked against his knees. Pa looked away, disgusted, picked up a wrench and stepped onto a side rail to reach a pressure valve poking out of the boiler top. He twisted the wrench. Hot steam spewed out.

The pressure valve had been broken for months. What with the sawing and releasing the pressure every few minutes, Pa didn't have time to feed the wood in. That was Johnnie's job. Rubbing his knee, he hurried to the woodpile as his father returned to mind the saw blade at the far end of the shed. The blade whirred into action and screamed its way into the log that Pa pushed into it.

Chunk by chunk, Johnnie fed wood into the boiler. He handled each piece gingerly, dropping several out of fear that a rat might be perched on the other end. When the boiler was roaring again, and his ears felt deafened by the noise, he stepped outside for a short break. That's when he saw the praying mantis.

It was climbing up a dogwood branch a few feet away from the boiler shed. Heart quickening, Johnnie drew closer. The bug was huge. Its lower body breathed in an out, like a bellows. Its big claws were folded up in front. Pa said the bugs were like Catholic priests, looking holy, but really just waiting to snatch you up.

The mantis had the biggest eyes Johnnie had ever seen on a bug, not ones you can see into like human eyes, but dead orbs on a head that swiveled from side to side, searching for things to eat. Johnnie leaned closer. The insect's head stopped and looked straight at him. The hairs on the back of Johnnie's neck rose. He knew it was silly, but it felt like that thing was about to grab him.

Then the mantis caught sight of a firefly sitting a ways up the branch. Its ugly head swiveled around and it began, ever so slowly, stalking the smaller bug. Johnnie held his breath. Then the claws flicked out. The little bug wiggled and twisted, but couldn't escape.

The mantis pulled it down and commenced to eat it alive, one bite at a time. The lightning bug kept struggling until its head got bit off.

Johnnie was as fixed on the mantis as he'd been on the book, lost in a dream cocoon. Then Pa's voice began to push through.

"Boy, get in here, quick!"

Johnnie ran back into the boiler shed. The sudden dark blinded him.

Pa's shout came from the side rail on the boiler. "I got the wrong wrench. Bring that eighteen-incher over there, the big one, and be quick about it."

Pa sounded scared, which made Johnnie scared. Pa's outline slowly revealed itself. He was pointing into a dark corner.

Johnnie ran to the spot, but his eyes didn't adjust fast enough. He tripped on a board and fell. He groped for the tool box, his fingers finding nothing but dirt.

"Damn ye, John, this thing's about to blow!"

Pa never cussed. Johnnie's throat closed up.

A god-awful sound roared through the shed like a mountain caving in. The blast of steam blew Pa clean off the side rail. He flew through the air and landed a few feet away on his back. His hands clawed up then fell down at his sides. He didn't move.

Down on the floor, Johnnie hugged dirt as the searing wave blew over him. When the steam cleared, he raised his head and saw his father's face lit up by a shaft of light. His eyes were shut. His face and neck were ugly red. His mouth opened. He shook a little and coughed. Little flecks of pink foam flew out and caught in his beard.

Johnnie knew he should run for help. But he couldn't tear his eyes away from that foamy, bloody spit. He couldn't tear his mind away from the growing horror that this was his fault.

After a long time—a minute? an hour?—Pa's eyes finally opened. Johnnie, released from his trance, scrabbled over to him. Pa's shirt was wet and hot. He smelled like scalded chicken.

"Pa? Pa!" Johnnie didn't recognize his own voice.

"Get Mama. Get Uncle Blackie." Pa's voice was weak, raspy.

He closed his eyes, and despite a few hard shakes Johnnie gave to his shoulders, kept them closed. Johnnie tore himself away and made for the door. The rats scuttled into the pile of boards. The boiler, its top seam split open like a cracked skull, leered at him through its still-smiling grate. Johnnie ran like the devil himself was about to snatch him up.

The wagon ride down the hill was the longest Johnnie had ever taken. Uncle Blackie drove the mules while Johnnie bounced around in the back, trying to keep Pa's head from hitting the wagon bed. When they finally wrestled Pa's still form out of the wagon, through the door and into the bedroom, Johnnie's trousers were spotted with blood. He watched the red dissolve into the faded brown fabric darkened by something else…his own piss.

Once inside the house, he stood against the wall with a wood crate pulled in front of him to hide the stains. Doc McGill arrived, black coat, black beard and black bag, looking like an undertaker. Mama ushered him into the bedroom where Pa lay.

Then the wait began.

"What happened, Johnnie?' Mama's mouth was all hitched up on one side. Her right hand twisted at her apron, her left cradled two-year-old Robert, wide-eyed, sucking on his booey rag for comfort.

Johnnie couldn't meet her eyes. "I don't know. I was outside, and, and there was this big roar, steam everywhere, and I ran inside and found Pa, and he…he…"

"What was you doing outside?" Jennie cut him off. His sister had that bird dog look for sniffing out lies. She was only nine, a year older than Johnnie, but acted as if she were boss of the household.

"I had to fetch a…a rag. From the wagon."

"Whatever for?" Jennie's eyes bored into him, icy blue, like Pa's.

"I…to, to wipe something up, an oil spill, and I ran back in, and Pa had red bubbles coming out of his mouth, and…"

"Why wasn't you in there with him, stoking that boiler?"

Johnnie swallowed hard. "I had to, you know, take a leak."

"You said you was getting a rag."

Johnnie felt like one of those rats trying to hide in the woodpile while Jennie pulled the boards back. He clamped his mouth shut and looked away.

"He's lying, Mama," Jennie said. She stepped between Mama and their two smaller sisters, Mattie, age four and Anna, age three, and stretched out her arms to enfold them. They all stared at him, stair-steps of accusation.

Johnnie let his back slide down the wall until the crate blocked them from view.

David M. Jessup

Then the bedroom door creaked open. Doc McGill came out wiping sweat from his face with a white handkerchief.

"He's going to live, Emma Jane, but his lungs have been scalded. There's some damage inside. Hard to say how much. His arm's been wrenched clean out of its socket, and his leg's broke. For the next couple of months he'll have to be mostly in that bed there. The biggest danger is he'll get down with pneumonia while he's healing." He rolled down his sleeves and buttoned the cuffs.

Johnnie swallowed hard. His story of the explosion would soon be contradicted by Pa. And he realized, with a guilty heave of his stomach, that he'd been half hoping that Pa wouldn't live to tell the tale. He wanted to crawl into the woodpile, disappear.

Mama handed little Robert over to Jennie. Her mouth twitched again, and her eyes got that same look as when Pa chastised her for some breach of his strict rules. Johnnie hated that look.

"He'll never be quite the same man, Emma Jane," Doc McGill said. "The scarring'll leave him short of breath. And he'll be crippled up some. Won't be able to do as much, especially for the next little while. You're going to need some help around here."

Johnnie shrunk back at the look Doc McGill gave him. Had Pa told him what happened?

"Maybe it's for the best," Mama said. "He was fixin' to join the Illinois Volunteers and go off and fight for Mr. Lincoln. We'd been short-handed either way."

"I'll help" Jennie said.

Johnnie stood there, tongue-tied.

Doc McGill walked to the door. "One last thing, Emma Jane. This climate is poison for folks with lung problems." He waved his hand through the thick air as if waving away a fly. "Too moist. Too hot. A miasma that makes things worse. I'm advising my consumption patients to move west where the air is dry and pure. Colorado Territory's a good place, they say. And it's growing fast. They have need of lumber in the settlements." He nodded and left.

Mama disappeared into the bedroom, followed by Jennie, Mattie and Anna.

Johnnie slipped out of the house and made his way into the back yard where Mac, his year-old Irish setter, bounded up with wagging tail and panting tongue. Johnnie knelt down, buried his face in the soft red mane. He felt like he was drowning.

"Good Mac, good Mac." The words changed to sobs.

Mac whined and licked his ear.

He felt a hand on his shoulder. Ashamed, he whirled around. Mattie stood there, brown eyes wide. He drew her in with a hug to keep her from staring at his tears.

'Twasn't your fault Johnnie," she said.

"Thanks, Mattie." He wished it were true, but inside, in that secret place where he hid things from the world, he knew it was his doing.

Two months later, Pa announced he'd be setting off for Denver City with a wagon load of goods. "Soon as I find a place to settle and build a homestead and new sawmill, I'll be back to fetch you. About a year, I expect." He cast a hard blue eye on Johnnie. "Suppose you can help your mama better than you helped me?"

"Yes, sir." The words came out strangled.

A week later, Johnnie watched from his hiding place as Pa rolled away down the road. Two black soot smudges peered like eyes on the back of the wagon's canvas cover. Just before it disappeared around a turn, Mac stuck his head out of the canvas opening. Johnnie had begged Pa to leave the dog with him, but Pa had refused.

"I'll be needing a watch dog," he said.

Johnnie slumped beside the tree trunk, throat burning.

5

Takansy
July 1862

Takansy stirred on the buffalo robe. It seemed unusually hot this awakening. At first she blamed the sickness that had laid her low these past six months, dried up her breast milk and left rough patches on her skin. Maybe the heaviness came from something in the July air, or the stillness. She lay there, listening to silence.

Her husband, Medina, was usually first up, but he was in Denver City buying trade goods. What of her children? Antonio was probably minding the trading post, Lena would be with the horses, Martín, her strange middle son, doing beadwork. And little Rosita? She cocked her head toward the bedroom door. Her squirrel-sized, frail daughter must still be asleep in her own sick bed, a nest of blankets in a dresser drawer in the next room.

Pale light slanted through the curtained window onto their

rope-weave bed. A gray, overcast day, robbed of Sun's energy. She stretched and rubbed sleep from eyes. She pulled on her moccasins, buckskin pants, and calico shirt. *Why am I so cold, even during the long sun days?* She wished again for the tiny blue healing roots that grew in the land of her birth.

Where is Miss Gracie? She should be padding around the other room preparing to breast-feed little Rosita. Takansy's heart felt both big and small thinking of the good-natured woman. Sarah Grace Boutwell. The light-skins called her Miss Gracie. She lived downstream with her husband and little Thomas, born a few days before Rosita, six months ago.

When Takansy fell ill and was unable to nurse, Miss Gracie took little Rosita to her own ample breast and kept the little girl alive. She would feed both children at once, like suckling lambs. This prompted frowns and murmurs among the settlers. Takansy was not sure why, since such things were common among her own Flathead people on the Bitterroot River far to the north. She felt grateful to Miss Gracie, but a little jealous as well, at being unable to provide what a mother should provide.

Is this sickness a punishment? The question nagged at her, a persistent reminder of the great sin she committed in the long ago.

She eased herself onto her knees, made the crossing sign and began her morning prayers. She asked Jésu to help Martín find his spirit path, to curb Antonio from his wild ways, to help Lena learn the way of the horse, to remove her own feelings of jealousy toward Miss Gracie. And, as always, she prayed most ardently for Rosita. Her mind swelled with the remembered sensation of those weak little hands clutching hopefully on her finger, the sweet smell of Rosita's black hair. She begged Jésu to breathe strength into the tiny child.

She waited for a sign from Jésu, but no answer came. The oppressive silence was beginning to unnerve her.

Rising, she hurried to comb out her hair and rebraid it. Slipping a leather ring over the end of each braid, she turned and opened the bedroom door.

Miss Gracie sat still as stone in the big chair beside the dresser. Her eyes, veined red and hollow above tear-streaked cheeks, held Takansy's for a moment then fell to the tiny child lying in her arms, death-gray, unmoving.

"Oh, Mrs. Medina, I'm so sorry."

Takansy gripped the edge of the dresser to keep from being heart-hammered to the floor. She crossed herself and plucked Rosita out of Miss Gracie's arms. Her fingers traced the girl's eyebrows, nose and ears. They rested for a moment on the tiny dew lip that had tried to draw life from Takansy's un-fruitful breasts. Then she laid Rosita in the dresser drawer, drew the girl's sleeping blanket over her face, and slumped into a chair. Her hands fell into her lap.

She knew she should say something, a comfort word, to Miss Gracie, but the talking way would not come. Miss Gracie leaned over, wrapped Takansy in her arms and began to cry.

Takansy wished she could cry.

At dusk, Rosita was laid in a pine box and set in a storage shed to await burial in the hilltop cemetery the next day. Takansy retrieved the obsidian blade she kept hidden in the back of her altar. It gleamed black in the fading light, round and flat, with a razor edge. She tucked it under her shirt, grabbed the foot-high silver cross from atop the altar, slipped unseen from their house and walked to the river, a black ribbon flowing between cobbled banks. She squatted facing the water, placed the cross on a rock in front of her and took out the blade. Bumps rose on her bare skin as she pulled off her shirt. She felt numb. Her right hand found the horizontal scar on her left arm just below the shoulder. Atonement for her great sin. She rubbed the ridged welt with her fingers. It comforted her, remembering how, on that black day long ago, Jésu had directed the blade to her arm instead of her throat.

"Jésu, I am asking you to guard my Rosita in the spirit world, to welcome her in your loving arms. Forgive me my sins."

She bowed to the cross and pressed obsidian into her flesh just below the scar. Blood trickled down her arm and dripped onto a stone. Strangely, she felt no pain. She tucked the obsidian back into a blanket fold, opened her mouth and began keening. The unearthly sound rose into the air and echoed against the great cottonwood branches thrusting skeleton-like into the near-dark sky. She rocked back and forth, catching her breath as she leaned back, crying out as she rocked forward.

After some minutes, her voice growing hoarse, she heard footfalls.

"Mrs. Medina?" The voice was Miss Gracie's. "Mrs. Medina? Are you...what are you doing here?"

Takansy made no response.

A hand touched her shoulder. "You're...you've hurt yourself! What have you done?" Miss Gracie moved around to face her. "You're bleeding! Come with me."

Takansy kept her eyes closed.

Then another woman's voice, low-pitched, heavy, breathless.

"Come, Grace, let's go get her husband. He'll know what to do. There's something...unnatural going on. She's hexed, maybe."

Takansy recognized Mrs. Blackhurst, another neighbor. She was glad when they hurried away.

Not long after, Medina arrived. He took her hand and tugged.

"*Mi amor*, come." His voice, his touch, were gentle.

She allowed herself to be pulled to her feet and drawn into his embrace. His body felt warm. Over his shoulder she saw Lena looking at her with fearful, wide eyes. Only then did the numbness leave her. She must return to this world, to the daughter that still lived. The last daughter. She must get well for the sake of Lena.

She turned from Medina, pulled her shirt on, picked Lena up and held her close.

"It will be all right, my flower. All right."

She felt Lena's arms tighten around her neck. A fear suddenly seized her, that things would not be all right, and the force of it nearly brought her down.

6

Medina
July 1862

"Enough! You must stop the cutting!" Medina pulled a cloth bandage around Takansy's arm, shredded the ends and tied them together. She sat, unresponsive, on their bed. "Rosita is with Jésu. Another scar on your arm will not help her. You hear me, woman?"

He shook her, made his voice stern, but realized he might as well be talking to a stone. Her gray eyes stared right through him, lost in another world. The same ghost eyes he'd seen when they first met, twenty years ago near Fort Bridger. Then, as now, she had cut herself with that cursed black stone. She had never told him why. Why was she reacting so strongly to Rosita's death? With five children, it was against the odds that all would survive. He looked at her weathered face, remembered its beauty when he had fought so hard to win her, and wondered at its mysteries.

He eased her down and covered her with a blanket, blew out the oil lamp, stepped into the main room and closed the door.

Lena jumped from a chair and ran into his arms. "Is Mami hurt? I saw blood."

He held her close. "She will be fine, *mi hija*. Her arm is bandaged. The resting, she needs. You, too." He led her into the side bedroom she shared with Martín. "To sleep now."

He helped her slip into the flannel nightdress he had bought at great expense from his friend Jones in Denver City. Such a beautiful little five-year-old, slender, light-skinned, large brown eyes, wide apart. Intelligent, too. Of all his children, she learned fastest in Miss Gracie's lessons. One day she would be educated, learn proper manners, charm the new settlers flooding in around them. He wished he could say the same for his other children.

"Papi, will Rosita go to heaven?" she asked as he tucked her in.

"Yes. We to bury her tomorrow. With prayers, to send her to *Diós*." He hoped he was right.

Takansy had asked him to get a priest, but the nearest one was in Boulder City, thirty miles away. He had refused, saying that God wouldn't allow an innocent child to remain in Purgatory even without last rites. He hoped it was true.

The next day the sun shone hot in the stone-walled cemetery he had built on the hill above their compound. The ground was drier here, away from the river. He and Louie Papa, Takansy's son from her first marriage, chopped through the hardpan with picks, then used shovels for the softer dirt underneath. In two hours they fashioned a grave big enough for Rosita's tiny body.

Eight of them gathered in a semi-circle as they lowered the shrouded body into the ground—little Lena, shy Martín, brash Antonio, quiet Louie Papa, stone-faced Takansy. Miss Gracie was there, too, teary-eyed, and the ample Mrs. Blackhurst, occupying more space than any two of them. They covered the little body with dirt, then stones. Medina recited a prayer in Spanish that he remembered from his boyhood.

Takansy just stared.

A month later, as mid-August winds began to dry the grama grass into brown flags on stalks, he and Louie Papa erected the grave stone. *Rosita Medina—Born and Died 1862.* Medina wiped his hands on his buckskin leggings and pointed to the four-foot high stone wall that surrounded his cemetery.

"One day we all to sleep here." He felt proud of the wall with its expensive iron gate arch with the cross on top. The late afternoon sun tinged it orange.

Louie Papa nodded. At eighteen, he seemed to be less talkative with every passing year. Like his mother, Medina mused. She had refused to come with them to plant the marker.

They turned and walked back down the hill. As they neared the trading post, a wagon rolled across his toll bridge and came to a stop at the hitch rail. He recognized the two soot smudges on the back canvas flap. William Alexander. He forced himself to smile as the Scot climbed off the wagon and limped toward him. He had known many of his kind during the fur trade days. This blue-eyed settler with the strangely mottled red and white beard was more unfriendly than most. Alexander had arrived last September to build a sawmill five miles upstream, but so far Medina had seen little of the man.

He put on his trading voice. "Señor Alexander. Good day. At your service."

William Alexander looked past him toward the store. "I'll be needing supplies. Long trip." He handed Medina a list on a scrap of newsprint.

Medina glanced at it, embarrassed by his inability to read. "Let us to go find Antonio. You travel far? Where?

"Back to the states. Illinois. To retrieve my family, bring them here." Despite his limp, the Scot's long legs carried him ahead.

"You to travel in this wagon?"

"I'll be selling the wagon in Denver City and buying a rowboat. It's faster. Another fellow is going with me. We'll float the Platte down to the Missouri and catch a river boat there."

They clumped up the stairs into the store. Antonio was not there, but Martín stood behind the counter, wavy black locks framing his pale face, like a girl's. Medina handed the paper to his son, glad he had persuaded Miss Gracie to begin teaching his children to read.

"Please to gather these for Señor Alexander."

Martín frowned at the paper, then nodded, turned and began lifting potatoes from a gunny sack onto the counter, counting as he went.

Medina asked, "Where is Antonio?"

Martín continued to count potatoes. "Fifty. He said he was going to the tavern."

Medina turned. "A thousand pardons, Señor Alexander. Please to seat yourself. I go to find my other son."

The Scot's bushy brows knotted up at the crucifix above the door as he sat down.

Medina bowed and hurried outside. As he strode through his compound, he took in his whitewashed log house, sturdy trading post, big barn, tavern and sleeping rooms where travelers on the Overland Stage Line spent the night. Of all the mountain men who had colonized the Crossing five years ago, he had become the most successful. The rest had mostly moved away, taking their Indian wives with them. Bill McGaa to Denver City, the Janis brothers to the Poudre, Tim and Jenny Goodale to Boulder Creek. He missed them, their easy camaraderie. In their place had come gold seekers, then people who wanted to plant crops and build homes and start towns. Lots of them. Good for business, but the rapid changes made Medina uneasy. Among the mountain men he had earned a place of respect. With these new settlers, especially men like William Alexander, the respect seemed to be missing.

The Overland Stage Coach was parked in front of the tavern, alongside three horses. He recognized Jack Slade's big dun gelding. Slade managed several stage stops along the Overland Trail. His visits were dicey affairs. The man was a good station master, but when he got liquored up he got mean. Medina heard stories about him, how he would shoot his pistol at bottles and mirrors and pick fights in saloons. Later he would apologize and pay the saloon owner for the damage. He had killed a man in Julesburg, it was said.

Medina pushed through the tavern door into the gloom. The sudden, sharp crack of a pistol shot and the sound of breaking glass sent him into an instant crouch. His tomahawk was in his hand before he knew it. He jumped to the side of the doorway, willing his eyes to adjust. When they did he saw Jack Slade, brown felt hat cocked on his head, squinting down a pistol barrel at a whiskey bottle on the shelf behind the bar.

"Stop, *hijo de puta*!" Antonio's voice!

Medina's throat closed. His fourteen-year-old son stood at one of the tables on the other side of the room with Medina's long-barreled

Hawken rifle leveled at Jack Slade's chest. The heavy gun wobbled in his hand. Takansy sat in a chair beside him, rooted, stone still like everyone else in the room.

Slade turned, black mustache twisted into a snarl. He raised his hat brim to get a better look.

"What'd you say, boy?" His words slurred together. His pistol swung around as he turned.

Medina's heart slammed as the big Hawken flashed and roared in Antonio's hand. But the bullet smashed into the ceiling. At the last moment, Takansy had thrust the rifle barrel upward. Splinters of wood trickled down onto the table through the smoke.

Slade blinked at Antonio. Medina, tomahawk raised, rushed him. But the stage boss raised his hand and smiled. "No harm done. I ain't going to shoot a boy." He reached back for the bar, lost his balance and fell, cracking his head on the brass foot rail. The pistol slid off his belly and thumped onto the floor.

Medina thrust his tomahawk back into his waist band and waved at Antonio.

"*Vente!* Help me to get him to a room, to sleep this off." They dragged the stationmaster to the porch and loaded him into a wheelbarrow. On the way to the sleeping room, Medina vented his fury at Antonio.

"*Idiota!* The man is dangerous! You have put our family at risk. You have not even the brains of a cockroach! For why you..."

"He was shooting our whiskey. A man has to defend our property, our honor." Antonio was smiling, pleased with himself.

"You are not a man! You are fourteen. And stupid! He will pay for everything, pay more than what he destroyed."

"But Papá, I'm..."

"*Callete!* You will not..."

Just then William Alexander came out of the trading post, hitching toward them on his cane, eyebrows arched.

"What is happening?" He stared at the drool hanging from Jack Slade's sagging lips.

"An accident. He fell, hit his head. He will to wake soon."

The Scot wrinkled up his nose. "That is what happens when you have a tavern, Mr. Medina. The devil's playground. Not fit for decent people."

He turned and limped toward his wagon, now filled with the

goods Martín had loaded. He pulled himself into the driver's seat and wheeled away toward the road to Denver City.

Decent people. They would soon outnumber the Slades. Medina looked at his son, at the smirk on his handsome face, at the violence in the boy's wild black eyes, and saw a reflection of himself.

7

John Alexander
September 1863

More than a year had passed since the boiler blasted Pa into an unconscious heap in the sawmill. Johnnie was dreaming about the explosion when he was jolted awake by the sudden stop of their wagon. It was around noon on a bright fall day on the last leg of his family's journey from Eden, Illinois, to their new homestead on the Big Thompson River in Colorado Territory. It had taken their sway-back horse, Old Dun, two months to pull them across the plains. They had rushed through sinful Denver City, travelling north sixty miles along the Overland Trail to the Big Thompson River, where it emerged from the hogback ridges onto the plains.

Johnnie pulled himself up to take a look around. Just beyond a pole fence bordering the road, he saw a young girl, no more than six or seven, racing across the pasture atop the most spirited horse he'd ever seen. He couldn't imagine being able to control such a horse. Yet the girl, dark hair flying, seemed glued to the magnificent animal's back. She rode without a saddle, bare feet hugging the horse's sides, brown skin on black hide. She smiled with such delight that Johnnie's breath caught in his throat.

He climbed out of the wagon, barking his shin on the way down, and made his way to the fence. A shout pierced the air to his right. He turned to see a tall Indian woman calling out in a language he didn't understand, her smile as delighted as the girl's. She waved at the girl. The loping horse pulled up sharp, digging black patches in the turf, snorting. There followed a musical, throaty flow of words that Johnnie took to be instruction. The girl nodded several times, then turned back into the pasture. The woman's gaze was so intense and adoring it made Johnnie look away. He wondered how it felt to be looked at like that.

When the woman turned to look at him, he was startled by her eyes, light gray. Spooky looking.

"My daughter." Her voice was breathy, with a funny accent. "She riding very good, yes?" The word "very" sounded like "berry."

"Yes, Ma'am." He turned back to watch the girl and avoid those gray eyes.

The girl guided the horse, a powerfully built black mare, through some quick turns, sprints and stops. Snorts gusted from the animal's nostrils. Sweat darkened its flanks. He took in the tangy scent of it.

The woman moved closer. Johnnie swallowed and glanced back at their wagon. He'd never been this close to an Indian. When savages had visited their wagon train—twice during the long trip across the plains—Mama had kept him, his brother and his sisters well back, huddled next to the wagon, while the men, guns at the ready, handed out gifts of beads and pots to make the Indians go away. They were Sioux. Afterward, Pa would grumble something like, "A little honest work wouldn't hurt those people."

To ease his jitters, Johnnie said, "I never saw a girl ride a horse like that."

The woman nodded and put her hand over the silver cross on her chest. She was tall; tall as his father.

"Best horse, best rider. She making big pride." She called out more instructions, and the girl somehow made the horse walk sideways.

David M. Jessup

Just then he heard Mama call. "Johnnie, come away from there now, you hear?" She was sitting on the wagon seat with little Robert fast asleep in her arms. "Pa wants you inside the store."

Johnnie tore himself away from the fence and started off to where Mama was pointing. He had learned not to tarry when Pa wanted him.

As he trotted past the wagon he took a quick glance around. He figured this was Mariano's Crossing, the place Pa said they'd have to stop at for supplies, despite it being owned by papists. On the side of the road opposite the pasture stretched a big open square with buildings on three sides. The barn at the far end looked fit for a king's herd. The horses in the corral were shiny enough to be in a parade. Straight across were three log cabins with the grass around them trimmed up real nice and the paths swept clean.

He hustled toward two big whitewashed log buildings on the north side. Giant cottonwoods made a kind of tent over them, green dappled with the first of September's yellow leaves. Their cool shade felt good on his arms. The building on the left had a covered porch full of chairs. Johnnie guessed it was the tavern Pa had warned about, the "den of iniquity."

He ran toward the other building. Bolts of bright calico and beaded leather shirts draped the porch rails. The walls were hung with pots and tools. Strings of red peppers dangled from the ends of the roof beams. He stopped dead when he saw the books. They lined the window ledges—dime novels about Kit Carson and Deadwood Dick. They gave off a mysterious, papery smell. Spellbound, Johnnie climbed the porch stairs to gaze at them.

Pa appeared in the doorway. "Johnnie, get a move on. Load these potatoes and beans into the wagon." His voice wheezed.

Johnnie felt the familiar queasiness in Pa's presence. He'd hoped Pa's lungs would be better in Colorado, but so far there didn't seem to be much difference.

He hurried to fetch the potatoes, but a flap of boot sole caught on a loose board and sent him sprawling at Pa's feet. The look on his father's face said it all: *There goes that clumsy son of mine, again.* Johnnie scrambled up, rubbing another dent in his shin, and made it through the door.

A young man stood there holding a big lumpy sack. He looked to be about fifteen or sixteen, with white teeth that gleamed in the semi-darkness. His smile didn't feel friendly. More like he was testing to see whether Johnnie could hold the sack he hefted over.

Johnnie staggered under its weight.

"Antonio Medina, at your service." The young man's tone sounded mocking.

Johnnie didn't answer. He gritted his teeth and vowed to get the potatoes into the wagon without dropping them or stumbling. He lugged them down the steps. Pa walked behind with his cane. Johnnie paused to let him pass, so his father's eyes would be watching something else besides his struggle with the potatoes.

As he strained to get the bag over the wagon's side rail, Jennie eyed him from the wagon bed.

"Be careful! Don't drop it."

The ever-helpful Jennie. Johnnie gritted his teeth, screwed up his courage and turned to his father.

"Pa, there's a book up there, about Kit Carson. A history book. Could we. . ."

Pa silenced him with an ice-blue stare. "I'll be back in a wag," he said, turning toward the store. "Be ready to go."

Johnnie stepped around the wagon for a last look at the horse and girl. The horse was tied to the fence rail. The girl stood between the Indian woman and a man he hadn't seen before. He was a tad shorter than the woman, lighter skinned, with thick black hair combed back over his ears. Johnnie stared at a tomahawk poking out of the back of the man's red sash, its blade within easy reach. In his hand was a black powder rifle with the longest barrel Johnnie had ever seen.

He and the woman were speaking in what Johnnie took to be Spanish. The girl turned first toward the man, then the woman, back and forth. Her eyes, wide apart, glistened.

The man pulled the girl toward him, gave her a hug, and with his hands on her shoulders, guided her toward the store. The woman followed, her face blank.

As the three approached their wagon, Johnnie heard Ma whisper, "Johnnie!" That meant Pa had arrived and he'd best climb aboard. But he couldn't take his eyes off the girl. He felt Pa come up behind him.

The man paused and smiled. "Welcome again, Señor Alexander." With a slight bow of his head toward Johnnie, he continued, "Mariano Medina, at your service." *Sairbeece* was the way he said it.

He held out his hand. His black eyes looked straight at Pa, bold as you please. Pa just grunted and stood there. Mariano Medina's

David M. Jessup

hand retreated to the girl's shoulder.

To Johnnie he said, "My daughter, Lena," and with a nod toward the woman, "My wife, Takansy." He said it with the accent in the middle, Ta-KHAN-see.

Johnnie silently mouthed the name, accenting the *kah*.

"Most people call her Maria. We call her John," he added with a smile that hinted of a private joke.

Why John, Johnnie wondered.

"My son, Antonio, you have met in the store, yes? And Martín, he is...somewhere." He shrugged, smiling.

Unnerved by Pa's silence, Johnnie blurted, "Very nice to meet you, sir. My name's Johnnie, and up there in the wagon. . ." Johnnie felt Pa's hand heavy on his shoulder, a warning.

Mr. Medina said, "How good for to bring your family to join your homestead, yes?"

"We got some supplies," Pa finally managed. His voice sounded strained.

"To come back anytime, you are welcome. We are to bring new trade goods all the Wednesdays, from Denver City. This Wednesday I will have some late melons."

Then Takansy, or Maria, or John, stepped forward and placed a hand on Lena's other shoulder.

Mr. Medina nodded at her and said, "My wife, she is to teach my daughter Lena the horse riding. Finest riding on the Big Thompson." They both hugged their daughter with their eyes.

Johnnie stared at them. *That's how a family should be.*

Then the girl looked directly at Johnnie and their eyes locked. A sudden current passed between them, a kind of quick understanding forged by those hands on their shoulders—caring hands on hers, a restraining one on his.

Pa steered Johnnie onto the wagon seat beside him. Johnnie stole a last glance at Lena. Her dark eyes held his as the wagon jolted forward.

When Old Dun neared the toll bridge, Pa said, in a voice Johnnie was afraid could be heard over the wagon noise, "Papists! Cursed papists!"

8

Medina
September 1863

Medina looked down into his daughter's big questioning eyes. Beautiful eyes.

"Papi, why was that man looking so hard at us?" she said.

"The bridge toll. He did not want to pay it."

He knew there was more behind William Alexander's hostile frown, but he couldn't figure out what it was. Some settlers didn't like buying supplies from someone they called a "Mexican," despite his repeated efforts to get them to call him a Spaniard. Perhaps that was what bothered the Scot. Or maybe it was being married to an Indian, being a "squaw-man."

He felt his jaw tightening. It was hard to work up smiles for William Alexander. Twenty-five years ago at a fur trade rendezvous he would have taught the man some manners. But those days were long gone. He glanced at the ax buried in the chopping block by the woodpile. A good thing to do, chopping wood, when muscles knot up after unpleasant encounters. He stroked Lena's hair and felt calmness returning.

"The boy seemed nice," she said.

"Yes. A little nervous. Polite, though." He touched her shoulder. "Come, *mi hija*, let us go to…"

Takansy's hand grazed his arm. "My husband, why you are taking her from her horse lesson?" Her gray eyes augered into him.

Medina forced a smile. "Miss Gracie is waiting. It is only an hour of tutoring. Then you can have her back." He let go of Lena and embraced his wife. "*Mi amor*, I am wanting the horse lessons also. You are making her into a wonder on that black mare, yes?" He felt her soften in his arms. "But there are other lessons needed. The numbers, writing. This is a new time. We are lucky to have Miss Gracie."

Medina didn't feel particularly religious, but he nevertheless lofted a sincere *grácias* heavenward for Grace Boutwell. She was the very opposite of William Alexander. The year before, she had befriended them, offered her breast to little Rosita, and was now teaching his remaining children the writing, and the reading. His children, he was determined, would not end up like him, unable even to sign his own name.

Takansy nodded and pulled away, looking resigned.

"Where is Martín?" he asked.

She raised her palms and shrugged.

"He's the one who needs horse lessons. The boy is still half afraid of them."

"The Horse Spirit is not with him."

As if that settled the matter. Medina managed a crooked smile. She was a more devout Catholic than he, pious to an extreme, yet she clung to her tribe's queer notions of animal spirits.

He said, "He still needs to learn. People will laugh at him if he cannot sit a horse."

He steered Lena toward their house with his hand on her slender shoulder. It surprised him how much he loved the touch of her. Holding her in his lap on their big porch chair, he would tell her stories of his fur trapping days, stories of animals with names, animals that could talk. He would invent some danger, causing her to wrap her arms around his neck and squeal, "No, Papi, no!" until he rescued the doomed creature.

Lena glanced back toward her mother, and the look in her eyes left Medina with an odd and slightly embarrassing feeling of jealousy.

9

Takansy
September 1863

Takansy watched Lena disappear into the trading post, then turned to retrieve the black mare. Wisps of steam rose from the horse's sweaty back into the crisp fall air. What a shame to interrupt her riding lesson.

"Shy Bird, you are needing a good rubbing. Come." She led the mare toward the barn.

Shy Bird. The same name as the horse she had ridden in the long ago, same glossy black color, same spirit. The thought of racing across the meadow on horseback tempted her like sweet honey. She banished it with a crossing sign. She had vowed to give up the horse-spirit path as repentance for her sin. Her vow would not be broken, not after so many snows of keeping it.

But that didn't mean she couldn't teach Lena the way of the

horse. Watching her daughter ride flooded her with pride and pleasure. The girl was a marvel, just as her husband said, a better rider than Takansy had been as a young girl, which was saying a lot. That Alexander boy thought so, too. What was his name? Johnnie? The look of wonder on the boy's face as he watched Lena made her proud... and a little uneasy.

From the barn came thumping noises. She hurried inside and found Martín dragging a saddle out of the tack room.

"Where you are going?"

"To help Louie Papa. With the cows."

Takansy reached for her son's curly black hair. "Not now. Miss Gracie, she is here for the tutoring. In the post. Go now."

Martín's thin arms gave way. The saddle *whumped* to the ground.

"But Mother, I've got to. Papá expects me to..." His voice trailed off.

Her son's resolve to please his father melted away. She saw the relief that lifted his dark eyebrows and softened his face. She touched a hand to his cheek then wrapped him in a hug. His long lashes fluttered against her neck.

"Another time. You going to Miss Gracie now." Her eyes followed his slender form as he slipped out. He was eleven, five years older than Lena, but around horses he seemed five years younger. His love was for growing things, plants, corn. And beadwork. So different from what his father wanted.

A *kacking* drew Takansy's eyes to a tree branch above the path where Martín walked. A crow. But not an ordinary crow. It had only one leg, and its beak held a strip of bright blue cloth. She recognized Martín's headband, lost the day before when his horse had run away. An involuntary quiver rippled across the back of her neck. *What is Crow saying?* Takansy's right hand reached for the beads dangling from her waist, her left found the cross around her neck.

Once inside their house, she walked to her altar. The crucifix on the wall had travelled with her all the way from the Bitterroot, given to her by the Blackrobe. She traced its familiar lines with her fingers. She knelt on the padded stool Medina had fashioned for her, crossed herself, and stared directly into the carved wood face of Jésu, her Christ. His smile was kind, forgiving. He was not remote like the Great Mystery. He had forgiven her on that day in the long ago when she almost ended her life with the obsidian blade. That lethal black stone lay wrapped in purple felt inside the drawer of the little table, tamed by the power of Jésu.

On sudden impulse she opened the drawer to look at the razor-sharp stone and immediately wished she hadn't. At the back, behind the purple wrap, a pair of tiny beaded moccasins came into view. Rosita's. The gift her little daughter never had a chance to wear. The moccasins stared like accusations. Her hand felt for the beads in the pouch at her side, and she wondered—not for the first time—if she was still being punished for her sins.

She touched the rough scars on her upper arm just below the shoulder. Rosita's scar was the lowest, still a bit tender even though more than a year had passed since her daughter's death. She welcomed the soreness. Bowing her head, she folded her hands and prayed for Martín, trying her best to banish Crow into the realm of silly superstition where the Blackrobes said he belonged.

10

John Alexander
September 1863

Pa's words, "cursed papists," burned in Johnnie's ears. He stopped himself from turning to look at the girl again. But her dark eyes floated before him as they approached the toll bridge to leave Mariano's Crossing.

Old Dun eyed the bridge's log side rails like they were mountain lions about to jump. Pa had to climb down and yank him forward. When he climbed back on the wagon, his forehead knotted up into the crooked letter A that meant angry. When Pa's forehead got its knot, everyone wanted to disappear.

Johnnie fixed his eyes on the road. Mattie crawled up beside him and pulled his arm around her shoulders. Little Anna rubbed her eyes. Jennie looked at Pa. Robert was still curled up asleep in Mama's arms. Mama's hands fiddled with his blanket. Johnnie wished her hands would stay still.

Pa clucked Old Dun into motion again, turning upstream toward the mountains to the west.

"That papist dunned me a dollar to cross his infernal bridge," he said. "A dollar! Said there was a ford a few miles downstream if we wanted to get across for free. As if that were a choice at this late hour."

Johnnie looked ahead at the sky. He liked how the setting sun gilded the cloud edges and lit up the trees and bushes with an orange glow. As they rolled along, he thought about seeing Mac again. The dog had been barely more than a puppy when Pa took him to find the homestead a year ago.

The wagon track followed the river west for about four miles, cutting through three sandstone ridges that ran north and south along the base of the mountains. Then it left the river, passed through a gap in a fourth ridge and turned north up a gentle slope. When they reached the crest. Pa's knot went away. He pulled Old Dun to a stop.

"Here she is."

On the left, pine-covered mountains sloped down to a grassy valley. From a towering canyon in the mountains, the river gushed out, flowed through the valley and disappeared into a smaller canyon to the east. The eastern ridge rimrock glowed red in the last of the sun. The scent of pine breezed around them. Johnnie stole a glance at his father's face and found a rare smile there.

"It's beautiful, Pa," he said.

"God's doing."

"Here at last," Mama said. "It's plumb pretty, Mr. Alexander."

"Listen," Jennie said. "It's Mac."

Sure enough, from somewhere down among the green and yellow leafed cottonwoods lining the river, Mac's bark drifted out. Mattie giggled. Anna smiled. Robert snuggled deeper into Mama's lap. They rolled on down the hill toward the sound. Johnnie's heartbeat quickened at the circles of trout rises spreading on the water's' surface.

Mac ran yelping across the bridge, flopping his long Irish Setter ears. Seeing the smile lingering on Pa's face, Johnnie decided it was safe to let his gladness show. He jumped off the wagon and grabbed Mac in a hug. The dog licked his face and bounded off to greet the others.

Johnnie let his eyes rove over their new homestead. On his left, a rickety barn tilted to one side. Next to it hunkered a sorry looking chicken coop. Two crooked corrals jutted out from the barn holding three goats and a milk cow. Just beyond, rough planks bridged the river, smaller here than at the Crossing. On the opposite bank of the river, a dugout was half-buried in the sloping hill about fifty feet from the water. Low and squat, its timbered doorway was flanked by sod walls that blended with the landscape. No windows. It looked like gloom itself in the deepening shadow of the big mountain to the west. Where was the house?

A young man walked out of the dugout and peered at them. He was lean with a straggly beard. He wore rough wool pants held up by red suspenders.

"That you, Mr. Alexander?"

"Hello Caleb. How're things?"

Caleb was the caretaker Pa had told them about.

Caleb said, "Good to middlin'. Lost a hen to a coyote is all. Got the barn finished, just like you asked."

Pa humpfed, eyeing the leaning barn.

Mama and the younguns got out of the wagon so Pa could walk Old Dun over the bridge. The planks sagged under the wagon's weight. Pa stopped in front of the dugout.

"John, Caleb, get this wagon unloaded,"

"Is this...home?" Johnnie said. The contrast with the fine buildings at Mariano Medina's Crossing made his heart sink. He felt his mother's eyes on him, a warning.

"It's a start," Pa said. "Took me till May to get this far, before I left to fetch you. The important thing was the sawmill." He pointed up the hill to a peaked roof that jutted into the darkening sky like folded bat wings.

Johnnie's insides rolled. He knew Pa had built a sawmill here, but he hadn't spotted the dark form of it. He swallowed his queasiness, jumped to and pulled the potatoes off the wagon.

The dugout had two rooms, one with a cookstove and table, the other with three straw-stuffed mattresses on the floor. One was for Pa and Mama and little Robert, another for Jennie and Anna, and the third for Johnnie and Mattie. Later that evening, after a supper of cornbread and beans that Johnnie couldn't eat, he lay on the mattress and tried to join Mattie in sleep.

Pa's voice rumbled its way to his ears. "John's going to have to pull his weight around here. Can't keep Caleb on much longer. Too expensive. Tomorrow I'll start John on the boiler."

Johnnie's stomach heaved. He scrambled for the door but only made it to the slop bucket beside the table. The spasms hit him in waves. He felt Mama's cool hand on his forehead.

"There, there," she said. She didn't ask why he was sick.

Back in bed, he tossed around, unable to sleep. Mattie finally rolled onto the floor to get away from him. To distract himself from the sawmill, he conjured up the brown-skinned girl on the black horse. *Nimble*, that's what she was. He repeated the word softly, savoring its sound, until it finally led him into sleep.

11

Medina
March 1864

Medina felt his face go hot. Veins bulged in his hands. Strain as he might, the ax blade remained stuck in the chopping block by the force of his wild swing. He felt like heaving the ax, block and all, into the river, still rimmed with ice along its edges. What stopped him was the presence of Louie Papa, his unflappable stepson, the bearer of bad news.

For a change, the bad news had nothing to do with his wife's over-protectiveness of Martin, her sly influence on Lena, or even the anti-Medina rumors that sometimes slithered through the settlement since William Alexander arrived with his family six months ago. This was about his land.

Medina gave the chopping block a vicious kick. Louie Papa looked away into the trees as if fascinated by the call of a mourning dove. His moustache drooped so far over his mouth that Medina couldn't tell if he was smiling or frowning.

"Who is this...land thief? His name?" Medina clipped the words out.

"Chambers. Abijah Chambers. New here."

A Scot, Medina suspected. A Scot would file a claim on land that wasn't his.

"He ain't actually filed it yet," Louie Papa said.

"Then there is time? We can to file first?"

"Yup. That's what Hiram Tadder said."

Medina trusted Hiram Tadder, the settlement's lanky postmaster and interpreter of territorial rules. But Miss Gracie's help would be needed for the homestead papers.

"Go to bring Miss Gracie. Hurry."

Louie Papa ambled toward the barn, his boots scuffing through moldy winter leaves still littering the ground. When he returned that afternoon with Miss Gracie, Medina gathered his family on the trading post porch.

Gracie Boutwell was a solid woman, no-nonsense, the kind you could count on to walk behind a plow as well as set a nice table. She hoisted a paper and read aloud: "The West half of the Northeast quarter and the East half of the Northwest quarter of Section Sixteen, in Township Five, North of Range Sixty-nine West. A hundred sixty acres. That's what you're allowed. That includes all of the Crossing, the river down to the lower ford and up to where Dry Creek comes in, about a half-mile north, and south to your butte over there." She handed the paper to Medina.

"A thousand thanks." Medina held the paper between his thumb and forefinger as if it were a rotten fish and pretended to read. It was all he could do to not tear it in two. "It is not much."

He remembered standing on the butte and bragging that he owned all the land he could see. That was six years ago, in 1858, when he first pitched his tent at the Crossing. Now, settlers were swarming in like grasshoppers and filing homestead claims. Abijah Chambers was one of them. In early 1864 he had snuck in and built a mud hovel a quarter-mile downstream. A squatter, hoping to prove up on land that included the very hill settlers had named after Medina, Mariano's Butte.

He returned the paper to Miss Gracie. "How am I to get it?"

"You have to get a land warrant. I'm sorry, Mr. Medina, but since you were born in Mexico, you can't file a homestead claim like the others. Do you know anyone else who already has a warrant? Maybe someone in the army, from your scouting days? If you can get them to sell, you can use it to trade for land here."

Medina's mind raced. Who? Not the settlers here. Then it hit him. "The widow of my old friend, Chepe Luis Tapia, has one. He died in the Navajo war. The Americano Army gave his wife the land warrant paper. Perhaps she will sell it to me." He turned on Louie Papa. "We go to Taos, tomorrow! Make ready."

The sudden announcement chased the vacant look out of Takansy's eyes.

"But husband, to the land of your birth you are never returning, so you are telling me."

"True. But now it is necessary."

She frowned. "But...your old enemy...he is there, no? You should not..."

He cut her off, irritated. "Miss Gracie has explained it. To get land, I must to have a land warrant. Another piece of paper." He spoke with more certainty than he felt, urgency trumping understanding.

"Taos?" Antonio spoke for the first time, dark eyes gleaming. His nose flared as if smelling adventure. "I can go, to help?"

"No, no. You must stay. With Louie Papa gone, you are the oldest. You to run the post."

Antonio sulked, unmollified by Medina's flattery.

"Papi, is it far?" Lena wedged into the circle between Miss Gracie and Takansy.

"Yes. Three weeks, maybe a month each way. We return in May."

A look passed between Lena and Takansy. Medina detected a horse-riding pact in the making.

"You will to continue your studies. All three of you." He made his voice stern as he locked eyes with each of them, until one by one, they looked down. "The writing, the numbers, you must to master them."

A pained look on Miss Gracie's face stopped him cold.

She stepped forward and laid a hand on his arm. "Mr. Medina, I am sorry to have to tell you this, but my husband and I...we are leaving the territory. Returning to the States."

"What? But the tutoring. It is just starting." Medina felt betrayed for the second time that day.

"I know, and I'm sorry. Your children have been good learners. But…the reasons are personal. The family we left behind needs us, and…well, I hope you'll understand."

At this news, Antonio smiled. Martín frowned. Lena darted another quick look at her mother. Takansy and Louie Papa remained stone-faced.

Medina pressed his hand to his head. It had taken him a year to find Miss Gracie. Not all settlers could read and write, and those who could weren't inclined to teach three half-breed children. He would miss her.

"We need a school," he said to no one in particular. "Thank you Miss Gracie for the time you have given us. And for Rosita, the nursing of her. We will not forget." He gave her a short bow.

She blushed and tucked a wisp of sandy hair under her bonnet. "You're welcome. Good luck with the land warrant. Mr. Medina, my husband and I, we think you and your family…are tops, the kind way you have welcomed us, and all." She turned away, lower lip aquiver, and hugged Takansy. "And Mrs. Medina, I sure am sorry about little Rosita."

Takansy's arm went around Miss Gracie's shoulder, but Medina saw the vacant look return to his wife's eyes.

"God's will," she said.

Medina turned to Martín. "With no studies, you will have more time to learn the horses, yes?" Martín's sullen look goaded him to add, "Maybe your little sister can teach you." Immediately he wished he could take it back. Martín colored and ducked inside. Lena looked down. Takansy and Miss Gracie stared at him.

He turned to Louie Papa. "*Vamanos*. We will take the big sorrel and your roan." With a nod to Miss Gracie, he said, "Goodbye, and may God walk with you." Then he turned and left the porch.

Later that night, he and Takansy made love. She seemed more responsive than usual, like in the old times.

Afterward, lying together under the blankets, she said, "My husband, you are sure about going?"

He patted her hand. She had never grasped the concept of land ownership. "It is necessary. We could lose our home."

"But…your old enemy, he is in Taos."

He felt his jaw tighten. No, he had not forgotten Ricardo Castillo, the patrón's son. He could picture his cockscomb of red hair, his disdainful eyes looking down his narrow nose, his Spanish aristocrat's sneer. He had not forgotten the childhood shame of betraying his little friend, Chepe Luis, to Ricardo Castillo and his toughs. He had not forgotten being chased out of Taos at age fifteen. What would he do if he ran into Castillo? The tightness in his body suggested it would be different this time.

He said, "Ricardo Castillo. That was, what, more than thirty-five years ago? He is old now, older than me, and I am fifty-two snows. Perhaps he is dead."

"Promise me you are not calling him out."

"I promise." He brushed her cheek with his lips and turned over. But as he lapsed into sleep, a picture formed in his mind of Ricardo Castillo's narrow eyes pleading for mercy while staring into the black hole of Medina's rifle barrel.

12

Takansy
April 1864

The one-legged crow crouched on the river trail, pulling strings of flesh from a dead toad. It cocked its shining eye at her. Takansy bent for a stone and heaved it at the black messenger. Crow laughed at the stone as it flew by. She ran forward, waving her arms. Crow lifted off the ground and flapped to a branch overhead, mocking her with croaks.

"Mami, what is wrong?" Lena's eyes were wide. The basket she held fell to the ground, spilling the healing roots they had gathered.

Takansy fingered her rosary beads and forced her shoulders to relax. *What am I doing? Martín is safe in the trading post.*

"It is nothing, my flower. That crow, he is a bother. I am sorry I am startling you." She bent down and placed the roots back in the basket. "Come now, we returning with medicine for that yearling."

Lena took her hand and they walked back along the trail. A meadowlark called from the flats above the bottomland, announcing his nesting territory. Spring's first mayflies danced among ripened buds on willow branches. Takansy drew Lena close and tucked a strand of her daughter's hair behind her ear. She used to leave her own hair uncombed—her "wild" hair, Medina called it. In her younger days she'd let it blow in the wind from the back of a running horse. Now, she kept it tightly braided.

They emerged from the riverbank willows into the clearing around the corrals and barn. Shy Bird nickered. A bay yearling limped up to the fence, its right foreleg marred by an ugly gash. Takansy guided Lena to a tree stump beside the barn.

"First we are cutting these roots into tiny pieces and mixing them with some yucca root juice."

They settled into a squat and began slicing the gray roots on the stump surface. Takansy's heart swelled as she watched Lena work, how her nose wrinkled in concentration. The girl had the horse healing spirit. Medina was still away in Taos, Miss Gracie had gone. *No more lessons. Only horse work. Alone, together.*

"Mami, how do you know so much about the healing plants?"

"An old woman is teaching me when I am a girl. Otter Woman. In the long ago, that root is helping my black race horse. "

"Why don't you ride anymore?" Lena stopped cutting and looked at her mother, head cocked.

Why indeed? It was hard to explain to one just passed seven snows. A sacred vow. A promise to Jésu, her savior. She fingered the top scar on her shoulder, hidden under her buckskin tunic.

"For the riding, I am old now."

Lena frowned. "But Mami, when did you stop?"

"That pan, my sweet, we need it now." Takansy pointed to a round enamel basin leaning against the barn wall. She didn't want to tell her daughter about her shame, how she'd caused the death of her village's finest warrior, how she had tried to end her own life until Jésu saved her from it.

Lena skipped over to the basin, brought it back to the stump and resumed her squat.

"When, Mami?"

Takansy sighed. She scraped the root bits into the pan, poured on a squirt of yucca extract from the flask she carried and began to mash the mixture with a smooth stone plucked from her possibles bag.

"When I am marrying my first husband, Papín, Louie's father. Papín is trader, traveling much. No time for riding." She handed the stone to Lena. "Your turn. Make paste, smooth, no lumps. Better healing."

"What happened to him, Mami? Papín." Lena tried to imitate her mother's French pronunciation.

"These questions, are they not stopping? Papín is leaving to Kaw River, and I am not staying with him. Too many people."

Papín's twinkle-eyed face and courtly bow suddenly bloomed in her mind. She damped it down with a touch on the rosary. *Deliver me from sin.* She was Medina's woman now, and she would be faithful, even in her thoughts. Her husband would be back from Taos next moon. She prayed daily that he would not run into his childhood enemy there.

"To the colt now. The medicine, it is ready."

Face glowing, Lena jumped up, basin in hand, and headed for the corral. Shy Bird arched her neck and flared her nostrils at the approaching girl.

Takansy watched, enraptured. *Graceful as the willow, lithe as a bobcat. So like me as a girl.* Then another temptation seized her, so powerful she had to catch her breath to stop herself. She wanted to loose her braids, leap onto Shy Bird's back and gallop across the pasture, hair flying in the wind.

13

John Alexander
September 1863 to April 1864

Seven months after they arrived, on a fine April day when sprouts turned the willow branches yellow-green, Johnnie heard a faint grinding noise in the big wheel nearest the sawmill boiler.

"Pa, what's that sound?"

Pa let go of the log on the sawing platform and cocked his head.

"Good ear."

Johnnie nearly burst out smiling. He had spent all winter mastering the sawmill machinery. His eleventh birthday came in November, and the extra year, he believed, would help him to be less clumsy. So far, it had worked. He'd only got two lickings with the razor strap that winter. For sloth, Pa'd said.

Johnnie didn't think he was lazy, just absent-minded and awkward, but Pa called it sloth. The other sins that merited the razor

David M. Jessup

strap were Lying, Taking the Lord's Name in Vain, and Fornication. Johnnie managed never to cuss or lie or fornicate—whatever that was—but had gotten the strap twice for sloth.

Pa pointed. "Grease. Over there."

Johnnie fetched the grease can and felt a tingle of pleasure as Pa's rough hand guided his own to the grease hole in the wheel. What a change from that first day at the sawmill back in September. The boiler had hulked black and angry in the rear of the shed as if waiting for Johnnie's mind to wander. He had struggled to keep his breakfast down. His hands had shaken like vibrating machinery as his father taught him about each valve, lever, and pulley. By the end of that first day he scarcely had the strength for chores. When he toppled into bed next to Mattie, he breathed a prayer of thanks that he hadn't done anything wrong.

As the snows came that winter, dustings at first, then a foot in November that shut things down for a week, his confidence grew. He learned to watch for any hint of things going wrong, any tiny difference in the roar of the fire, the humming of the belt, the tilt of the sawblade. Now, after seven months of anxious concentration, Johnnie's hands no longer shook.

Pa nodded at him. "Ye may be old enough to log the mountain with me after Caleb leaves."

Johnnie returned the grease can to its place against the wall. His stride suddenly felt longer.

Emboldened, he asked, "Me and Mac, could we go fishing come Sunday?"

"Mac and I."

Pa was forever correcting his speech, and Mama's, who came from backwoods stock.

"Come Sunday, we go to church."

"There's a church?"

"Buckhorn Presbyterian. New, it is. Not a building, but a gathering on Buckhorn Creek. More folks arriving every month, and now there's enough Presbyterians for services."

Johnnie's heart sank. If church here was like back home, it might take most of the day. Pa himself often got wound up like a preacher, not one of those fire-breathing, hell-and-damnation Baptist ranters he'd once heard, but a sober, Presbyterian highbrow who talked forever.

Would Lena be there? No, the Medinas were papists, who bowed down to graven idols. He had never seen a graven idol, and wondered what they looked like and if Lena bowed to them.

Pastor George didn't look like much. His chin and hairline fell away in equal measure from a possum nose that stuck out a good two inches in front of lidded eyes. But he sure could preach, for glory sake. Kept everyone awake right up to the last "Amen."

He told about a Negro named Moses who smuggled his family out of Kentucky to Illinois with the help of Presbyterians. He said that violence was wrong, but Christians should get behind President Lincoln because the commandment to Love Thy Neighbor was tops in the Holy Book.

During the sermon, Johnnie stole glances at Pa. Hands clasped over his cane, black coat buttoned, Pa nodded an exclamation point to every pronouncement. His eyes gleamed blue approval. He'd been ready to join a Union regiment back in Illinois before Johnnie's carelessness left him crippled and short of breath.

On the way out, Pa said to the preacher, "We Alexanders left South Carolina back in the forties to get away from the slavers. We called our new town 'Eden.' Can't claim it was a sinless place, but it was free of the sin of slavery." Pa smiled a touch at his own humor, a look Johnnie almost never saw.

Pastor George nodded and shook Pa's hand. "I try my best to keep this little flock attuned to the great moral issues back in the States." He poked his great nose a little closer and lowered his voice. "Around here, people pay little mind to the war. They're mad at Lincoln for pulling soldiers out of the territory to fight back east. Indian depredation is their concern, out on the Platte River Road."

Johnnie recalled their trip along the Platte River, which had been free of depredation.

"The only savages we seen out there was beggars," Mama said. She leaned in, bonnet nearly touching Pastor George's black hat, like she wanted to be part of the men's talk. Johnnie stared at her. Mama never spoke out like that.

Pa gave her a look and she pulled back. "This is Mrs. Alexander," he said, "and these are our children, Jennie, our oldest, then John, Mattie, Anna and Robert. Robert just turned three. You already know our man Caleb."

The hired hand hung back. Pa had given him his notice, and he looked glum.

Pastor George chucked Robert under the chin and patted each child's head in turn, gently pushing them along toward the door.

Next in line came a tall man with a big mole on his cheek. The black hair around it twitched like a spider when he frowned. Johnnie tried not to stare at it. Behind him stood a pretty, brown-haired woman who had a bruise on her cheek the size of a baseball and the color of spoiled cabbage. He tried not to stare at that, too. Johnnie caught a whiff of the powder she had patted over it.

The man said, "I'm Henry Howard. This here's my wife, Susan."

Pastor George shook hands and gave Susan Howard's bruise a long look. "Nice to have you. Welcome to Buckhorn Presbyterian."

Outside, the March sun drove the chill out of Johnnie's bones. Some twenty people stood talking in clusters. Most of them, he noticed, wore better clothes than his family. Then the biggest woman he'd ever seen left one cluster and came toward them. Her feet had to swing wide to move herself along. Her long, pink skirt was wide as a tent, and her white blouse was stretched so tight it looked as if might bust its buttons. Her arms, outstretched in greeting, looked big around as telegraph poles.

Johnnie gawked. Jennie's sharp elbow dug into his ribs to make him stop.

"The Alexander family!" the woman said, her face folds parting to reveal an even row of white teeth. "Your father said you'd be joining us about now. I'm Mrs. Adam Blackhurst. Welcome to the Territory!"

She pumped Pa's hand, gave Mama a squeeze, and bear-hugged each child as Pa supplied the names. Johnnie stiffened, but still got squashed like a bedbug. Her bosom smelled of powder and sweat. When she let go, he almost lost his footing. It was embarrassing, because people were watching.

"My two girls are right over there." She pointed to two young ladies standing off by themselves looking bored. "That's Sarah Jane, my oldest, with the auburn hair, and Della's the shorter blond one. Della's eleven, probably about your age, Jennie."

"I'm twelve," Jennie said. "Johnnie here is eleven." She made it sound like a defect.

Mrs. Blackhurst said, "We live down by the Crossing, right close to the trading post. You've been to Mariano's Crossing, I suppose?" She made it sound like a girl's name, *Marianna.*

Johnnie nodded and looked at Pa. He scowled.

Mr. Howard, spider twitching on his cheek, wandered up. "I heard that Mexican squaw-man shot one of his hired hands a year ago, right off a ladder where he was fixing the roof, ain't that right?"

Mr. Howard had such a deep south accent it took Johnnie a bit to figure out that "hawd hands" didn't mean the opposite of soft.

"Not true, not true!" Mrs. Blackhurst waved a stout finger. "Mariano shot a hawk off the roof. Just protecting the pigeons he's got up there. That poor Mexican fellow got such a start he fell off the ladder all by himself. Broke his collarbone, he did. I know, I was there when it happened, and I'm the one who helped his wife wrap his shoulder, poor man. That's a fact."

Mr. Howard's cheeks turned red. Johnnie got the feeling he wasn't used to being talked to that way by a woman.

He said, "Just don't seem right, him and his squaw and them half-breeds owning the only store hereabouts. I got no truck with Injuns. Injuns attacked our wagon on the way out here. Made off with the Chilsun boy, the lad not five years old."

Mrs. Blackhurst beamed at him. "Mr. Howard, you and Susan are new here, so let me explain. I'm sorry to hear about that Chilsun boy, but to most folks around here, Mariano Medina is a hero. You probably heard of the rescue of Captain Marcy in the winter of fifty-seven?"

Mr. Howard stared straight ahead, not wanting to admit he hadn't.

"That was six years ago, before anyone was settled here. Captain Marcy tried to lead his platoon across the mountains from Fort Bridger down south to Fort Massachusetts. After supplies for the U.S. Army, he was, but the silly man started off at the end of November! Snow got so bad they near froze to death. Had to eat their horses and mules, and some say they came close to eating each other. Mariano Medina showed them the way out, then rode ahead to Fort Massachusetts and brought back the rescue party. Several soldiers near perished in the snow. He saved a bunch of them."

Johnnie felt his admiration for Mr. Medina grow.

"That don't make him any less of a squaw-man," Mr. Howard said.

Mrs. Blackhurst beamed right back at him as if he was a slow learner who needed her cheerful help. "There's good and bad among the tribes," she said. "Around here the Arapahoes are friendly, under Chief Friday, who speaks the King's English as well as you and me."

Johnnie wondered if Chief Friday spoke better English than Mr. Howard.

"We've not had trouble from them, except for some begging, being they's so poor and hungry," Mrs. Blackhurst said.

Mama stirred a bit, glad to hear her opinion confirmed.

"Now the Utes, that is another matter," Mrs. Blackhurst said.

"Horse thieves," someone said behind them.

"Captain Jack's band," another man said.

"Mariano Medina is the sworn enemy of Captain Jack, the Ute," Mrs. Blackhurst said. She dropped her voice a bit and people had to gather closer to hear. "Captain Jack abducted Mariano Medina's wife back in the forties, before they was married. Up around Fort Bridger. Medina rescued her and that Ute chief has sworn revenge. That's a fact."

"That don't mean…"

"What it means, Mr. Howard, is that Mariano Medina is the one we count on for protection against depredating savages. Take a look on the back wall of his trading post. You'll see three scalps there! He's a crack shot with that Hawken rifle of his. If that Captain Jack and his Utes come poking around here, you can be sure Mariano Medina will be first in the fight."

Johnnie felt his eyes grow round hearing about the scalps.

"Now that wife of his, she's real quiet, but she makes the prettiest beaded leather you'll ever see, and folks pay plenty for her outfits, especially greenhorns passing through on the Overland Stage. That's one of the reasons the Medinas are so rich. Plus his fine horses and cattle."

"And his toll bridge." Pa's sudden words made Johnnie jump. Pa's bushy brows were hunched below the A-knot.

"That, too," said Mrs. Blackhurst. "Don't get me wrong. The Medina bunch is not our kind. I'm not saying my daughters should marry one."

A titter passed through the crowd. Sarah Jane and Della still stood off a bit. If they heard their mama, they didn't show it.

"All I'm saying is that when it comes to Indians, you don't have to worry about Mariano Medina or his wife. Who, by the way, is a Flathead from way up north. They are peaceable savages, too. Folks call her Maria, and her husband sometimes calls her John. Can you imagine? John? I have no idea why, but I'll find out one of these days."

Mr. Howard scowled as if he didn't give a hoot what kind of savage she was or what she was called. Johnnie didn't remember Mrs. Medina's head being flat, but vowed to study her closer when he got the chance.

"The problem," Pa said, "is not that they're Mexican or Indian. The problem is, they're Catholic."

At this, Mrs. Blackhurst seemed taken aback. "Why I suppose they are." She puzzled a moment, then said, "There's no Catholic church around here. Nearest one's in Boulder City, about thirty miles to the south. They never go. Besides, Mrs. Medina's the devout one. Has herself an altar inside the house. Saw it with my own eyes. So, Catholic or not, that woman is a step above the rest of her kind who are totally ignorant of our Lord and Savior. Wouldn't you agree, Mr. Alexander?"

"No, Madam, I…"

Pa's speech was cut off by the approach of a tall, dark haired man with a jutting jaw and hands the size of bear paws.

"Why here's my husband, Adam. Mr. Blackhurst's the finest carpenter along the Big Thompson, and that's a fact. Adam, meet the Alexander family, and Henry and Susan Howard." Mr. Blackhurst's hands engulfed those of the other men. Johnnie was glad for the interruption. It spared them from Pa's sermon about idol worshippers, indulgences, the Pope and the inquisition.

"Adam, we were just talking about the Medinas," Mrs. Blackhurst said. "They certainly are different from most folks, but once you get to know them, you get along just fine. Isn't that right?"

"Yep, that's right."

"The oldest boy, Louie Papa, is real quiet, but knows his cows better than anyone around. If you want tender beef, you buy it from the Medinas."

"Real tender," Mr. Blackhurst said.

"He's named Louie Papa on account of his true father is not Mariano Medina but some Frenchman named Papa who traded the Flathead woman to Medina for six horses when she was already with child. That was back in forty-four."

"Six horses and some blankets," Mr. Blackhurst said.

"What about the girl?" Johnnie asked, then regretted it. He could feel the burn of Pa's eyes.

"That Lena girl is just a sprite, but she can ride a horse like no other," said Mrs. Blackhurst.

"Don't even use a saddle and bridle," said Mr. Blackhurst. "She's the apple of her parents' eyes."

Johnnie remembered the proud look Mr. and Mrs. Medina gave to their daughter. He remembered the way Lena looked at him.

"They had another girl named Rosita, but she died last year, just a baby. And, oh my goodness, that is quite a story." Mrs. Blackhurst wound up for another telling. "Maria near came apart after that. I was there and…"

Pa cut in, his voice impatient, "We must be going. Logs to saw tomorrow. Mr. Blackhurst, I'd be pleased to supply you with all the boards you need for your work."

Mr. Blackhurst stuck out his hand and Pa's own disappeared into it. "Sure, Bill. We can talk price next time you come to the Crossing."

Pa didn't look too pleased about the meeting place, or being called by his first name.

Johnnie climbed into their wagon and Pa clucked Old Dun off for home. Johnnie had forgotten about fishing. He was bursting with curiosity about Mariano Medina, his strange Indian wife, Louie Papa, Antonio, Martín, the little dead child named Rosita, and especially the brown-skinned girl named Lena who rode the spirited black horse.

14

Medina
April 1864

Taos was so dry the defeated shoots of new grass crackled underfoot as Medina and Louie Papa walked toward the Taos land office. If not for the date on Medina's new land warrant, it would be hard to believe it was April. They paused at the plaza's edge to eye the line of petitioners crowding under the shade of the adobe building's green awning. The late arrivals wilted in the sun on the adjoining boardwalk, licking dry lips. Medina's eyes jumped from face to face, looking for the red hair and hawk-beak nose of his old enemy, Ricardo Castillo.

"We should just go home," Louie Papa said.

"This will not take long."

Medina glanced at his stepson. Dull brown boots, pants, shirt, skin, mustache. Blending with the background. Avoiding trouble. He's probably right, Medina thought as he fingered the land warrant tucked inside the leather pouch at his waist. It felt satisfyingly thick. That he couldn't read a word of it made it all the more precious, his ticket for saving his land. Yes, they should get home fast. But he couldn't resist the temptation to watch Ricardo Castillo get what was coming to him.

The opportunity had arisen two days ago after he obtained the land warrant from Candalaria de Tapia, Chepe Luis's widow. Short and broad, with an open, trusting face, she had offered to sell the land warrant at a low price, obviously unaware of its value.

"Chepe Luis would have wanted you to have it," she said in Indian-accented Spanish. "He always said you were his hero."

Some hero. A flush crept up Medina's neck as he recalled cringing before Ricardo Castillo and his toughs while they tormented Chepe Luis as a child. He paid her double what she asked, hoping she wouldn't notice his shame.

The widow continued, "Chepe Luis died from a Navajo arrow. He served bravely under Captain Luna. He earned this paper."

Then she had added something that stopped him cold.

"Some are not so deserving. Ricardo Castillo is one of them."

"The patron's son?"

"Yes, that one."

"He is to get a land warrant?"

"Yes. He bribed Captain Luna. I have a witness."

The story she told washed over Medina like a warm bath in winter. Castillo had obtained false papers identifying him as a member of Ramón Luna's Sixth Company of the New Mexico volunteers. But the bastard had never served in the American Army. In fact, he had opposed the American takeover of New Mexico in 1846. He had been clever about it, speaking with two tongues until he figured out which side would win. But he never joined the Army. She knew this for a fact. A young man she knew was present when the bribe was paid to Captain Luna.

That got Medina thinking about redemption. And settling old scores. He had hunted up his old boss, Charlie Autobees. Together they interviewed the witness, took him to the Governor's office in Santa Fe and succeeded in cancelling Castillo's warrant. And just in time. It was due to be picked up at the land office the next day.

Medina wanted to watch Ricardo Castillo receive the bad news. Watch his face. Wanted him to know who had done this to him.

So, here they stood, he and a reluctant Louie Papa, waiting in the dusty street outside the land office for Castillo to arrive.

Castillo blustered into view around ten. He had grown flabby and lost some of the red in his hair, but not his swagger. Nor his cronies. They strutted on either side, smiling, all teeth and no humor. People stepped back, eyeing the three as if they were a pack of feral dogs. One thug was tall, heavily muscled, with a stick-thin mustache. Medina recognized the other. He was pudgier than when he had kicked and beaten Medina at age fourteen, but he was the same tough, no doubt about it. This time, Medina thought, there will be no running.

"Cover me," he said to Louie Papa. He stepped into the middle of the street.

Cutting into the line, Castillo pushed his way through the land office door. Pudgy followed, fat wobbling over the top of his too-tight pants. A pistol bulged under his waistband. Mustache-man leaned against the wall and began picking his teeth with a large knife.

Minutes passed. A church bell chimed, muted, as if dulled by a crack. Then the door of the land office flew open and slammed against the side wall. Castillo stormed out, his face twisted. He pushed aside a man in sandals, nearly knocking him down. Into the street he fumed, looking up and down as if seeking someone to hit. He spotted Medina. His face showed no recognition.

Medina spoke into the sudden silence. "What happened, Castillo? You lose your land warrant?"

That brought a sharp squint his way. "What do you…who are you?"

Pudgy and Mustache formed ranks on either side. Medina stepped close. Castillo's face sagged, his eyes spidery with red veins. Under the silky white shirt, muscles had turned to flab, strangers to hard work.

Medina smiled. He was enjoying this. At fifty-two years, he felt fit, his own muscles hard and practiced. He doffed his hat and bowed low.

"Mariano Medina, your father's former stable boy, at your service."

Castillo drew back, confused. Then he drew himself up to full height, mouth hardening into a familiar, arrogant sneer.

"Ah yes, now I remember. The protector of my sister."

The derision brought a smile to Pudgy's face and a turning of heads from the line-standers. This was turning into a show.

David M. Jessup

The old impulse to flee caught Medina by surprise. He had to force his gaze to meet Castillo's. Why had he sought this confrontation? He should have finished his business and left. His mouth went dry.

Castillo filled the silence. "What have you to do with my land warrant?" He sounded genuinely curious.

Medina wished he'd thought this through. If he told what he knew, they might go after his dead friend's widow. He forced a smile back onto his face.

"I know you lost it. I know you do not deserve it." To his dismay, his voice sounded weak. He cleared his throat.

"And how do you know this?"

Medina stood mute, wishing he were somewhere else.

Castillo stepped closer. Without looking at them, he said to his cronies, "*Muchachos*, this little bastard needs our help to loosen his tongue."

Pudgy smiled and pulled the pistol from the under his shirt. Mustache drew his blade.

Medina's instincts took over. His own knife flicked out quick as a snake's tongue, and Pudgy, looking surprised, dropped the pistol. A widening red slash on his wrist spurted blood.

"Shit," he said, grabbing the wound.

Mustache raised his knife arm, but paused as the intruding barrel of Louie Papa's rifle waved him away.

Castillo, left without protection, stepped back, but too late. Medina's blade sliced through his silk shirt from its collar to where it disappeared under his leather belt. A red stain butterflied outward.

"You have…God, I am…" Castillo sank to his knees. His hands groped at the fabric along the cut, opening it to his horrified eyes.

"You are not dying," Medina said. "It is only a little cut. Something to remind you…"

He never finished. Out of the crowd rushed a boy with a flag of flopping red hair. The boy threw his arms tight around Castillo's neck.

"Papá, Papá," he screamed.

Through hot tears the boy's eyes fixed on Medina's. The force of their hatred caused Medina to shrink back. He turned, grabbed Louie Papa by the arm and ducked into the gathering crowd.

15

Takansy
May 1864

Takansy turned to the four directions, peering with hawk eyes. *No one around.* She plucked the beaded wraps from her braids and drew an old comb out of her belt pouch. Carved from the tine of an elk antler, the comb's blunt teeth raked against her scalp. She bent and shook her head. Electrified tresses cascaded over her eyes, flaring out in mutual repulsion, as if alive to the thrilling risk she was about to take.

She placed a shaking hand on Shy Bird's glossy shoulder. At her touch, the mare twisted her head. Takansy combed the mare's sleek neck, which was blacker than her own gray-streaked hair. She led her daughter's horse alongside a stepping stone.

Woman and horse stood in the far pasture just beyond the graveyard. A curtain of green hid the compound below, cottonwoods and willows fully leafed out. She took a deep breath, stepped onto the boulder and swung herself onto Shy Bird's back, feeling the remembered wonder of a horse between her legs.

Horse Spirit had come to her in the night, a dreamlike horse's head and a single word that tolled like bell: *Ride. Ride. Ride.* Unable to return to sleep, she rose in growing excitement and waited for the dawn. Now, here she sat on Shy Bird's back, riding a horse for the first time since vowing not to. Her shoulders shook with her own daring.

She was on the verge of urging Shy Bird forward when another image suddenly came to her. A smiling Jésu, radiating love and compassion...and reproach. Her throat tightened. Her shoulders slumped. She slipped from Shy Bird's back and leaned with her arms around the black neck. The wind lifted a strand of hair and cooled the tears on her cheeks. She led the mare back down the hill toward the barn.

"Mami, look! Papi is back." Lena pointed from atop Shy Bird, now returned to the lower pasture.

Jolted, Takansy shifted her gaze. Over the crest of the slope rode Medina and Louie Papa, silhouetted against a blue sky scalloped with afternoon clouds. Their long rifles rested horizontally across their saddles, two crosses bobbing down the hill. Takansy saw the thrust of her husband's chin and the straightness of his back. *He has counted coup.*

Lena's shout brought Martín, Antonio and a half-dozen ranch families into the courtyard. Lena slipped off Shy Bird's back and ran toward them. Takansy followed. Medina dismounted, scooped Lena into his arms and waved a paper in the air.

"The land warrant!"

Antonio clapped his father on the back. "Did you shoot anyone?" His eyes glowed above an eager grin.

Medina laughed. "No, *mi hijo.* And you did not, either, I am hoping."

He clasped Antonio, then Martín, and last, Takansy. She let herself be drawn into his embrace.

"You are safe," she said. "You did not call out your enemy?"

Medina pulled back, eyes shifting toward Louie Papa.

"I saw him."

"You did not...speak with him?"

"Ricardo Castillo is old, fat. No longer *patrón*. When the *Americanos* took over New Mexico, they put all the *patrónes* in their place. He is hamstrung."

"Did you fight him?"

"Not really." He shrugged her off and moved to greet Valdez, Garcia and the other ranch hands and their wives.

She stopped Louie Papa with a hand on his sleeve. "I am glad you are back safe."

Louie Papa gave her a closed-lip smile under his mustache.

"What happened between Medina and Ricardo Castillo?"

Louie Papa shrugged. "The red-hair had two bodyguards. I made sure they done nothing." He patted her hand and pulled away.

She knew it would be no use to press him, quiet-tongued as he was. She released him and turned to follow the chattering bunch to the trading post. Her husband had never told her exactly what Castillo had done to him when he was a boy. Some youthful torment—shoving, stealing a ball. But she knew it was more than that. She had seen his anger, seen what it could do. She hoped he had kept it in check.

16

John Alexander
May 1864

In May 1864, not long after Mr. Medina returned from Taos and church folks were buzzing about whether he had cheated Abijah Chambers out of his land claim, Johnnie took a chance. Pa had got an order for lumber from Mr. Medina. After chores the next morning, Johnnie worked right smart to help Pa load the wagon. His father's bad leg was hurting, creating an opening.

Johnnie sidled up and said, "How about I come along and help you unload those boards? I'm almost twelve." He tried to sound offhand.

A knot worked itself up on Pa's forehead. "You can carry the potatoes and unload the boards," he said. "But keep to yourself. No idle talk with those papists."

Johnnie struggled to keep from dancing a little jig.

They rode to the Crossing under a sky so blue it made Johnnie's breath catch. Skies in Illinois were never like that. Whiffs of the last wild plum blossoms filled his head. It was hard to sit still. At the hitch rail in front of the trading post, Johnnie gaped at the rich calicos, colored blankets and red peppers hanging from the roof beams. Their own homestead was dull as a tintype photo by comparison.

The Kit Carson book was still in the window. He hopped down a little too eagerly and vaulted up the porch stairs for a closer look. Before he got there, Lena and Mr. Medina appeared in the doorway. Lena's dark eyes locked on his, and he felt that same disquieting current pass between them. Conscious of his father limping up the stairs behind him, he forced his gaze back toward Mr. Medina.

The trader smiled, but didn't extend his hand.

"Señor Alexander, welcome. With your permission, the boards you are bringing are to unload at the house behind. Perhaps your son does this while we talk about more orders? Two new families from the states, to want your lumber."

Pa looked a bit doubtful, but finally nodded permission.

"Lena, *mi hija*, please to show young Mr. Alexander the place."

Johnnie didn't wait for Pa to change his mind. He jumped down the porch steps, climbed on the wagon seat and clucked Old Dun into motion. Lena walked ahead, her glossy black hair swinging between her shoulder blades. Johnnie couldn't stop staring at her nimble stride, as graceful on her feet as she was on horseback. Twice, she looked back to make sure he was following. Johnnie grinned at her.

She stopped in front of the Medina's big whitewashed house. Johnnie marveled at the size of it, its trim neatness.

Lena pointed to the side of the house. "The big boards there." Her voice had a husky sound, free of her pa's accent. "They are for a woodshed. Those smaller boards are for inside. A new table. Louie Papa is making it."

Just beyond the barn, Johnnie spotted Lena's mama walking up the road to the south. Her hands fingered a string of black beads.

"Where's your mama headed?"

Lena's face turned cloudy. "The cemetery. There. On the hill."

His gaze followed her pointing finger to a row of gravestones above a low stone wall. He raised his eyebrows into a question.

"Rosita. My little sister who died. It still makes Mami sad. She..." Lena's voice trailed off.

"Sorry." Johnnie wanted to give her a hug.

He hefted the small boards and followed Lena through the door. Their house smelled of soap and wet wood. Sun streamed in through two real glass windows. A fine, cast iron stove stood in the room to the left. A darker room to the right revealed the corner of a bed. The middle room, where Johnnie stood, was big enough for a table, six chairs, and a polished wood cabinet with glass doors. He stared at the blue and white china plates inside.

"You eat off those?" he said.

"Sometimes. They come from Holland."

Johnnie thought of his family's dented tin plates and the tree stumps they used for chairs.

"The small boards go here." Lena pointed to a space on the floor.

Johnnie laid the boards down almost reverently. Above him on the wall hung two long rifles, three tomahawks, a beaded pouch and three knives, one so big it looked like a sword.

Not wanting to stare, he shifted his eyes to the other wall and found something else to stare at: a wood chest about three feet tall covered with tiny candles. In front stood a small padded bench, on top, a two-foot-high silver cross and a wood statue of Jesus. On the wall above hung another cross with Jesus nailed to it, bright blotches of red on his hands and feet and side.

Johnnie gaped. He was face to face with a graven image, a site of papist rites. The hair stood up on his neck.

"Mami set it up." Lena eyed his face. "It's nice when the candles are all lit."

"Nice." Embarrassed, he said, "The outside boards. I'll unload them now."

She followed him outside and stood there while he finished stacking.

He said, "You sure know how to ride that black horse."

"Thank you." She looked down and toed a small stone from the swept path. The corners of her mouth lifted a bit, making little creases on either side.

Just then Mr. Medina bustled up. He poked his head inside the door, then stepped lively over to Johnnie and Lena.

"*Bueno*. Stacked so square I almost not to want Louie Papa to touch them. A thousand thanks." He pumped Johnnie's hand.

Johnnie felt his face blush. "Yes, sir." Getting his hand shook for a good job made Johnnie want to hug the man.

The trader eyed him a moment. "The books in the window. You can read them?"

"Yes, sir. Most of them, anyway. Some words I don't know."

"You can do the writing also?"

Johnnie nodded.

"Maybe you can teach my daughter and sons, yes?"

Johnnie couldn't think of anything he'd rather do. Then he remembered Pa waiting at the trading post.

"I'd like that but…well, there's a lot of work, at the sawmill I mean…and Pa…"

"I can pay. We to talk with your father, yes?"

"No!" Johnnie fought to dampen his alarm. "I mean, that wouldn't be a good idea."

Mr. Medina nodded and shrugged. "I understand. No important."

He walked off toward the barn, shouting something to a couple of Mexicans leaning on the corral fence. They jumped and ran into the barn like they'd been poked with a stick.

Johnnie felt like he'd been poked with a stick, too. He turned to Lena. "Well, I best be going."

"Thank you." Her eyes caught his in the familiar hold.

This time he didn't look away.

"Maybe some day we'll do the teaching thing your Pa asked about."

"That would be nice." The creases around her mouth crinkled up again. Johnnie wanted to see her full-out smile.

On the way home, Pa grilled him. "Ye didn't talk to them, did ye?"

"Just enough to get the boards unloaded."

"What's their house like?"

"Fancy. Real china plates from Holland."

Pa snorted.

"They had a bloody statue of Jesus hanging on the wall inside. It was awful looking. And another statue on a desk, a graven image." As he said it, Johnnie felt low as a snake.

"Idol worshippers. The work of the devil, boy."

"And that Indian woman, the way she plays with those beads. Gives me the willies."

"Rosary counting. Part of their ritual."

With each lie, Johnnie's spirits sank. He was gaining Pa's confidence, making a return to the Crossing more likely. But he felt like a conniver, all the same. He pretended to listen to Pa's anti-papist lecture, but found his thoughts drifting to Mrs. Medina and how sad she must have felt about losing her little Rosita. It would be like Mattie dying. He thought of his own mama, how sad she would be. He wished he could talk more to Lena about what happened. Then he remembered how happy Mrs. Medina seemed training Lena on that beautiful black mare. They both wore the kind of smiles that make a body want to sing. Maybe the Rosita sadness would go away with time.

17

Takansy
August 1864

Takansy stitched another row of tiny blue beads on Mrs. Blackhurst's elk hide coat, but her heart wasn't in it. Sadness, like her finger joints, had swollen in the two years since Rosita's death. Some days were harder than others. This was one of them, a hot day in late summer. She blinked to wet her eyes from the dry heat, and sighed. From her rocking chair on the trading post porch, she could see the pasture where Shy Bird grazed. Teaching Lena the way of the horse was about the only thing that gladdened her heart these days. They would have another session late this afternoon, when the cooling started. She stopped her beadwork long enough to fan away the sweat on her forehead.

In the dusty courtyard next to the porch, Henry Howard and William Alexander were arguing over the price of some boards in

Alexander's wagon. Mole-cheek pointed out flaws. Blue-eye watched him with a bushy frown.

Medina walked out to help settle the argument with some charm talk. It seemed to Takansy that his stride had turned to a near swagger since his return from Taos.

Mole-cheek cast a mean eye at her husband.

"You got that land warrant signed by the President yet?"

"Not yet, Señor. But it is filed before anyone else. I will soon be owner of the land you stand on."

Medina told her the land warrant would give him new respect. With mole-cheek, at least, it hadn't. She watched the men smile at each other, two wolves with bared teeth. It set off an apprehensive flutter in her chest.

Before the argument could be settled, Martín stepped out of the doorway. He was dressed in riding boots and a broad-brimmed hat that made his face look too small. A lock of black hair hung down his pale forehead. Takansy resisted the urge to brush it back into place.

Martín walked down the stairs into the courtyard. "Papi, I'm riding the big bay today."

"Good. You to practice. Soon you to ride with Louie Papa for the cattle."

The boy hesitated, glanced back at Takansy and headed toward the barn.

Not that bay! A powerful horse, prone to spooking. Hard to control. Takansy tied off her bead stitch and shoved the coat into a basket on the floor.

Lena burst from the doorway and ran past her to catch her brother.

Alarmed, Takansy went after them. Neither Blue-eye nor Mole-cheek would look at her as she passed, but she felt their eyes on her back. And Medina's. She turned enough to see him following about twenty paces behind.

By the time she arrived at the corral gate, Martín emerged from the barn leading the big bay stallion. Lena held the reins as he mounted. The stirrups were too long for his short legs.

Takansy grabbed the bridle. The big horse tore a furrow in the dirt with an impatient front hoof. She skewered Martín with her eyes.

"Not riding this animal. Not ready."

"He is fourteen. Past ready," Medina had come up behind her. He reached around and patted his son on the leg.

She put hard eyes on her husband "Not the boy, the horse. It is needing more of the training." Martín was not ready either, but she didn't say so. She didn't want to embarrass the boy in front of his father.

Medina turned on her. "The horse is fine. Five years, lots of training. Lena rides him this morning, no problem."

Lena looked at her feet. Martín stared at the stallion's ears. The bay waggled its head from side to side, shaking off flies.

"The storms. Lightning. He might spook," Takansy said.

"Martín knows what to do if the lightning comes close, yes? Tell it."

Martín's fingers tightened around the big Spanish saddlehorn.

"You get off quick, duck into low ground and let the horse go." His voice, thin and nasal, sounded uncertain.

"It is the stinging season," Takansy persisted. "Yellow jackets…"

"*Por el amor de Dios*, woman! Never there is to be a safe time for this boy to ride? Will you keep him forever shucking corn? Sewing pretty beads?"

Medina's tone left no doubt about his opinion of his boy doing beadwork. He switched to his warm-eyed look, the one calculated to soften her. His hands found hers, and she let him take the reins.

"For why you to fear?" His voice was soft, cajoling.

"Just…a worry." She could not tell him about Crow. He did not believe in such things, and she tried not to, either.

"I will be fine, Mother." Martín pulled back on the reins and turned the big animal toward the gate. Thin white lines rimmed his pressed lips.

She stepped aside, defeated. "Go with God, my son." Her heart beat fast as Martín rode toward the river trail, passing Blue-eye and Mole-cheek, still dickering over the logs. They each gave Martín a look. Alexander touched his hat. Howard pulled his down.

Lena ducked back into the barn.

Medina put on his smile and strolled back toward the two men.

Takansy trudged back to the porch, slumped into her rocker and resumed her beadwork as Medina settled the dispute between William Alexander and Henry Howard. She stitched on through the afternoon, waiting for Martín's return. She stitched until her fingers ached and the bead rows became so ragged she had to tear them out.

Just before supper she heard the clop of hooves near the barn. The bay stallion. Riderless. She jumped up. Beads peppered the porch floor. Heart pounding, she rushed the side-stepping bay. A loose rope trailed along the ground from the saddlehorn. Dark splotches stained the pommel. Her fingers came away from them, sticky and smelling of blood. A vice clamped her head and spread down her spine to her feet. Her cry lofted out through the cottonwoods. Medina, Louie Papa, Lena and Antonio stumbled out of the house and rushed toward her as she collapsed to the ground.

18

John Alexander
August 1864

Johnnie heard about Martín's death from Henry Howard a few days later. Sweat trickled around the big man's hairy mole as he drawled his story to a cluster of twenty churchgoers.

"That Mexican tied the boy onto the saddle with a rope. Slapped the horse on the rump and sent his own son off to his death."

Mr. Howard's mouth twisted into the kind of smile Johnnie once saw on a fellow who tricked a boy out of a dime.

Gasps and tuts sounded through the church crowd. Someone said, "Anyone tell the sheriff?"

Pa, standing next to Johnnie, said, "I didn't see any rope."

Henry Howard frowned. "You wasn't looking."

"I was as close to him as you." Pa pulled himself to full height and turned on his blue blaze.

Johnnie pulled his shoulders back and took a step closer to his father.

Pastor George said, "Could be you saw different sides?"

Pa and Mr. Howard ignored him. Mrs. Howard glanced nervously at her husband, then at Pa.

Mrs. Blackhurst barged in. "I was there when they brought that poor boy in." Her bosom heaved. "Louie Papa found him in one of those ravines that wash out from a hogback. Poor boy's head was pummeled to a pulp. Like it was pounded by a rock."

"Or the saddlehorn," Mr. Howard said.

"Was he tied to the saddle?" Johnnie asked, then shrunk back from his own boldness.

Mrs. Blackhurst unfolded a smile. "The horse came back alone, blood on the pommel. They didn't find the boy until noon the next day. No way to know about a rope."

"I saw it," Henry Howard said.

"Could be the boy tied himself on," Mrs. Blackhurst said.

"What the hell does that mean?" Howard's face purpled.

"He was a delicate child, more like a girl than a boy. Scared to death of horses. My guess is the boy was just trying to live up to what they all expect over there. You know. They got the finest horses around, and they all ride like top hands. Boy wanted to fit in, is all. He may have tied the rope himself."

"You believe that?" Mr. Howard shook his head like he was talking to dunces. He turned and dragged Mrs. Howard away by the arm. A dozen people followed, mumbling about Mexicans and half-breeds. The congregation seemed split about even.

Johnnie felt worried. He didn't want to believe Mr. Howard. But what if it was true? He wanted to ask Lena about it.

The next day he got his chance. Pa's arm was hurting, and glory be, he let Johnnie drive to the Crossing, all by himself.

As he pulled up with a load of boards for Mr. Blackhurst, he found Lena pumping water from the courtyard well. Her face was glum. Johnnie could make out tear streaks under her dark eyes. He climbed down, uncertain.

"I heard about Martín, and I'm real sorry."

Lena set down the bucket. She managed a nod, but no words. Her eyes pooled.

Johnnie wanted to hug her, but just stood there, feeling awkward.

"Lena, excuse me for asking, but some folks are saying your pa tied your brother onto the saddle with a rope on the day he...on the day of the accident."

Her eyes flashed sparks. "No, that's not...that is a lie!"

The force of her denial sent Johnnie back a step. "I didn't mean to...I don't think it's true, not at all. It's that Mr. Howard, he says all manner of things that aren't true and most folks don't..."

"I helped Martín with the saddle and bridle. The lead rope was tied to the saddlehorn. Papi didn't do...he didn't even touch the rope." Her eyes wetted up again.

She hefted the water pail and headed for their house. Johnnie followed. At the door she turned.

"You tell them, John Alexander. It's not true."

"I'll sure do that, Lena. You can count on it."

She disappeared through the door. Johnnie stood there feeling bad. Then anger began to flood into him. Why would Henry Howard tell those lies? And why would some people—too many people—believe him?

David M. Jessup

19

Medina
August 1864

From his chair at the head of the supper table, Medina surveyed his family. Lena pushed a potato around her plate with a fork. Louie Papa chewed slowly, wouldn't meet his eye. Antonio's knee bounced crazily. Takansy stared out the window toward the cemetery where they had laid Martín to rest a week ago. Medina followed her gaze. Bloated August flies buzzed against the window pane.

Medina poked his fork into a bite of stew meat, lifted it to his mouth, then set it back down.

"People are acting strange. Ever since Martín's…accident."

Antonio was the only one to meet Medina's gaze. "What do you mean, strange?"

"First the Sheriff asked a lot of *loco* questions about ropes. Then no one came to the burial, not even Blackhursts. Adam Blackhurst came today, bought a coffee pot. Would not look at me. What is happening? Does anyone know?"

Lena stirred in her seat. "There is some…" She trailed off. To Medina it looked as if she wished she hadn't opened her mouth.

"Go on."

"There is some talk that you tied Martín onto the saddle. That you caused him to…die."

"Who is saying this?" Medina felt his hand squeezing his fork.

"It's just…talk."

"Who?"

"Mr. Howard."

"That pig!" Medina slammed his fork down and rose, sending his chair crashing to the floor. "How you to know this?" Seeing Lena flinch, he softened his voice. "Who told you?"

"The Alexander boy. John. He says only some people believe this."

"But some do. I will kill Henry Howard."

Antonio's eyes blazed. He jumped to his feet. "I will help."

Louie Papa put out a restraining hand. "You stay out of this."

Lena, eyes wide, said, "Papi, don't do anything. Please."

Medina turned to Takansy. "I did not tie Martín to his saddle. You were there."

She twisted slowly around to stare at him, through him, ghost eyes sunk into bruised hollow sockets. Her silence knifed into him. She turned back toward the window.

Medina struggled to get the pleading tone out of his voice. "It could have happened to anyone. Fate. God's will." He sought the eyes of each remaining child, but they flickered away. "*Mierda!*" He stalked out the door to the woodpile and grabbed the ax. By dusk, a cord of split wood lay jumbled on the ground.

Later that night, drained, he watched Takansy slip off her shirt. A new scab flared on her arm, red and angry in the candlelight. It paralleled the other two, as if a three-toed bear had raked her.

He touched her arm and said, "I wish you would not do that."

She pulled away. "I wish you are going to get a priest for Martín." She lay down on their bed.

"It was too late for a priest." He wanted to say he was sorry. Wished he had sent for one, no matter how long it might have taken. A priest would have comforted her. Maybe even him. A sudden memory came to him of being rocked in his mother's arms, frightened of the great aloneness of souls in limbo without last rites. Maybe there was something to those stories.

He lay down beside his wife and tried to draw her to him. She pulled away and curled into a crescent.

She said, "I should have stopped Martín. God tried to warn me. I did not listen."

He knew what she really meant. The ropes binding Martín to that saddle were invisible ones, woven from Medina's demands on his son. He sighed and stared at the *vigas* in the ceiling, unable to sleep.

20

John Alexander
August to November 1864

In late August, a few weeks after Martín's death, Johnnie heard something that nearly caused him to choke on the beans he was shoveling into his mouth. They had just begun their evening meal under the big cottonwood in front of their dugout. Johnnie couldn't get over how the air cooled off as soon as the sun dropped behind the big mountain.

After a few bites, Pa said, "There was a raid last night. Captain Jack, that bloody Ute chief, snuck down from the mountains and made off with eighteen of Medina's horses."

Everyone stopped eating. Mama's hand flew to her chest.

A fearful image of mutilated bodes flashed into Johnnie's mind. Lena's body.

"Did they scalp anyone?" He tried to sound calm.

"Medina and his woman were down in Denver City at the time."

"What about…the girl. And the brothers."

"Slept through it, I reckon. No one hurt."

Johnnie felt himself breathe again.

"Will they come after us?" Mattie asked, her eyes worried.

Johnnie was glad she was the one to ask.

"Don't think we have anything those Indians want," Pa said, looking toward the corral where Old Dun stood in a droopy snooze. But that night he had Johnnie run the milk cow, goats and hog into the barn with Old Dun, and instead of sleeping, he propped himself up against the wall with his old muzzleloader across his lap. Johnnie didn't hear any snoring that night.

On Sunday, Mrs. Blackhurst reported that Mr. Medina got most of his horses back.

"Most folks were too scared to chase after Captain Jack, but not Mariano Medina," she said. "Him and his friends, Tim Goodale and Jose de Miraval and some others—Louie Papa, too—chased those savages clear up into the mountains and rescued twelve horses."

For once, Henry Howard kept quiet. He picked at his mole and looked down.

Johnnie felt proud of Mr. Medina. In the circle of faces he saw growing respect.

"What happened to the raiders?" someone asked.

"They got away, but they'll be back. Mariano Medina and Captain Jack are avowed enemies. Only a fight to the death will end the matter. That's a fact."

"I heard Captain Jack scalped three children up on the Oregon Trail," a new settler named Ed Clark said. "That's what they said when we came through Fort Laramie."

Mothers pulled their children close. Johnnie patted Mattie and tried to swallow the dryness out of his throat.

"Should we…you know…do something to protect ourselves?" Susan Howard asked, wide eyed.

"A fort. Some place we could go if there's an attack," Adam Blackhurst said.

Heads bobbed in agreement.

A fort was what they got, courtesy of Mariano Medina. Johnnie watched it go up on Medina's property across the river from the trading post. It took all of September and October to build. About ten feet high, its rock walls were slotted with rifle holes. Mrs. Blackhurst said Mr. Medina was "civic minded" to supply the land and pay for the wood roof. Except for Pa and Mr. Howard and a few others, most folks seemed to agree.

"It's mostly stone," Pa said, disappointed that more lumber wasn't needed. He didn't seem mollified by Medina's paying him a good price for the roof boards.

A couple of weeks before Thanksgiving, folks gathered under a pale gray sky to finish the fort's roof. The Blackhursts, Mr. and Mrs. Howard, Pastor George, Hiram Tadder, the postmaster, and some fifteen others. Mama and Mattie came, too, with Pa and Johnnie.

The men hauled log beams up by means of pulleys. The chill wind moaned through them. When all were in place they started nailing boards across the beams in layers, first going one way, then the other.

At noon they all climbed down and gathered on stumps set around a huge cast iron kettle resting on a bed of glowing coals. Sarah Jane Blackhurst, dishing out stew, tossed her hair as Antonio Medina went through the line flashing his white smile at her. Mrs. Medina gave him a hard look. He winked and went right on smiling.

Lena sat down beside her mother, who wrapped an arm around her. Mr. Medina joined them and wrapped his own arm around Lena. She looked like the prize in a tug-of-war.

Lena bobbed her head at Johnnie, "Hello, John Alexander."

He liked the way her black hair glistened. Liked seeing her there, snuggled between her mama and pa.

He said, "I skinned and hauled those beams myself." It didn't feel like bragging, saying it to her. She gave him that secret half-smile he liked.

When lunch was finished, settlers gathered around to thank Mr. Medina for the fort. He shook their hands one by one. Johnnie had never seen him look so pleased, smiling and puffing his carved ivory pipe.

Then a man came riding in on a lathered-up horse. He wore

fringed buckskins and a fur cap atop a head full of gray hair and bushy whiskers. Mr. Medina stepped out to meet him.

"Tim Goodale," he announced to the crowd. "A friend from the fur days."

Mr. Goodale dismounted. He was older than Mr. Medina, with weathered crinkles fanning out from lively blue eyes that hinted to Johnnie of adventure…and maybe trouble, from the harried look of him.

Mr. Medina said, "For why you are hurry?"

"There's been a massacre. Hundreds killed. Wiped out."

A murmur broken by intakes of breath spread through the gathering.

"Captain Jack?" someone said.

Mr. Howard stepped up, face red. "Guns. Time to hunt Injuns."

"No, no, not Captain Jack, not any Indians doing the raiding," Mr. Goodale said. "Indians was the ones kilt. Out east of Denver City, on Sand Creek. Women, chilluns, shot and scalped. Black Kettle's Cheyenne band. Hundreds of them, murdered."

Everyone started talking at once.

Pastor George's voice finally cut through the clamor. "Who did it? When?"

"Colonel Chivington. First Colorado Volunteers. Two days ago, November eleventh," Mr. Goodale looked grim.

Johnnie watched everyone's face for clues about whether he should be scared. Mama's face worried up under her bonnet, but that was nothing new. Mrs. Blackhurst, wide-eyed, grabbed Sarah Jane and Della and drew them close. Adam Blackhurst picked up a hammer in his bear paw. Antonio's smile disappeared. Pa stamped his cane hard on the ground.

Pastor George shouted, "Quiet, quiet!" but his plea got lost in the shouting.

Mr. Howard's rough voice sounded through the din. "It ain't murder! Killing savages ain't murder."

Mr. Goodale fixed him with a frown. "'Twas murder, plain and simple. Black Kettle's Cheyenne band was peaceable. They was flying the flag of the United States, and they was camped right where the U.S. Army told them."

"Cheyennes been doing plenty of raids along the Platte," Mr. Howard said.

"Not Black Kettle's band, but they probably will now, the survivors."

"Lord a'mercy," Mrs. Howard said.

"How come you takin' the Injun side? You a squaw-man, too?" Mr. Howard's jaw jutted out, mean-like, toward Goodale.

Everyone got real quiet. Mr. Goodale gave Henry Howard a look that made Johnnie shrink back. Despite being old and thin, Tim Goodale had a way of moving that made Johnnie glad he wasn't Mr. Howard.

Mr. Medina reached for his tomahawk. Mr. Howard's eyes shifted between the two mountain men. He looked like a man wishing he'd kept his mouth shut.

Pa waved his cane into the thunderous silence. "Let's hear what this means for us. What might happen next, do ye think?"

Mr. Goodale, his eyes still hard on Henry Howard, said, "Chivington is a fool. Instead of chastising the Cheyennes, he has stirred them up. They'll be wanting revenge."

The women moved a little closer to their men. The men looked every which way but at each other, as if wondering if they had what it takes to fight Indians. A sudden gust grated along the eaves and sent a loose pile of shingles into a clattering collapse. Everyone jumped.

Mr. Howard shifted from mean to hangdog. "Injuns killed the best friend I ever had. Kidnapped his boy."

Hiram Tadder stepped forward, dark brows hunched over his thin nose, smile gone. "I heard that Captain Jack once cut up a man into pieces and sent his scalped head to Fort Bridger in a bloody sack."

Johnnie shuddered. No one spoke for a long moment.

Then Mr. Goodale said, "Captain Jack hates the Cheyenne worse than Chivington. If he attacks, won't be for revenge. Or at least not revenge for what Chivington done at Sand Creek." He looked at Mr. Medina as if they shared a secret.

Mr. Medina gave a grim little nod.

"We'll need to organize patrols," Mr. Howard said. "No point waiting for the savages to attack." He was trying to regain his footing, but no one seemed to take up his suggestion.

"Let's get this fort finished," Mr. Blackhurst said.

They went back to roofing. When they were finished, everyone filed out of the barn and got to hitching their wagons for the ride home.

In the bustle, Johnnie sought out Lena. "Are you scared? About Captain Jack, I mean."

"Papi is not worried." She didn't say whether she was, but Johnnie couldn't help notice the two little winkles that creased the skin above her nose.

21

Takansy
April 1865

Drips of fat spattered on the hot coals, sending puffs of venison-scented smoke across the courtyard toward the waiting crowd. Building the fort had changed the way the settlers treated her husband. Respect, he called it. Emboldened, he had invited neighbors to a *fiesta* to celebrate Lena's eighth birthday. It was April 11 on the light-face calendar, five months since the fort was finished.

Takansy gave the spit another quarter turn. The roasting was near done. She launched another prayer of thanks for the deer's sacrifice. Antonio, proud of his kill, had brought the young buck to her late the previous day. When she picked up the knife to skin it, as she had a hundred others, the deer's staring eyes had caught her off guard. Huge and brown under long lashes, they reminded her of Martín. She had to sit a minute before beginning the task.

What was it? Eight? Nine moons since Martín's passing? Rosita was hard to lose, but the little girl had been scarcely six moons old when she died. Martín had been with Takansy for fourteen snows. Long enough for her to feel a hole in her heart every afternoon when she stitched beads or peeled dried corn for dinner or did any of the countless other things that reminded her of him. The image of Martín's soft eyes seeking Medina's approval haunted her. She fingered the latest scar on her arm.

Takansy forced herself to think of Lena. Soon they would gather along the pasture fence to watch Lena perform some new riding tricks Takansy had taught her. Her spirits began to rise. The glowing coals felt good against the April chill.

Two groups had been invited to the *fiesta*. In one clump, bedecked in beaded buckskins, moccasins, and colored calico, stood friends from the fur trapping days: Tim Goodale and his Jenny come up from Boulder Creek, José Miraval's family and the Janis brothers from La Porte. The men laughed, backslapped, swapped stories and surreptitiously passed a leather-covered bottle around.

In another clump stood the settlers, stiff as trees. Except for Mrs. Blackhurst in her pink dress, they dressed in wool and cotton, mostly brown and black and white. Besides the Blackhursts, lanky Hiram Tadder was there, affably shaking hands and introducing two new families, the Bartholfs and the Clarks. Pastor George did not come. Neither did Henry and Susan Howard. She was glad not to have Mole-cheek there.

The Alexander boy came, minus his family. A nice enough youngster, Takansy thought, awkward and shy. Recently he had found his tongue, hanging around and asking about her husband's adventures. Asking her about horses. And Lena. He seemed hungry for connection. Maybe too hungry. She watched him climb the fence rail, face rapt.

When Lena began her horse-riding show, Takansy allowed her heart to swell. Her daughter wore the new outfit she had made of white doeskin. It looked like snow against Shy Bird's black hide. Her riding way seemed to knit the settlers and the mountain men together. They whooped and clapped, and the bottle soon made its way into hands of male settlers and back. Medina intercepted it and handed it to Louie Papa, who carried it off to the barn.

Takansy watched her husband's head incline toward the Janis

brothers for a few quiet words. She guessed he was trying to avoid offending the settlers' wives, who had different notions about liquor than the trapper crowd.

When Lena finished riding, John Alexander clapped harder than anyone else.

Takansy lofted a thank-you prayer to Jésu. Her daughter did everything she had done at age eight, and something more, a horse bow, that Takansy hadn't mastered until she was sixteen. She was transported back to her village on the Bitterroot. Chief Big Face had written a song about her racing victories. She sighed, then remembered her vow. Training Lena was the next best thing to doing it herself. It was enough.

Later, around a campfire in the courtyard, they feasted on roast venison. Hiram Tadder played the fiddle. Settlers and trappers danced. Antonio strummed a guitar while Sarah Jane Blackhurst tapped her foot. Takansy moved among them exchanging full plates for empty ones. The settlers stayed until after dark, except for the Alexander boy who left right after Lena's ride.

As the crowd drifted off, Takansy saw her husband pull Mrs. Blackhurst off to the side. A dark look came over his face. She moved closer to listen.

"Mariano, I tried, but…"

"You mean my Lena is not selected? But she is the best rider."

"No one disputes that. It's just…well, the committee decided to have a parade king this year. Do something a little different."

"A parade king?" Medina's voice rose. Takansy moved in and put a hand on his sleeve. The muscles in his forearm knotted.

"A man. Boy actually. The Bartholf son, Bisam. They're new here and, well, folks thought it would be a good way to welcome the newcomers, to have one lead the Fourth of July parade."

"Can he ride?"

Actually, it'll be a wagon. He'll ride in a wagon. Very fancy. Red, white and blue bunting. And we'd like your family to ride in a wagon, too. Right at the end of the parade. It's a good way to end the…"

"We will be busy that day." Medina turned and stalked away from the campfire.

"Oh, Mariano! I'm sorry…" Mrs. Blackhurst called after.

Takansy caught up with him halfway to the tavern.

"My husband, please to not being angry. It is not important."

"Not important?" He whirled on her, jaw tight.

She pressed on. "The important thing is happening here, today. Lena is becoming a marvel and people are cheering her. Parade is not important."

"If Lena is not enough good for them, then neither is my fort. To the devil with them! They can get scalped by Captain Jack for all I care."

At the mention of Captain Jack, Takansy glanced around for Lena. The fire had dwindled to flickering coals. The settlers had gone home. The trappers had moved inside the tavern. No Lena.

"You think he will come back, Captain Jack?"

"Of course. Have you forgotten what I did to him?"

Takansy had not forgotten. She had been married to Papín, Louie Papa's father, at the time. The fat Ute abducted her from Bridger's Fort, carried her off into the mountains and had just stripped off her skirt and spread her legs when Medina had come shouting into the raiders' camp pretending to be a horse trader. He had tricked the Ute into letting her go. Captain Jack would not let such a humiliation rest.

Takansy clutched her shivering shoulders. "I must find Lena."

"Do not worry," Medina said, pulling her close. "He will not get near you again. I will kill the *hijo de puta*."

But Takansy wasn't worried for herself, any more than she'd been when Captain Jack kidnapped her the first time. What sent the cold chill into her body was the thought of Lena in the clutches of the vicious Ute. A premonition worse than kacking crows seized her and kept her awake long into the night.

22

John Alexander
April to August 1865

About a week after Lena's birthday show, Johnnie returned to the Crossing with his father to buy new hinges for a gate and a barn door. As they pulled up to the hitch rail, Mr. and Mrs. Howard walked out of the trading post. Mrs. Howard's arm was in a sling. Mr. Howard stared straight ahead, and Mrs. Howard looked down. Mr. Medina followed the Howards down the steps, his yellow pant stripes folding and unfolding in quick rhythm. His dark eyes gleamed out of narrowed lids at Henry Howard's back.

Pa's eyes alighted on Mrs. Howard's arm sling. "What happened?"

"Fell down the steps. Just sprained," Mr. Howard said.

Mrs. Howard didn't say a word.

"You heard the news?" Mr. Howard said. Without waiting for an answer, he went on, "The War's finished and done with. Lee's surrendered to Grant." He didn't sound any too happy. Then he added, "And Lincoln's been shot dead."

Pa's jaw dropped. "Killed? Who?"

"Don't rightly know yet. The stage driver told it. Just left."

Pa looked like he'd been hit by a board. Honest Abe Lincoln grew up near Eden, Illinois, and Pa was proud of that fact.

Mr. Medina said, "Good man, Mr. Lincoln. To free slaves."

Mrs. Howard shot him a quick look. Her face was even prettier with no bruises.

Mr. Howard noticed his wife's glance. His face colored up.

"Maybe now we'll get some nigras out this way, to join up with the Mexicans and Indians."

Mr. Medina stared at him hard, and despite Mr. Howard's being a good foot taller and big as a bear, he was the first to cast his eyes down.

Pa's eyes shifted between the two of them, as if trying to decide whether to take sides between a papist and a cracker.

Finally he said, "Wonder what this might mean for us?"

Mr. Howard seemed relieved to have someone to face besides Mr. Medina.

"Hard to say. Maybe one good thing'll be to get some more U.S. troops out here to handle the Injun depredations."

That made Johnnie wonder about Captain Jack. He'd made himself scarce since the raid. Now, nine months later, folks were going about their business. They also had the fort, which made them feel safe.

Pa nodded. "Well, we'll be getting on." He tipped his hat to Mrs. Howard. "I am sorry about those stairs, Madam."

"Thank you. I'll be all right," Mrs. Howard said.

Johnnie tried to recall if the Howard home had any stairs.

Pa bought his hinges and they headed home.

Pa said, "Cursed crackers. The killers of Abe Lincoln will burn in the fires of hell."

In August 1865, three months shy of his twelfth birthday, Johnnie once again headed to the Crossing for supplies, alone this time. It was hot and uncommonly hazy. Grasshoppers swarmed like a Bible curse. The fields crawled with them. Millions. They ate everything in sight, especially the new-fangled alfalfa that some folks claimed made twice as much hay as regular grass. The grasshoppers made short work of that idea. Johnnie had liked bugs one at a time, but the 'hoppers gave him the willies. They crunched under the wagon wheels and jumped every which way as he passed. No matter how he tried, he couldn't get used to them crawling on his skin. By the time he reached the Crossing he was jumpy as a rabbit.

So when he first sensed something was wrong, he figured it was only his grasshopper edginess. Then the trading post door slammed open. Antonio burst out, struggling to jerk free from his mama's grasp.

"Let go!" he shouted, but Mrs. Medina yanked him to the floor of the porch.

She pinned him for a moment, but he kicked out and caught her in the chin with his foot. He squirmed free and lit out for the barn. She yelled something and ran after him.

Antonio was too fast for her. He jumped astride a horse and galloped away over the toll bridge.

"Antonio!" Her wail had no effect. Her shoulders slumped. She crossed herself as her son disappeared into the trees on the north side of the river.

Lena rushed onto the porch. The look on her face sent a fearful chill down Johnnie's spine. He wanted to be a protector, but he felt afraid, himself.

"What's wrong?"

Lena's hands gripped the porch rail. "Captain Jack came in the night. Many horses are gone. My Shy Bird, stolen. My Papi is chasing him. Now, Antonio, too." Her worried eyes lingered on the trees where Antonio had disappeared.

Johnnie felt the blood drain out of his face. An image floated into his mind of Captain Jack cutting off Mr. Medina's head.

Mrs. Medina walked over and touched her daughter's hand. She said something that caused Lena to jump down the stairs and trot toward the barn.

She turned to Johnnie. "Young Alexander, you are needing something?"

Johnnie opened his mouth but it took a moment for words to come out.

"Mrs. Medina, shouldn't we get some help, a posse or something?"

"All is in the hands of Jésu now." Her face got its blank look. She crossed herself. "My husband is having Tim Goodale helping him. And Louie Papa, and Valdéz."

"And Antonio?"

Something flickered across her face. "In the hands of Jésu." Her hand clicked through her beads.

"Is it true what they say about Captain Jack? Does he…torture people?"

"It is true. I knowing what he does." Her voice was flat.

Johnnie couldn't figure why she seemed so calm. But before he could ask another question, Lena's piercing shriek reached them. Mrs. Medina jumped like she was poked with a stick. She ran toward the barn, Johnnie close behind, his heart pounding.

Lena stood pointing along the corral fence. Johnnie caught sight of something red. He ran closer before it dawned on him what he was seeing. The top of a skull. Peeled. Blood still dripping into a dark pool buzzing with excited flies.

Johnnie turned and heaved up breakfast into his outstretched fingers.

Mrs. Medina knelt by the body, felt for a pulse, then covered the horror with a horse blanket pulled out of the tack room. She hugged Lena close and stroked her hair a long moment. Then she shooed Johnnie and Lena away and called out something in Spanish. Two ranch hands came running, passing Johnnie and Lena on their way back to the store.

Johnnie pumped some water from the well and scrubbed his hands hard to get rid of the stink. He sat down on the porch steps with Lena. He tried to wish away his shakiness.

Lena said, "Poor Juan García, he was…probably trying to save the horses." She looked toward the corral, where the ranch hands bent over the body.

"Will they come back?" Johnnie asked.

"Mami says no."

"Aren't you scared?" She shook her head. But her fingers twirled her hair into a tighter and tighter twist.

He put a hand on her busy fingers. They quieted right down, and that helped him quiet down too. Their eyes locked together for a long moment. "It'll be all right," he said, trying to act reassuring, her brave protector. It was easier to imagine before seeing the bloody head.

It wasn't long before folks started showing up at the Crossing. Johnnie watched the men bluster about organizing a posse. The women brought things to eat, although no one was hungry. The men began to argue.

Mr. Howard boomed out, "...just a few miles out east, on the plains. If we attack now, they won't be expecting..."

Another voice cut in. "They's Arapahoe, not Utes. It was Utes done this."

"It don't matter. We'll not be safe until all them Injuns is cleaned out."

"Yeas" and "nays" muttered their way around the circle.

Mrs. Blackhurst waded in, her husband Adam in tow.

"We'll not be having another Sand Creek here on the Big Thompson."

More muttering. Folks were still divided about Sand Creek, some calling it a massacre and others a victory.

Mr. Blackhurst took over. "We'll divide into three groups. Henry," he said to Mr. Howard. "How about you taking six men to ride out and warn people and get them over here to the fort. I'll take another bunch to follow Medina and chase down those Utes. The rest of you stay here to protect against another attack. Get everyone into the fort. Bring food and water. Let's not leave anyone out."

That seemed to get people moving. Mrs. Blackhurst began shooing people toward the fort. The men sorted themselves into two groups, checking their guns and mounting up. That's when it dawned on Johnnie that his family might be in danger.

"I'd best be going to fetch my family," he said to Lena.

She stood up and shook his hand in that formal way.

"Go safely, John Alexander." Her voice was grave. She jumped off the porch and ran to where her mother was talking to some of the women.

Johnnie hurried to his wagon and climbed up onto the seat, but Hiram Tadder stepped over and put his hand on Johnnie's leg. His sleeves were rolled up. Big veins pulsed in his bare arms.

"Whoa, young fellow, where you off to?"

"Got to warn my folks."

"You hop off and wait here at the Fort. We're heading out your way. I'll make sure they come on in."

"But...I'll need to come with you and..."

David M. Jessup

"Boy, no time to argue. That horse'll slow us down. Now get off there." His voice was kind but firm. He reached up and pulled Johnnie down.

Tears flowed suddenly, and Johnnie turned away, not wanting Hiram Tadder to see. Or Lena.

"Go on now," Mr. Tadder said.

Johnnie headed for the fort. He fought to keep his shoulders from shaking. He felt like a little boy again, the last thing he wanted to be.

Mrs. Medina cut him off. "Young Alexander, the other horses, bringing them in, you please helping?" She pointed to the corral where two Mexican ranch hands slung halters over their shoulders and headed toward the far pasture.

"Yes, Ma'am." Johnnie felt a wave of relief at having something to do. "Thank you. Thank you, Ma'am." He looked square into her gray eyes and saw kindness there.

Wiping his cheeks, he ran after the ranch hands and tried his best to stop thinking about Captain Jack and what he might do to Mr. Medina, about his family, about Shy Bird. About how he'd thrown up and cried in front of Lena.

23

Medina
August 1865

The fort loomed gray-white beside the river, its row of gun holes staring black and sightless as Medina rode past. The churned earth from sixty stolen horses made an easy trail to follow in the August moonlight. Medina calculated they could catch Captain Jack's band in a couple of hours, but he held them back. He wanted the raiders to think they had made a clean getaway. He wanted them to relax, bed down for the night. He wanted to surprise them. He wanted Captain Jack on foot.

Beside him, Tim Goodale slouched forward in his saddle, looking practically neckless. Getting old. Or still hung over from their previous night's drinking. Drunk or not, there was no one he'd rather have at his side than Tim Goodale. It was good he'd been visiting the night of the raid.

"That fat sonofabitch surprised us," Goodale said. "Injuns ain't supposed to attack in the dead of night." Strands of his unruly gray hair danced from side-to-side as he waggled his head in disgust.

"It did not help that we were both *borracho*."

Medina was not a heavy drinker, but last night he had tipped a few for old times' sake. Then, he was ashamed to admit, they had snored half-way through the raid. Takansy had been the one to awaken him. In one hand she held a frightened Lena, in the other, one of his pistols.

"Raid," she whispered, pointing toward the pasture.

By the time he and Goodale stumbled out of the house, the raiders had already galloped off with sixty of his horses, including Shy Bird.

It had taken a couple of hours to round up spare mounts from the far pasture and prepare his team. Besides Goodale, he selected Valdez, the best shot among all his hands, and Louie Papa, always cool and steady in a crisis. Others had clamored to go, but he ordered them to stay to protect the Crossing. Not really true, as he was sure the Utes would not return. His real motive was that too many men would make it harder to sneak up on the raiding party. There were no more than six or seven attackers, according to Valdez's daughter who'd had the presence of mind to count them from her hiding place in the woodshed.

Antonio had been difficult. Medina was proud of the boy's boldness, but couldn't afford his impulsiveness. Not on this venture.

"Your Mama needs you to stay. You will be the man of the house while I am gone," he offered.

Antonio, looking sullen, had not believed him.

The trampled trail led straight through the cottonwoods across the river bottom heading north. At the last line of trees, Goodale reined up and pointed to a dangling woodpecker feather strung on a branch.

"There's his calling card. Ain't that the bodacious limit, leaving us a taunt?" He plucked it down and handed it to Medina. "It's been, what? A good twenty years since you spoiled his fun up on Green River? And here he is, coming back for more."

Medina ground his teeth. "This time will be different." The memory of the last time burned in his mind. Takansy on her back, legs forced apart by Captain Jack's meaty hands, his fat body kneeling over her, his woodpecker headdress swaying obscenely.

Stay calm, he told himself. *Anger causes mistakes.* How many times did he have to learn this lesson?

They followed the trail past LaPorte, up the Cherokee Trail and into the Laramie River Valley. Just before dawn, they spotted the raiders' camp—shadowy lumps in a clearing below a wooded hillock, the herd grazing on grass still fresh at that altitude. The raiders had chosen new mounts from Medina's bunch and picketed them close. Medina squinted at the clearing, but could see no lookout. A a glint near the smoldering campfire caught his eye. A bottle. Had they been drinking? Let down their guard?

He signaled his three companions to creep onto the hillock to await the sun's rise. Then he dismounted and slipped in among the picketed horses. Familiar with his scent, they made no sound. He pulled picket pins and sliced through hobbles. Shy Bird was not among them.

When the rising sun touched the tops of the pines, the lumps around the dead campfire began to stir. Six figures rose from the ground to start their day. The meadow grass turned from silvery to green in the growing light.

A sudden clamminess came over Medina. Not again. The fear that had paralyzed him during his first encounter with Captain Jack threatened to return. He shook his head to banish it, willed anger to take its place.

He leveled his Hawken at one of the raiders and waved his hat at the hillock. Shots popped. Three of the raiders dropped like stones. Medina shot another. The two remaining Utes bounded off in opposite directions. The slender one ran into some pines and disappeared. The chubby one, his woodpecker headdress flapping, ran toward a clump of willows. Medina yanked out his pistol and charged after him.

"Mine!" he cried.

At Medina's shout, Captain Jack whirled around, crouching low. His heavy eyelids lifted when he saw who it was. He pulled something out of his belt and swung it toward Medina. Medina fired. Captain Jack's startled eyes rolled back into their sockets as the slug crashed into his forehead. He toppled backward onto the grass. A spray of red fanned into the grass behind him.

Panting hard, Medina knelt down, grasped his enemy's greasy black hair and lifted his head.

"You are killed, you focker."

The eyes stared back, sightless.

Medina reached for his skinning knife. It was only then he felt the pain in his side and saw what lay in Captain Jack's splayed fingers. A tiny silver derringer. He set down the knife and lifted his shirt. Captain's Jack's bullet had entered his side just above his hip bone. The wound hardly bled, and the pain, though sharp, would soon subside. There was no exit hole, which meant the lead was still inside. It wouldn't be the first. Another bullet had been lodged in his shoulder since his fight with Curfew at Fort Bridger, the same fight that cost him the tip of his finger. He pulled some wadding out of his shot pouch, stuffed it into the wound and hitched up his belt.

Just then Goodale and the others ran up to gawk at the dead Ute. Blood oozed from the hole between his staring eyes.

Medina picked up his knife and went to work. Captain Jack's scalp came off with a satisfying rip.

An hour later, Antonio galloped up, pistol drawn.

"Shooting's all over," Goodale said.

Antonio's face drooped. "How many?"

"Five. One got away."

"Let me go after him." Antonio wheeled his horse around.

Medina put a hand on his reins. "No, Antonio. It is better he tell his band about what happens. Help us to look for Shy Bird." He had to stare his son down.

They circled the camp site in widening spirals with no sign of Lena's mare.

By mid-morning, his mood sagging, Medina said, "Better we to head back. The people will be wondering." *And pleased when they hear what we did.*

Antonio was no horseman. He charged this way and that, spooking the nervous herd. Medina had him ride in front where he was less likely to cause difficulties.

About halfway back, Louie Papa shouted, "There she is!" He pointed to a black horse trailing its picket rope and heading homeward. He caught up with Shy Bird and snubbed her picket rope to his saddlehorn.

Medina's spirits swelled. He imagined Lena's smile at the safe return of her mare. Imagined Takansy's smile when she saw the two scalps dangling from his rifle barrel. Imagined the smiles—the respect—of the settlers. He rubbed his dust-gritted eyes, wiped the crusty ring of dirt from around his mouth, and ripped out a yell. Antonio yelled back. Goodale grinned and waved. Valdez gave him a thumbs up. Louie Papa's mustache twitched. Even the rising swarms of grasshoppers, stirring to voracious life in the morning sun, seemed to cheer his triumph.

Late in the day, Adam Blackhurst's rescue party found them a few miles out from the Crossing.

"Saw your dust cloud," Blackhurst said.

The settlers' horses were lathered up. The men gawked at the scalps. They looked relieved to be taking part in the rescue without actually having to fight Indians.

Adam Blackhurst asked, "What happened?"

Medina started to reply but Goodale cut him off.

"They was hard to follow in the dark of night, but Mariano Medina is an expert tracker. We found those horse stealers up on the Laramie. They was waiting for us and they had us outnumbered, but Mariano knows how to fight Injuns, he does. Been with him during the trapper days, by God. So we split up and three of us worked our way up on a hill while Mariano, single-handed, drew their fire and finished off two of the buzzards. We got the rest, except one we let go on purpose."

Medina went slack-jawed at the telling. Later, he whispered, "*Amigo*, that story you told was good. Too bad it is not true."

Goodale said, "Leave me be, you little cuss. Just give me a cut of all the extra plunder you'll get as folks traipse into your store to buy something from the famous Mariano Medina."

Medina chuckled. Goodale could always get a laugh out of him. It was Goodale, in fact, who had come up with the name "John" for Takansy. "Iffen they's going to call you 'Marianna,' we might as well call her 'John.'" It was a private joke that somehow compensated for Medina's own lack of education. He might not be able to read or write, but the settlers could neither pronounce nor spell his name correctly. He took perverse satisfaction in the way they swallowed the fiction that he had a woman's name and Takansy, a man's.

They arrived at the Crossing to a tumult of greetings. Women and children poured out of the fort. Men from the three riding groups gathered in the courtyard. Goodale dismounted and gathered them around for another telling. Medina smiled at the sight of Henry Howard and William Alexander in the crowd. Goodale's embellishments may shut them up for a while, he thought.

Louie Papa and Valdez maneuvered the herd into a corral. Medina grabbed Shy Bird's rope and rode straight for the store's porch where Takansy and Lena waited, along with the Alexander boy. Lena jumped down and grabbed Shy Bird around the neck. Her hands roamed over the mare's black hide.

"Oh, Papi." Her eyes filled as they locked on his.

His own eyes threatened to spill over. His voice came out gruff. "No hurt." He had to quickly shift his gaze to Takansy.

Smiling, he slowly raised his rifle barrel. The two bloody trophies swung like pendulums.

"Revenge. For what he did to you."

Takansy's eyes seemed to recognize the scalp with the shorter hair. But instead of a smile, her face froze. The ghost stare again. Her right hand went to work on her rosary.

He felt the smile slide off his face.

John Alexander stepped back, color draining from his face. Lena stared at the scalps and climbed back onto the porch. Takansy reached out and pulled her closer.

A grasshopper sailed through the air and landed on Medina's lip. He bit it in two and spit the still-fluttering halves into the dirt.

"Captain Jack will never bother us again." Deflated, he turned to join the crowd gathering around Goodale.

24

Takansy
August 1865

Takansy eyed the scalp swinging from the gun barrel, its bloody patch of skin already beginning to dry to a leathery darkness. She took note of its familiar short hair, its dull greasiness. The fear that had kept her body tight for the past two days drained away. She felt exhausted.

Her husband's eyes gleamed, a hawk returned from a hunt. The same look she had seen upon his return from Taos. The settlers will be impressed. His pride will grow.

She wished she could share his elation. Her indifference puzzled her. Then she recalled her apathy when Captain Jack had captured her years ago. She bore no anger against her captor, took no satisfaction in his death, felt only relief that Lena was safe. She tried to muster a thank you for her husband, but could not work one up.

When her husband's gaze shifted to Lena, she pulled her

daughter close. The girl should not have been shown those scalps. Then he'd bitten the grasshopper in two. She groped for the comfort of the cross hanging from her neck. The grasshopper swarms made her uneasy. Were they also an omen?

Her husband turned away to join Goodale, who was waving him over to join the audience of eager settlers gathered in the courtyard. She watched Antonio, flashing his brash smile, swagger into the circle opposite his father.

She spotted Valdez and Louie in the corral. Stone faced, Louie busied himself with the horses, well apart from the crowd. How different Louie was from Papín, his friendly, back-slapping father. She missed her first husband at times. She wondered whether he still ran the trading post with his brother on the stinking Kaw River, where she had refused to stay. She did not regret her decision, but sometimes she missed his lively wit.

Young Alexander stirred beside her, coming out of his white-faced trance brought on by the sight of the scalps.

"Excuse me, Ma'am, I'll be going to hear what they say."

She gave him leave with a nod and turned to re-enter the store, pulling Lena behind her. Inside the welcoming dimness, she sent Lena for some water and began re-arranging goods on the shelves. From an inner room she brought out some beaded pouches, arrows, tomahawks and several buckskin shirts. The settlers, upon hearing the story of Captain Jack's death, might be in the mood for some genuine Indian wares.

Lena returned with a bucket of water and hefted it onto the countertop.

"Mami, shouldn't we go where Papi is? To…be with him?"

Takansy drank in her daughter's slender frame, her lithe movements, her luminous eyes. She did not know what she would do if she lost Lena.

"Yes, I thinking we should." She hugged Lena one more time and walked out to stand by her husband in his victory appearance before the settlers. She bent her knees slightly so she wouldn't be taller than he was.

Later that night as they prepared for bed, she discovered his wound. He let her tend to it with her special leaves and powders she had brought from the Bitterroot. It reminded her of his long convalescence from far more serious wounds in Fort Bridger, when he had spent over a month in her care. The memory made her feel warm toward him, and the next morning when they awoke, she pulled him close and stroked him into hardness and guided him into her.

"Like times before," he said, and slid back into sleep.

25

John Alexander
August 1865

Seeing those scalps almost made Johnnie throw up again. He clenched his jaws together to quell the nausea. When Mr. Medina turned to walk back to where the crowd was gathered, he followed, just to get himself moving.

Mr. Medina had a way of walking, quick and smooth, that caused others to sit up and take notice. The circle of people opened to let him pass. Johnnie hurried to dodge in behind him. Adam Blackhurst and his wife started clapping, followed by Hiram Tadder, and before long everyone was stomping and cheering. Well, almost everyone. Mr. Howard's hands were stuffed into his overall pockets. He stood back a ways with two men Johnnie had never seen, standing stiff as posts. Mrs. Howard didn't clap either, but she sure had some kind of grin on her face, pretty as a picture.

Johnnie looked for Pa, but couldn't see him. Maybe Pa would change his mind about Mr. Medina, what with all this cheering and hero welcoming.

Adam Blackhurst waved his hands in the air and called for quiet.

"Folks," he said, "we have among us some intrepid fellows who have rid us of a scourge. Let us get them all together here so we can…here's Tim Goodale, many of you know his adventures as trapper and guide, and…where's Louie Papa? There, in the corral. come on over, Louie. And of course, the leader of the rescue party, Mariano Medina, the builder of the fort. Come on in the center here. Spread out, folks, make some room here in the middle. Who else? Where's that other Mexican fellow I saw with them?"

In response, Antonio strutted into the open space. Mr. Blackhurst, suddenly frowning, said, "No, I mean the other one, the hired hand who rode out with Mariano Medina."

"Valdez, his name is," Mr. Medina said. Then he called out the ranch hand's name, and Valdez followed Louie Papa out of the corral, looking embarrassed.

Antonio didn't let this stop him. He came farther into the circle, walked right up to Mr. Blackhurst, grabbed his hand and pumped it once, then turned around and waved to Sarah Jane. She started to wave back, but stopped herself after catching the look on her father's face.

For a moment it looked like things might come to an awkward stop, but just then Mr. Blackhurst caught sight of Lena and her mama coming over from the trading post.

"We might as well get the whole family over here. Make way, give some room." he said.

Mrs. Medina walked with Lena over to her husband, gave him a little squeeze on the arm and said something in his ear. A big grin spread over his face. Lena, standing between them, got a half smile on her face, too. Louie Papa stepped up to one side, mustache twitching, head lowered, while Antonio assumed a pose on the other. Antonio waved as the clapping started up again.

Johnnie clapped loudest of anyone. He glanced around again for Pa, feeling vindicated at thinking Mr. Medina a hero. He felt proud for their family, getting applause like this. And as he watched Lena, standing between her mama and pa, flanked by her two brothers, he wished again that his family could be more like theirs.

He felt a hand grab his shoulder. Pa spun him around.

Pa said, "Where have ye been boy? We've been searching high and low." The knot wrestled up on his forehead.

Jennie stood beside Pa with her hands on her hips.

She said in that oldest-child voice that Johnnie hated, "We've been waiting and waiting. We've got chores."

Johnnie pulled back. "But Pa, can't we stay and hear a little…"

The hand turned into a claw that jerked Johnnie out of the circle and propelled him toward their wagon where Mama waited with Mattie, Robert and Anna. Sudden ire seized him.

He raised his hand to bat away the hand and muttered, "Leave me be!" But the claw only tightened, and the starch went out of him. As he trudged along he heard Mr. Blackhurst's voice rumbling out over the crowd.

"…some might say men such as these aren't civilized. But I say to you, without them, civilization could never come to this land. They are the pathfinders, the advance guard, whose steely courage clears the land of the wild savage and makes it possible for settlements, for tilling the soil, for the building of churches and the advance of culture across this great nation…"

What would happen to the "Advance Guard," Johnnie wondered, after "Culture" moved in. Then they got too far away to hear, and Johnnie climbed into the back of the wagon and sat there with his chin on his chest feeling whipped. On the way home, Pa let fly with another Catholic lecture. And Johnnie, to his great shame, said he agreed.

26

John Alexander
June to October, 1867

In the two years after Captain Jack's scalping, Johnnie worked hard at growing into the kind of man he could respect. He hadn't liked getting all squeamish in front of Mr. Medina, or crying in front of Lena, so he had vowed to become more stout-hearted. He took to doing things he'd normally shy away from, like chopping heads off chickens or shooting a hog to be butchered. Pulling guts never bothered him. He'd been cleaning trout since he was little. Killing was the hard part. With the hog he had to shut his eyes as he pulled the trigger.

He offered to put down one of their sick goats, a pet named Henry. He pulled Henry to his wobbly feet and led him outside the corral. The idea was to strike a hammer blow between the eyes to stun the animal, then cut its throat. When he raised the hammer, Henry looked up with such trusting gold eyes that Johnnie eased up at the last instant. The poor animal thrashed around something awful as Johnnie pulled out his knife to finish the job. He got astraddle of Henry, but a hoof caught him in the elbow, numbing it. It took three cuts before the blade found the neck artery. Blood sprayed all over. After what seemed forever, Henry finally went still.

Pa, watching from the barn, said, "Pay attention, boy. Ye are near fourteen! Your mind still wanders, that is your problem."

For once he was wrong. Johnnie's mind was about as focused as it could get. He just didn't have the gumption to do what needed to be done.

Other times, though, his mind did wander, especially when he was working. Hauling logs, sawing boards all day, chores morning and night. It got tiresome. Johnnie's mind would gallop off with Mariano Medina to fight Indians, or mount up with Louie Papa and Lena to herd cows. Before long he'd be stumbling over a rock or rolling the wagon down the wrong track or standing beside a whirring saw blade with no log on the platform. Pa's voice would slap him awake with a "Get a move on, boy" or a "do I need to get the razor strap?"

Sometimes the slap was more than spoken.

Johnnie wanted to stand up to Pa. But he couldn't seem to get up the gumption for that either.

What he liked most was visiting the Crossing, which he managed to do every other month or so. The more he liked it, the more he told Pa he didn't. He fibbed to Mr. Medina about Pa, and fibbed to Pa about Mr. Medina. He became a pretty good liar.

In the fall of 1867, a real English Lord moved into the valley just to the east of the Alexander place. Mrs. Blackhurst said he was the youngest son of a duke who'd given all his property to the oldest, so the younger son had to come to America to seek his fortune. Folks called him Lord Ogelvie. Despite his living close, Johnnie never saw the man. He didn't belong to their church, and sent his hired hands directly to Denver City for his goods instead of going to the Crossing.

"Too good for us," Pa said. In Pa's eyes, Englishmen were even lower than Catholics. Johnnie'd cut his eye teeth hearing stories about English crimes, stories handed down through generations of

Alexanders. He could still hear Grandpa John, whose name he carried, going on about his great-great grandfather being forced off his bonny farm in Scotland by greedy English landowners to live in a slum in Antrim, Ireland, and later was herded onto a stinking ship bound for America. Until he heard Pastor George preach, Johnnie thought all sermons included stories about the sins of the English.

Pa always said, "If you're an Alexander, you don't consort with Englishmen."

To Johnnie, such stories were old tales having nothing to do with their life here. So naturally, Johnnie was curious about Lord Ogelvie.

One Sunday afternoon he hiked through the short canyon downstream from their place and snuck up close to Lord Ogelvie's stone house. Frustrated by not being able to see over the surrounding stone wall, he made for the red sandstone cliff to the east. It was the tallest of the five hogbacks that paralleled the mountains.

He'd always been curious about what lay atop that towering cliff. He scrambled up through the mountain mahogany and pulled himself up and over a low spot in the rimrock. Panting hard, he stopped, transfixed. Before him lay a hidden valley forested with pine and juniper. It sloped away from the cliff edge, then rose to a second cliff on the east. The two rimrocks made it impossible to see the hidden valley from below. In all his trips to the Crossing, he'd never guessed it was there.

He walked along the clifftop feeling a growing sense of liberation. To the west, high peaks rose up with bits of snow still on them. To the east, past the second rim of cliffs, the plains stretched away forever. Closeby, to the southeast on the other side of the river, Mariano's Butte poked up, a Chinaman's hat kind of a hill, and at its base, hidden in some trees, was the Crossing.

Johnnie forgot about Lord Ogelvie. He walked down slope into the trees and began exploring the magical valley. It was tumbled with broken slabs of sandstone, some big as wagons.

Between two of them was a narrow cleft. Squeezing through, he discovered an opening big as a barn enclosed by sandstone walls, open to the blue sky. A private hideaway. A hidden room inside a hidden valley. Johnnie's breath caught as he took it in. Clean sand patches filled the spaces between juniper bushes. Bunches of yellow sunflowers sprouted from the sandy floor. Rocks covered with dry moss were shaped like fantastical creatures.

He sat down on a sandstone slab and whispered, "My hideout."

Every Sunday thereafter, Johnnie made for his hideout. Shelf-like cavities in its sandstone walls became hiding places for his collections: curious pieces of driftwood, dried bugs pinned with cactus spines to a wood board, stones, and his prize, a scraper tool some Indian had cast off after it had broken. There were bones, including a human finger bone which became—in the story he made up about it—the finger of a famous Apache Indian killed by Kit Carson. He named the Indian "Red Feather" due to a flicker feather he'd found near the bone.

Safe within his hideout, Johnnie practiced knife fighting and spear throwing. Mac would light out after the homemade spears and drag them back through the bushes, getting all tangled up in the process. Johnnie acted out scenes from books, his fists punching away at imaginary outlaws. He hoped to gain the fighting skill and cat-like grace of Kit Carson, who was the all-time champion Indian fighter, a man so clever he could wiggle out of most scrapes and fight his way clear of those he couldn't.

In a notebook he'd fashioned out of butcher paper, Johnnie wrote a story about the final battle between Mr. Medina and Captain Jack. Knives, tomahawks, rifles, and teeth all came into play. Mr. Medina came within a hair of death, but finally stood victorious over the dead Captain Jack, who deserved what he got because he wouldn't fight fair.

One Sunday as he was leaving for his hideout, he caught a glimpse of Jennie ducking behind a bush. Trying to follow him! Alarmed, he dawdled along, studying the black and blue jays that acted so bold, and playing hide and seek with a yellow-breasted bird that hid in the willows and made all sorts of strange calls mimicking other birds. Then he meandered off in the wrong direction to throw her off. Jennie stumbled along behind, making noises Johnnie pretended not to hear. Once on top of the forested ridge above the canyon, he doubled back and hid in some rocks. From that perch he watched her follow the false trail he had laid. Freed of her prying eyes, he hoofed it east and reached his hideout undetected.

On the days Mac came along. Johnnie would tell him things he couldn't tell anyone else. Mac would cock his head and wag his tail.

Johnnie told him how he read forbidden books, consorted with papists, and admired the Medina family. How Lena's glossy hair framed wide eyes with long lashes, how the little creases on either side of her mouth dimpled up when she smiled, how she rode horses, and how he would soon develop that same easy way of moving. How he felt guilty for wishing he could switch families.

In late October, 1867, Johnnie made a haul to the Crossing. He unloaded boards and loaded up some onions and potatoes. He spotted Louie Papa's new wife standing in the doorway of their cabin. Her name was Eleanor, from Denver City. Her stomach seemed bigger. Johnnie guessed she was going to have a baby.

As he turned past the pasture east of the trading post, Johnnie saw Louie Papa and Lena separating cows from their calves. Weaning time. He pulled Old Dun over to the fence to watch.

Louie Papa crooned low from beneath his long mustache as he eased his roan into the herd. The horse nosed out a calf and pushed it out toward the holding pen. Panicked, the calf tried to dart back, but the roan kept ahead of every move. Dancing low on its front legs, the reins slack, that horse seemed to have a mind of its own. Finally, the calf gave up and trotted into the pen where other calves bawled in protest.

Lena closed the gate behind it. She spotted Johnnie and waved, smiling that way she did whenever she was around horses. At age ten her cheek bones were showing more, and her face looked even prettier now that she was more girl than child.

It was quite a sight, them working together. Johnnie wanted to ask them to teach him to herd cows, but he didn't have the gumption.

It was late. He shook the reins and clucked Old Dun into motion.

27

Takansy
January 1868

It was an unusually warm day in January, the month her people called the Freezing Moon. A Chinook's warm breath had shrunk the snow into a few dirt-layered drifts. Takansy hauled some pans, blankets and books onto the trading post porch. Settlers would be buying today, lured by the false spring. She breathed deeply, almost exultant. It was the third winter since the raid. Her spirits were on the mend. The pain of losing Rosita and Martín had lost its knife edge. Lena would soon be eleven, a prodigy on horseback. The thought made Takansy's heart grow big.

Medina walked out to join her, a cup of coffee steaming in his hand. He winked at her. Their pleasuring under the buffalo robe had grown more frequent since she tended his wound from Captain Jack's bullet. Among the settlers he was a rooster again, preening under their mostly approving eyes. His fort, the killing of Captain Jack, the quality of his trade goods, horses and cattle had won over all but Mole Cheek and Blue Eye.

She turned to see John Alexander striding toward them from his dilapidated old log wagon. He had grown a bit taller in the last several years, but not filled out much. To Takansy, he still looked boyish for his fourteen years. His sandy hair was cut short, his smile-crinkled cheeks had not yet felt the scrape of a razor.

"Good morning, sir. Ma'am." He bowed slightly, first to Medina, then to her, polite as ever. "Just saw your daughter out there in the pasture. She's something. Got that black mare stepping sideways."

Takansy felt herself warm to him. "She racing tomorrow. Like me when young, winning many."

"Why don't you ride? I'd like to see that."

Takansy groped for an easy answer. "Lena having horse spirit now."

He gave her a puzzled look, and she was glad when the books she had set out on the window ledge caught his eye.

He said, "That's a new Kit Carson book." He began thumbing the pages. "By Ned Buntline!" He grinned as if he'd just found a gold nugget. He was not handsome, exactly, with a large Adam's apple that bobbed when he swallowed, but his smile gave him a pleasing face.

On impulse, she said, "You taking book."

The young man looked startled. "Oh no, Ma'am, I'd never take anything from you." He held the book out to her.

She felt herself come close to laughing. "You taking it, bringing it back." She patted his arm and pushed the book back toward him.

He grinned. "Why thank you, Ma'am, but...well, I'd best leave it here, read some on it when I come over." He set it back on the window sill.

Medina raised his cup. "You to have some coffee with me?"

John Alexander's smile now threatened to split his face. "Yes, sir!"

They pulled up chairs as Takansy went inside to the cookstove, poured the steaming brew through a strainer into a cup and added some fresh cream. The boy never tired of listening to Medina's stories. Medina never tired of telling them.

As she stepped back onto the porch, John Alexander said, "How'd you lose the tip of your middle finger, sir?"

Medina held his hand up and turned it over. "Long ago I lose him. A man jump me at Fort Bridger. Nearly kill me. Later, he die."

"Did you...kill him?"

He smiled and waved his hand, dismissively. "He freeze in Bear River."

The boy took a stub of a pencil from his shirt and a scrap of butcher paper from his pants pocket.

"Do you mind? I'd like to write that story down."

Medina raised his cup as if in a toast. "You are a curious boy. Curious is good. Sure, you can write him. But first..." He tossed out the last bit of coffee, walked into the trading post and emerged a moment later with a brand new pencil and notepad. "For the writing, you to have the best tools."

"Oh no, sir, I couldn't take that home. I..." The boy's face screwed into a frown. "Could I please keep it here, and use it when I come?"

Medina nodded and cocked his head. "Your father?"

John Alexander swallowed hard. "No, it's just...it might get lost if I took it home." Then his face brightened, as if remembering something. "But there is a place I could...why yes, I can use this. Thank you, sir." His smile returned. He fanned the notepad pages with his thumb. "The book, too." He smiled at Takansy, retrieved the Kit Carson book and tucked it into his shirt front. "I'll have it back in a wag," he said.

Medina said, "*Bueno*. But the story to wait. Buyers here." He thrust his chin toward the courtyard where two wagons rolled up. He clapped John Alexander on the back and stepped down the stairs. At the bottom he turned. "Maybe you to write a story about Kit Carson. He to visit the Crossing soon, maybe tomorrow or next day."

The notepad flopped to the floor. Takansy retrieved it and handed it to the dumbstruck boy.

Over seventy people came to the crossing to see Kit Carson. Takansy was amazed. *He is only a trapper and scout, and they act like he is General Grant!* Her wonder increased when he stepped out of the stage coach into the fading winter light.

What she saw was not the man she remembered from her days at Fort Bridger. The pallor of his forehead, the droop of his jaw, the hollows under his eyes and cheeks transformed him. Pain gripped his features. A short man made shorter by sagging knees, his step faltered as he moved toward the welcoming committee. Shadows from the bare tree branches spidered over his face.

People drew back when they got a look at him, then clapped. He gave Takansy a weak smile of recognition when he got to her place in the receiving line.

Lena curtsied beside her. At Medina's insistence, Lena wore a frilly blue dress instead of the beaded white buckskin garment Takansy had made. It rankled. But she forced herself to be agreeable.

There were speeches. A news man asking questions. Fiddle music. Takansy paid scarce attention to the words and the fanfare. What she noticed were people's eyes. How Henry Howard, bypassed by Medina and Kit Carson in the receiving line, bored holes in her husband's receding back. How pretty Susan Howard's eyes followed Medina, rather than Kit Carson, as they walked by. How Antonio, chin thrust up as if wanting to pick a fight, fixed bold eyes on Sarah Jane Blackhurst, and how she batted her eyelashes and flipped a lock of auburn hair with a toss of her head.

And how John Alexander's eyes seemed riveted not on Kit Carson but on Lena. Takansy fixed him with a stone stare. His brows curled into question marks, then he quickly looked down at his notepad and began to write.

28

John Alexander
June 1868

In June, 1868, five months after Kit Carson's visit, word got out that the famous scout had died. Johnnie wasn't surprised, remembering how Carson had looked that day. But he felt low. Heroes get old and die like everyone else, he figured. But that was no comfort. He wondered if he would ever do anything heroic.

For sure, it wasn't going to happen hauling logs with Pa all day. That's what he mostly did, up on Alexander's Mountain, as folks now called it. Pa would walk ahead marking the next tree to cut, while Johnnie drove the wagon. Then they'd pull a two-handled saw through the trunk, ax off the branches and heft the tree on board.

Pa had gotten stronger in the Colorado air, sure, but still was short of breath. Johnnie took over hefting the heavy end. He was growing stouter, that was the good thing about it. When no one was looking he'd sometimes take off his shirt and bend his arms to watch his muscles flex.

Pa's wagons were built narrow to move along the skinny tracks they hacked into the mountain. When loaded, they got top heavy, hard to manage. One day, instead of paying attention, Johnnie started daydreaming about galloping off on a fine horse with Lena and Louie Papa. His mind drifted away like the clouds of yellow pollen that puffed up when the wagon brushed a pine branch.

That's when the right front wheel dropped into a runnel and twisted to the side. Lost in thought, Johnnie flew off the wagon seat and landed, knees first, on rocky ground next to a patch of prickly pear. Pain stabbed through him. He bit his arm to keep from crying out.

Four logs toppled off the dangerously leaning wagon and rolled to the bottom of a draw, tearing out bushes and making an awful commotion.

Pa didn't speak a word. His weary sigh said it all. *Clumsy and absent-minded, same as always.* He pulled Johnnie up and looked at the blood spots seeping through his son's torn trousers.

"Let's have a look."

Johnnie rolled up his pants and bent his legs. Nothing seemed to be broken. Pa brushed the dirt off the cuts.

"Ye'll live," he said.

Johnnie gritted his teeth.

It took the better part of the afternoon to drag the logs back up to the wagon. By the time they finally got down the mountain, dark had closed in.

"Think you can manage unloading by yourself?" Pa's wheezy voice, weakened by the added exertion, stung. He walked away rubbing his bad arm.

Johnnie felt sorry for his father and glad to be alone at the same time. The odor of biscuits and gravy drifted out of the dugout, making his mouth all runny. He led Old Dun to the sawmill platform and lowered the wagon's side board. Crashing like thunder, the logs rolled into place. He yanked at Old Dun to move him to the barn to unhitch the wagon. The horse balked.

He yelled and swatted the horse's rump. Too late he realized a corner of the side board was pinched between two logs. The wagon tipped over. Old Dun snorted and yanked at the harness, his eyes wild white in the near dark.

"Goddammit sonofabitch." Johnnie kicked at an upturned wheel and felt hot tears well up.

"You cussed!" It was Jennie's voice, loud, accusing.

Johnnie whirled around. There stood his sister with a plate of biscuits and gravy. Her hand covered her mouth, but not far enough to hide the smirk that signaled she was itching to tell Pa. Instead of handing over the plate, she set it on the sawmill platform and backed away.

"Jennie! I didn't..." But she was already turning back toward the dugout. "What am I supposed to eat this with?" he shouted at her retreating back.

By the time Johnnie freed Old Dun and untangled the harness, the gravy had turned into a gloppy, quivering ooze. He stuffed the mess into his mouth and thought about what awaited in the dugout. Probably the Old Testament: *Thou-shalt-not-take-the-name-of-the-Lord-thy-God-in-vain* commandment, followed by a sermon on how the Israelites got smited for the same transgression, and ending with the razor strap, wielded in "sadness-not-in-anger."

What Johnnie hated most was getting chastised in front of the others. Mattie and Anna would hug each other and cry. Little Robert would stare and vow never to do what Johnnie did. Mama would hover and wring her apron. And Jennie, the good child, would gloat. Right then, Johnnie hated Jennie, and Pa, too. Most of all he hated his own clumsiness, his daydreaming foolishness. His weakness in standing up to Pa.

He decided right then and there to sleep in the barn. He crawled up on a pile of hay over Old Dun's stall, pulled a smelly horse blanket over his legs and despite being all tuckered out, laid there awake, knees hurting, worrying. About cussing. About what he might do if Pa came with his razor strap.

Before long Mama's quavery voice called out, "Johnnie? Johnnie?"

He burrowed down into the hay. The door hinges groaned. Old Dun snorted.

"Johnnie, you all right? I been worrying about you."

"I'm fine, Mama."

"How're them knees?"

"Just scratched."

"You best come, Johnnie. I've got your Pa calmed down now, but you still need to take your licking."

"I'm not coming."

He could hear her fumbling around in the dark for the ladder. The thought of her climbing up there was more than he could take.

"Stop, Mama. I'll come down."

When he got to the bottom, she hugged him. He pulled away. They walked toward the dugout. Pa was leaning on his cane next to a lantern on the porch. Mac stood still beside him, his ears cocked forward. Robert, Annie and Jennie were nowhere to be seen, thank the Lord.

Pa skipped the lecture. His face looked drawn, his body all tuckered out.

"John Alexander, it's my duty as a father to punish ye for blasphemy, but I take no satisfaction in it. Bend over the stump."

Brave thoughts of rearing up on his hind legs and telling Pa a thing or two just frittered away when the strap came out. Johnnie got down on his smarting knees, bent at the waist so his chest rested on the stump, and wrapped his arms around the rough bark.

The strap came down with a *whop*. Ten licks in all. Mac whined. Johnnie dug his fingers into the bark, gritted his teeth, and didn't cry a single tear until afterward, when they'd gone inside and Mac laid his head on his leg.

Next morning, Johnnie loaded the wagon with rough-cut boards and climbed into the driver's seat.

Pa limped out and rubbed the boards with his hand. "Mind ye get full price for these boards—twelve-fifty, not a dime less." Pa's face was hard, his eyes brittle blue, his voice harsh. He wanted to make sure he got his money's worth for the extra annoyance of selling to a papist. "And go slow. No more spills." His finger wagged from side to side like an upside-down pendulum.

Although Pa stood square on the ground looking up, to Johnnie it felt like he was glaring down. Johnnie couldn't meet his eye. His backside still burned from the razor strap.

"I don't hear an answer," Pa said.

"Yes, sir. These here boards'll stay put. Got 'em roped down tight."

"These boards. It's time to be using proper English. You're fourteen."

"Yes, sir."

Johnnie caught sight of Jennie standing in the doorway. Getting scolded like a child was hard to take, especially in front of her. But he couldn't blame Pa after what happened yesterday. So he gave Pa a nod that he hoped wasn't too bootlicky and turned Old Dun toward the Crossing.

His spirits rose with every clop of the horse's hooves. A whole day away from home, free of blue-eyed disapproval, a day—if Johnnie worked fast—with time left over to watch Louie Papa and Lena working the Medina herd. He pushed Old Dun to go faster. The horse snorted disapproval. The wagon lurched. Wheels squealed like a hog rousted from slumber.

Mariano's Butte came into view. It wasn't much to look at—a scrubby little mound with a rocky point on top—but to Johnny it signaled the welcome boundary between the dreary world behind, ruled by his dour preacher of a father, and the exciting world ahead, led by a fearless hero.

Of a sudden there was a big twisty jolt, and Johnnie jerked hard on the reins. Too hard. Old Dun pulled up short, and the boards moved forward with a sickening sliding sound. They cracked hard against the wagon headboard. It splintered loose from its angle-iron frame, lifted Johnnie out of the seat and shoved him forward. Twisting around, he grabbed the bar on the wagon top with both hands. His arms near ripped out of his shoulders, but he managed to hold on. Old Dun, feeling the reins go slack, lurched forward. The wagon caught up with the sliding boards and the load held.

"Whoa. Easy, whoa." Johnnie tried to sound calm despite his heart leaping clean out of his chest. The wagon slowed to a stop. He got off. The damage wasn't too bad. He pulled the boards back into place and wired the headboard back on its frame. He gave Old Dun a long pat on his neck. The horse hadn't panicked, glory be. He'd saved Johnnie's bacon.

Johnnie looked at his hands. They shook like aspen leaves. Mariano Medina's hands never shook, he felt sure.

As he set out again for the Crossing, Johnnie got to figuring the accident might be a blessing. He could borrow a saw from Louie Papa and replace the headboard. He could tell Pa he'd seen it was weak and replaced it before it could break loose. That way Pa couldn't get mad when he got back late. He smiled at this bit of cunning.

As he hoped, Louie Papa and Lena were working cattle in the big pasture east of the trading post. Johnnie pulled up to the fence and waved. They rode over. Louie Papa's high-top boots rested easy in the stirrups. Lena's brown moccasins dangled free against Shy Bird's bare sides. She wore buckskin pants topped by a short skirt.

She gave him a little nod. "Hello, John Alexander."

Johnnie liked how she always called him by both names. He said, "Them's sure some fine horses. I'd give a lot if could ride like that."

"You got a horse," Louie Papa said.

"You mean Old Dun, here?" Johnnie laughed. "Those cows of yours could run around him twice before he could take three steps with those big old cloppy feet of his."

All three looked at Old Dun's feet, trees planted in the road. Louie Papa's mustache twitched. Lena laughed. It lit up her face like sunrise on the mountain.

Emboldened, Johnnie said, "Say now, "I don't suppose you could teach me. I mean, I don't want to be a bother, and if you say no, that won't make a bit of difference, but…" He trailed off, feeling like he'd stepped too close to some edge. Then he thought of the licking he'd just got, swallowed hard and went on over. "I'd sure like to learn to ride like you."

Lena looked at Louie Papa. He looked at Johnnie, then back at her. "Shoot, we can teach you." He nodded toward the corral. "Maybe Buckskin Joe over there."

"That one. By the water trough." Lena let out a low whistle.

A compact buckskin raised his dripping nose from the horse tank and peered at her with ears pointed.

Johnnie said, "Well, he's not as spry as Old Dun here, but I reckon he'll do."

That got another smile. It spread to show her white teeth. Johnnie felt like dancing.

Then Lena's eyes caught sight of something beyond the corral, and Johnnie turned to see Mr. and Mrs. Medina coming toward them from the trading post. His face was all smiley, like he'd just won a horse race. Hers was unreadable, but her step had a nice bounce to it.

Johnnie squared his shoulders and wiped his hand on his pants, hoping Mr. Medina would shake it or maybe even give him one of those half-hug, back slapping greetings he used with Kit Carson and other friends.

29

Medina
July 1868

Medina hurried toward the pasture fence. Louie Papa, Lena and the Alexander boy stood there looking quizzical. His excitement must be showing. Takansy's, too. He glanced at his wife as she strode along beside him. As close to happy as he'd ever seen her. All due to the letter he carried in his hand.

A twinge in his right side reminded him he was still packing Captain Jack's derringer bullet. He seldom noticed it, except when he got moving fast. He took a deep breath.

At the fence he greeted young Alexander with a wrap-around, two-handed back-slap. The boy blushed. From the other side of the fence, Lena and Louie Papa stared at him.

He waved the letter in the air. "You are to witness. We have good news!"

Their eyes followed the waving paper. He had made the stage driver read it to him four times while he savored the imagined reaction of the settlers.

"The Denver City committee is make a big decision. Lena, you to lead the parade. The big one, Fourth of July. Our friend Jones has arranged it."

He stuffed the letter back in his pocket, reached over the fence and pulled Lena off Shy Bird. The black mare edged away as he lifted her over the fence.

He shouted, "*Viva* Lena, queen of Big Thompson!"

Takansy stepped forward to hug Lena. "Big pride. My heart so large, my flower."

Lena beamed, a smile that reminded Medina of his wife's smile in the early days. Takansy smiled back. It felt good to be celebrating the moment together.

Takansy patted her daughter's shoulders. "I making you new white doeskin dress for the parade. Best bead dress ever."

Medina's mood dropped. Why was Takansy presuming to dress Lena Indian style? He had something else in mind, something like what the Denver City ladies were wearing. He shook his head to shoo away a fly.

"Your clothes. Later we will decide."

To change the subject, he turned to John Alexander, "You have brought wood, yes? After unload, you to come see my new guns— Henry repeaters, very good. I to show you." He knew the lad admired his collection of firearms and the stories that went with them.

Louie Papa stepped forward. "Boy wants to learn cattle work. We're trying him on Buckskin Joe."

Medina took in the boy's eager eyes. They peered from under a mop of sandy hair like a near-grown puppy's. The boy didn't seem quite up to his fourteen years, a slow grower. He flashed the youngster a smile.

"Good to learn. You get good enough, you to come work for me, yes?"

"Yes, sir."

Medina liked how the boy stressed the "sir." He smiled at the thought of what the boy's dour father might think if his son came to work for Mariano Medina.

John Alexander said, "Mr. Medina, sir, you don't suppose I could go with you. To the parade, I mean. I won't be a bother. I could help, you know, like loading the wagon, hitching up...and brushing the horses...and all that."

Medina looked at his wife, shrugged, and said, "Why not? We will to leave early on July three. Just before sunup. You will to ride the wagon, yes?"

"Yes, sir. Anywhere you say." The lad looked as if he'd been handed a hundred dollars.

Medina headed back to the trading post. It would be a good thing for John Alexander to return and tell the settlers about Lena's triumph. He savored the thought of turning Frank Bartholf down when he asked, as he surely would, for Lena to lead their puny Fourth of July parade there on the Big Thompson next year.

30

John Alexander
June to July 1868

"You pleased?" Johnnie asked Lena after Mr. and Mrs. Medina left.

Lena stroked Shy Bird's neck. "Yes, but…Denver City is noisy, lots of people, buildings. Shy Bird may not be…you know…used to it. A parade."

"You'll do great. That horse does whatever you want." He studied her face. Her brow remained furrowed, so he added, "Besides, if my folks ever grabbed me up and carried on like that, I'd be so busting out with happiness you'd have to tie me down with ropes to keep me from floating away."

That got a faint smile. "Yes, that part is nice."

Louie Papa twitched his moustache toward Buckskin Joe and said, "Better get moving if you want a drover lesson."

That brought Johnnie back to glorying in his new, imagined life as a cowhand. Mr. Medina had said he might work for him! Johnnie felt like Lazarus must have felt when Jesus raised him from the dead.

He soon got lost in a world of saddles and cinches and reining and stopping and turning. He tried to keep his horse at a distance that caused the cow to move in the right direction. Buckskin Joe was so quick that he near fell off several times when he signaled with too much force. "Easy," Lena would say. "Just a light squeeze, not a kick." Or, "Just give him his head." It was hard to get the hang of it. He bounced around on that horse's back until his hind end was even sorer than when he'd arrived.

Time flew by without so much as a howdy. June's trick is to make it seem earlier than it really is, what with daylight lingering on and all. It wasn't until the shadow of the western mountains took the bright out of Lena's face that Johnnie realized how late it was.

Alarmed, he blurted out something about chores and asked Lena if she could take care of Buckskin Joe while he ran to unload the boards. He collected the money at the store, told Mr. Medina he'd have to look at his guns some other time, shouted a bunch of "thank yous" and "I'm sorrys" to Louie Papa and Lena, and wheeled Old Dun around toward home.

By the time the horse clip-clopped past their darkened barn, Johnnie's heart was hammering. He had plumb forgot to fix the wagon's headboard, which was going to be his excuse for getting back late. He felt its broken edge with his fingers and wondered if another whipping would cure his absent-mindedness. It hadn't so far.

Maybe he could slip in and spend another night in the barn. But it was too late. A lantern bobbed in the barn doorway, its light flickering across Pa's livid face. He leaned forward, his good hand gripping his hickory cane. Mama held the lantern beside him. Her face looked wrung out.

Johnnie hauled Old Dun to a stop. He felt his face go hot. He couldn't—wouldn't—take another chastisement, even if he deserved it. He was fourteen. Fourteen! He would snatch up that razor strap. He would face Pa down. Push him, by God, if he had to. He would leave. He would… go work for Mr. Medina. The blasphemous thought took hold of him as if the devil himself was waltzing him around a dance floor. He felt a drop of sweat trickle down the side of his face and cool in the night air.

"Where in God's green earth have ye been?" Pa's voice was angry, but Johnnie was surprised to hear a hint of worry as well. Pa added, "I was just rigging up to go look for you."

Mama ran over and squeezed Johnnie hard against her. The devil was no match for that hug.

"Johnnie, Johnnie," she said. "I was a mite worried about you. After that whuppin'…I'm glad you're home."

"It's all right, Mama."

At Pa's approach, her voice quieted to a whisper. "Don't rile him, Johnnie. He's hard, but he don't want you to go, neither. He's…"

He patted her as Pa limped up. The darkness didn't dim the blue sparks burning in his eyes. As usual, Johnnie's own eyes wavered and dropped.

"Where have you been?" Pa said.

Johnnie's mind clawed for purchase like a squirrel falling through branches. He couldn't think of what to say.

Mama prompted, "What happened, Johnnie?"

"The wagon broke." He pointed to the headboard. It wasn't a lie, at least, and it got Pa looking somewhere else besides at him.

Pa walked over and poked his cane at the loose headboard, which let out an accusing creak. He swung around, brandished the cane for a moment, then limped away.

"You can fix it in the morning."

They watched him disappear into the dugout.

Mama said, "Johnnie, he's plumb scared, though he don't show it." She took his head in her hands and gave him a fierce look. "He needs you, Johnnie. His arm and all. He can't…"

She didn't have to spell it out. His arm, his lungs, the boiler accident…it was all Johnnie's doing. There was no getting around it. He sighed and pulled away to take care of Old Dun.

"Don't leave us, Johnnie," she said, in a voice that near broke his heart.

It took some smart stepping on Johnnie's part to finagle his trip to Denver City. The sawmill, he told Pa, could use a new, fine-cut blade. According to Mr. Blackhurst, folks wanted better wood for cabinets and such, now that their main homes were built with the rough-cut lumber from their sawmill. Denver City was a long way to go for fine-cut wood, and they could expect a high price for good boards from a local mill.

Pa's eyebrows lifted into bristly question marks.

"Which store?" he asked.

Johnnie took this as a good sign. "Jones' Mercantile is where…"

"Don't ye be going to just one store. Shop around. Compare." He scribbled some figures on a piece of butcher paper and handed it over. "No more than twenty-five dollars."

Johnnie took the paper and tried to keep his expression business-like. Apparently, Pa hadn't heard about the Fourth-of-July parade.

"Talk to your Ma about food and supplies. Ye'll need sleeping gear. Tent. No hotel. Can't afford such niceties."

Johnnie took a deep breath to stop himself from running to the kitchen. Mama's first yen was to get Pa to go, too, but Pa wouldn't have it, praise the lord. She put on that "Oh-Johnnie" worried look, wrung out her apron until it was as wrinkled as a prune, and finally got busy stuffing food in a seed-sack duffel bag.

"I don't like the idea of you going all the way down there alone," she said.

He patted her. "Others are going. I won't be alone."

"Who?"

"Oh, several I heard about. The Bartholfs, I think. It's a holiday. Lots of folks." In truth, he didn't know of anyone going besides the Medinas. The local folks had their own parade to attend to.

"Where will you stay?"

"Folks say there's a tenting ground near the…" He almost said, "parade," but caught himself. "…stores. It's only for a couple of days, Mama. Come on, help me find that canvas for a tent, and I'll need a bedroll."

That kept her busy. He kept telling her she needn't worry. Not that it did any good, because worry was just something she did. Milk soured. Mama worried. She finished packing, then pressed an extra five dollars into his hand.

"Just in case," she whispered.

The coins felt hot. "What'll Pa think?"

"We won't tell him."

Surprised, he looked at her tight-lipped, determined face.

"Thanks, Mama." He gave her a squeeze.

The money, thirty dollars in all, went into a belt pouch.

Later, he fetched his church-going clothes—Pa's hand-me-down white shirt, black pants and oversized coat—and stuffed them into the duffel. For the grand parade, he wanted his best outfit.

He didn't have to argue about the trip's timing. His family never even celebrated birthdays, let alone the Fourth of July, despite its marking America's defeat of the British, which Pa would naturally want to celebrate if he believed in celebrations at all, which he didn't. In his view, celebrations were the work of the Devil, a diversion from the sober and frugal pursuit of work every day except Sunday, when God could be celebrated in the same sober and frugal way.

Johnnie managed to set off before dawn on the morning of July 3, trying to look sober and frugal and feeling just the opposite. The good feeling lasted all the way to the Crossing. It was unusually warm for the pre-dawn time. The smell of horses and leather wafted out of Mr. Medina's open barn door as Johnnie reined in Old Dun. Before him stood Mr. Medina's fine army ambulance wagon, used for hauling trade goods from Jones's Mercantile.

"My 'avalanche,'" Mr. Medina called it in his accented English.

The wagon was draped with red, white and blue bunting. Shy Bird was tied on behind, a team of matched grays was hitched to the front. All three horses were so well groomed their coats shone in the lantern light.

In front of the grays, hands holding the harness, stood Mrs. Medina in a plain buckskin outfit, tunic and pants. Lena hovered by her side. Oddly, they paid Johnnie no mind as he unsaddled Old Dun and turned him out into the pasture. When he walked up behind them, he could see why. Their eyes were fixed on Mr. Medina and Antonio, faced off about twenty feet away, bristling at each other like two hounds.

Mr. Medina shouted something in Spanish. His words spewed out like stones. A vein pulsed in his neck. The knuckles on his left hand squeezed white on his Hawken rifle. His right hand, balled into a fist, hammered the air, coming down again and again on an invisible target that Johnnie reckoned might soon be Antonio's head.

The sneer on Antonio's face was scary to behold. He stood, loose and easy, but coiled like a snake. He was thinner than his pa, but quick, with muscles that would make a body think twice about tangling with him. He was full grown, twenty years old.

He shook his head slowly and said "no" a couple of times. His smile seemed intended to aggravate his father.

Seeing Antonio stand up to his pa like that gave Johnnie a thrilling fright, like watching a daredevil walk a stretched wire.

Mr. Medina took a step forward. Before he could close, Antonio let out a dog's bark of a laugh that silenced the birds awakening in the trees. His white teeth flashed a smile that seemed to say, "Let's not fight…this time." He turned aside and walked—*sauntered*—away.

Mr. Medina stood there for a full minute. His right hand reached for his tomahawk, but just rested there, as if seeking comfort. Then his shoulders relaxed. He turned and walked toward the wagon, head down. Mrs. Medina and Lena glanced at Johnnie for the first time, relief on their faces.

Part of Johnnie felt satisfied to realize that his wasn't the only family with father-son trouble. Another part was disappointed. His notion of the Medina family being a happy affair was shook up.

When Mr. Medina finally spotted Johnnie, his face did a quick little dance in reaction to an unexpected audience.

He managed a smile and said, "John…good day. We are ready to go now, yes?"

Johnnie stood there a moment too long before hefting his duffel onto the wagon. By that time Mr. Medina had come up in front of the three of them. The shout had gone out of his face but the snarl was still there.

"Never to bring shame on your family," he said, looking first at Lena and then at Johnnie. "And never, ever, to dishonor your father."

"Yes, sir," Johnnie mumbled. He looked sideways at Lena.

"Yes, Papi," she said, looking down.

"The family is all," Mr. Medina said. "*La familia.* Together we to get respect. Alone, you…" He trailed off for a moment, then said, "Antonio is much in danger to bring shame on our family. If he does, he must go. *Exilio.*"

Of a sudden he gripped Lena's arms so hard her thin body jerked forward. "Lena, *mi hija,* listen. You must to promise me. Bring pride on your family. Promise!"

Lena nodded, her eyes round.

"Say it."

"I promise." Her voice could barely be heard.

His eyes bored into her. Finally, he let go, and she sagged back to recover her balance. Johnnie glanced at her mama. Mrs. Medina's gray eyes lingered first on the girl then on her husband, but her expression was blank as a frying pan.

Mr. Medina climbed into the driver's seat. Mrs. Medina pulled herself up beside him. Lena and Johnnie settled into a little depression in the canvas tarp covering the load. Underneath, Johnnie discovered later, were potatoes, onions and some of Mrs. Medina's fine beaded shirts to drop off at Jones Mercantile.

As the wagon jounced down the road, dust rising on both sides, Johnnie sat in silence, waiting for a chance to ask what the fuss was all about without seeming too nosy.

The morning sun bore down on them through the opening under the wagon's roof. Johnnie took off his boots and wiggled his toes in the air. He unbuttoned the top of his shirt.

Lena took off her moccasins and rolled her pantlegs up to just below her knees. She pulled her legs toward her and wrapped her arms around them, knees sticking up. Johnnie stared a few seconds too long at the smooth brownness of her calves and ankles, then fixed his eyes on the sky.

"Hot," he said, for something to say.

She gave him a shy sideways glance, "A breeze would be nice."

"Or some clouds. Maybe this afternoon. If we don't get some clouds, then you and me, we're going to melt." He swiped a hand across his forehead and flicked some sweat onto the tarp.

Her face looked red.

He said, "You feeling all right?"

She nodded, but not very convincingly. He couldn't decide if it was the heat or the Antonio business that was bothering her.

"Where's Louie Papa?" he said.

"He couldn't come. His wife...the baby is sick. If she needs a doctor..."

"Your little cousin."

"Yes. In a few years I can teach him to ride. Like I was hoping with Rosita."

"Well, I guess you're stuck with me for now."

The corners of her mouth turned up a bit, but she didn't smile. They talked about horses for a while.

Finally he said, "I don't see Antonio riding much."

She gave him a guarded glance, then looked at her parents bouncing along on the seat in front. They were talking, intense-like, but only murmurs could be heard over the wagon clatter.

Lena leaned a little closer and in a low voice said, "Antonio rides very good, but…he likes city things."

"So what's he gone and done? Why's your pa so mad at him?"

Lena waited a long time before answering. "The Blackhurst girl."

"Sarah Jane? What about her?"

She frowned and put a finger to her lips. "He's sweet on her, and she on him."

Johnnie recalled Sarah Jane's cow-eyed response to Antonio's flirty smile at the Kit Carson visit.

"Nothing wrong with that," he said, trying to sound experienced in such things. "They're both old enough. What's your pa got against them?"

"Not Papi. It's her parents, especially her father. They don't want Antonio coming around, because…" She looked down.

He waited, letting her find the words.

"He's Spaniard. And Indian. Like me."

Johnnie could feel her eyes on his face.

"That's about the worst reason I ever heard."

"Doesn't your father think the same?"

"He's got nothing against Spaniards, or Indians, for that matter, except the savage kind, raiding and all. He's mainly…" Johnnie felt embarrassed to go on.

"What?"

"He's…well, he don't cotton to Catholics."

"Why not?"

"It's a long story. My grandpa, our whole clan, came from Scotland, then ended up in Ireland where the Catholics…well, let's just say they beat up on our kind pretty bad. But it was long ago, clear across the sea, and now it's just a bunch of old stories. Why he keeps on about it, I'll never know. It's just foolishness." He felt a little disloyal saying this, especially after Mr. Medina's lecture about honoring your father. But he didn't want Lena to think he had some kind of narrow-mindedness when it came to her family.

"You are…what are you?"

"Religion-wise? Oh, I'm…our family…we're Presbyterian. Protestant. My pa preaches sometimes." He wanted to get the conversation back on Antonio. "Shoot, if Antonio wasn't Catholic, my pa'd marry him to my sister Jennie right off." He gave her a little smile.

The corners of her mouth lifted a tad, then she became serious again.

"It's not just that, with Antonio, I mean." She bent her head down to her knees and said to him sideways, so her parents wouldn't hear, "Antonio and Sarah Jane…my papa caught them in the barn, and you know…" She trailed off, blushing.

Johnnie looked away. *That* would be a horse of a different color.

"Shoot," he said, unable to come up with something that would make him sound wise.

At noon they stopped to water the horses in Boulder Creek. When Lena stood up, her knees shook. His own knees felt stiff so he didn't think much about it.

She said, "I will ride for a while."

She scrambled down, said something to her mother, walked over to the creek and splashed water on her face. When they set off again, she pulled herself onto Shy Bird and rode alongside the wagon, bareback. Neither she nor her horse looked to be their usual spirited selves. Her face was still flushed. The heat, he guessed.

31

Takansy
July 1868

At the watering stop, Takansy watched John Alexander watch Lena. The boy's eyes lingered on her daughter. Too long, she thought.

When they started down the road again, Takansy worked her way back to sit next to the boy.

He scooted aside to make space. "Ma'am?" His Adam's apple bobbed.

She sensed his discomfort. Her eyes often did that to people. She shifted her gaze to where Lena rode off to the side, beyond their wagon dust. Her daughter's face looked unusually flushed, even for such a hot day.

"Like Flathead people she riding, no saddle. I teaching her."

"Yes, Ma'am." He turned to face her. "Ma'am, I've been wondering...I don't want to cause offense, or anything, but...

your people, do they have flat heads, and if they do, how come, well, yours isn't...you know...flat?"

The boy was so serious she almost smiled. "That name coming from the Coast People who are tying their babies' heads onto a board so they pointing on top, like this." She formed a tipi shape with her hands. "To them, we are the ones having flat heads. You, too."

"So that's it." He smiled, then fixed his gaze back on Lena.

Takansy turned the talk back to her daughter.

"Riding like her, no one is doing it. In the parade, she wearing Flathead dress. Indian ride, Indian dress." She jutted her chin toward Medina and added, "She wearing lady dresses only to *fiesta*."

"Like the blue one she wore when Kit Carson visited? I like that."

She shook her head. "My dress finest beads, bells from Denver, very expensive. To an English Duke I can be selling it one thousand dollar. One thousand!"

She was pleased to watch his jaw drop.

He said, "For glory sake. That's more money than our family ever scraped together in a whole year. I can't believe...well, I reckon maybe English Dukes can do such things. He shook his head, then added, "You said something about a *fiesta*?"

"In hotel. After parade. Denver City big men and wives." She thrust her chin again toward Medina. "A *grande tertulia*. It is all he is talking about."

John Alexander glanced at the patches on his pants.

Then she fired her question.

"My Lena. You are liking her?"

The boy jerked like he'd been stuck with a needle.

"No, Ma'am, I mean...well, yes, I do like Lena, and Louie Papa and, well, your whole family, you know, you've been so kind... helping me learn horses and...she's so...nice, for a little girl, I mean." The boy squirmed as his eyes slid away from hers.

She liked this boy, but his reaction did nothing to relax her vigilance.

Before she could say more, however, she was jolted by the sudden flight of a large hoot owl, spooked by the wagon, flapping silently out of the tree branches above them. Takansy's mouth went dry. She crossed herself and grabbed her rosary beads

"What's wrong, Ma'am?"

"Bad Medicine." She whirled around to check on Lena. Her

daughter's face had lost its color. The girl leaned to one side, and for a moment, Takansy thought she was going to fall off Shy Bird. Then Lena's head jerked and she heaved a stream of yellow vomit down onto a bushy tuft of grass. It hung there, quivering in droopy strings.

"Stop, Mariano! Stop!"

Takansy jumped down, landed hard on the road and ran to her daughter. Lena slid to the ground and stood bent over the grass with her hands on her knees. Her neck and head spasmed. Shy Bird sidestepped and turned, ears pointed.

Takansy cupped Lena's forehead in her palm through the next several spasms.

"Hold on, my daughter, it will soon pass," she crooned. Lena's head felt warm, but not feverish.

Medina's shadow fell across them. "The stomach sickness?"

"I am hoping that is all, but…"

Lena heaved once more and pushed herself upright. Takansy took the water jug from Mariano and passed it to Lena. Shaking, she rinsed and spat, then rose from her knees.

Medina reached for her, but Takansy said, "You getting Shy Bird. Lena riding with me in the wagon." She pulled Lena to her and helped her back to the wagon.

John Alexander, eyes round, stood holding the team.

"What happened?"

"Lena sick. You riding the wagon seat now."

Medina lifted Lena into the wagon.

"It is just the stomach sickness, like Louie Papa's baby, yes? Lena will be better by tomorrow night, to meet the governor at the hotel *fiesta*?"

Takansy stared at her husband, annoyed at his focus on the big man event. She gave him a curt nod and pulled herself into the wagon beside Lena. The boy climbed up beside Medina, and they set off again.

Along the way, Lena threw up two more times. Finally, she fell asleep.

As Takansy gazed at Lena's flushed face, images of Rosita and Martín pushed their way into her mind like dancing demons.

32

John Alexander
July 1868

Johnnie kept wanting to steal glances at Lena, but every time he turned around, he ran smack into Mrs. Medina's stony stare. After a while he kept his eyes on the road. He asked Mr. Medina if he was worried about Lena.

"She sick sometimes," he said. "Short times. Usually better in one day."

Johnnie hoped he was right. He remembered the red splotches of scarlet fever that had killed his cousin in Illinois. He stole another look at Lena, but her face was shaded under a strip of calico.

The road entered a flat stretch of plains. The sun, halfway down toward the western mountains, lit up the green grass from behind. Several hundred cattle spotted the land. They had longer horns than any Johnnie had seen. Along the far edge of the herd rode several men.

"John Wesley Iliff. His beeves, his riders," Mr. Medina said. "Come up from Texas. The Goodnight Trail."

Johnnie had heard of John Wesley Illiff, the biggest cattleman in those parts. His mind drifted into a daydream of becoming a top hand, riding a fine horse, swinging a rope, rescuing calves from mountain lions. Then he remembered his duty to his family.

They arrived in Denver City late at night. Johnnie gawked at the stores, houses and saloons lining the street. And the people. Why were they still up? Dust rose around them, heavy with smells of manure and sounds of laughter, curses and occasional fighting. Fiddle music sounded from an open doorway. Three men in rough boots and wool shirts staggered out. Miners, he guessed.

They passed an open area filled with tents and campfires. His mouth watered at the smells of sizzling meat and coffee.

"That's where I'll be staying. I brought a tent," he said.

Mr. Medina nodded and pointed ahead. "Our hotel, it is there, just another street more."

Johnnie peered at the grand-looking building. Oil lanterns shone from windows.

"Could I come and...I could tend to the team and wagon so you can get on inside and, you know, with Lena. I'll walk back here after." He didn't want Mr. Medina to see him unroll the ragged square of canvas he called a tent.

"Yes, good idea."

They rolled toward the hotel. The words *American House* were carved into a big stone across the top of double doors. Couples strolled the boardwalk in front. The men wore polished boots, creased pants, long-tail coats and silk top hats. The ladies wore white gloves and dresses wide enough to take up two spaces. One woman's dress was so low-cut it made him blush.

Mr. Medina pulled the grays to a stop. A man dressed in tight pants, shiny boots and a black vest stepped up to hold the horses while another walked toward Lena and her mama, gloved hand outstretched, to help them out of the wagon. Lena looked pale as a skinned cottonwood.

They climbed the steps toward two doors tall as houses. A thin, hawk-like fellow in a fancy purple coat with gold sleeve braids pulled a door open. He turned up his beak of a nose as the Medinas passed in front of him. Johnnie didn't like his look, not one bit.

The doors opened into a towering room with a huge brass chandelier and leather couches all around. Fancy-dressed people clustered near the bottom of a long, curved stairway. Johnnie looked at his patched pants and faded shirt and decided not to go in.

Mr. Medina turned in the doorway.

"Until tomorrow, then. God willing, my Lena will soon lose the sickness.

Johnnie hoped he was right. She looked like a fallen bird in her mama's arms. He gave her a little wave, but her eyes were closed. Were streaks of red inching up her neck? He couldn't tell for sure.

33

Takansy
July 1868

Takansy hugged her daughter close, pressing her cheek into Lena's sweaty hair.

"Resting soon, my flower."

Lena nodded but made no sound. They followed Medina as he pushed through the hotel lobby toward a hotel man, thick-necked and official, standing behind a counter.

Before Medina could get to him, A.H. Jones rose from a heavily cushioned chair.

"Late again, I see." He grabbed her husband in a back-slapping hug. "Just like a durned Mexican." His infectious grin revealed a gap between his front teeth.

"I am Spaniard, you Irish drunk." Medina grabbed Jones's burly shoulders and held him at arms length.

Jones's grin faded. "What's wrong, *amigo?* You don't look so good."

"Lena sick. We need to get room, quick."

Jones bowed low in Takansy's direction, "Ma'am? What's wrong with your girl?"

"The stomach sickness, I think."

"Not scarlet fever, is it? We've had some cases here."

Takansy's throat closed. She had not thought of that deadly sickness. She placed her hand on Lena's forehead.

"No fever." It was as much a prayer as a statement.

Medina turned to Jones, "A doctor. You can get one?"

Before Jones could answer, the thick-necked hotel man bustled out from behind the counter, a frown on his sweaty face.

"Excuse me sir, but we are full and the lobby is off limits to…people who aren't guests."

Takansy watched the muscles bunch in Medina's back, a dog bristling.

Jones brandished a large brass key at the man.

"I have their room already rented, courtesy of the parade committee. You can go back to your cage."

"But, sir, I have…"

"Ask Mr. Bartholomew about it. Go on."

The hotel man's frowning brows lifted into a wheedling arch.

"Yes, sir." He backed away with a little bow and winced when he bumped into the sharp corner of the counter.

Takansy reached to calm her husband. "Come, now we going to room. Resting for Lena."

They followed Jones up the curved staircase, ignoring the stares of the other guests. In their room, Jones lit the oil lamp as Takansy eased Lena down on the edge of the bed. A white ceramic chamber pot jutted from underneath. Takansy placed it on Lena's lap, then settled down beside her. She watched the tenseness leave Medina's shoulders as he surveyed the big four-poster bed, the elegant armoire, leather chairs and lace curtain that graced the window.

"*Bueno,*" he said.

"Best room in the hotel," Jones said. He turned to Takansy. "Ma'am, it's Saturday night. I know where to find Doc Crabtree, but I don't know as he'll be in any shape to help your daughter."

She grasped Jones's hand. "Thanking you. She is resting. No

parade tomorrow." Saying it made her wince inside. How she had wanted her daughter to ride! She scanned her husband's face.

"No parade?" Medina repeated the words slowly. Then his face lifted. "But *la fiesta*...tomorrow night, here in the hotel, with the Governor, the parade committee." His eyes found hers. "You have the healing touch. Make her well enough for *la fiesta*, at least."

She fixed him with her hard eyes. "Only if the sickness is gone."

His eyes shifted to Jones. "Come, let us to find the *médico*, yes?"

Jones bowed. "Ma'am, taking your leave." He clapped Medina around the shoulder and guided him out the door.

Takansy poured water from a pitcher into a glass, raised Lena's head and pressed it to her lips. Lena took a greedy drink and collapsed back onto the bed.

"You sleep now." She began crooning a sleeping song.

Lena's breathing slowed, became regular. Takansy peeled back the covers and the collar of Lena's shirt. A vein pulsed in her slender neck. There was no sign of telltale red splotches. Relieved, Takansy knelt and offered thanks to Jésu. *She is in your hands.* Then came the voice in her head: *so were Rosita and Martín.*

34

Medina
July 1868

"Much thanks, my friend." Medina gripped Jones' arm. Being with him felt easy, like with the old trappers. Not like with the newcomer settlers.

They descended the curved stairway into the hotel lobby. Medina's hip bones hurt after a long day of wagon seat pummeling.

Jones said, "Bad luck, your girl getting sick."

"Yes. Especially after you push the parade committee to have her. A thousand thanks."

"Shoot, I was glad to do it. Besides, a lot of those big wheels are eager to show they don't hate Indians after the Sand Creek business. Easterners won't let them hear the end of it." Jones let out a gap-toothed chuckle.

Their partnership had begun nearly ten years ago when Medina hauled his first load of trade goods from Jones' Mercantile to the Crossing at the beginning of the gold fever. Jones had somehow gained the confidence of all the jostling city factions: politicians, wary Mexicans, gaunt Confederate miners, cattlemen, the strike-it-rich crowd...even the sorry looking Indians that hung out like camp dogs on the fringes of town.

"Lena usually to get better quick, but...the *grande fiesta*, it is tomorrow." Medina had so savored the notion of seeing the settlers' shocked looks when they heard about Lena being honored at the Governor's reception. Now it might not happen.

"I'll see if I can find Doc Crabtree." Jones' didn't sound hopeful. He waved Medina past the doorman onto the hotel landing. "Say, who's the lad I saw riding on your wagon?"

"John Alexander. Son of a sawmill man. Poor, but good boy." He pictured the young lad's threadbare pants and tin-patched shoes. "Maybe I send him to you for some new clothes."

"Sure, I'll be there tomorrow. Speaking of clothes, you brought the bead shirts?"

"Five. In the wagon."

"Big sales tomorrow. Lots of eager buyers in town. Your wife's beadwork is the best." Jones rubbed his thumb and first finger together and laughed. They walked down the steps into the street. Jones whistled for his driver.

He asked, "Louie Papa and Antonio?"

"Louie, his baby sick, like Lena. And Antonio, he has head of burro. I catch him, hands all over white girl." Medina's neck tensed remembering the sight of Sarah Jane Blackhurst's white breasts cupped in Antonio's hands when he found them in the barn.

Jones grinned. "Shoot, we're all Americans now. I'll bet she wasn't unhappy about it. To girls, Antonio's like honey to flies."

"Not to laugh. That girl's mama and papa, they are to me, a friend. But not if Antonio gets her with baby. And the others? *Diós*! Not like you, smiling friend at all the people, even Mexicans."

"Spaniards," Jones corrected, then turned to look down the street. "Where the hell is my driver?" He whistled again, then turned back to his friend. "There's a new school here, two actually, one for boys and one for girls, both Catholic, both very high falutin'. Good education and manners to boot. Best learning in the Territory, even better than the high church Episcopal bunch. Maybe you send Antonio there. Let the Jesuits keep him out of trouble."

The idea took root in Medina's mind. Get Antonio away before he did anything more to shame them. The problem was that Antonio was a little too old, and probably too stubborn, to go. But Lena...

"Maybe Lena, too."

"Sure. Father Machebeuf'll be at the hotel reception tomorrow night. The Mother Superior of the girls' school, St. Mary's Academy, she'll be there, too. You can meet them. Oh, by the way, Lena's dress is all ready, just like you asked. The seamstress will bring it over first thing for a fitting. Your girl will be the hit of the party."

"Much thanks for that."

Jones's buggy wheeled into view from behind a bar down the street. Lamplight reflected off the harness silverwork. Jones frowned.

"The sonofabitch has been drinking." He cupped his hands around his mouth. "Hey you bum, get here quick or get a new job!" The slumped driver jerked erect and whapped the buggy whip hard on the startled horse's rump.

Medina grasped his friend's arm. "The doctor. You to get now?"

"Yeah, sure." Jones pulled himself onto the buggy seat and elbowed the driver. "Doc Crabtree, on the double." He turned to Medina. "Saturday night. I'll try, but…" He shrugged, and they set off.

"God go with you." Medina turned back and entered the hotel.

Lena lay on the bed beside Takansy. He stepped closer and laid a hand on his daughter's head. It was sweaty, but cool to the touch.

"No fever?"

Takansy shook her head no.

"The doctor, he is coming."

He pulled up a chair and took her hand in his. His thumbs felt the knobs of her knuckles. She winced. The rheumatism—"the sore bones," she called it—was beginning to affect them both.

They sat in silence for a while. Night air stirring through the window curtains cooled his face.

"Jones told me about a school here, St. Mary's," he said. "For girls, to get very good lessons. Maybe good for Lena."

She pulled her hand away and looked at him as if he'd handed her a dead toad.

35

John Alexander
July 1868

Johnnie propped up his sorry excuse for a tent on a bare patch of grass between a farm family and a group of three young miners. The farm family had turned in for the night. The miners laughed and passed around a brown jug. Their eyes fixed on him, glowing with reflections from their campfire. Johnnie quickly looked away.

Mama had packed some stew fixins, but there was no wood for a cook fire. Instead of asking the miners, he tip-toed over to the tent where the farm family slept and set his stew pan on the still-glowing coals of their fire. Then he returned to his tent, rolled out his blanket, set the duffel inside and sat down to wait. His stomach pulsed with hunger.

One of the miners, a black-haired man with a wicked smile and a missing tooth, stared at him. Johnnie studied his own boots like they were made of gold ore, then unease got the best of him. He rose to go for a stroll.

The next street was lined with saloons. A lone church with a wooden cross had elbowed in among them, an unwanted preacher among unrepentant sinners. Carousers lounged outside each saloon. He wondered how whiskey tasted.

A group of hangdog Indians trudged by dressed in shabby blankets and stained buckskins. A reveler in red suspenders raised a bottle and shouted, "Long live Sand Creek! Long live Chivington!" Laughter echoed down the street. The man stepped into the street and waved something dark at the Indians. "Your mother." His teeth flashed yellow in the lamplight.

Johnnie's mouth flew open. It was a scalp, crusty brown, with long straight hair. Suddenly, he wasn't hungry anymore.

The Indians, about ten of them, kept on walking. Maybe they didn't understand. Or maybe they just wanted to stay low.

Another man, stocky and tough-looking, stepped out and yanked the first man's arm down.

"Hell, McGinty, taking a woman's hair ain't nothing to brag about. Iffen you ain't got a brave's scalp, I'd keep it hid if I was you."

Red Suspenders whirled and staggered, a mean snarl on his face. A third man with a lop-sided smile stepped between them.

"C'mon boys, it's too early to fight."

The three walked back to the saloon, laughing.

Johnnie moved on. He hoped the drunks would be too hung over to show up at the parade tomorrow. The thought of Red Suspenders waving that scalp at Lena made his face hot. He kicked a stone across the street. It hurt his toe.

He circled back to his tent. The three miners were gone, the farm family still asleep. He fetched the stew pot and sat down to eat. The potatoes were still hard, but he was drooling, too hungry to care. A hunk of meat fell and rolled down his shirt. It landed in his lap, oozing grease onto his crotch. Thank the Lord he had a fresh shirt and pants in his duffel. He glanced inside the canvas tent.

His mouth froze in mid-chew. The duffel bag was gone!

The money! Johnnie's heart leapt clean out of his chest. Then he remembered Mama had made him carry the money in a belt pouch. His shaking hand found it there. Praise the Lord and Mama, both! He jumped up and did a quick turn around his campsite. No duffel.

The miner's fire had gone out. Johnnie peeked inside their tent. No sign of them. He ducked in and began rummaging through the jumble of blankets and gear. The smell of unwashed men assaulted his nose, along with the odor of his own nervous sweat. Every rustle and clink from the surrounding camp, every murmur and shout, caused him to jump. Near as he could see, which wasn't much, the duffel wasn't there. His tongue felt like paper.

He ran back to his tent, rolled the blanket into the canvas and found another spot on the far side of the tenting ground. Even then, he couldn't sleep, what with thinking about Pa's reaction to the stolen duffel, and Jennie's superior smirk.

Finally, in the wee hours, he dropped into a fitful doze.

In the morning he headed straight for the hotel, his thoughts on Lena. At a water trough he glimpsed his reflection. The stew stain still darkened his clothes. Trying to wash it out only made things worse. On top of it all, the tin on his left boot was gone, leaving a flapping sole. He slicked his hair back, lamenting his sorry state.

The hotel doors were shut and the doorman gone, glory be. The lobby was empty. Everyone was at the parade, he figured. If he didn't get a move on he was going to miss Lena's ride. If she was well enough.

He hustled on down to Larimer Street and found the reviewing stand. The Medina's weren't there. A man in a top hat and black frock began shouting through a bullhorn.

"Ladies and gentleman. Please clear the street; the parade is about to begin."

Spotty applause broke out as folks moved to the sides.

"Ladies and gentlemen," he continued, "I regret to inform you that the young lady selected to lead the parade, the eleven-year-old riding sensation from the Big Thompson Crossing, Lena Medina, will not be with us this morning due to illness." A little murmur of "Ohs" and "Ahs" rippled along the street.

Alarmed, Johnnie ran back to the hotel. Mr. Gold Braids was back on duty, guarding the massive doors. He took one look and moved to block Johnnie's way.

"State your business," he said. The fake smile was gone.

"I'm with the Medina family. Their girl is sick and I need…"

"No visitors. The girl is confined to her room at her parents' request. They are supposed to attend the Governor's reception this evening. I'm sure she will be better by then." He looked Johnnie up and down and added, "There is a little matter of proper clothes."

Johnnie retreated down the steps, face burning. His shoe sole caught on the bottom step, and he fell down on all fours. He picked himself up, hands and knees skinned, and forced himself to walk, not run, out of the doorman's sight.

Johnnie wanted to go back to the parade, but time was running out for getting the saw blade. Only one store, the Denver Mercantile, had a blade the size they needed. It cost twenty-eight dollars, more than Pa had figured, which made Johnnie nervous. The store owner, a jowly man who chewed on a pork rind the whole time, smiled at Johnnie's feeble attempt to talk him down.

"You can get one cheaper in St. Louis," he said, his face smug. Then he softened a bit. "This here's still a gold town. Prices are high. Most goods have to be hauled across the plains, and what with Indian attacks and lost wagons, everything costs more."

Johnnie was in no shape to argue. He paid the man and left with the saw blade, wrapped in butcher paper, tucked under his arm.

Johnnie felt hungry. He had two dollars and a dab left in his money pouch, enough for a couple of meals. Did he dare spend it? The idea of accounting for it in front of Pa's stare made him sweat. He found a street vendor selling corn, ham and beans, and said goodbye to seventy-five cents.

Medina's wagon was parked inside the hotel's corral, guarded by Mr. Tight-pants. Under his watchful eye, Johnnie wedged the saw blade in next to the sideboard. Then he strolled back to his campsite to wait for the reception, wracking his brain for a way to slip into the hotel to see if Lena was all right.

When the heat ran off with the last of the day's dwindling light and oil lamps flared, Johnnie returned to the hotel. He fell in behind two chattering couples as they climbed the steps.

The doorman, skin yellowish under the flickering lamplight, spotted Johnnie right away.

"You again?"

Johnnie worked hard to meet his eye but only got as far as his chin.

"The Medina family. I'm with them."

The doorman's thin lips twisted into a non-smile. "I know. Wait here." He walked into the lobby, leaving the door open.

Johnnie spotted Mr. Medina near the bottom of the curved staircase, dressed like a Spanish *grandee*. Dark blue pants with a yellow stripe down the side, red waist sash, white shirt and crisp dark vest. On his head jaunted a narrow-brimmed black hat. He turned as the doorman pointed Johnnie out. His eyes told Johnnie to stay put. Hotel guests nodded as he walked over. Men tipped their hats, some women curtsied. He smiled at each in turn. They returned looks Johnnie had seen at carnivals, like people viewing the tattooed man or the fat lady.

Mr. Medina's smile got tighter as he drew close. He took hold of Johnnie's shoulder and guided him onto the landing.

"Johnnie, when we return to the Crossing, you to do some work for me, yes? Make fences, build sheds?"

Johnnie nodded, surprised but pleased. "Yes, sir. I mean, I'll have to ask, but…how is Lena? When she didn't ride this morning I got real worried and thought…"

"Lena rides tomorrow. The sickness, she is gone. They make special time for her. Same street as parade. You to come sit with us, on the benches, yes?"

"The reviewing stand? Why, sure. That's great, sir, about Lena I mean. I was worried about her, and, well…sure, I'll be there." So Lena was all right after all. Johnnie felt ten pounds lighter.

Mr. Medina reached into his belt pouch and pulled out ten dollar bills. "Jones Mercantile. You know it?"

Johnnie nodded.

"This dollars advance pay. You go to Jones. To get new pants and shirt. And new boots. Yes?"

Shame took hold of Johnnie. "I can't do that. Thank you, sir, but…"

Mr. Medina stopped him with a pat on the back. "You to take the dollars. To get new clothes. Lena happy with that."

Johnnie swallowed and took the money.

Mr. Medina said, "Cut hair. Get a cut hair, too." He turned and headed back into the hotel.

Johnnie stood there a moment, ears burning. Mr. Medina was right, of course. These grand doings were not for the likes of him. But it hurt, just the same.

Applause sounded from the lobby. Lena had appeared on the balcony at the top of the stairs. Her dress shone pure white. The upper part hugged her like it was sewn on. The sight of her bare shoulders caused his breath to catch. He forced his gaze down to the vast circle of fabric fanning out from her waist and ending at the floor. With each step down, a pointed slipper, sparkling like diamonds, poked out from under the dress. Her right hand, gloved in pure white, caressed the massive railing. On her head sat a crown that sparkled like her shoes.

Lamplight flickered on her still-pale face. Her smile looked forced, uncertain, maybe even scared. Johnnie wondered how it felt to be on display like that. On impulse he stepped forward, wanting to tell Lena how pretty she looked, like a princess. Then he remembered his clothes. He took a last look inside as Lena reached the bottom of the stairs and disappeared among the onlookers. Then he noticed her mother standing back in the shadow of the stairway, alone and stone faced.

For the past six years, Johnnie had a notion about how nice it was for Lena to be the daughter of two such loving and wonderful people. Enough to make him wish he were their son. Now, he wasn't so sure.

He turned to leave. The doorman stood at attention, the nasty smile still on his face.

36

Takansy
July 1868

Takansy stroked Lena's hair and lifted a hot cup of smooth-stomach root tea to her daughter's dry lips. Last evening's big-man *fiesta* had put a strain on her daughter. Lena's mouth twisted as the bitter liquid slid down.

"She to be well enough to ride?" Medina's question grated. He was pacing a few feet away from where she and Lena sat on the hotel bed. Morning light filtering through the lace curtains gave his face a jumpy look.

"Still sick. Last night, it was bad for her." Takansy wanted him to worry, even though she felt her daughter was recovering well. The night before, her own worry had stampeded like an edgy horse, spooked by Owl and thoughts of Rosita and Martín. Yet Medina had insisted on Lena's appearance at the event. Resentment pulled down the corners of her mouth.

Medina stopped pacing and leaned toward Lena.

"Last night, you look so beautiful. The people, they cannot stop talking about you. The Mayor. The Governor, even. You bring much pride to our family."

Pride is more important than your daughter's health, Takansy thought.

"When Lena is on the stair, the Mayor say that she to make a fine lady. The Mayor!"

"These city people are speaking with two mouths." Takansy had seen the Mayor's smiles, watched how the men had shaken her husband's hand and clapped him on the back, how the women had bobbed elegant curtsies and spoke compliments. But she had seen other things as well: covert glances, smiles not meant for Lena, whispered exchanges behind fans.

Medina flicked his hand as if brushing a fly. "Mother Superior say Lena is acceptable to St. Mary's Academy. Best boarding school in the Territory."

There it is again, the school talk. The run-away feeling clutched her chest.

She pulled Lena closer. "It is time to preparing for your ride." Her voice came out pinched. She rose and set the cup on a table. "Your riding dress, I getting it now."

Lena smiled and rose. Her eagerness gladdened Takansy's heart.

Medina said, "Are you sure you are well? The ride, we can skip if you are not."

Takansy's throat seized. *Why this sudden protectiveness?* She wanted him to worry, not cancel the ride. She had invested too much of herself in preparation for this moment to have it cut short now. She felt her face go hard.

"She is well, look at her! She not skipping the ride." She pointed her eyes at him.

Medina backed away, looking startled by the sudden change in his wife's evaluation of Lena's health.

"I thought you said... Good, good, we go. I will get Shy Bird. Ride well, my daughter."

He reached for a lock of Lena's hair, giving it that gentle, intimate tug Takansy used to enjoy, but now found annoying. She resisted the urge to push his hand away.

Lena brushed her lips against his palm. "Thank you, Papi."

His face softened. It was the same gentle look he'd worn when Takansy nursed him back to health after the beating that took his finger tip and nearly his life, the same gaze he'd cast on her after he'd risked his life to rescue her from Captain Jack. And suddenly, in the aura of that look, Takansy felt herself relenting. Despite this new fixation on fancy schools and white-lady dresses, he always arched proud at Lena's horsemanship. Soon they would be together, husband and wife, proudly watching their daughter's triumph. She would find a talking way to stop the boarding school idea.

Medina raised his palm in farewell and disappeared through the doorway.

She retrieved Lena's riding outfit from the clothes-hanging chest. Blue and white beads glistened like slithering snakeskin as she moved her hands beneath the white doeskin on which they were sewn. Tiny brass hawk bells, nearly a hundred of them, tinkled from sleeves, tunic hem and leggings. She allowed the leather fringes, soft as rabbit fur, to slip through her fingers.

Lena pulled the leggings over her slender legs.

"Mami, Shy Bird has never done our tricks in these streets, with all the strange noises. And people, what if they shout or throw things, or scare her?"

"That's why we going early to the street, so Shy Bird can get ready." Takansy adjusted the tunic as Lena tightened her belt. "Are you with jumping stomach, my flower?"

Lena pulled on the fringed shirt. "A little, Mami."

Takansy pulled her close and brushed her cheek. "Shy Bird solid, not jumpy. Today you riding like Indian princess."

"Yes, I hope." But Lena's brows wrinkled into a frown as they left the hotel room and headed for the corral.

37

John Alexander
July 1868

Johnnie walked to the reviewing platform dressed in new black pants, white shirt and shiny black boots. Despite the blisters forming on his heels, he refused to limp. No one stared at him. He liked it that way.

The crowd was smaller than it was yesterday. Many had hightailed it home, others went about their business. Three no-account drunks sprawled on the sides of the street. The smell of cooking bacon drifted out of an open doorway. For once Johnnie wasn't hungry, having bought a steak dinner the night before with some of Mr. Medina's money.

A bunch from Iliff's cattle ranch gathered across the street, sporting wide hats and bright neck scarves. Two cowboys held a canvas banner with the ranch brand painted on it. They joked and carried on in a way that made Johnnie want to be a part of them. He could hear their spurs jingling.

Two groups of students in fancy school uniforms gathered beside him. Their signs said, "Regis School for Boys" and "St. Mary's School for Girls." One of the male students caught Johnnie's eye. Tall and straight as a ramrod, his brown eyes roved over the crowd as if people were lucky to have a glimpse of him. Girls cast covert glances his way. He was kind of Mexican-looking, but his skin was real light, lighter even than Lena's. But the most striking thing about him was his hair. Most was black, as expected, but a swatch on the left front side was dark red in color. It reminded Johnnie of a rooster's comb.

The young man's eyes locked on his for a moment. Johnnie quickly looked away.

On the reviewing stand, the announcer sat beside a brown-suited man with a sign in his hat band saying, *Rocky Mountain News*. A handful of folks sat in chairs. Some he recognized from the hotel lobby. Mr. Medina sat in the front row beside Mr. Jones. Mrs. Medina sat behind them.

Johnnie felt reluctant to push his way up there, even with his new outfit. Truth be told, he still felt a little miffed about getting shooed out of the hotel.

The announcer raised his bullhorn.

"And now, ladies and gentlemen, the moment you've been waiting for, the child riding sensation all the way from Big Thompson, here to astonish and amaze you with feats of horsemanship, the lovely Lena Medina, only eleven years old, daughter of Mariano Medina and his wife, sitting here beside me. Let's give them a warm Denver City welcome."

The applause again, reminded Johnnie of a carnival. People hauled up and gawked at the Medinas as if they were on display. Mr. Red Suspenders, the drunk scalp-fellow, elbowed to the front. Johnnie's throat tightened. Surprisingly, the man started clapping. Johnnie stared, confused.

Heads suddenly turned toward the end of the street. Lena had appeared from behind a building atop Shy Bird, her doeskin outfit white against a red tasseled blanket.

From a standstill, Shy Bird leapt into a dead run. Down the street they galloped toward the reviewing stand, Lena's long black hair flying. She sat upright, arms stretched overhead, fingers extended toward heaven, that astonishing smile on her face. Johnnie's breath caught in his throat.

Folks' eyes went wide, mouths opened. Some jumped to get out of the way. Red-top pressed in for a closer look.

A student said, "She's got no bridle."

At the reviewing stand, Lena brought Shy Bird to a sudden, dust-churning stop. "Wows" and "ohs" filled the air. She posed there, all blue beads and feathers and tinkling bells, and Johnnie could see her face had mostly lost its sickly look.

Then the show began, Shy Bird side-stepping, twirling around in circles on her hind legs, weaving in and out down the street and back, switching her forward leg at every turn, loping, trotting, stopping, backing up, and dancing back and forth on high-arched legs.

The Illiff boys waved their hats in the air and shouted huzzas.

Johnnie couldn't contain himself. He waved his fists and busted out with a shout. "Isn't she something?"

The students turned to stare. Johnnie felt Redtop's gaze linger.

A bowlegged little man dragged a metal trough into the street and dropped a lit match into it. Flames flared, smelling of kerosene, and settled into a three-foot high burning wall. Lena wheeled away, turned, and trotted Shy Bird toward the flames. Most horses would spook at such a fire. Not Shy Bird. At Lena's signal, the mare sailed clean over it. Cheers sounded from all around, Johnnie's loudest of all.

Mr. Bow-legs snuffed out the fire with a blanket. Through the billowing smoke, Lena rode right up to the reviewing stand. With a squeeze of her right knee, barely noticeable unless you knew what to look for, she got Shy Bird to step out with her left leg and buckle the right into a kneeling position. Lena leaned backward and raised her hands. Horse and girl bowed before the stand. The smile on Lena's face lit her up like a lamp.

Folks clapped and cheered. Mr. Medina stepped forward, waved at Lena and bowed, smiling at the crowd. Mrs. Medina stood with folded arms, eyes dancing.

Johnnie suddenly wanted to be up there with them. He waved to get their attention, but they didn't see him, so he set out for the platform. As he passed, Redtop tugged his arm.

"Do you know them?" He tilted his head toward the Medinas while keeping his intense brown eyes on Johnnie's. He flashed a set of perfect white teeth.

Despite himself, Johnnie felt the young man's pull, got an inkling of why other students circled in his orbit.

"Yes! I came here with them. He's the famous mountain man, Mariano Medina, and that's his wife, she's a Flathead Indian woman, and he owns a bunch of fine horses, fine as you'll see anywhere, and beeves, too, and they've got a trading post at Big Thompson, and he was friends with Kit Carson, and..."

"And the girl?"

"Why sure, I know her, Lena, and her brothers Louie Papa and Antonio, and I'm learning to ride with her and..."

"Lena, you say?" Redtop shifted his eyes to watch Lena ride away toward the Elephant Corral. "Perhaps she will come to Denver City for school one day, when she is old enough." He turned to gage Johnnie's reaction, a smile playing on his lips.

"Why no...she won't," Johnnie said, with more certainty than he felt. He remembered Mr. Medina talking about education. Could he be planning such a thing? Then, for no reason other than to bolster his own statement, he said, "Come on. You can meet them. They'll tell you."

Redtop's face clouded. "No, that would not be a good idea."

"Why not?"

"Nevermind," he said.

"What's your name?

The young man turned and walked away without answering.

Another student, a short boy with blond hair, stepped up. "He's Richard Castillo. Richard Castillo Junior. He's our star baseball player." The short boy, along with the other students, fluttered after Castillo, moths around a lantern.

"We're home."

Lena's whisper awakened Johnnie. He sat up in the rolling wagon and peered through the gathering dusk at the familiar gate posts coming into view. They had been traveling since before dawn, Lena sleeping much of the way. Then Johnnie had drifted off, too.

The glories of yesterday's events flooded back into his mind. He nudged Lena's arm.

"You were great," he whispered.

She stretched, calico sleeves slipping down to reveal bare arms.

"Shy Bird was not scared at all. She did everything I asked. Everything!"

"You see those Illiff hands cheering you on?"

"No, but I saw you, John Alexander. Saw you jumping." She paused a moment. "In your new clothes. Papi called you a true *caballero*."

Johnnie grinned, remembering how the high-falutin' doorman had bowed when he walked into the hotel after Lena's ride.

"Your mama and pa sure looked pleased. Proud of you."

Lena's eyes clouded.

"Something wrong?"

"No. It's just..."

"What?"

"That Catholic girls' school in Denver City. St. Mary's. Papi said something about sending me there, but Mami...They argued about it."

"Would you like to go there?"

"No."

"Maybe it's just talk. Say, your pa said I could do some work for him, earn some money to pay off..."

He was cut short by a shout. Mr. Medina pulled the grays to a stop at the entry gate. The team fidgeted, eager to get to the barn. Shy Bird whinnied to the horses in the pasture, who lined up along the fence like so many school kids. Dry dust roiled in the shadows around them.

Louie Papa ran toward them looking more hang-dog than usual. Something was wrong. His baby? He reached them, panting, bushy eyebrows bunched.

"Antonio's done run off with Sarah Jane Blackhurst. Worst part is he took a shot at Adam Blackhurst. With your Colt 45. Didn't hit him, just shot to run him off. Right over there." He pointed toward the barn.

Johnnie could almost feel the wave of anger pulsing out of Mr. Medina. He looked as if he might bite the stem off his ivory pipe.

"The Sheriff'll be paying us a visit, I expect," Louie Papa said. "I was standing right next to Antonio, but didn't jump him soon enough. Too surprised. Never thought he'd do such a thing." He paused. The strain of such a long speech showed in his face.

Mr. Medina got down from the wagon, took his pipe out of his mouth and spit. His voice sounded thin, strangled.

"John, please to help Louie unhitch the wagon. Then water, some hay. Make sure the team to get brushed down."

The expression on his face made Johnnie scared for Antonio.

"Yes, sir." Johnnie fumbled with the lead reins as long as he could, trying to hear more.

"The girl. She being here?" Mrs. Medina asked.

"In the barn," Louie Papa said. "Antonio done hid her there. Two horses. All packed, ready to go. Had it all planned. When the girl's papa called out from the bridge, I went to see. Antonio come out of the barn. Shoulda noticed he had his hand behind his back."

"*Carrajo!*"

Mr. Medina spat the word out like poison, a cuss word, Johnnie figured. He paced in a tight little circle. Johnnie started pulling the team toward the store, slow as he could.

"Mr. Adam Blackhurst. He is not hurt?" Mrs. Medina's hand roamed over her rosary like a fluttering sparrow.

"Maybe scuffed a bit. Hit the ground pretty hard, ducking. Scrambled on hands and knees before he got up and started running." Louie Papa's moustache couldn't entirely hide what looked like a twitch of a smile.

Mr. Medina reared on him. "Nothing goddamn is funny! To where they go?"

Louie Papa went deadpan again. "Couldn't say. Lit out south."

Johnnie looked at Lena. Her frightened eyes jumped from her parents to Louie Papa. Mrs. Medina's face got that grim, far away look.

"The wagon. Get the load out."

Mr. Medina turned around and set out for their house, his wife a few steps behind. Lena led Shy Bird toward the corral. Louie Papa and Johnnie started unloading the wagon. Johnnie couldn't get any more out of him except the comment, "Antonio's stubborn as a mule and hot-tempered to boot. Bad mix."

As they finished up, Johnnie grew more and more alarmed. What would the Blackhursts do? Would Mr. Medina get arrested? Instead of celebrating Lena's triumph, everyone would be carrying on about Antonio, bad news pushing out the good. He could hear Pa's righteous anger, Mr. Howard's foul talk.

And yet, as he fetched his saw blade and saddled Old Dun for the ride home, a guilty little thought burrowed through his mind, a thought about how it might feel to run away from home.

38

Medina
July 1868

Thick smoke coiled around Antonio's chaps, but the leather refused to burn. Cursing silently, Medina poked some more sticks under them, removed his hat, knelt, and fanned. It would take a bonfire, he decided, to rid himself of his son's belongings. He pulled the chaps off the feeble flames and walked over to the woodpile for some larger logs.

His face was hot, and not just from the fire. He had barely slept. How could the ungrateful whelp do this to him? Shame their family? He had worked so hard to build respect for the Medina name, for a place of honor. Now, he would have to find a way to make things right with Adam Blackhurst and his big talking wife. Beg apologies from all of them, the whole English-speaking, scandal-gossiping, behind-the-hand-whispering bunch. He imagined Henry Howard raving about

David M. Jessup

"Mexicans" and "half-breeds." He could hear William Alexander's raspy talk about "papists."

All because of Antonio. The thought of his son shooting at Adam Blackhurst sent a hot jolt up his spine. With it came another: Antonio's fits of anger were not unlike his own.

He strode back to the fire and tossed on three logs. When the flames finally built up, he tossed the chaps back into them.

A heap of memories, now turned bad, lay piled beside the fire. Three fine shirts he'd bought for Antonio. A toy gun he'd carved himself and hauled all the way from Bridger's Fort, where Antonio had spent the first years of his life. Pants, leather belts, his son's accumulated possessions. The pair of fine boots he had given Antonio for his fifteenth birthday. One by one, he tossed them to the eagerly licking tongues of flame. Brown smoke coiled up into the sunlit cottonwoods. Ugly smoke.

A sudden prickling signaled someone's presence. He turned to see Lena watching him, eyes filled with tears. His anger cooled as he pulled her close. She felt stiff in his arms.

"Antonio dishonors us."

No response. He turned her around.

"Come, *mi hija*, let us to go to the store. I have something for you. A surprise."

There was a slight resistance as he tried to lead her away. He gently turned her head away from gazing at the fire.

"Lena, you remember how the people in the hotel clap for you when you to come down the stairs? My daughter, you catch their hearts. I full with pride for you."

She shrugged and allowed him to pull her to the trading post.

Once inside, he handed her the book he had secreted away. Her slender hands, so much fairer than his weathered ones, brushed the cover, a photo of a fine lady with her hair in an elegant swirl, a parasol over her head and a glorious dress swelling out from her waist. Lena shot him a questioning glance.

"*Miss Abigail's Book of Etiquette for Young Ladies.*" His fingers brushed the raised gold words he'd memorized with Jones's help. "In school, you will learn to read so you can tell your Papi what it says. Even better, to show me with your dressing and good talk." He smiled and gave her hair a gentle tug.

"Thank you, Papi." Lena wouldn't meet his gaze. She tucked the book under her arm and walked out of the door.

He wished he could get a smile out of her. Still recovering from her illness, maybe. *At least she is a child I can be proud of.* With a jolt, he realized that, aside from Louie—who wasn't really his—she was the only child he had left.

39

Takansy
July 1868

"Mami?"

Startled, Takansy turned to see Lena in the doorway, staring with troubled eyes. She rose from her altar with a last quick touching of her forehead, chest and shoulders. Her knees hurt. She creaked over to enfold her daughter.

"What troubles you, my flower?"

"Papi has burned all of Antonio's things."

"Where?"

Lena pointed to the black smoke rising behind the long bunkhouse where Antonio stayed.

Takansy pressed Lena's head into her bosom, as if hiding the smoke would somehow blot out her husband's action.

"Do not trouble yourself, my daughter. They are only things."

"But Mami, Antonio will need them when he comes back."

"They can be replaced. Your father's anger going away soon." Even as she said it, her heart told her she would never see Antonio again. Another child lost.

She tried to reason that Antonio would have left anyway, as boys do when they become men. Antonio had always followed the swaggering way, a boy who recklessly climbed rocks and thwacked sticks into bushes to challenge bears. And risked his life to challenge Jack Slade. It was his time to go, a young bull leaving the herd.

But she could not silence the whispering voice that accused her of failing, once again, to guide a child away from trouble. She sighed and massaged her eyes with her thumb and forefinger. To change the subject, as much for her sake as Lena's, she put on a smile.

"Do you know, my daughter, how wonderful is your riding on Shy Bird? My eyes, they are not staying off you, even though I am trying to make them look at the people watching."

Lena's face relaxed a bit. Takansy gripped her arms in both hands.

"But afterward I am seeing the people cheering. The cowboys, the good riders. In their faces they are seeing a marvel. Your riding, no one is better." She took Lena by the hand and led her inside. "Come, I having something for you."

From her altar chest, Takansy withdrew a delicate chain holding an inch-long silver cross. A bluish center stone gleamed in the window light.

Lena bent close, then drew back, eyes wide.

"It's beautiful! It looks...alive. Those lights inside. Blue, and green and white. Like stars."

"God's fire. That is what a Blackrobe is telling me in the long ago. When I first learning of Jésu." Takansy clasped the chain around Lena's neck. "It has the protection power. I am giving to you, for safe."

"Thank you, Mami. Thank you."

Takansy tucked the cross under Lena's shirt. "Not for showing. For keeping close to heart." She patted Lena's chest. Then she drew out a black rosary and pressed it into Lena's hand. "Keep these with you also. More safe."

Lena's smile faded. She backed toward the door.

"I'm going to feed Shy Bird, now."

Takansy followed her onto the porch. That's when her eyes found the book Lena had left against the door frame. She ran her fingers over the parasol lady, frowned, and put it back down.

40

John Alexander
July 1868

The sun was well set by the time Johnnie rode Old Dun toward home, clutching the paper-wrapped saw blade under his arm. The string the package was tied with hurt his fingers, and he had to stop now and then to rest it against the saddle.

Antonio's caper weighed on his mind. Would Mr. Medina try to chase Antonio and Sarah Jane down? Would the settlers blame the whole Medina family? What would the Blackhursts do? He didn't want to hear what Pa would say.

Pa. He glanced around at his new boots dangling from a saddle tie against Old Dun's flank. How was he going to explain them to his father? And his missing duffel bag? His new clothes, at least, were hidden in his saddle bag. He felt dirty, dressed in his stained shirt and filthy pants again.

When he reached the base of his hideout cliff, he got off and untied the boots. The rimrock beckoned against the starlit sky, but there wasn't enough time to hide the boots up there. Instead, he stashed them beneath the jutting edge of a broken chunk of red sandstone about as big as Mr. Medina's wagon and piled on a few smaller rocks to hold them down. He clucked Old Dun into motion toward home, feeling gloomy as could be.

When he arrived at the dugout, Mac wagged his way over. He didn't bark, for glory sake. Johnnie scratched his floppy red ears while Mac slobbered his tongue over Johnnie's face.

The front door creaked open. Lantern light spilled out and captured him in its glow.

"That you, John?" Pa called out.

"Yes, sir." Johnnie tried to sound glad to be back. "I got the saw blade." He fetched it up toward Pa, hoping to make it the subject of conversation.

Pa limped over, trailed by Jennie, Mattie and Robert. Mama followed, tucking wisps of hair under her night cap. Little Annie, he guessed, was asleep.

Johnnie unwrapped the brown paper and held up the blade.

"This here'll make some fine boards." His voice rang with forced heartiness.

Pa tested the saw teeth with his work-hardened fingers. "It'll do." A stiff little smile twitched onto his face.

Johnnie began to relax.

Robert, emboldened by Pa's mood, touched the blade and said, "This'll make some fine boards." His dark eyes shone.

Johnnie rubbed his brother's hair, black like his Uncle Blackie.

"We'll hook her up tomorrow. You can help. Someday you'll be able to run the sawmill all by yourself." But that day, Johnnie knew, would be far off. Robert's thin little arms could barely heft a fireplace log. Seven years, maybe eight, before he would be much help. Eight long years.

"How much?" Pa's smile dissolved into a hard-eyed squint.

Johnnie could feel the good will seeping away.

"A little more than we thought. But it's high quality tempered steel, and we got ourselves a year guarantee." Johnnie spouted this out in a hopeful rush, repeating the hardware man's words. "Only five dollars more." It was really three dollars, but he didn't want to own up to squandering two dollars on a meal.

"Thirty dollars!" Pa's eyes flared. "When ye going to learn to bargain? Ye got to be tough with these Shylock merchants. They'll nick ye every time if ye give them a chance. Ye got to learn to deal with them, to walk away, call their bluff. What's the matter..." He paused, as his forehead knotted up. "Wait...I only gave ye twenty-five."

"I used the travel money, Pa." Johnnie felt his voice grow strained. "I didn't buy a meal, so nothing's lost."

"What travel money?"

Johnnie looked at Mama, realizing he'd betrayed her. Her face flickered pale in the lantern light.

"He had to eat." For once Mama's voice had a stubborn tone.

At that moment Jennie's voice pierced the air.

"Johnnie, where'd you get these?" He whirled around. Jennie waved his new pants and shirt from where she'd fetched them out of Old Dun's saddlebag. They dangled from her upraised hands like wanted posters.

"Jennie, you...give me those. You've no right..." He choked back a cuss word.

Jennie danced away, waving the new clothes like captured battle flags. Mac barked.

Hot rage seized Johnnie. He lunged for her. If his wild swing had connected it would have knocked her down, for sure. It was one of the few times he saw real fear in her eyes.

The smack of Pa's cane on his back brought him up short.

"Enough!" Pa's bellow stilled the bird calls in the night air. Johnnie spun around to face him. The cane waved in the air above Pa's head. Little gobbets of spit flecked his beard. His breathing rasped into the silence.

Jennie's question hovered in the air. Johnnie's mind raced for a story. "Hiram Tadder loaned them to me." Even as he said it he knew he was digging his own grave. "For the parade. I mean, for watching the parade. My own clothes was ruined, so..."

"Were ruined?" Pa corrected. "What parade?"

"My pants were soiled, and my shirt had a big food stain on it..."

"You said you didn't eat," Jennie said.

"Only the stew Mama sent, not a meal." Johnnie's voice went soft with self-incrimination.

"What parade?" Pa said.

"Fourth of July. Mr. Tadder was kind enough to loan me…"

"John!" Pa cut him off with a wave of his cane. "Hiram Tadder was here every day this week."

Johnnie's stomach did a somersault.

"Falsifier!" Pa shouted. "Therefore will I scatter thee as the stubble that passeth away by the wind of the wilderness. This be thy lot, the portion of thy measures from me, saith the Lord; because thou hast forgotten me, and trusted in FALSEHOOD." His sermon started low, crescendoed to an enraged shout and ended with the crack of his cane on Johnnie's elbow.

The shock wave of pain sent Johnnie to his knees. A cawing sound came from somewhere deep inside him.

Robert started crying. Mattie buried her face in Mama's sleeve. Mama's eyes turned accusing. *I help you, and you betray me*, they seemed to say.

"I'll have the truth now," Pa said, his voice low, except for the "now."

Johnnie struggled to his feet, his elbow on fire. Hot tears welled, rage flared in his throat.

"Mariano Medina bought the clothes for me!" He paused for control, then spilled out the story of the wagon ride, the invitation to work for Mr. Medina, the ten dollars advance pay.

Pa's eyes narrowed. "Ye'll be working for no papist. Ye'll be paying Mr. Medina back out of what you earn elsewhere. Ye'll not be accepting charity from anyone, let alone a papist. Ye'll not be hauling more logs over there, either." He turned and limped out of the lantern light.

His words closed on Johnnie like a padlock on a prison cell.

Mama left without a backward glance, dragging Robert toward the dugout. Jennie had disappeared. Mattie hung back, worrying a small stone with her bare toe.

"I got a new pet," she said finally. "A cottontail. I'll show you how I tamed it."

"Tomorrow, Mattie."

She turned and slumped away.

"Thanks, Mattie." Johnnie stuffed the new clothes back into his saddlebag. The ache in his elbow spread to his whole body.

In church, all the talk was about the Antonio-Sarah Jane scandal. On Johnnie's first day back, Adam Blackhurst showed up with a gravel burn on his cheek and a bandage on his hand. Pastor George preached about the sulfurous fires of hell that awaited those who became the Devil's Disciples by fornicating. Mrs. Blackhurst's fan waved faster every time he said the word "fornicate."

That word troubled Johnnie, too. A year or so back, a Mexican boy at the Crossing had showed him a drawing of a lady with exposed breasts, private parts and a disconcerting smile. Pointing to the fur patch between her legs, the boy said that was where men put their peckers when they got hard. Shocked, Johnnie flat out didn't believe him. He'd seen goats and dogs and horses do such a thing, but not people. It was unthinkable. But lately his own pecker sometimes got hard at night, and he began to wonder if he might be a Devil's Disciple. *Maybe that's what Antonio and Sarah Jane did. Maybe that's what "fornicate" means.*

After the sermon, folks surrounded the Blackhursts in the shade of a cottonwood. Della stood off to the side, looking uncomfortable without her sister.

"Missed me by a hair," said Mr. Blackhurst, measuring his narrow escape from Antonio's bullet with his thumb and forefinger. "No provocation at all. Didn't know Sarah Jane was even there till afterward, when she rode out of the barn with that renegade." Anger flared in his face. "I was walking to the trading post, minding my own business, and that ornery little Mexican just opened fire."

Johnnie remembered Louie Papa saying Antonio had only shot into the air.

"It's what I been a-saying," said Henry Howard, a self-satisfied smile on his hard face. "They're scarce civilized, those goddam breeds."

Pastor George gave him the eye, but before he could say anything, Pa cut in.

"Papists. Blood and violence in all they do."

"The sheriff came out, but it took him a whole day and Antonio was long gone by then," said Mr. Blackhurst, his jaw muscles knotting.

"And Sarah Jane?" Susan Howard stepped out from her husband's shadow to put in this quavery question.

Mr. Howard's smile turned to a frown.

For once Mrs. Blackhurst didn't have much to say. Her reddened eyes oozed fat tears, which she dabbed at with a handkerchief.

"Haven't heard," was all she said.

Johnnie heard suffering in her voice.

"Learned shooting from his pa," said Mr. Howard. "That old Mex is hot-headed, shot his share of people. I say the sheriff ought to lock him up for egging his boy on."

"Or at least we should all stop buying from him," said someone from the back.

Nods and murmurs of approval sounded through the crowd.

Johnnie couldn't abide the unfairness of what they were saying.

He blurted, "Mr. Medina's madder than anyone about Antonio. He didn't…he didn't egg him on."

Stares shrunk him down, especially Pa's. He wanted to crawl into a hole.

On the way home Pa grilled him. "How do ye claim to know so much about papist doings?"

"Louie Papa told me, when I passed through the Crossing after Denver City. He said Antonio just shot into the air. When Mr. Medina found out, he was fit to be tied. And ashamed."

"And why am I only now hearing this?"

"Hard to talk after a caning." Johnnie blanched at his own boldness. He rubbed his still sore elbow.

Pa fixed him in his blue stare. "Ye sassing me boy?"

"No, sir." Johnnie kept his eyes on the wagon track.

"Don't ye be speaking up for those Medinas or ye'll have another caning to worry about."

"Yes, sir. But…it's the truth, that's all."

"Ye aren't one to be talking about truth."

Jennie, sitting behind them, kept quiet during this verbal caning. But Johnnie had no trouble imagining the smug look on her face.

In the weeks that followed, Johnnie took to sleeping outside under a cottonwood tree when the weather was good, and even sometimes when it wasn't. Having to work all day with his father, he couldn't bear being with him at night, too, hearing his wheezy breath, remembering the injury he'd caused, calling to mind his duty to stay.

The days dragged by like slow ticks of a clock. Chopping,

trimming, hefting, hauling, unloading, sawing, loading. Johnnie didn't know what level of Hell was reserved for falsifiers like him, but at age fourteen, being stuck on their hardscrabble homestead felt like the very lowest.

He treated the new saw blade like gold, sharpening it every week, making sure boards didn't bind on it, being extra careful not to do something clumsy. The smooth-cut boards brought Pa extra money. That anger knot in his forehead went away whenever he got back from selling them.

Johnnie hoped Pa would relent and let him go back to the Crossing, but it never happened. He would try not to think about herding cattle with Lena and Louie Papa or the comings and goings of people with interesting lives. About Lena's ride, and how she had widened the eyes of the Illiff cowboys. How she widened his eyes.

Whenever he got the chance, he'd light out for his hideout. He would walk through the narrow rock gap, pull off his boots and wiggle his toes into the cool sand. The chipping of sparrows and the *kewwww* of soaring redtails comforted him. The scent of pines floating on the late afternoon breeze calmed him. He watched bugs to figure out what they ate and how they made baby bugs. He wished he had some books to read. He wished he could show Lena his bone collection and tell her stories about them. He imagined her jumping catlike from boulder to ledge, exploring the hideout.

So it went for the rest of July and most of August. Long hot days of work, exhausted sleep, and Sunday trips to the hideout. Now and then Pa would get suspicious.

He would ask, "Johnnie, where are ye wandering off to?"

"Just walking," Johnnie would say. "Good for the soul, being up in the hills." Pa couldn't argue with that. It was what the Sabbath was for. He would give Johnnie one of his "the Lord is watching you" looks. Johnnie wondered how long he could lead this double life.

Then, like a blessing, the English tenters came.

41

Takansy
August 1868

The dreams started during the Moon of the Afternoon Showers, weeks after Takansy returned from Denver City. They came in the sleep-awake time just before the sun begins its sky journey. The dreams were always the same. She would be threading her way between broken sandstone slabs tall as the porch roof. The sand on the path would feel warm and soft between her toes. The boulders would glow red from the westering sun, seeming almost translucent as she passed slowly between them. She would finger their rough sides in wonder, and rub the patches of green, black and orange lichen crusting their surface.

The boulders would speak to her in low, humming voices, barely audible, telling her to seek a place among them safe from discovery. A "resting place." Sandstone spirits, calling to her. Then she would wake and wonder, with a twinge of unease, why she might need a "resting place."

The intensity of the dreams impelled her on a daily search of the sandstone ridges between their house and the base of the mountains. Because of her vow, she travelled on foot. The first ridge was low and unimpressive; the second, the Devil's Backbone, was spectacular but the wrong color. From the third, also low, she could see the fourth and tallest crest, whose rimrock was the closest in color to the one in her dream. It appeared to be the work of a giant flint-knapper who had struck the ridge into a knife edge. The next day she packed her possibles bag for a trip there.

Her preparations caught Medina's attention.

"For why you to go walking so long?" he asked as he carried a sack of beans out of the trading post.

"Looking for calm-stomach root. My supply is lowering." She wanted to keep her dreams to herself.

He raised an eyebrow. "It is so rare that it to take such long time?"

"Yes. Hard to find. I looking along the river, higher up."

He shrugged and carried the beans to a small buckboard driven by Susan Howard. It was the first time Takansy had seen the woman alone, without Mole-cheek hulking nearby. Medina hefted the beans onto the wagon, then stood a long time—longer than necessary— nodding and talking.

Susan Howard seemed captivated by whatever he was saying. Her laugh was throaty and musical, her bangs fluttered against her forehead as she nodded at him.

Takansy saw the attraction, but jealousy flickered feebly in her breast. *Why?* She wasn't sure.

She glanced toward the corral where Lena was brushing Shy Bird to a black sheen. Lena was what quickened her heart. Having her here, with her horses. Not at some far-off school. She wished she could fly with her, side by side, across the meadow on horseback. Would Jésu mind if she broke her vow after all this time?

She filled her leather bag with beef jerky and currants and set off for the tall rimrock. At the spot where the river cut through it, she picked her way through mountain mahogany, up its east slope toward a saddle in the ridge crest. Passing through it, she discovered a hidden valley nestled between the crest behind her and another, taller rimrock to the west. The ridge-top valley could not be seen from either side.

As she made her way across it through a forest of dwarf pine and juniper, her heart quickened. There lay the broken slabs of red sandstone she had seen in her dreams. The valley ended abruptly at a cliff edge. It made her queasy to look over the edge. Far below, the silver ribbon of river disappeared into a dark, impassable canyon that marked the western boundary of the Alexander homestead. She retreated from the cliff edge and headed north through a jumble of red rock slabs.

A bird's squawk from a nearby juniper made her heart jump. *A gray jay! Can it be?* She had not heard its call since childhood. *Why so far from its homeland?* It fluttered off, flashing the pale tips of its dark tail. She followed.

Little by little, it led her to a cabin-sized slab of sandstone leaning against another, creating a small, tipi-shaped opening nearly hidden by a small juniper. The jay perched above the hidden opening as if waiting for her. Not until she pushed aside the branches and stepped into the space between the stones did it fly away. The opening was barely head high and about a body-length deep, a small cave with a sandy floor. The "resting place" of her dream?

The realization that then flooded into her was so powerful she sank to her knees. The gray jay was Otter Woman, her girlhood guide and medicine woman, returned from the Great Beyond to show her this spot.

But why?

42

John Alexander
August 1868

The first bunch of tenters drove up to the dugout in a grand wagon with white canvas stretched over arching oak staves pinned to polished sideboards. At the sight of it, Johnnie dropped the empty water pail he was carrying. The wagon was pulled by a team of Belgians every bit equal to Mr. Medina's grays. On the driver's seat sat a portly, clean-shaven fellow in a gray silk hat. His shiny brass buttons strained against the bulging cloth of his traveling suit. Beside him sat a lad about Johnnie's age. He had fair skin and wore brown riding breeches, flared at the thigh. Next to him perched a thin woman in a fancy dress shaded by a wide, flowery hat brim. Her cheeks flushed red against a deathly pale face. She coughed into a lace handkerchief. The sound was not ladylike, but deep and urgent.

Johnnie felt his family gather beside him to stare at the strange

David M. Jessup

visitors. Jennie eyed the young man. She patted her loose hair into place and swiped her apron across her sweaty face. She pulled Mattie in front of her to shield her stained, flour-sack dress from the boy's gaze.

"Hello, hello," said the man, his voice hearty. "May I have a word with you?"

Pa stiffened at the English accent. Mama gave him her pleading look. After a long, uncomfortable silence, Pa answered.

"What will ye have, then?"

If Pa's Scottish accent affected the man, he didn't show it. He climbed down, beaming. The wagon rose a good six inches when rid of his bulk. He doffed his hat, revealing a wave of dark brown hair, and grinned.

"My good sir, I am Nigel Winterbottom, and you are, I presume, Mr. William Alexander? I have been informed by a Mr. Tadder at the post office that you own the finest section of this beautiful stream (he gestured toward the river) that can be found in this magnificent country. My request to you, sir, is for the opportunity to pitch our tent on the bank over there for six weeks." He lowered his voice and tilted his head toward the wagon. "My wife suffers from consumption, and our physician has prescribed the bracing air of the Rocky Mountains as the most likely cure for this onerous malady."

He paused for a moment, his face perfectly arranged to gain sympathy, then continued, "I would, of course, be prepared to pay you a handsome rent for the privilege of encamping on your fine land." He patted a coat pocket bulging with financial promise.

Johnnie watched two mental armies battle for control of his father's face. The Scottish hatred for the English seemed to be gaining the upper hand, then Pa's eyes shifted to the man's pocket. Finally, he nodded agreement, but the word "yes" seemed to stick in his craw.

Mama spoke for him. "Why yes, I believe that if you make yourselves agreeable I reckon we could allow a space for you."

To Johnnie it sounded as if she wanted to welcome them without seeming too eager.

Mr. Nigel Winterbottom smiled and bowed. "Good, good. We will be most appreciative."

There followed a back-and-forth. Pa demanded ten dollars a week. Mr. Winterbottom agreed, if they were provided daily bread, milk and eggs, which Pa agreed to for an additional two dollars per day.

Mr. Winterbottom stuck out his hand to close the deal. The handshake, English meat on Scottish bone, felt like a peace treaty.

Inside Johnnie's head, numbers swarmed like bees. Two dollars a day, plus the weekly ten, came to twenty-four a week, times six weeks made for a hundred forty-four dollars! More than lumbering earned in a month. What if more tenters came? What if they showed up in June and stayed all summer? The possibilities swooped to and fro in his head like cliff swallows over the river. No longer would they depend on logging. No longer would Pa depend on him. Jennie or Mattie could take care of the tenters. Anna—even Robert—could carry eggs. Johnnie could...leave!

As Mr. Winterbottom re-crossed the bridge, Jennie said, "Pa, may I please be the one to take care of them? Take them the eggs, I mean, and the daily other things, and collect the payments and all. I'll do a good job." Her voice wheedled.

Pa appraised her with one bushy raised eyebrow, then nodded yes. She was his favorite, and he seldom told her no.

"Only what we agreed, though. No extras."

"Of course, Papa." Jennie glanced toward the wagon, where the boy, now on foot and holding the team, looked back with friendly curiosity.

After an hour, the Winterbottom's tent rose on the opposite bank like a white sail. By that time, Jennie had scrubbed herself pink and changed into a faded calico dress that had belonged to Mama before she broadened out. Jennie's attempt to look fetching was a miserable failure, in Johnnie's opinion. Pulled into a tight bun, her mousy hair topped a heavy brow and a square jaw that made her look middle-aged instead of fifteen. Pitiful...if he'd been inclined to feel pity after what she'd done to him.

The lad, with the name of Basil, was also fifteen, but seemed as gullible as a trusting four-year-old. He hungered for stories about Noble Savages, and Fierce Wild Beasts, and Desperado Outlaws.

"Do you know Kit Carson?" he asked in his funny accent the first time they talked. "We heard about an Indian attack here, a fierce warrior named Captain Jack. Did you see him?"

Johnnie did his best to oblige Basil with answers. What he didn't know, he made up. Basil would sit by the campfire with his mouth so wide open you could stash a sack of potatoes in there. Before long he was following Johnnie around like a friendly dog.

It felt strange to be doted on by a rich boy all decked out in flared riding breeches and fancy boots. Basil's folks were nice to him, too, not at all what Johnnie had been taught to expect of the English.

Jennie would often come mooning around, trying to push into their talks with comments Johnnie often found embarrassing. Like the time she called Ulysses S. Grant an Army General.

"He's President now," Johnnie said. In an aside to Basil, he added, "Jennie doesn't hear much news." Even in the firelight he could see the color rising on both sides of her strained smile.

To curry favor with the Winterbottoms, Jennie started bringing extra eggs and baked treats free of charge. Johnnie knew Pa would have a fit if he knew, so he tried to make sure he did. Little Anna became his chosen messenger.

He would say things to her like, "You see how Jennie is giving them extra eggs and not getting paid? That worries me, 'cause Pa may find out. So don't say a word of it, Anna, will you?" She would nod in solemn promise, one too big for a young'un to hold.

Pa wasn't blind, either. It was plain as day that Jennie was sniffing around young Basil, and Pa didn't like it.

One evening in late August, Jennie invited Basil to pick wild plums. Johnnie watched them disappear then ran to get Anna.

"You want to go fetch some plums?" Anna's brown curls bounced as she smiled and nodded. Hand in hand they made their way through the plum thicket to a small grass clearing. There sat Jennie, cross-legged on a blanket, with Basil kneeling in front of her, where she had pulled him. Their clasped hands flew apart like startled pigeons. The look of guilty panic that blotched Jennie's face was worth a hundred dollars to Johnnie. Basil just looked surprised.

"Oh, excuse us," Johnnie said, faking surprise. "Didn't mean to intrude." He winked at Basil and hauled Anna out of there. On the way back, he said, "This will be just our little secret, yes Anna?" She nodded, her eyes bulging with the hugeness of the discovery.

Two days later it all came out. As he passed by the dugout, Johnnie heard Pa holler, "Young lady, ye'll give me no back talk. There will be no more of your taking care of the English. I won't have it." Jennie's whining protest got a thunderous "Silence!"

Jennie stumbled out of the doorway right into Johnnie. He let the smirk linger on his face a little too long.

She huffed up and leaned in close. The look in her eyes set his neck a-prickle.

"You!" She hissed out the word so Pa wouldn't hear. "You… hell-damned snake viper."

The force of this never-before-heard cussing made Johnnie recoil. He shrugged, trying to look innocent.

"I didn't say anything to…"

"You will pay." Her face screwed up into an awful mask. "I hate you!" She turned and ran, shoulders shaking.

Johnnie's mouth went dry. He felt bad about what he had done, and had an inkling that the price of revenge would be high.

43

John Alexander
June 1869

After the tenters left in September, Johnnie spent a lonely winter lumbering, doing chores, and going to church. He escaped to the hideout whenever he could. He taught Mattie how to fly fish, and he tried to teach Mac how to herd goats, but the dog wasn't the herding kind.

Next spring, the river swelled to overflowing with the June rise, making fishing difficult. Johnnie felt so bored and alone that he almost wished Jennie would pick a fight just to spark up something interesting. But she didn't, and he gradually relaxed his guard.

After nearly a year of banishment from the Crossing, he hinted around to Pa to let him take up hauling again, but no ice melted in those hard blue eyes.

When summer arrived, four new tenter groups camped along the river, one from England, the others from New York, Pennsylvania and Virginia. The southern folk were few and far between after the whipping they got from General Grant and their big plantations all taken apart and such. The northerners boasted about the war, which folks in Colorado Territory were mostly left out of, what with only Indians to fight.

By that time Jennie had wormed her way back into Pa's good graces. She begged Pa's forgiveness for the Winterbottom business, served him up with every kind of doting attention, and before long it was Jennie this and Jennie that, just like before. She worked her tail off serving those tenters, and found several beaus who lasted a week or so before they wanted shut of her.

Johnnie mostly stuck with lumbering. He didn't much take to waiting on travelers, but he was glad for the money. With it, Pa bought a new horse from Hiram Tadder, an eight-year-old gelding named Horace, to pull the wagon up the mountain, although he still used Old Dun for the easier hauls. He even bought white blouses for girls, white shirts for Johnnie and Robert, and a new brown dress for Mama—he didn't much cotton to colors. Everyone got new footgear as well, except for Johnnie, who, according to Pa, could get by with the boots he had. Johnnie figured he was still being punished for lying about his Medina-bought clothes. He felt bad about not repaying Mr. Medina.

The tenter money got Pa in a better mood, and soon he started talking with a man named Lucas Brandt about a school. Lucas Brandt first came to their place in June looking to place a special order for lumber. Johnnie had heard some about him at church. Folks seemed to like him because he had a good word for everyone.

When he visited to talk about a school, he would ask Johnnie things like, "How's that red setter of yours? A good retriever?" Or, "You catch good-size fish here in this part of the river?" He actually listened to the answers like he really cared about them.

Once he asked Johnnie if he'd like to go to school. Johnnie said, "Yes, sir," and meant it. He couldn't think of anything he'd rather do, save riding herd with Louie Papa and Lena.

Frank Bartholf was just the opposite. He had come by in early March to buy boards for a new barn, but his eyes quickly slipped away from Johnnie to Pa and to their sorry dugout with a hole in the roof, which Pa hadn't fixed yet despite having more greenbacks. Mr. Bartholf paid Johnnie no mind and made him feel like a no-account kid. According to churchgoers, he had a reputation as a sharp businessman who would make his mark in the Territory.

Mr. Bartholf had a pretty daughter named Julie, who, like Johnnie, was fifteen. She had blond ringlets that bounced beside her temples when she bobbed her head. Her presence in church created disquieting sensations in Johnnie, who stole glances at her and carried mental images of her to his hideout, where his pecker sometimes got hard thinking about her.

When it came to girls, Johnnie was what Mama would have called a "late bloomer." He was half-way to fifteen before he started "interfering with himself," as the preacher called it. A sin. Still, he couldn't imagine doing such a thing with a real girl. The devil's temptation made him feel guilty, and strangely enough, disloyal to Lena, although that was silly, seeing that she was just twelve, still a girl. He wondered when he would ever be able to talk to her again.

44

Medina
June 1869

Medina felt the heat creeping up his neck as he tried to reason with his wife.

"She is not too young. She is twelve. Close to becoming a young woman." He spoke in Spanish to make his meaning as precise as possible. "Many younger girls are at St. Mary's. You met Mother Superior, you heard her tell about how they supervise the students, watch them day and night in the boarding house. Lena will be safe." He paused a moment, then added, "Safer than here." He left unspoken the names of Rosita and Martín.

Takansy refused to look at him. She sat at her usual spot on the trading post porch, hands busy with the latest buckskin shirt. The only indication that she heard him was a speeding up of the slight rocking motion in her upper body as she bent over her beadwork.

"Jones is there. He will help watch. Damn, woman! Just as good to talk with a rock." He spun around and clomped down the stairs, striking the railing with his fist as he left. Pain flared in his hand, payback for his anger.

He stalked toward the tavern where he found Louie Papa and his new friend, Lucas Brandt, straddling barstools. Some brandy, he decided, would cheer him up. A couple of strangers sat smoking at a table in the back. Otherwise, the place was empty. Business had been bad after the Antonio trouble nearly a year ago. The settlers had boycotted Lena's twelfth birthday in April. His family—what was left of it—had celebrated privately this year, along with his Mexican hands and their wives and children. And this new fellow, Lucas Brandt, who seemed to be spending more and more time with Louie even as Louie spent less and less with his wife and little boy, who had gone off to visit her parents in Denver City, and seemed to be staying an unusually long time.

Lucas Brandt grinned at Medina and raised his glass. "Hello there, Mr. Medina. You look like you might need one of these." Brandt was tall, single, energetic, and friendly. Everyone seemed to trust him. He had that same ease with settlers as Goodale had with mountain men. Medina had warmed to him right away.

Medina nodded. "Yes, I will join you." He turned to his new bartender, a drifter named Eusebio, and pointed. "Brandy. That one."

Eusebio was wiping out glasses with a dirty towel and putting them up on a rack. Medina made a note to talk to the idiot about using clean towels. The bartender, catching the tone in Medina's voice, did a bootlicking bow and mumbled his thousand pardons. He was a cringer. Medina couldn't stand cringers.

"Louie here was telling me about how your boy Antonio took a shot at Jack Slade in here." Lucas Brandt pointed to the hole in the ceiling.

The last thing Medina wanted was to discuss Antonio. He raised his glass and said, "To your health, Señor Lucas Brandt. And yours, Louie." He tossed down the brandy in one swallow.

Louie Papa squirmed on the barstool.

"What do you hear about a new store downstream?" Medina said.

Brandt brushed a hand through his sandy hair. "Yes, there's talk. Down by the Osburn farm. Lots of newcomers there. But it's mostly going to be farm tools, seeds, barbed wire and like that. You'll still have the travelers. And all the fine leather work no one else has." He swigged his whiskey and grinned. "And you know, Mr. Medina, that whole Antonio business, it's wearing off. Adam Blackhurst's still a mite touchy, but Mrs. Blackhurst, why, she's gone back to telling folks it weren't your fault."

Louie Papa said, "There's talk of building a school, too."

Medina eyed his stepson. Trying to steer talk away from Antonio, he guessed.

"Why, that's right," Lucas Brandt said. "Frank Bartholf mentioned it just the other day. Asked me to get folks together up this way to see whether we could get up some funds for a school. And find a place." He leaned closer to Medina and confided, "Say, why don't you join us? Be a good way for everyone to get past that Antonio business and, you know, find something we all want to do, better the community, and all."

Medina held out his glass for a refill. The idea of building a school appealed to him. It might repair the family honor. Give Lena a way to start her studies without leaving home. Although he didn't want to admit it, he shared Takansy's worry about Lena being too young to go off to Denver City. This way she could learn the basics here and go to St. Mary's later.

He said, "School, a good thing, yes."

"You know, those flats above your place here?" Lucas Brandt pointed toward the south beyond the cemetery, "Good place for a school. Hope I'm not being pushy or anything, but…well, just think about it." He got up from the bar and grabbed Louie's hand. "Louie, nice talking, but I best be going before dark. See you tomorrow for that fencing up the canyon. Sure is pretty up there."

"You to go past the Alexander place?" Medina asked.

Louie nodded.

"Give my curses to that Scot," Medina set his glass down hard. Ever since the Denver City parade, the bearded lumberman had been coming alone to the Crossing, without his son. Medina would rather have young John deliver boards.

Lucas Brandt tipped his head back and wrapped them in a laugh. "He's a tough old crow, and that's the truth." They walked out of the tavern, said their goodbyes and set off in different directions. Medina headed back to the trading post, less moody after the brandy and the talk.

Chill had driven Takansy inside the store where he found her rearranging blankets on shelves.

He said to her back, "They to build a school here. Lena can go to it, not to Denver."

She turned and for the first time since they'd been arguing that day, looked him in the eye and nodded.

"Let us to eat," he said, and left for their home.

When he entered the kitchen, he found Lena stirring a stew pot on the stove. She turned and smiled, the savory-smelling vapor rising behind her. He would never admit it, but he felt relieved. Arguing with his wife would be over, at least for now, and he could keep Lena close another year or two. He took out his pipe and absently tapped in some tobacco from his pouch. The brandy suffused his stiff knuckles with warmth and his mood with well-being.

"I will eat Louie's share, too," he said with a smile as Louie came in the door. "I am hungry like a bear."

Louie Papa grunted and sat down at the table. Takansy, looking placid, floated in and sat beside him. Lena dished chunks of meat and potato into their bowls. Casting a sly glance at Medina, she gave Louie an extra large portion.

Medina laughed out loud. "We are going to have a school here, *mi hija*, for you to learn. Close by." At that, Lena stopped spooning stew and looked first at Medina then at her mother. And like fire being smothered by a blanket, Medina's mind suddenly called up the sour faces of William Alexander and Henry Howard, and maybe Adam Blackhurst—and who knew what others—reacting to the presence of Lena Medina, Catholic half-breed, sitting next to their children in school.

45

John Alexander
June 1869

When Johnnie heard about plans for a school, it felt like getting out of prison. The news came early on a Sunday morning in June, after the crops were all planted and folks had a little time on their hands. He was milking their cow when he felt Pa's tap on his shoulder.

"After church, there's a school meeting at Frank Bartholf's new barn, and I need you to drive the wagon."

Johnnie nearly spilled the half-full pail. He didn't believe Pa needed him for driving. But Pa's forehead was free of the knot and he looked to be in a fine mood.

"Why sure, Pa." Could Pa actually want his company? He finished the milking and ran inside to change. He put on his best clothes, which meant the britches with the fewest patches and his new white shirt. Mama starched the collar up so much that it rubbed his neck red. He wondered if Lena would be there.

They set off right after church. Along the way they talked about the grasshoppers being gone without Pa preaching about the Will of God. They talked about the need for a school and about Frank Bartholf's barn, which was now the grandest in their corner of the territory.

Pa said, "Now we've got a good place to meet that isn't run by papists." After the Antonio scandal, Johnnie could understand why folks might want a new meeting place, but no one else seemed to share Pa's reason. Still, it felt good to be talking with Pa like that. He wondered if his father was treating him different because he was fifteen, but he didn't want to ask, for fear of getting a sermon.

As they rolled past Mr. Medina's toll bridge, Johnnie snuck a look toward the pasture where Lena sometimes rode. She wasn't there. But he did see Mr. Medina bringing a horse out of the barn, all saddled up and ready to ride. Johnnie wondered if he was coming to the school meeting, but didn't dare ask.

About twenty people were already in the barn when they arrived, most of them dressed up in Sunday clothes. They sat on three rows of benches and chairs arranged in a semicircle around a table close to the back wall. The ceiling beams were higher than any Johnnie had seen, save the hotel in Denver City. The barn smelled of new wood instead of manure. If livestock had yet been in there, they'd left no sign.

Lucas Brandt sat behind the table facing the people. Mr. and Mrs. Howard sat on the left side of the front row, and Mr. Bartholf on the right. A stiff-backed Mrs. Bartholf sat next to him, and beside her sat Julie. Besides Johnnie, she was the only other young person there.

Julie's blouse was pulled tight into her skirt, accenting the transfixing swells of her breasts. She turned and fixed Johnnie with her pretty blue eyes. He looked away and hoped he wasn't blushing. His neck had gotten skinnier as it grew longer, and Jennie often made fun of his bulging Adam's apple, which bobbed when he swallowed and enjoyed such a life of its own he wanted to keep it hidden. He buttoned his shirt collar.

Pa walked right up to the front row and sat down one chair away from Frank Bartholf. Despite his new shirt, he still looked poor compared to the others. His frayed black coat had a hole burned into the sleeve from the day he fell asleep with his pipe in his mouth. He wore an old-fashioned tall hat like the ones you saw in pictures of Abe Lincoln. Some people looked sideways at him as he took his seat. He paid them no mind and just sat there in blue-eyed stiffness, waiting for the meeting to start.

Mama would always tell Johnnie he should hold his head up and remember they were just as good as anyone else, no matter how poor they were, but right then, as he sat down beside his father, he gritted his teeth and hoped no one would notice.

Mrs. Blackhurst, who was hard not to notice, entered with her usual commotion and said in her loud voice, "Johnnie, my boy, come to offer your opinion on the school building, are you now?" She nodded to Julie and continued, "Well, well, Miss Bartholf. It's always good to have the young people represented. Have you met Julie Bartholf? Julie, meet John Alexander."

Heads turned. Eyes pried. Johnnie scrambled up, his ears burning. "Hello, Miss Bartholf."

She nodded her yellow curls into a bounce, rose and extended her hand. "Pleased to meet you." Her hand was as soft as her voice.

He quickly sat down. His hand tingled. If there'd been a hole close by, he'd have crawled right into it.

Mrs. Blackhurst plopped down next to him and pulled her husband into the chair on the other side. Her thigh spilled over and pressed into Johnnie's leg.

Lucas Brandt rapped on the table and started the meeting, so that all the gawking faces turned to him. Johnnie breathed easier as Brandt went on about the kind of school they needed to build and what kind of materials had to be bought and how much things would cost.

After about five minutes, the door swept open and who should come in but Mr. Medina. Heads twisted around and mouths opened, Johnnie's included. Instead of his usual moccasins and Spanish pants with the sash, he stood there in shiny black boots, dark blue pants and a new topcoat over a white shirt. He looked like any other well-off settler, except for his black hair and dark features and the Hawken rifle that rested easy in the crook of his arm, like a natural part of his body.

His eyes roamed over the room. Then he worked his way up to

the front. As he glided past, Johnnie caught a whiff of mint leaves mixed with tobacco. He hadn't seen the trader since the Antonio incident, but once again felt the weight of his presence. It wasn't his height or his new store-bought clothes, or even the rifle. He just had a way about him, a kind of commanding air, like Johnnie imagined President Ulysses S. Grant would have when he walked into a room.

Mr. Medina picked up the empty chair next to Pa, moved it against the wall a little to the right of Mr. Brandt's table and settled into it facing them. He removed a new, flat-brimmed felt hat and rested it on his knee. His eyes, black as beads, seemed to dare anyone to question his right to show up late. When they spied Johnnie they softened, and he nodded and smiled.

Pa's knuckles went white on his cane. His jaw tightened. From the side, Johnnie could see that anger knot lumping up on his forehead like he'd just spotted a polecat. It made Johnnie nervous, and secretly pleased, as he had always felt a kind of polecat kinship with Mr. Medina, from the first moment when Pa had hissed, "Papist."

To his left a chair scraped against the floor, and Johnnie glanced around to see Adam Blackhurst looking daggers at Mr. Medina. Mrs. Blackhurst put a meaty restraining hand on her husband's arm and he settled back down. Antonio and Sarah Jane's absence shouted silently through the room. Rumor had it that the wayward couple had been spotted way down south in Pueblo.

Mrs. Bartholf, sitting close to Mr. Medina, clutched a white kerchief to her nose. A fly buzzed through the silence and, lit up by a shaft of sunlight filtering in through a slat in the wall, landed on her hand. She jumped as if a mouse had run up her leg. Mr. Bartholf's mustache twitched. Julie stared.

On the other side of the front row, Mr. Howard's face twisted into a disagreeable frown while Mrs. Howard, in her usual position slightly behind her husband and safely out of his eyesight, actually shot a quick welcome smile at Mr. Medina. He smiled back. Her face froze as Mr. Howard turned to look at her.

Mr. Medina nodded to Mr. Brandt, as if giving him permission to continue. Mr. Brandt crinkled his eyes and face into a smile and cleared his throat. Johnnie started breathing again.

"As I was saying," Mr. Brandt continued, "about the school. It's going to cost around four hundred and ninety. The committee…" He paused to point out three people in the room. "Frank Bartholf, Adam

Blackhurst, and Ed Clark, the Committee, has come up with four ninety, that's for a log school, as we talked about, so if we want it built…" He paused to see if anyone would object. "If we want this school built, the fairest way to drum up the money is a tax on property, just like we did last fall for other expenses. That way the folks with the most valuable property pay more than…"

"Hold on a minute."

A tall man rose from one of the chairs on the left side of the room. His brown hair was slicked back in what Johnnie imagined to be New York fashion, or maybe London, England, and his swell clothes—matching brown pants and coat, a white starched shirt and shiny brown boots—were every bit as fancy as Mr. Medina's. Johnnie wondered who he was, and Mrs. Blackhurst, as if kenning his mind, leaned over and whispered, "Lord Ogelvie."

So that was him, the English gentleman that Pa liked to lambaste whenever he went on about the sins of the English. Johnnie had never laid eyes on the man, despite him living in the valley Johnnie went through on the way to his hideout.

Lord Ogelvie adjusted the spectacles on his thin nose and said, "To be fair, shouldn't the families with children pay more? After all, they are the ones who will benefit from this school." His voice was high-pitched with the same funny accent as the Winterbottoms.

His words caused some folks to get the fidgets. Johnnie hunkered lower in his chair since there were five Alexander kids and worried that Ogelvie was talking about them.

Pa rose from his chair, wood cane clutched in his right hand, beard aquiver, blue eyes blazing. "Lord Ogelvie," he began, with a stress on the word "Lord" that left no doubt of his scorn for English lords. "Let me remind you of how much you—how much all of us (the wood cane swept around in a big arc) depend on the youngsters in this community for our future." He fancied his deep baritone to be as irresistible as the flood of mighty waters in the Bible verse he was so fond of quoting.

Despite Pa's speechifying, Johnnie liked what he was saying and sat up a little taller.

"Who will help Hiram Tadder deliver mail? Who will keep stock of the goods in Frank Bartholf's warehouse? Who will mind the accounts in the new bank coming to our fair settlement?" Pa paused long enough to fix an eye on Lord Ogelvie, still standing. "As an

English gentleman, with plenty of money to put in the new bank, don't you, sir, wish to have your accounts managed by someone who can read and write and calculate?"

A titter of appreciation rippled through the room. Johnnie allowed himself a little smile and, just then, didn't mind so much if people knew who he was.

But then Pa looked Johnnie's way and said, "And how will we produce our next generation of preachers, to promulgate God's word?"

Johnnie's toes curled. Pa would like nothing better than to turn his son into a Presbyterian preacher, the last thing in the world Johnnie wanted to be.

"What kind of future community do we want? One where our youngsters can read the Good Book and live by its word?" He reached into the side pocket of his coat and fetched out his dog-eared bible. He brandished it like a weapon. "Or one in which ignorant yokels live in sin and degradation?"

They were in for it now, a full-throated preach. Johnnie sank back down. Then Pa had to pause to take in a raspy breath, and Lord Ogelvie jumped in.

"Excuse me a moment, Mr. Alexander, but could you tell us how many children you plan to enroll in our new school?"

The knot in Pa's forehead pulsed purple. "That's got nothing to do with…" he began, but the English Lord reared up and raised his whiney voice to a near shout.

"Five. Correct me if I'm wrong, but you have five of the sixteen children who will be attending this school, correct?" Lord Ogelvie sat down, a nasty smile lifting the corners of his thin mouth.

Before Pa could round back on him, Mr. Blackhurst hoisted his tall self up and said, "Maybe this would be a good time to present the results of the tax appraisal."

He waved a sheet of paper in the general direction of Pa's still open mouth. Johnnie wondered what an "appraisal" was, but folks seemed to want to hear about it, if the murmurs of approval were any guide. Glowering, Pa sat down with a last flourish of his Bible.

Mr. Blackhurst began to read off names and numbers. Mr. Brandt wrote them down on a slate board in three columns. The first name was Pa's. "William R. Alexander, property valued at $840, tax is two dollars and eleven cents."

"About forty cents for each child," Lord Ogelvie said, setting off a wave of grumbling because the last thing anyone wanted was another round of argument.

"Next, in alphabetical order, is Frank Bartholf, property $1,200, tax $7.40." The chalk scratched against the slate. "Adam Blackhurst, $1,200, $7.40."

As the list grew, people got real quiet. It was turning into a contest, a score card of folks' value.

After about five or six names, the Alexanders were still ranked at the bottom. Johnnie looked down at his boots held together with tin strips and hoped someone else would take their place at the low end. Then Clinton Farrar's name was read.

"Property, $50, tax, 31 cents."

Johnnie didn't know Mr. Farrar, but he was sure glad he existed and was poorer than they were.

The list grew to ten names, then fifteen, with no one's property value topping that of Bartholf and Blackhurst. Then, at sixteen, Lord Ogelvie edged them out with property valued at $1,490. People stirred. Who would turn out to be Big Thompson's richest settler?

Next, the name Mariano Medina was read. Mr. Blackhurst paused to clear his throat. "Four thousand, seven hundred dollars."

You could hear gasps as all eyes turned toward Mr. Medina.

"Tax, $29.14."

It was more than three times the tax on Lord Ogelvie. Mr. Medina didn't so much as twitch an eyebrow. He just sat there, face still as a rock, and waited.

Seven more names were read, but except for the Smith brothers with $3,000, which was really only $1,500 each, no one came close to matching Mr. Medina's value. Johnnie felt like cheering. Pa looked snake bit. Everyone else just stared at the blackboard like they expected the chalk marks to fetch up and fly away.

"What's the total?" someone asked. Mr. Brandt drew a line under the column of tax figures and wrote $125.17.

"That ain't enough," another voice said.

Mr. Brandt just smiled and said, "It's just the first round. Come October we'll do another assessment after the season's over and we should have enough to finish. With this, we can buy us a piece of land and get the logs bought."

At that remark Pa's face brightened, and Johnnie knew why. Their sawmill, he hoped, would get paid to supply the logs. Johnnie's heart sank thinking about hauling all those trees down the mountain, then felt guilty because he should be glad to be helping build their school.

"We can't wait till October to start building," said Mrs. Blackhurst. Her thigh bulged over the edge of her chair and came alarmingly close to Johnnie's. "You all know what the weather can be then. We'll need shelter."

At that moment Mr. Medina stepped to the center of the room next to Mr. Brandt. You could have heard a grasshopper sneeze. His eyes moved easily from Adam Blackhurst to Pa to Lord Ogelvie and back to Lucas Brandt. The corners of his mouth lifted ever so slightly.

"No is necessary to buy land," he said. His voice was soft but firm. "I will to give two acres of land on the hill south of Crossing. Free, no charge." To quell the commotion that started up, he raised his right hand with the missing end joint of his middle finger.

He continued, "My men will to build the school for free. You to pay the wood. The school we will have before the first snow." He had the look of a man pleased with himself for being able to do something no one else could do.

With that, he gave a friendly nod and made his way to the exit. He didn't seem hurried, but he got to the door with surprising speed where he turned and said, "A thousand pardons, but the stage comes. I am to welcome it."

As he opened the door to leave, Mr. Brandt called out to him. "Mr. Medina, your generosity is…well, we just want you to know how much we appreciate your help."

Several voices echoed his thanks. A couple of people clapped then quickly stopped. Henry Howard glowered. Pa's knot got bigger.

Mr. Medina's smile flashed wide. He bowed slightly and said, "It is nothing," then left and shut the door behind him.

In the hubbub that followed, Pa's voice boomed, "Mr. High and Mighty, thinks he's better than the rest… ."

"Tut, tut." Ogelvie's high-pitched whine cut in. "If he thinks he can buy his way into our good graces, I say let him try."

Other words flew around. "Generous." "Ill-gotten gains." "Stolen horses." "Why would he want a school on his place?" "A good man." "Catholic influence." Johnnie heard Mr. Howard mutter, "He's up to no good."

Mrs. Blackhurst leaned toward Johnnie, her thigh warm against his, and said with a fat-lipped smile, "You have to understand,

Johnnie, that some folks here have a hard time accepting the idea that a Mexican—with an Indian wife, to boot—can be richer than anyone else." She chuckled. "Some of us wouldn't invite him to dinner, me included, after what Antonio did, and here he is paying for our school." She shifted back onto her chair which made a worried sound, like it was about to collapse.

Mr. Brandt rapped on the table to quiet everybody down and started writing on the slate board the names of the children to be enrolled in the new school after it was built. The first name to go up was Sarah Jane Blackhurst. Johnnie couldn't figure why Mr. Brandt put her name up since she was long gone. Maybe he thought she might come back sometime. Heads whipped around to watch the Blackhurst's reaction. Mrs. Blackhurst colored up. Mr. Blackhurst just stared straight ahead.

Next came Della Blackhurst, followed by Katie and Lilly Clark. Then three Barthoffs: Bisam, Eugene and Julie. Johnnie stole a quick glance in her direction. Then Hannah Warner, and two children with the curious names of Montana Kilbourne and Johnlittle Sise. As Lord Ogelvie had pointed out, the Alexanders filled five slots. Mr. Brandt wrote them all down: Jennie, sixteen, Johnnie, fifteen, Mattie eleven, Anna ten, Robert nine.

At the bottom of the list he wrote "Lena Modeno, twelve."

He spelled Lena's name wrong, but Johnnie kept his mouth shut.

"Only sixteen youngsters?" someone said.

"That's it so far," Mr. Brandt said. "Some folks's families are still back in the States, remember that. By the time she's built, our school's numbers will climb."

When the meeting ended, people moved the benches and chairs over to the side and walked out to their horses and buggies. Johnnie glanced over at perky Julie Bartholf and vowed to pay more attention to girls his age. But when she returned his gaze and smiled, he looked quickly away and swallowed, his Adam's apple doing an out-of-control jig.

As he and Pa funneled out, Mrs. Bartholf lowered her kerchief from her stern mouth long enough to say to no one in particular, "That Lena Medina is half Mexican, you know, and her mother's an Indian."

"A double half-breed, you mean," Mr. Howard said. Then he paused and added, "Guess that makes her a full breed." He smiled like he just made a funny joke.

David M. Jessup

Without thinking, Johnnie said, "She really knows how to ride horses." It just came out. Pa gave him the eye and guided him onto their wagon. On the way home, Johnnie thought about school, about getting time away from home. And about Lena, and the feeling that always fluttered in when she came to mind. Twelve years old now. Would she look different after nearly a year?

46

Medina
September 1869

Medina grasped his daughter by the shoulders and slowly turned her. The dress was perfect. Light green, silky to the touch. He rubbed it between his thumb and forefinger. Jones had assured him it was the latest in fashion, the best fabric, what schoolgirls in the finest stateside academies were wearing. Judging from the cost, Medina believed him.

"Now let us see your smile." He tickled Lena under the chin.

She pulled away.

"What is wrong?"

"Nothing, Papi. I will be fine." She twirled around once more for his benefit.

Takansy stepped forward and hung the silver cross with the blue stone around her neck. "Her spirit is not in this school of yours."

There it was again, the meddling, a buzzing fly that wouldn't go away.

"But of course it is. Tell her, *mi hija*."

Lena's eyes darted from one to the other. "I'm fine, Mami. Ready to go."

"Look at me, Lena." He tugged her chin back in line with his, drew her close. "You are to remember this: You are as good as any other child in the school. Better. You to be proud, to hold your chin high. Your *abuelos*, they come from Spain. Proud people, important people." An untruth, it came out all the more forcefully. "You are to learn the reading, the writing, to bring pride to our family, yes?"

Lena nodded.

He grabbed her shoulders. "And to remember this. The respect, it is above all. If anyone—anyone!—casts on you the disrespect, you are to tell to me, right away."

"Yes, Papi."

"Now, we go." He nudged her toward the door.

Takansy intercepted her. "Taking these also." She pressed a rosary into Lena's hand. "More protection. With the cross."

"*Dios mio!* She is only going up the hill." The ice in his wife's eyes silenced him. *I'll let her have her way in this small thing. The big thing is going to the school.*

He walked Lena to the buckboard, helped her into the seat, and set off up the road, leaving Takansy standing in the doorway. Lena shot her a goodbye nod, and waved.

Only up the hill. They could have walked, but he wanted Lena to arrive in style. He clucked the horse through the golden cottonwoods, up past the cemetery and onto the flats. The September sun warmed his back, the intense blue sky gladdened his spirit.

When the new school came into view, gleaming white with new paint, Medina felt a rush of pride. His crew had worked hard on it all summer. Instead of crude logs, it had real siding, smooth-cut by William Alexander's new saw blade. Luckily he had not had to deal with the cold-hearted Scot. Lucas Brandt had done the paying and hauling. He also headed up the school committee and served as skilled go-between with the settlers.

"Everyone is pleased as punch with the school," he assured Medina. "And a heap grateful to you for building it. Nothing has done more to bring us all together."

Medina let himself believe this was true.

Arah Sprague, the newly-hired teacher, stepped out of the school door. Dark haired, handsome in a *gringo* way, suited with tie, he looked the way Medina thought a young teacher should look.

He stepped up to the buckboard and offered Lena a hand. "Miss Medina. So pleased to have you. You are the first to arrive."

Respectful, too.

"I to leave her in your hands."

"She will be a fine student, I'm sure. And Mr. Medina, I'd like to thank you, again. For all this." He swept his hand back toward the school.

Medina allowed himself a smile. The Antonio business was finally behind him. He nodded and wheeled back down the road. A song suddenly found its way to his lips, an old Taos drinking song. *Strange.* He never sang.

A wagon approached. The words died in his throat. Mr. and Mrs. Blackhurst, with Della, their remaining daughter, between them. Mrs. Blackhurst gave him a nervous smile, Adam Blackhurst a frown. It was Della's hostile glare that spoiled his mood. As if it were he, not Antonio, who had run off with her sister. He tried to smile as they passed.

"Good morning, Mariano," Mrs. Blackhurst chirped. A brittle sound.

Then, a second wagon. The Alexander family. The bearded Scott kept his eyes straight ahead, as did the oldest daughter sitting next to him. The younger children gaped. The mother straightened her bonnet. Only Johnnie, sitting in the back, met his eyes with a smile.

"Good morning Johnnie, nice to see you again." Medina's voice came out loud, almost aggressive.

To the devil with them. He jerked the reins, turning the buckboard back toward the barn.

47

John Alexander
September 1869

Johnnie bounced along in the back of the wagon, trying to contain his growing excitement. The first day of school! He sniffed the warm, dusty odor of fallen leaves carpeting the river bank. Cottonwoods fluttered in golden glory, backlit by an autumn sun shining down from a cloudless, deep blue sky. Old Dun seemed to catch his excitement, stepping lively along the road. Pa's erect form swayed on the driver's seat, flanked on the left by Jennie's broad back and on the right by Mama's even broader one. The younguns bounced on the blankets in front of him.

As they turned into the Crossing, he spotted the Blackhursts just ahead. And beyond them, Mr. Medina coming down the hill in his buckboard. Johnnie tensed.

As if reading his thoughts, Pa said, "Ye'll not be traipsing down here just because school is close by. Ye'll be eating your lunches up there, studying if there's any free time, and coming home right after school. Chores will be waiting for you." Johnnie knew this was aimed at him. And with Jennie serving as Pa's eyes and ears, the rule would be hard to break.

He gave Mr. Medina a nervous wave as the trader shouted a greeting. Pa refused to look at the trader.

They topped the hill and piled off the wagon in front of the school, alongside a dozen other students. Mama fussed with their clothes, brushed them with her hands, straightened Johnnie's collar. Kissed him, for glory's sake. Right in front of Della Blackhurst!

At last Mama climbed back aboard and Pa wheeled the wagon away back down the grade.

Johnnie turned, and there stood Lena. He had to work to keep from staring. Her face had the same high cheekbones, wide brown eyes and little mouth creases he remembered, but she had grown taller since her parade ride, and her waist seemed narrower. Maybe it was the dress she wore, a light green ankle-length affair with sleeves that only came to her elbows. He took in the silver cross around her neck and the bead pouch on her belt.

Their eyes met. She gave him a little nod. Quizzical, Johnnie thought.

Before he could speak, Mr. Sprague ushered them inside and showed them their seats.

A stove occupied the far end of the room. Windows looked out on either side. There were three rows of benches on each side, fronted with a taller bench for a desk. The school smelled of fresh-cut lumber. Johnnie felt proud. He'd sawed most of those boards, himself.

Mr. Sprague rapped on his desk. He welcomed them, had them each say who they were, then started them off on a spelling lesson. He wrote on a chalkboard, they copied the words onto slates. He had an easy way about him, confident, friendly, but brooking no nonsense. Johnnie liked him immediately.

The lesson was easy. Too easy. From his seat in the back, Johnnie let his eyes wander over the room. Nine girls sat on one side, eight boys on the other. Three students to a bench. They ranged from seven to sixteen, with Jennie the oldest girl and Johnnie the oldest boy. Jennie sat up front next to Della Blackhurst. Della's hair was done up with hanging curls to rival those of Julie Bartholf.

David M. Jessup

She made a point of fluffing her new dress, as if to proclaim the importance of its owner.

Julie Bartholf was there with her brothers, Bisam and Eugene. Julie was prettier than ever, ringlets bouncing hypnotically. There were newcomers, too: Charlie and Billy Rist, Johnlittle Sise, Montana Kilbourne. Johnnie watched them struggle with their chalk. For the first time in his life, he felt competent, a step ahead.

Mr. Sprague rang a little bell. They set down their slates and rose to fetch their lunches. Johnnie drifted toward Lena.

She gave him a shy look. "John Alexander, why haven't you come to the Crossing for so long?"

He kept his eyes fixed on her forehead, ashamed to admit he'd been punished for lying about the parade.

"I've been real busy, logging and all. And Pa...well, he's doing the hauling now."

"Buckskin Joe misses you."

"I miss riding that good horse." And I miss our lessons, he wanted to say. "You still helping Louie Papa with the herd?"

"Yes, but now with studies I can't do so much." Her face brightened. "Mami is teaching me horse healing. We gather medicine plants along the river, some close to your place. I'm learning so many new things."

"Maybe we could..." He started to say he'd like to see those plants, but felt Jennie's eyes boring in.

"Got to get my lunch. Nice seeing you again."

His abruptness brought a puzzled frown to Lena's face. She shrugged and turned to fetch her own lunch from the back of the room. Johnnie joined Mattie, Anna and Robert to dig into the beans Mama had fixed. He watched Lena as she sat by herself in a corner. Mattie caught the direction of his stare.

"Eat your beans," he ordered.

In the other corner, Jennie and Della ate together. He watched Della's eyes rove over the room. They lingered on Lena, narrowing into lidded slits.

By the time a month had gone by, Della managed to divide their class into two groups separated by their clothes: the hand-me-downs and the store-boughts.

Among hand-me-downs, Johnnie knew he stood out for having the most ill-fitting pants. He was still a good two inches shorter than Pa, whose cast-offs he wore. He also held the prize for the ugliest pair of boots. His new boots from Denver City were still leading a lonely life holed up under the boulder at the foot of Hideout Ridge.

Della's store-boughts included Julie Bartholf, her brothers, and the two Rist boys. Della set herself up as Miss Prim and Proper. She would cast her keen and critical eye on everyone else, commenting on their state of dress and grooming, and the quality of their English. Johnnie sometimes wondered if she was trying to put some distance between herself and the scandal of her sister's running off with Antonio Medina.

Julie Bartholf paid her no mind, but others preened and vied for Della's attention, including Jennie, who, of all people, had the least chance of joining her circle. Della played her along, sometimes fixing her hair in a style which only served to draw notice to her square jaw. Jennie lapped up the attention like a pet. Johnnie had the feeling that Della fussed with Jennie as a way to entertain her circle of admirers.

Lena posed a quandary for Della. On the one hand, Lena's dresses were real fine, and she was the prettiest girl in the school in Johnnie's opinion, although Julie Barthoff could also turn heads. Adding to Lena's pull was her horse riding fame, which she never talked about, even though everyone else did.

On the other hand, Lena was part Indian and part Mexican. A half-breed. The only Catholic. The rosary drew stares. And she was the sister of Antonio, the cause of the Blackhurst's shame.

It only took a couple of weeks for Della to figure out how to cut Lena down. It happened during a spelling quiz. Each of the students had to go to the chalkboard and write five words spoken at random by Mr. Sprague from a vocabulary list he'd given the day before. When Lena's turn came, she approached the front of the class like a deer walking through a forest full of hunters. She picked up the chalk as if it might bite her and turned her wide eyes on Mr. Sprague.

"*Thorough,*" he said.

She raised the chalk and froze. Seconds ticked by. No one stirred.

Finally she wrote, *thouro*.

"Can someone help?" Mr. Sprague asked.

A half-dozen hands waved. Lena kept her face to the board. Bisam Barthoff supplied the correct spelling. The next three words gave other students the chance to show they knew more than Lena. Finally, out of pity, Mr. Sprague said, "cat." That Lena was able to write that word served only to drive the point home. She couldn't spell.

As Lena turned to take her seat, Della said in a loud whisper, "Princess Dumbell."

That got a titter out of the class, especially from Montana Kilbourne, who, Johnnie figured, was getting even with Lena for ignoring his flirtations on the first day of school. Jennie laughed. too, eyes glowing mean. Lena walked real stiff back to her seat with her eyes cast down. Johnnie felt downright low for her. He felt like strangling Della Blackhurst.

Mr. Sprague rapped his desk. "Class, we will have none of that. There is no shame in not knowing something. You are all here to learn, and everyone comes from different backgrounds. There is only shame in making fun of those whose background may have set them behind. What matters in this class is effort. Practice. Improvement. That is what counts."

His little lecture cut both ways. It drew attention to Lena's "background" while claiming it didn't matter.

Mr. Sprague was in his late twenties. His dark hair and straight white smile caused girls to bat their eyes, and his skill with a baseball bat earned admiration from the boys. Plus he knew full well that Lena's pa had paid for the school. And most of his wage.

His manly charm carried the day. But Della's nasty little seed needed only a few sprinkles to sprout into a weed. Before long, "PD" became Lena's whispered nickname among the store-bought set.

One day Johnnie asked Lena why she wore such expensive clothes that made her stand out so.

"Papi," she said.

"Why? How come it's so important to him?"

"He...I am his... ." She searched for the right word.

"Pride?"

"Like in Denver City. I am the family...representative." She sounded the word out carefully. It had been on their vocabulary list a week or so before.

"And the beads? The cross?"

"For my Mami," she said.

"What about you? What do you like to wear?"

She looked downhill toward the Crossing.

"When school is over, I go put on my skirt and pants. The ones you see when I work with the horses."

A picture formed in his mind of her easy grace on horseback. But what with Jennie always present and Johnnie responsible for driving them all back home, he hadn't figured out a way to spend any time after school with Lena and Louie Papa and the livestock.

But that was sure what he wanted to do. More than anything.

As the oldest boy in school, and already knowing how to read and write and cipher, Johnnie got named the class tutor, to help the younger ones catch up. This happened in November, around the time Johnnie turned sixteen. Lena, at twelve, was the oldest student assigned to his group, followed by Johnlittle Sise and Charlie Rist, both ten, and eight-year-old Lilly Clark.

For an hour each day Johnnie would gather them around to read books together. Sometimes he would have them write, although he needed Mr. Sprague's help on the finer points of grammar. Jennie should have been there, too, but as he explained to Mr. Sprague, the last thing she would take would be any instruction from the likes of her brother. Della, two years her junior, became Jennie's tutor, in more than reading and writing.

Johnnie discovered he was pretty good at tutoring, that he had a knack for cheering kids up when they felt dumb. He always found a way to point out the things they were learning, the progress they made. It made him feel swell when they got the hang of how words were strung together, and that light would go on in their eyes and they would stand a little taller.

Of all those in his group, Lena learned the quickest. She blossomed like the prairie flower her mama sometimes called her. Once she learned a vocabulary word, she never forgot it, and weeks later out it would pop in some sentence or other, and she would get that pleased look on her face. Then Johnnie would use the same word in another sentence, and before you knew it, they'd get a game started about who could use the word in the most unusual way.

David M. Jessup

The others weren't dumb, either. They worked hard, adding another half-hour together after school, practicing reading aloud to each other, then writing and spelling. After awhile they made a joke about Della's nasty label and began calling themselves the Dumbbell Posse. Lilly Clark made some sheriff's stars out of starched cloth to pin to their chests, with the words Dumbbell Posse written on them. Johnnie rustled up a Kit Carson book, and they acted out parts, with Johnlittle Sise playing Kit Carson and Lena the maiden in distress and Charlie Rist the bad Indian. Lilly was the narrator.

By Christmas, Charlie's brother Billy and Julie Bartholf asked if they could join their group, along with Johnnie's sister Mattie. Mr. Sprague not only agreed, but suggested they put on the Kit Carson play for the whole school and invite everyone's family to come. The date was set for April 12, two weeks before the last day of school.

"That's my birthday," Lena said. "I'll be thirteen." The pleased look on her face reminded Johnnie that birthdays were a lot more important in her family than in his.

When the plan for the play was announced by Mr. Sprague, Della looked as frosty as the February icicles hanging outside their schoolhouse windows. That look meant trouble, Johnnie knew.

Along about then it started getting into Johnnie's head that Julie Bartholf liked him. At times he could feel her eyes on him and when he glanced around, she'd smile at him until he would feel flustered and look away. During outdoor reading sessions, when weather allowed, she would sit beside him on the ground, arms wrapped around her legs, resting her head on her knees and letting her blond curls spill down over her dress. In response to almost anything he said—no matter how plain—her face would get all "rapt" (to use one of their vocabulary words). Whenever they paired off for a moment she would talk in low tones and call him "Johnnie," despite Mr. Sprague's rule that they call each other "Mister" or "Miss."

Julie's attentions raised Johnnie's spirits, but also made him uneasy. Compared to Charlie Rist or Montana Kilbourne, and especially Mr. Sprague, he felt skinny and clumsy, with ears too flappy and the world's biggest Adam's apple. He figured that if Julie Bartholf was attracted to the likes of him, there might be something wrong with her.

One day in March, when the blowy remains of winter had everyone hankering for spring, Julie sidled up and said, "Johnnie, some of us…you know, my sister and brother, and Charlie, Hannah, and Della…are coming over to our house this Sunday for my birthday. There'll be popcorn and some games and a taffy-pull." She paused a moment, eyeing him. "I was thinking, maybe, you'd like to come?"

This invite came with a smile as bold as you please. He looked down and shuffled along, feeling like a big dope.

Her arm brushed against his. He could see the little blond hairs on her cheek stand up against her face's rosy glow. His eyes shifted to the swelling under her sweater, and he had to tear them away. His mind scrabbled around for something to say.

Julie let out an unfunny laugh. "Well don't just jump at the chance," she said.

He finally said, "Why Julie, the thing is, I'll have to ask my pa, you know, we have a lot of work to do, and usually he has me working, but I'll find out and sure, I'd like to come. If it's possible."

Did I really say that? The lie was outlandish, as they never worked Sundays.

Julie pulled away, pink cheeked. "Well, let me know. I just thought it would be swell."

"It would be, Julie, and I'll try to come, that's for sure."

But he wasn't sure. Not at all. Julie triggered unthinkable thoughts, and the more he thought them, the more embarrassed he became around her.

With Lena, it was different. There was an ease in talking with her that Johnnie had only felt with Mattie, which didn't count because she was just a little sister. During rare moments when he and Lena were alone, she would sometimes tell him things that bothered her.

One day in February, as they warmed their hands around the cast iron stove, the last two to walk out into an icy gray afternoon for the trip home, Lena said, "I saw you watching me from the hotel door in Denver City, when I came down the big stairs in that white dress. Do you remember?"

"Sure do. You looked grand."

"I felt so…strange. My papi…sometimes it feels like I'm one of his prize horses, or something. All those people, staring."

He said, "Shoot, Lena, that's better than having a father who's ashamed of you."

She gave him a look, half curious and half worried. "Is your father ashamed of you?"

"My Adam's apple is too big," he said, grinning and pointing at it. He was trying to keep things light.

That got a faint smile. "I think it's just right," she said.

Later he confided, "I'm pretty clumsy sometimes. That bothers my pa."

He went on to talk about his bouts with Jennie, his low mood about a life of lumbering. And his dream about owning a ranch some day. She listened, intent, head tilted to the side in a way that kept him talking. He didn't know why he told her those things, her being just a little girl. But it felt like an escape from prison.

As the school year wound on toward spring, Lena went from outcast to center stage, much to Della's disgust. Instead of looking down their noses at her, the other students would gather around and ask Lena about horse riding, or her Indian mama, or the doings of Catholics. Once they asked about her cross and rosary beads, and she explained how they helped protect her. She made it all sound mysterious and exciting.

During breaks, she would be the first to be chosen for games like hopscotch, because her feet were quick as rabbits and she never stepped on a line. Everyone looked forward to the Posse's upcoming play and Lena's starring role in it as the maiden rescued by Kit Carson. Whenever they were within earshot and eyesight of Lena, Charlie Rist and Montana Kilbourne would start throwing balls, cavorting around, punching each other's arms, and laughing loudly, all the while looking to see if she was paying attention.

There were two strong reactions to this change. Della and Jennie began stalking around with dark looks, huddling together in conspiratorial knots, their group having shrunk to just the two of them.

The second confounded Johnnie. He started feeling outlandishly jealous when the other boys got Lena's eye. The truth was, he had started thinking about Lena in ways he had previously thought about Julie. Images of Lena's hands holding a book, her little mouth creases, the soft hair on her forearms, her quick step and dazzling smile, flooded into his mind at unexpected times.

Worse, he thought about touching her.

It was wrong. She was three and a half years younger, and despite telling himself she was almost thirteen, he knew she was still a girl, the daughter of two people he felt closer to than his own parents. The idea of them finding out his secret thoughts was worse than Pa finding out.

Back in Eden, Illinois, Uncle Blackie once told him about a man he and some other fellows had whipped up on and run out of town. "Won't see any more of that pre-vert," he said.

"What's a pre-vert?" Johnnie asked.

"A pre-vert is a slimy rat who touches little girls. Ye'll understand when ye get older," he said.

It scared Johnnie to death, thinking he might be a pre-vert.

To drive away temptation, he started acting more like a teacher, going over spelling words and grilling Lena on vocabulary, setting himself up as the authority and her as the student, the opposite of the way they were during their horse-riding lessons.

Lena noticed the difference. She would look quizzically at him as he stuck doggedly to the lesson.

Mr. Sprague sometimes assigned them poems to memorize. They were supposed to figure out what the poet was saying. One day in early April, when the pasqueflowers were blooming and the perfume of wild plum blossoms began to stir undefined yearnings in Johnnie's soul, the teacher gave them a poem by John Yeats.

Johnnie took his Posse just outside the schoolhouse door and sat them in a circle in the warm sun. He read the first few lines aloud: "A thing of beauty is a joy forever. Its loveliness increases; it will never pass into nothingness."

When he asked what it meant, Lena raised her perfectly shaped arm. "I think it means remembering something pretty in your head, and it stays with you even when it's not there anymore…like my horse."

Or like you. Johnnie gazed seconds too long at how her hair was swept behind into a glossy black braid that exposed her graceful ears and neck. *A joy forever.* Johnnie swallowed hard, his Adam's apple pushing into his shirt collar. He quickly called on Johnlittle Sise before anyone noticed the flush creeping into his neck.

But someone had. As he walked with Lena back through the

school door, he found Jennie sitting there, staring flint at them. He jumped away from Lena.

"Time to go," he said, grabbing his empty lunch sack. Jennie's eyes cut from him to Lena and back again, calculating. He had to brush past her to get back out the door.

48

Takansy
April 1870

Takansy hunkered between the graves, her right hand on Rosita's, her left on Martín's. Tiny shoots of new blue grama brushed her fingers as she prayed. The New Grass Moon came early in that part of the country. At her girlhood village on the Bitterroot, snow would still be hiding the ground.

She inhaled the April air and slowly released it. No vapor cloud formed in the noon-day sunlight.

Over the top of the cemetery's rock wall, she watched a group of students emerge from the schoolhouse about a hundred paces to the south. Lena and John Alexander moved among them as one creature, as if encased in a bubble. They found a rock and sat down close together.

The Alexander boy was thinner than when he'd accompanied

them to Denver: all bone and stringy muscle and knobby neck. She couldn't see his features very well, but the shadows under his cheekbones and the angle of his jaw signaled the change from boy to man. His walk was different, too—less awkward and hesitant, a longer, more confident stride. A tutor now, according to Lena.

The front and sides of Lena's hair were swept behind and pinned in the light-face girls' way that Medina liked. It made her seem even taller than she already was. Her dress, belted at the waist, hugged tiny swells of developing breasts.

Near the pair, two boys tossed a ball back and forth, their eyes shifting toward Lena so frequently that they missed several catches. Their prairie dog barks of laughter reached Takansy over the cemetery wall. Lena ignored them.

John Alexander pulled a book from his pack and opened it on his knees. Lena edged closer to see. Their knees touched. The boy's finger pointed to the page as he spoke the words. Lena's eyes moved from the open book to John Alexander's face, back and forth.

Takansy had watched Lena fall under his influence, little by little. Her eager reading of the books he gave her, her efforts to please him. And the boy's obvious interest in Lena went beyond learning, despite his clumsy attempts to hide it.

Takansy knew the danger signs. The same feelings she had felt as a girl for her young brave, Charges Ahead. The same yearnings that had led to her sin and shameful separation from her people. Lena must not make the same mistake.

49

John Alexander
April 1870

At home, Jennie planted notions in Pa's head against Lena. It was Lena this and Lena that. Lena the teacher's pet. Lena getting the prize role in the school play. Lena the princess, lording it over the plain folk. And worst of all, Lena showing other kids how she counted the rosary.

That last bit spewed out one evening at the supper table just as Mama was fetching a pot of simmering turnips from their new, cast iron cook stove. Jennie put on her mother hen look and wrapped a protective hand around each of the younger children's heads, as if to cover their tender ears.

"Right in front of all the younguns, she clicked those black beads and did her chanting."

Pa's beard bristled. "Not you three, you didn't watch," he said, nailing Mattie and Robert and Anna with an accusing stare.

"Johnnie let them watch," Jennie said.

Pa's blue-eyed blaze turned on Johnnie.

Johnnie kept his on Jennie. "Did not!"

"Did, too."

"Pa, she only did it once or twice. The other students kept asking her. I can't watch Anna and Robert and Mattie every minute," Johnnie said.

"I had to pull them away from her, Pa, just yesterday," Jennie said. "Johnnie was watching her, too. She was going on about the hail Marys and all that mumbo jumbo they do. The younguns was lapping it up like spilt milk. That girl has cast a spell on the whole school."

The A-frown knotted Pa's forehead. "That teacher." He spit out the word like it had a bad taste. "He allows this to go on? He allows our school to be turned into a school for papists?"

The idea of Lena being an agent of the Inquisition would have made Johnnie laugh coming from anyone but his father.

"Pa, Please. Mr. Sprague…"

"John William!" Pa's sermon voice filled the air, drowning out his. "Ye'll not be associating yourself with that temptress. She'll not be in your little group. She'll not be poisoning the minds of the children. I'll be having a word with your Mr. Sprague, I will. And not just me. It's time for the convening of a committee."

Johnnie stared at him. He could feel heat rising in his neck. He pushed back from the table.

"He's sweet on her, Pa," Jennie said. "He's plumb gone on her."

"You liar! She's just a little girl, she's…"

"He's with her all the…"

"You…" *Bitch* Johnnie wanted to say. He lunged at her.

She screamed and jumped up, knocking her tin plate onto the floor. Anna started crying. Robert scooted into the corner, wide-eyed.

Mattie said, "Johnnie, no."

Mama held up her pot of turnips like a shield. Johnnie tripped, and his hand, seeking balance, found Pa's shoulder. Pa batted it off like it was a snake and lurched to his feet. Johnnie turned and stumbled out of the dugout into the night.

Two hours of pacing failed to settle him down. Jennie had exposed something best kept hidden. Even to himself.

The next week at school, Johnnie upped his resolve to stay distant from Lena. He made sure everyone in the Dumbell Posse got equal treatment.

During breaks he would stay to himself or run off with Johnlittle Sise to check the trout rising to bugs hatching on the river down below the schoolhouse. Every day after class he would bundle his brother and sisters into the wagon and head straight for home. He could feel Lena's big, questioning eyes on his back as they left. The week seemed to last forever. And despite himself, during chores or settling down to sleep, Lena's face would appear in his mind like a pond reflection that shimmers back into being after the rock-splash ripples subside.

When Saturday finally came, he hurried through chores and the day's quota of log sawing. The whining blade grew hot and the fresh sawdust mounding under the saw table took on a slightly burnt smell.

Mattie brought him lunch so he didn't have to go inside.

"Don't pay Jennie no mind, Johnnie."

"You're a peach, Mattie." He gave her a hug. "I'll be back tomorrow. I'm going to be alone for a while. Got some thinking to do."

Mattie looked alarmed.

"Don't worry," he said. "I'll meet you tomorrow at church."

An hour later he walked between the sandstone slabs that guarded his hideout. He unpacked his sack, set up a small campfire, and boiled up some coffee in a tin can. From a cavity in the wall, he fished out the *Little Women* book Mr. Sprague had given him. He figured it could teach him something about girls. Then he rolled out his blanket on the sand next to the sandstone wall that still glowed in the rays of the late afternoon sun. He leaned against it, soaked up its warmth and opened the book. Just as he arrived at the part where Beth is dying of scarlet fever, he heard a scraping sound. His neck prickled as he scanned the low ledge that encircled his secret place. Then he saw her. Lena was looking down on him with grave, questioning eyes.

He jumped up. The book flew off his lap and *thunked* into the sand.

"Lena! How did you find me here?" His voice came out funny, almost a shout. She turned as if she might bolt.

"Wait!" He stretched out his hand.

She hesitated a moment, then squatted down, took his hand and jumped down onto the sand, graceful as a fawn. Her touch felt cool in his campfire-warmed palm. She pulled away. A gleam of sunlight reflected off the silver cross that dangled from a delicate chain around her neck. She brushed aside a strand of glossy hair, still looking uncertain.

"How did you know I was here?" he repeated in a softer voice.

"You come here often. I sometimes see you when…"

"You followed me?"

"No, John Alexander. I saw you leave here one day last fall. From down there." She pointed down the hillside to a dense clump of trees where Shy Bird was tethered. "I peeked in here, saw where you, your tracks, your sign. I have never come in here. Until now."

"And now?"

"And now…I thought I might find you here today. I'm sorry if I have…"

"But why?"

She looked at a rock and took a deep breath. "Our Posse. So changed. I am worried that I have done something. Something wrong that has made you angry." Her eyes, uncertain, swung back to his. "I can leave. I didn't mean to…to bother you."

"Lena, no." He grasped her arm, then pulled away after the touch sent a tingle down his spine. "No, you haven't done anything, you…it's not you at all. You're swell, the best student in our group."

She looked unconvinced, so he blundered on.

"Lena, you know Jennie, how she is, and Della. They spread gossip, and lies. Jennie told my pa…" he almost repeated what Jennie had said about his being sweet on Lena, but pulled back from that cliff.

"What did she say?"

"Nothing about you, well, except when you showed your rosary beads to the others and answered their questions—that's what Jennie told him about, but then he goes on about priests and nuns and idol worship and secret Catholic cults and…it's all folderol. It's just… "

"But you don't believe that, do you? Why are you so changed?"

Why indeed? Because I'm plum gone on you, like Jennie says. Because if I don't stay away from you, I'm going to do something I'll be sorry for. His mind scrabbled for words, a prairie dog caught out in the open, looking for a hole to dive into. He found one.

"Lena, your papa, he dotes on you. He loves you. My pa, he hates me. You can't understand what that's like. It makes me… Sometimes, I just get to feeling lower than a snake."

"Why does he hate you?"

He gazed at her a long time, and of a sudden he wanted to tell her the whole story about Pa and the accident. It felt like a boil ready to burst. He guided her to a spot on the worn blanket.

"Come, let's sit. I'll tell you."

She squatted down, buckskin skirt fringes brushing the ground, and stretched her hands over the little blaze. He fed it some sticks and sat down to face her. The blanket was in shadow, a winter compared to the summer above, where the April sun still warmed the rimrock. The coffee started to boil. He only had one cup, so he settled the grounds with a splash of cold water, filled the cup with steaming coffee and gave it to her.

She bobbed a thanks and held the hot cup with both hands wrapped around it for warmth. She sniffed the coffee smell and her nose wrinkled up in that way she had.

He took a deep breath, and started. "You see my pa's arm, his limp. You hear how he breathes. I did that to him." He looked into the fire and saw another fire, long ago, in a boiler, and the story began to spill out, first in rivulets, then in torrents, melting ice. The forbidden book, the praying mantis, the rats in the woodpile, his awkward fumbling for the wrench, the blinding roar, the bloody foam. Especially the bloody foam.

"Lena, I was never so scared, before or since."

She leaned toward him, eyes full of tears. His own cheeks were wet. A tear splashed on his hand. His? Or hers? She put her hand on his arm and this time there was no pulling away. His head swirled. He felt himself pulled into a perilous current.

"But he lived." Lena rose from her squatting position, stretched her legs one after the other, then hunkered back down.

"But I didn't know he would. Doc McGill came to the house after we got Pa down the hill. He was with Pa for the longest time while the rest of us waited outside the bedroom door, not knowing."

"What did you tell them?"

Something forgiving in Lena's eyes helped him say what he said next. "I lied. I told them I was outside when the boiler exploded. I thought…I thought Pa would die, and no one would find out it was my doing. Lord help me, I hoped he *would* die."

What had started as a diversion had become a confession. Lena's intense listening was beyond anything he had ever experienced, a listening that stripped away his reserve and led him, step by step, into the deep pools of her luminous eyes toward the opposite shore, crossing over to reveal his last and most dangerous thought.

He reached for her. "Lena, there's something I..."

Then he saw the little girl in her, a current too treacherous to cross, and he pulled back to the safety of his riverbank. He grasped the coffee can and took a drink. It was cold and bitter. He set it down with a shaking hand.

She cocked her head, waiting.

He stood up, feeling cold. Little prickles ran down his legs into numb feet.

"You'd best be going. Your folks'll be worried."

Her brows bunched into a frown. "You work so hard, for your father. Shouldn't...isn't he glad for what you do?"

"That's the difference between your pa and mine."

"It is not so different as you think," she said in a small voice.

"What do you mean? I've seen the way your pa looks at you, all proud, so full of... ."

"It's true, but..."

"He'd do anything for you."

"I can't explain it," she said with a little shrug. She stepped close, gave him a shy hug and stepped away. "John Alexander, thank you for telling me all that, but..." She paused, searching for words. "I still don't understand why you...at school...I mean, why you are so changed...toward me."

He looked at her a moment trying to figure out how to explain that the school tutor shouldn't be having the kind of thoughts he had about a twelve-year-old student. The same thoughts he was having, Lord help him, as he stood there next to her fighting the urge to reach out and pull her close.

What he said next surprised him. "Lena. I'm leaving the school. I'm leaving our family. I've decided to hire out to the Illiff outfit. If they'll have me, I mean. Or some other ranch. Anything, really. I have to get away."

Her eyes widened as she backed up a step.

"So, you see, I haven't been myself this last while, been thinking, figuring things out."

"So no more lessons? No more Posse?" Her face got a stricken look. She whirled around and climbed up the low hideout wall, quick as a squirrel. At the top, she gave him a last tearful look, then disappeared. He pulled himself up over the ledge in time to see her run into the little grove of pines below.

50

Takansy
April 1870

Takansy stared at the feather duster flicking mechanically over the wooden statue of Jésu and wondered how long she had been holding it. Her mind dwelt in dark corners, wrestling with what to do about her daughter and the Alexander boy. In a few days Lena would enter her thirteenth year. Her journey into womanhood would soon follow. If Lena stayed here, her love-blindness would grow, her knee-touching with young Alexander would soon enough turn into babies. *Too soon.* Babies would mean the end of the Horse Spirit path. The end of special closeness with her only remaining daughter. The Alexander boy was nice enough. But he had no money. No way to own horses. And his family! She shuddered at the kind of welcome Lena might receive from Blue-eye.

Could she stop Lena from seeing the boy? Might she even team up with the boy's awful father to end all contact? The memory of her own youthful defiance cast a shadow on that path.

What, then? Send Lena to a place where boys like John Alexander would not be allowed? What had been unthinkable before, now opened as a possible path, a lesser of bad choices. Could she bear sending Lena to the Denver City school? For a while, at least, long enough for her daughter's love sickness to wilt.

Medina's satisfied grunt jarred her out of her thought cave.

"*Bueno.* The store sales, better than ever. Antonio's insult, it did not last." He sat at the table, drawing a circle around the number at the bottom of a ledger. *He cannot read or write the words, but with the numbers, he is a calculating coyote.*

He glanced toward her.

"You have that ghost stare again." He sighed, closed the ledger and looked out the window at the hint of green flashing on the cottonwood branches in the slanting afternoon sun.

The door slammed. They both turned. Lena rushed past them, tossed a school book into the corner and disappeared into the bedroom. Her face was a tumult, her mouth a thin line.

"Lena?" both said at once.

Medina rose from the table at the same time Takansy tossed aside the feather duster and both of them rushed after their daughter. Lena lay facing the wall. Takansy sat on the edge of her bed and placed her hand on her back.

"What is it, my flower?"

Medina came up beside them.

For a long moment Lena lay there. Then in a quavering voice she said, "Mr. Sprague is leaving. The school play I was…that will not be. They have stopped it."

"Why is the teacher to leave?" Medina asked.

"He says to take care of his sick aunt in Denver City. But I do not…Della says it is because he…because the play is…"

"Is there to be another teacher?" Medina asked.

"Yes, Papi, he is already there but…"

"Then this is not so great a tragedy for such a sad face. Yes, my daughter?"

Lena pushed herself up and turned to face them in a sitting position, her hand reaching out to grasp Takansy's arm.

"Oh Mami, Papi, it is all my fault! Della says it is because

I…because Mr. Sprague let me tell about…these!" She tugged the black rosary from her belt pouch and flung it against the wall.

"What? How can that…" Medina's voice grew edgy.

"And this." She yanked at the silver cross hanging from her neck, but the chain held.

Takansy caught Lena's hand in her own and held it. "Because we are Catholic?"

"Yes, and because I was telling them—they asked me, the others—and I told them about the Virgin Mary and St. Francis and how we say the rosary, and Mr. Sprague said it was all right when Della told him to stop me, but it wasn't all right, and there was a committee, and our play—we cannot do it—and now he's leaving and…"

"A committee? Who?" Medina, voice thickening, leaned close and seized Lena's arm.

"Papi, don't…"

"Who? On the committee?"

Takansy pulled at his fingers. "Let go! You are hurting her."

"Della did not say. She…maybe there is no committee. Maybe Mr. Sprague just… ."

Medina let go of Lena's arm and began pacing in a tight circle beside the bed.

"Lucas Brandt. He will know about this. I will find him and make him tell." He turned and stalked out of the room.

"Husband! Not the anger way. Stop and think."

The front door crashed closed. Needles pricked at Takansy's spine. He would need to be stopped from acting in haste, if she could find a way to do it. She turned back and smoothed Lena's hair.

"What else, my daughter? There is more?"

Lena looked as if she'd just watched her horse die.

"The Posse. John Alexander's tutor group. It is no more."

She leaned forward and laid her head on Takansy's shoulder. A tear rolled down the side of her face, hung a moment, then dropped onto Takansy's buckskin shirt.

"He is…leaving the school."

But not the Crossing. Still too near.

"Mami, we must ask John Alexander to stay as a tutor, here. Separate from the school. Papi asked him once. He will do it if you and Papi ask."

Takansy lifted her daughter's face and captured her gaze. "You are having the love feeling toward John Alexander?"

Lena stiffened. A hood of caution slipped over her eyes.

"No, Mami. I just...he can teach me, that is all."

But it was not all. "We shall see, my flower." But she was already seeing more than she wanted to see. "Rest here. I must going to your father before he is doing the anger." She patted Lena's hair and walked out into the April air to find Medina.

51

Medina
April 1870

As he expected, Medina found Lucas Brandt sitting at the bar with Louie Papa. Brandt drew back as Medina approached.

"You look snake bit. What happened?"

"The school committee, you are there, yes?"

"Well, yes, I was on it for a while. Why?"

"You to send the teacher away, to Denver City?"

"Not me. The committee's changed some since I...say, did this just happen, sending Arah Sprague away?" Brandt raised his eyebrows at Louie Papa as if asking for an explanation.

Louie Papa shrugged.

"Who is the committee?" Medina asked.

"Well, let's see. Mrs. Bartholf's still there, and William Alexander with that passel of kids, and, I'm not sure about Ed Clark, and I'm pretty sure Henry Howard's on it, new this year, and…that's all, I think."

"Many thanks." Medina turned and headed out the tavern door toward the barn.

"Where you going?" Lucas Brandt said.

"Wait for me," Louie Papa said. He started to rise, but Medina glared him back onto his stool.

Medina arrived at the Howard place around supper. Its appearance surprised him. He expected something more in line with Henry Howard's slouch. Instead, there were chicken pens, goat runs and corrals, all in neat squares, surrounding a plank-sided barn with painted black door trim. A small but well-built log cabin stood next to a straight-rowed, weedless garden. The porch was swept clean, the yard empty of trash, the corrals raked free of manure. Susan Howard's doing? Medina knocked on the door.

Henry Howard pushed through it. Up close he seemed bigger than when Medina had last dealt with him across the store counter over a year ago. Howard thrust his hands into his pockets and stood there like a tree, shoulders bulging under his thin shirt, red suspenders straining to keep his pants from being pushed down by his protruding belly. He looked like a man who didn't like being disturbed during supper.

"Well, if it isn't Mr. Medina, come for a visit," he said, with just enough sneer in his voice to rankle without being openly insulting.

Susan Howard appeared in the doorway behind him. Worry lines bunched her forehead when she recognized Medina.

"What you want?" Henry Howard said.

Medina wondered if the man's face muscles had ever experienced a smile.

"The school committee. You are there, yes?"

"What of it?"

"For why you send the teacher away?"

Henry Howard shifted his bulk from side to side. "For why? Because he wanted to leave, that's for why."

Medina took a slow breath and forced himself to stay calm.

"You to stop the school play, for why?"

"Teacher did that all by himself. Thought it best."

The weight shifting continued, from one big foot to the other, then back. The late afternoon sun played across the mole on his cheek every time he swayed out from under the roof's shadow.

"My daughter. Lena. Your committee to have some problems with her? You do not like?" Medina had to clear his throat. It always seemed to tighten in situations like this, thick and less coherent. His English always got worse. It was very annoying.

The big man's swaying increased. "Why no, Mr. Medina. No problem. No problem at all."

From behind her husband's right shoulder, Susan Howard began shaking her head in a vigorous "no." She was still pretty, Medina thought, despite her worry lines. He realized, too late, that he was staring at her.

Henry Howard stopped swaying and swiveled his big head around. "You saying something different, woman?"

"Why no, Henry, I'm just... ."

"Then why you shaking your head, no?"

"Well, it's just that you said earlier that the girl is Catholic and that Bill Alexander..."

"Shut up, woman."

"...said she's corrupting the minds of the other... ."

"I said, shut up!" Henry Howard reached out a meaty paw and shoved his wife in the chest. She staggered back, her body bouncing off the door frame with a crunching sound and sharp exhalation of breath. As she regained her balance and danced away from him, her eyes blazed with sudden fire.

"And you called her a little half-breed slut."

Medina saw color flare on Henry Howard's cheek as if he'd been slapped. The big man cocked his arm back for a sledgehammer blow and balled his hand into a fist the size of a pumpkin.

Medina was faster. He slipped the tomahawk out of his belt and whipped it around in a short arc to intercept Howard's blow. The big man saw it too late to stop his swing. Knuckle and bone cracked against the flat side of the blade. Henry Howard let out a sound somewhere between a scream and a bellow.

Medina didn't wait for him to recover. He whapped the flat of the tomahawk against the top of Henry Howard's skull. Howard slumped down on his hands and knees, his head swinging back and forth like a bear.

Medina swapped his tomahawk for his hunting knife, crouched down, grabbed the brute's hair in his free hand and jerked his head up. With his other hand he pressed the knife against Howard's thick neck. Panting, he fought the instinct to slit the man's throat, to finish him before he recovered enough to retaliate.

Medina didn't like the odds if he didn't at least cripple the man. Instead, this time he tried to scare him.

He leaned close to Howard's ear and said, in a voice thick with battle heat, "No to fucking hit her again or I to kill you *muerto* and to hang your hair with other scalps, and maybe your balls, too. *Comprende?*" He pushed the heavy head down to make sure Henry Howard could wrap his eyes around the ten-inch skinning blade. "I will to stick you clear up to Green River," he added.

Henry Howard held very still for a moment, then, to Medina's surprise, burst into sobs.

"No, no, please, I won't, I'm sorry for what I said, won't do it again, just let me alone, don't..." His mountainous body heaved.

Medina was too shocked to move. Before he could say anything, Susan Howard knelt at his side, leaned against him and pushed his knife hand away. The press of her body against his unraveled him.

"Henry, Oh! You're hurt, oh my darling, your hand, it's bleeding, your head, let me..." She held his bloodied head in her hands and lifted it to peer into his eyes. "Come inside, now, so I can bandage it."

He staggered to his feet and let her guide him toward the cabin door. Just before disappearing inside, she twisted her head around and locked eyes with Medina. It was a confusing mixture of gratitude, reproach, and what else? Defiance perhaps. Medina couldn't tell.

He rose, tucked the knife back into his belt and made for his horse. His body felt cold and a little shaky. He mounted and set out for the Crossing. Reason slowly returned, and he thought—not for the first time—that his outbursts often brought him a lot more trouble than he wanted. He decided against riding up to William Alexander's place.

It was dark when he returned. He handed his mount over to a stable hand and hurried to the house. He had gone off without a coat, and the early spring plunge from day to night temperatures had set his teeth chattering.

He found Takansy kneeling by her altar. Soft candlelight erased time's wrinkles from her face, and he was suddenly transported back to the day twenty-five years ago when she had left Papín and come with him, an event that left him dumbstruck with joy. She crossed herself, rose, and the spell was broken.

"Lena?" he asked.

"Asleep. She will be fine. She is young."

"She may be fine, but I am not fine. I found out…Henry Howard's wife told me all I need to know."

"You spoke with her?" Takansy's eyebrows arched with sudden curiosity.

Medina, remembering the Howard woman's closeness, felt discomfited by her stare.

"And her husband, that bag of *mierda*."

"Did you…hurt him?"

"I hope so." Medina didn't want to go into detail, so he switched topics. "Lena can no longer attend this school. The school committee has dishonored her, and our family. They do not deserve her. Or our money." He paused a moment before saying the next words. "This fall, Lena will attend St. Mary's Academy in Denver City. It is time. I have decided."

Again the raised eyebrows. He braced himself for the expected protest. Then he got his second big surprise of the evening.

"Yes," she said. "I suppose it is time."

52

John Alexander
April 1870

Three days after Johnnie talked with Lena in his hideout, Mr. Sprague announced he was being replaced by a new teacher. He said he had to leave to care for a sick aunt in Denver City. He said the school play would have to be cancelled because it would take too much time away from studies. He said all this with his face fixed in a false grin.

Johnnie knew he was lying.

Della and Jennie walked around with superior looks on their faces that said they knew things no one else did. But the story finally leaked out. There had been a meeting. Pa got it together. Mrs. Bartholf was there, so was Henry Howard. Probably Mr. Blackhurst, too, judging from Della's knowing nods.

Johnlittle Sise bawled when he heard about the play. His mood didn't improve when Johnnie told his students that he would be leaving, too, come the end of the month. The whole Posse was pretty glum. Johnnie pointed out that school was almost over anyway, so it didn't matter. But he didn't believe that, himself. He felt low for them, low for himself.

Lena never came back to school. Johnnie worried she might be sick, but two days later, traveling back through the Crossing on the way home, he saw her on Shy Bird out in the pasture, riding with Louie Papa. She spotted him and turned away without waving. It was April 12, her birthday, the day of the school play. He felt empty.

A few days later, Johnnie managed to get Louie Papa alone. He was walking by himself on his way to the well in the courtyard when Johnnie caught up to him. He mostly kept his mouth shut as Johnnie babbled on about trying to hitch up with the Illiff outfit, and how much he needed his help.

Finally, Louie Papa said, "I'll see what I can do."

The next few days stretched long in the waiting. Chores at home seemed to take forever. Up on the mountain, Johnnie cut and loaded logs fast as he could, afraid he'd miss Louie Papa if he came looking. Then, five days later, he showed up around dusk just as Johnnie was forking some hay over the fence to their milk cow.

"You start with Illiff tomorrow. Ain't much. Mostly horse chores, the remuda. It's a start. Bring your gear and meet me in the morning."

"I don't have a saddle," Johnnie said. "Or bridle."

"Come anyway."

"I thank you. This means a lot."

Louie Papa touched a finger to his hat brim, wheeled around and rode off, straight-backed, long legs resting easy against his horse's side, seat glued to the saddle even at a trot. Johnnie wondered if he would ever be able to ride like that. At least now he would have a chance to try. Heart quickening, he tossed the pitchfork aside and ran into the barn. The word "gear" overstated the contents of the small, makeshift canvas bag he had packed up and hidden there. He looked through it one last time, tucked it back under a pile of hay, and geared himself to face his father at supper.

That evening, before Johnnie could swallow the first bite of turnips and pig knuckles, Jennie said in her accusatory voice, "What was Louie Papa doing here? Down at the barn, I saw him talking to you."

They were sitting around the old wood door that served as a dinner table. Pa bristled up at Jennie's question, then turned to Johnnie. Mama stopped eating. Johnnie felt the little ones' eyes on him, nervous, their forks suspended in mid-air.

Johnnie stared at his plate as if the pig knuckles were going to haul up and walk away.

"He...I got a job. At the Illiff Ranch. I'll be leaving tomorrow. Louie Papa's taking me. I'll be working cattle." He had to clear his throat three times to get this out.

Mattie stared at him, then pushed away from the table, tears in her eyes. He vowed to go to her later and let her know he would visit often. Anna and Robert stared, waiting for an explosion. Mama's eyes got that pleading look, but she didn't say anything. In a way, that was harder on Johnnie than if she'd carried on more. He had to grit his teeth to keep his resolve.

With a straight face, Jennie said, "You're leaving? Who's going to do the lifting and the sawing and log loading?" She let that question hang for a moment, then she turned and patted Pa on the arm. "Pa, I'll fill in as best I can. We'll make do somehow." A little smile pulled up the corners of her mouth.

"There's a way," Johnnie said. "I mean, I'll be sending some of my earnings home. That, plus the tenter money. Should be enough to take on a hired hand. Like Caleb." He was babbling, his eyes jumping between Mama and Pa. "I'm sixteen. It's time to get out on my own." He tried to sound sure of himself. It was what he'd practiced.

Pa, his voice strangely calm, said, "What do ye know about cattle?"

Johnnie, expecting a rant, said, "I been learning. I know more'n you think."

Pa smiled. He put on a kind face, but his eyes narrowed down.

"Cowhands need to know about cows. And horses. They own saddles and bridles and ropes and chaps. Ye have none of these things. Look at ye, boy. Pure mountain. Ye know about logs and sawmills. What makes ye think John Wesley Illiff will hire the likes of you? Not to mention ye are still as clumsy and absent-minded as the day ye were born."

Something snapped inside Johnnie. He jumped up so suddenly his knee upended the table. Wooden bowls flew through the air, turnips spattering everywhere. A glob landed square on Pa's beard.

Mama let out a holler. The younguns scattered like chickens. Jennie jumped back and let fly at him with her fork. It stuck in his shoulder, wobbled a bit and fell to the floor. Johnnie didn't feel a thing.

Next thing he knew he was flying out of the door. He ran to the barn, fetched the canvas bag from under the hay, and set out on foot. Mac padded up, tail wagging.

Johnnie knelt down, gave the dog a hug and said, "Stay, boy. Stay." His breath caught in his throat as Mac's ears drooped. All the way to his hideout he argued with himself about whether Pa was right.

In the morning he walked to the cliff edge and looked back toward his homestead.

"Goodbye, Mama," he said aloud. "Goodbye, Anna and Robert and Mattie. Mac. And you too, Pa." Then he turned and set out for the Crossing.

At the base of the red cliff, he retrieved the boots he had bought in Denver City with Mr. Medina's money.

He found Louie Papa in front of the wagon shed, hitching up a small two-seater. He looked for Lena, but saw only Medina's stable hands.

Louie Papa gave Johnnie's canvas bag and boots a quizzical look. "In there," he said, nodding at the buckboard.

Johnnie tossed them in.

"Got a saddle for you. Not fancy, but it'll do." Louie Papa walked into the shed and came out hefting an old saddle and bridle. He tossed them in the wagon where they landed with a thud in a puff of dust.

"I'll pay for it, first chance."

Louie Papa waved him off. "Thank Lena. She's the one who rustled it up."

"How is she?" Johnnie had tried to wrangle her out of his mind, but she had trotted back in, and he was picturing her eyes and her hint of a smile and her smooth skin…his heart hammered with quick, sweet guilt.

"Fine, I reckon. More horse time."

"Not sad?" Johnnie was hoping she'd been missing him.

"Nope."

Getting information from Louie Papa was like digging for gold along the Big Thompson. You could starve between nuggets.

"Her pa and ma?"

"Mama's fine. Medina's heap angry."

"About what happened at school?"

"Yup."

"He going to do anything?"

Louie Papa twitched up a trace of a smile. "Paid a visit to Henry Howard. Decided to send Lena to school in Denver City come fall. St. Mary's."

Johnnie tried to cover up the sinking feeling inside. He remembered the well-dressed bunch of students from the parade. He remembered the young man with the strange red hair asking about Lena.

"I reckon she'll do well in school, no matter where she goes," he said.

He fished the new boots back out of the buckboard. Mice had chewed the leather near the top of the left boot. Still, they were better than the tin-strapped contraptions on his feet. He sat down and pulled the new ones on. He tossed his old boots into a trash-filled box next to the shed. Starting fresh, he thought.

"From Mr. Medina," he said to Louie Papa, indicating the boots as he pulled them on. "I'll need to speak with him. I'll be quick."

"At the fort. Hurry."

Johnnie trotted across the bridge and found Mr. Medina standing on a stool beside the fort's wood balcony at window level. He had some pigeon coops there. The birds fluttered around him, fighting for whatever he held in his hand—corn, Johnnie reckoned. When he saw Johnnie he tossed the yellow kernels on the balcony floor and the birds fluttered down like gray leaves. With a wave he stepped down from the stool and greeted Johnnie with a shoulder-patting hug and *saludos* in the Spanish custom.

"Johnnie," he said. "For why you are not stopping here so much anymore?" Pipe smoke was strong on his breath.

"I quit school."

"Ah, yes. That school. A good thing to be gone from there."

"Good?"

"Yes, yes. That school, it is not good enough for my Lena. She will have a finer school. In Denver City. Where I want her to go even before. Now, she goes. Very expensive." He rubbed his thumb and forefinger together, like he was counting coins. He didn't seem to mind the cost.

"Saint Mary's Academy, yes. A proper school. There she will

become a fine lady. Music. Art. She will be with people who know how to dress. To read and to write. Better than this school." He gestured with his chin up the hill and waved his hand dismissively.

Johnnie swallowed. "Sir, I don't hold with what they did, to Mr. Sprague I mean, and stopping the play and all. My pa, he and me don't see eye to eye on…"

"Not you to worry, Johnnie." He winked and waved his hands as if brushing away gnats. "You are welcome here. My house is your house."

He smiled and clapped Johnnie on the back. "And you, Johnnie, you are to become a *vaquero*, Louie Papa tells me."

"Yes, sir."

"John Wesley Illiff. He owns many beeves. Thousands. But rough Texas cattle. Not to match my cattle for…how you say?…the quality." He swept his arm toward the pasture, just beginning to green up after the first spring showers. About thirty cows stood in a corral with their heads over the fence, eyeing the new grass. One of Mr. Medina's Mexican hands, pitchfork slung over his shoulder, strode toward a stack of last year's brown hay just outside the corral and began tossing bunches over the fence. The cows, big bellies ready to calve, shoved each other to snatch mouthfuls.

Medina laughed. "Soon little beeves to be on the ground. Then those cows to eat twice as much as now." His hands moved to measure an imaginary mound of hay about four feet high.

"Sir, there's something I'd like to say."

He gave Johnnie a questioning look.

"You remember these boots?" Johnnie pointed. "And the clothes? The one's you loaned me money for in Denver City?"

He nodded, but Johnnie could tell he'd forgotten all about it.

"I aim to pay back the ten dollars."

Mr. Medina's hands flew up in protest. "No is necessary."

"Sir, it's necessary for me. What I aim to ask is, what I'd like to do, if it's all right with you, is come here when I can, when I get some time off, to help you out on chores, you know, like chopping wood, tending cows, loading, hauling, cleaning the barn, whatever you need done, so I can work it off. Ten dollars worth."

Mr. Medina thought a moment, then broke out in another grin. His mood seemed to be all smiles that day.

"Good. Good. You come. The work here, we have it always."

"It may be a while. I'll have to buckle down and get settled into the Illiff bunch."

His hand reached out and Johnnie shook it. The knuckles were bonier than Johnnie remembered. He bowed.

"*Con tu permiso*, I go now. Trade goods." A chin thrust pointed to the store where a loaded wagon pulled in from the Denver City road.

They walked together across the bridge, back to where Louie Papa waited in the wagon.

Then Johnnie spotted Lena.

She stepped out onto the trading post porch about a hundred feet away. He felt his breath catch. She didn't see him, and began arranging some baskets of what looked like onions on the porch display shelves. Her glossy black hair swung from side to side. He felt Mr. Medina catch him staring.

Johnnie said, "Does Lena want to go to St. Mary's?"

Mr. Medina's eyebrows rose up as he stepped back to look at Johnnie. "But of course. She is eager. Who would not want to go to such a school? She tells me she wishes to learn the mandolin, to become a lady. Of course she wishes to do well for herself. And to bring honor on our family. There is no question." His voice was hearty with certainty.

"Good. She is very smart. I could tell, when I was her tutor, in the Poss...in the group I helped with."

"Ah, yes, yes, and I thank you for your help, thank you very much, Johnnie. And now she will be learning new things. Things you cannot teach her, yes?"

Johnnie forced his chin to stay up. "True. I wish her well."

They arrived at the wagon and Mr. Medina walked on.

Louie Papa said, "*Vamanos*. We'll meet the Illiff boys about an hour east of here. They'll take you the rest of the way."

Johnnie thanked him and climbed aboard. Wind gusts stirred the new April grass as they drove away. Freshly sprouted cottonwood leaves flickered lime green. Spring, a hopeful time. He tried to work up the kind of excitement that used to fill his dreams of this day, now that it had finally come, yet his eyes were drawn back to the store. Lena was looking his way. He waved, but she didn't wave back. He vowed to forget her.

53

Takansy
September 1870

Everything was ready except Takansy's state of mind. She pawed through Lena's clothes in the wooden chest one last time. Her mind galloped about for things she might have forgotten. She lifted the cloth covering on the basket of sweet cakes, then covered it again.

"Papi is waiting, Mami." Lena stood in the doorway dressed in white-lady traveling clothes: lace boots, long black stockings, gabardine skirt, white blouse, jacket, hair gathered under a tiny oval hat with an egret feather that proclaimed is uselessness for anything practical. She was ready for the trip to St. Mary's.

Takansy forced herself to smile, a betrayal of her heart. *Why did I agree to this?* John Alexander had left, no longer a danger. Over the summer her daughter had reconciled herself to him being gone. Unfortunately, she had also reconciled herself to boarding school.

Perhaps the first had led to the second.

Takansy had argued with Medina. Oh, how she had argued! But he was stone.

"For why you change your mind?" he said. "The money, she is all paid. I even get Jones to let her ride the horses, as you want. She is not baby anymore. Thirteen. Time to learn as young woman."

TaKansy had given up. And now it was time. She looked at her daughter standing there in her strange clothes and tried to picture her in buckskins.

"One last thing, my flower." From the altar chest she drew out a beaded leather pouch. Its worn otter skin felt soft to the touch. With her thumb she traced the familiar red and blue otter pattern beaded on its surface. She handed it to Lena. "You see the beads? They form the otter sign."

Lena traced the curved pattern with her forefinger. Takansy squeezed Lena's fingers into a tight grip around the pouch.

Seized by a sudden fierceness, she said, "Daughter, this was given to me by Otter Woman in the long ago. It has powerful medicine to keep you safe. Do not forget the spirit of your people. Wear it always. Promise!"

"Yes, Mami. Thank you."

Takansy tied the pouch around her daughter's neck and tucked it inside her shirt, invisible under the silver cross. She wrapped her arms around Lena and squeezed, then pulled away, a little too roughly.

"Go now." She spun Lena around and guided her out into the waiting September sun.

"I love you, Mami."

Takansy closed the door. She didn't want to watch her daughter climb into the wagon next to Medina and drive away.

54

John Alexander
September 1871

John slit through the belly hide of the stillborn calf, being careful not to puncture its gut. The reek of steaming afterbirth, slung along the ground on the other side of the corral fence, clogged his nostrils. He held his breath, hefted up the dead calf and looped the rope connecting its hocks over a corral post. Grasping the hide where he'd cut circles around both legs, he pulled. The hide peeled off with a hissing rip.

A year ago his hands might have been shaking, his stomach queasy. But not now. Over a year spent working on John Wesley Iliff's ranch had taken care of that. He hung the calf hide over a rail, lifted its little carcass off the post and slung it onto a trash pile at the end of the corral. Flies settled on it in a cloud.

On the other side of the fence, the calf's mama bawled her

confusion. A brindle-coated longhorn too young for calf-bearing, she was one of twenty-some heifers bred early by an over-eager young bull who had torn through a five-rail fence to get at them. Six had stillborns. This was the last one, calving in September, way out of season. The mama approached the fence and sniffed at her calf's hide. You'd best remember that smell, John thought.

He ducked into a shed next to the corral. A motherless calf lay there on a pile of straw, shivering despite the September warmth. Its own mama, another of the young heifers, had refused the calf's feeble attempts to suck, kicked the poor little guy in the face, jumped the fence and run off to rejoin the herd.

John swept the abandoned calf up in his arms, carried it to the fence and maneuvered the dead calf's hide over its body. He opened a gate, set the calf down and backed away from the suspicious mama, who gave him the cow-eye. He eased back through the gate and shut it.

"Come on, girl, come on." John made his voice sing-song, low. The brindle lowered her head, stepped up and sniffed the bloody-robed calf wobbling on thin legs. Three deep snorts and a lick. The calf tottered back along the cow's flanks, found an engorged teat and gave it a feeble head butt. The adopted mama cranked her head around to look at the little creature, then let out a soft *maaaa*. The calf latched on, and the brindle stood there, instinct taking over.

John climbed the fence for a better look. The brindle swung her head around and snaked a horn between the rails that caught him on the thigh.

He jerked back. "Damn you! That's the thanks I get?" He rubbed the sore place, feeling it starting to swell. No broken skin, thanks to his leather chaps. He took a deep breath, and despite the pain, smiled.

A year had passed since he'd ridden away from the Crossing. A year since Lena had gone off to school in Denver City. He'd made it as an Illiff hand. He'd survived the hazing of the other hands, gotten bucked off too many horses to count, gotten back on, been allowed to help move bunches of cattle from time to time, riding drag, eating dust, low hand on the ranch. But he had proved up. Learned about cattle. Sent some of his earnings back to Ma, and stowed away quite a bit for himself, despite getting ribbed by the Illiff hands for not blowing his earnings on Saturday-night frolics in the bars south of the Union Colony, like they did. He had proved Pa wrong.

He had tried to forget about Lena. She would have probably come back to the Crossing for the summer and would now be getting ready to go off for her second year at St. Mary's. Or maybe not. He couldn't seem to stop wondering about her.

He wiped his bloody hands on his chaps, leaving a satisfying smear. The dirtier they got, the better he liked them. The better he fit in. He set off for the bunkhouse to wash up before supper. The chaps flapped against his boots as he walked. He looked down to make sure the boots' pointy toes aimed straight ahead, not splayed out to the side like they did when Charlie Hardwick had owned them. Charlie sold him the boots after he'd broken his foot in a stampede and couldn't wear them anymore. The tops had butterfly stitching, yellow thread on brown.

Looking down, he almost ran into Leather Bill. The ranch foreman held him off with a calloused hand.

"Whoa there. Lucky for you I wasn't a bull. You mighta got yourself stomped."

Surprised, John backed up a step. "Sorry." He was relieved to see the crinkles fanning out from Leather Bill's eyes. They were the closest thing to a smile the foreman ever wore.

"She took the calf. The brindle."

Leather Bill rolled a cigarette, lit it and regarded him through the smoke. "That last bunch of Texas beeves we got form Charlie Goodnight have been nothing but trouble."

"Well, that's the last of those heifers."

"You made short work of it."

John jumped into this opening. "Say, I was wondering…what with the calving all done and us still a ways out from fall roundup, I was wondering if I might take a couple of days? Got some business to attend to."

"What kind of business?"

"I owe some money. To a friend. Need to work it off." John didn't know what to make of the man's hard stare, so he added, "It's close by, Mariano's Crossing, a couple of hours. I'll be back first thing Monday morning."

Leather Bill let the smoke curl up through his handlebar mustache. "You'll need a horse."

"The red roan?" It was John's favorite.

Leather Bill actually grinned. "Who you trying to impress?"

John felt himself color. Was he that obvious?

"I could take the pinto."

"Better. You don't need a cutting horse for a trip like that. Besides, girls like pintos."

John wasn't sure how his face betrayed him, but however it did, it caused crusty Leather Bill to laugh out loud.

"What's her name?"

John looked down at his boots. "Julie," he said. "Julie Bartholf." But that was a lie.

55

Medina
September 1871

    Medina strode onto the porch of the post office and felt the chill on his back as the roof's shadow blocked the September sun. He was in a hurry to finish his business with Hiram Tadder and get back home where Lena was preparing dinner. She would soon depart for her second year at St. Mary's. She was becoming a refined and well-educated young lady, and to his delight, had learned to play the mandolin.

    As he reached for the post office door, he heard a soft clink behind him and felt eyes on his back. He whirled around and dropped into a crouch with his Hawken raised, and immediately felt foolish. Here he was in the middle of civilization, reacting as if he were alone in Indian country, thirty years ago. That business with Henry Howard had left him jumpy, even after a year and a half. He peered at the figure who had come up behind him. Then his jaw dropped at the sight of his wife's former husband.

"Papín! Is it you?"

"*Mon ami!*" Papín swept the cap off his head and made that elaborate bow Medina remembered from their days together at Bridger's Fort. The fringe of hair around his bald head was white, the familiar charming smile accented by age lines and hollow cheeks. He had shrunk, but he hadn't lost his showman's swagger.

Medina strode forward and grabbed his old friend in a back-slapping embrace. Papín's shoulders felt bony thin.

"For why you come here? To trade, yes?"

Papín laughed "My trading days are gone. The business, she was good for many years, the war, she bring lots of soldiers to my store, both sides. Then the Mormons come, the Oregon travelers, I get plenty rich, move to St. Louis. Now, I tell tall stories to my grandchildren to watch their eyes grow big."

Medina smiled. Papín hadn't lost his knack for roping people in with his talking way.

"If not to trade, how do you plan to get your wife back?"

"Sonofbitch! You take her away from me for some lousy horses and blankets. I try hard for her to come to my trading post, but she say too many mosquitoes on the Kansas River. But I know real reason. You steal her heart with that rescue from Captain Jack. Sonofbitch."

Medina laughed. He wished the Frenchman's tale were true. Medina had never felt that Takansy returned his early passion for her.

Papín went on. "Speaking of that sonofbitch Indian, I get some news you kill him dead. Is true, or just another of your lies?"

"Come, I to show you his scalp, tell you the whole true story. Then you can tell your grandchildren." Medina pointed through a gap in the cottonwoods where the corner of his barn could be seen. "Over there is my place, across the bridge."

Then he grabbed Papín's arms. They felt scrawny beneath the dark wool coat. "I am happy to see you after all the years. You look different in city clothes."

"Ah, truth is, I am sick, my friend. That is why I travel. To Bridger's Fort, even to the Bitterroot, and now here. To see once again my friends, to visit the places we lived. We had some times together, no?"

"Yes, good and bad. Ripe for the telling after dinner. But come now, you must be tired. I have nice room for you, a tavern, whiskey, a hot bath. You rest." Medina felt alarmed for his friend's health. "Is that your rig?"A fine rig—like Papín's coat, very expensive.

At Papín's nod, they walked to the horse and buggy beside the post office. Papín struggled to pull himself into the driver's seat. Medina almost gave him a boost, then thought better of it. He climbed up to the other side of the seat. Papín, breathing heavily, clucked the horse toward the bridge.

"My son?" Papín said.

"Louie Papa. That is how the settlers call him. He is up in high pastures, to bring down herd. I to send for him *pronto* for you to see."

"He is well?"

"He is not sick, if that's..." Medina looked at Papín and grinned. "Your son is much different from you. To get a word from him, a smile, it is like digging rock. Maybe you are not his true father, yes?"

Papín shot him a glance.

"Maybe his true father is short, brown and ugly."

Medina slapped his knee and laughed. He hadn't felt this good since the last time he bantered with Goodale.

"I only wish!" he said. Then he sobered with what he needed to say next. "Louie is married. You have two grandchildren, but they are in Denver City with their mama and her parents. There is big problems."

"What problems?"

"Shouting. Fights. Louie not to say why. Maybe he will tell you. I think they are finished."

Papín maneuvered the buggy onto the bridge in silence.

Then he said, "And Takansy?"

Medina's mood sagged. He wondered whether to tell Papín about his wife's change of mind about sending Lena back to Denver City for her second school year. Her argument about Lena's unhappiness made no sense. Hadn't Lena herself said she was pleased to be there? Of course there had been the usual problems of getting used to a new school. Some pining for home. All to be expected. But Lena loved learning, loved playing the mandolin. She would always play for him when he visited. She said she wanted to stay in school.

Takansy accused him of being selfish. "You big pride," she would throw in his face, over and over. But he had sacrificed much for Lena, worked hard, paid big money for her sake, so she could learn all the things he never could.

Then there was the issue of Shy Bird's new foal. Medina had bred the mare to Hiram Tadder's black stallion with a notion of surprising Lena when she came home for the summer. The surprise worked. Lena was delighted with the little filly, but now was so involved with Takansy in gentling and training the foal that she didn't want to leave. Medina hoped he hadn't made a mistake.

"Takansy, you know her, how she drift off into silent spells. Hard to know what she really thinks. Two of our little ones in the grave, and she..." he almost said, "blames me for Martín's death," then changed his mind. "She is much sad, and now worries about our daughter, Lena."

"Is your girl sick?"

"No, she is fine. Ah! you will see for yourself, she is the image of beauty, like her mother was when we... ."

"When we were both silly in love with her, no?"

"Yes, like that. And smart, too. I send her to a school in Denver, very expensive. She is home now, for summer. She will play the mandolin for you, which she learns there."

Papín laughed. "Too bad your daughter is such a disappointment to you."

Medina felt himself flush. How much his enthusiasm must show!

"She is how old?" Papin asked.

"Fourteen. You to meet her, there, at our home." He pointed to the cabin as the buggy rolled into the courtyard of his compound.

Papín let out a low whistle. "Sonofbitch! You do well, my friend. Rich, like me."

"You were my teacher." He told Papín of his land title, his success with the toll bridge, his fine livestock, his trading post. It felt good to tell this to someone who could appreciate what he'd done.

"Our old friend Kit Carson visited here a few months before he died. Then I have General Sherman, General Grant."

"You fill your store with trade goods for the crowds, no?" Papín gave him a shrewd look.

Medina nodded. "I miss out on Kit Carson, forget to stock enough Carson books and Carson hats, but with the generals here, I sell plenty, like bandit."

"And how are the Americans? How they like you being so rich?"

"To my face they are mostly polite. 'Mr. Medina this' and 'Mr. Medina that.' But... "

"Behind your back they talk shit?"

"They are cowards."

"It is the same in St. Louis. Even with us French."

"I take my Lena out of their sorry school here, my money, too."

At that moment, the door opened and Takansy stepped out onto the porch, shading her eyes from the morning sun.

"*Mon Dieu*, there she is." Papín said.

56

Takansy
September 1870

Takansy bustled onto the porch and turned to rearrange the blankets on the wall, hoping work would lighten her heavy heart. The days of the Yellow-Leaf Moon were shortening, and with them the time of Lena's departure for her second year at St. Mary's. The horsemanship lessons were coming to an end. Her mind scrabbled for a way to stop Medina from sending Lena away again.

The creak of buggy wheels caused her to turn and squint into the sun's slanting rays. Through the filter of her fingers, she stared in wonderment at her first husband as he struggled off the buggy seat and made his way toward her. Her reserve nearly crumbled.

"Papín," she whispered as she stepped down the stairs to meet him. How old he looks! How thin his face! Yet the same crinkly smile, the same wink, the same jovial greeting.

"Still the great beauty, my Indian princess." He swept his fine beaver hat out to the side and bowed his low bow. Pointing to his bald head, he said, "Here am I, Mister Upside Down Face."

Takansy giggled for the first time in years. She had bestowed that name on him when she first caught sight of his bald head and full beard from her hiding place in the berry bushes near her people's village on the Bitterroot.

Medina called from beside the buggy.

"I to take care of this old nag. You to take our guest inside, but not give him any of my good brandy."

Her husband's grin matched Papín's.

Papín allowed her to remove his coat and guide him up the steps into their home, to a big chair with cushions. He collapsed into it. She pulled up a chair to face him. She was shocked at his frailty, so different from the robust man who had taken her in thirty years ago when she had left her own people after her great sin.

As if reading her mind, Papín said, "I come from your people's home on the Bitterroot not thirty days gone."

Takansy's heart skipped a beat. She had put all that behind her. Now, she found herself gripped by curiosity.

"Your papa, the great Ironhand, is long dead, as you probably know. Passed into the Great Beyond the same year you left me for that rascal Spaniard."

He said this with a smile, but she sensed regret, which, to her surprise, pleased her.

"Snow-cave Man married your sister, SoChee, and had a son, Charlo, who is now Chief. Your sister asked about you, and I told her I would send word. But there is sadness." His face turned grave. "The army plans to move them to a reservation north of the Bitterroot, near the big water they now call Lake of the Flatheads."

"Their horses?"

Papín's smile returned. "They have managed to keep their fine animals, and they still race, crazy as wind, like you once did, no?" He reached over and patted her hand.

An idea sprouted in her mind and grew like a weed, a sudden desire to visit her homeland, to see her sister and Snow-cave Man once more, to see the great horse herd that was the pride of her people. To show Lena.

The door swung open. Medina walked in leading Lena by the hand.

"My daughter, meet Señor Louis Papín, the father of our Louie, our old friend from Bridger."

Lena, dressed in her white-lady dress, bobbed a perfect curtsy. To Takansy's eyes, it looked ridiculous. She pictured her daughter in buckskins galloping through the meadows of the Bitterroot. She couldn't get the image out of her mind.

Papín heaved himself up for another elaborate bow. "Your papá did not lie. You are pretty as your mama." His wink got a blush out of Lena and a smile out of Medina.

Medina said, "But no more talk. Our guest must rest from his travels. For supper, we talk, and to drink top brandy, no charge."

Later that evening after dinner, Takansy reluctantly pulled a chair in between Papín and Medina to hear Lena play the mandolin. Medina had insisted their daughter wear her school clothes that evening. Takansy thought Lena looked uncomfortable as she started picking at the strings of the lacquered wood instrument. The music, written by someone named Mozart, sounded alien to Takansy.

When she finished, Lena gave a stiff little bow. "I am still learning."

Medina clapped and thumped the floor with his feet.

Papín applauded and said, "You have mastered much in only one year. You will start again your lessons when you return, no?"

"Papi will take me next Sunday."

Takansy kept her face still. *Maybe not.*

Papín went on. "And the Academy, you like it there, study hard?"

"Yes, the nuns are excellent. I am learning difficult books, arithmetic, manners. I share a nice room with another girl."

Takansy stared at her daughter. *Why is she saying these things?* Only yesterday she had spoken of her unhappiness at St. Mary's, the harshness of the nuns, the aloofness of the girls, the confinement inside the Academy walls, how she missed her horse lessons.

Takansy rose from her chair and turned to Papín. "You are wishing more coffee?"

Papín appraised her. "Thank you, but no, you have filled me up with that wonderful rabbit stew, just like the old times."

"Then I wishing you a night of good sleep. I going to sleep now." She managed a feeble smile, walked into their bedroom and shut the door.

She stared at the pallet she had dragged into their room a week ago when she told Medina she would no longer share his blankets. Her mind drifted over their early life together, his desire for her, his bargain with Papín. *How has it come to this?*

She lay down without removing her clothes, pulled a blanket around her and tried, unsuccessfully, to sleep.

The following day she brought Papín to the pasture to watch Lena ride Shy Bird. The temperature had plunged and the yellowing cottonwood leaves rattled on their branches, sullen reminders of Lena's impending departure. Takansy hunched into the blanket she'd wrapped herself in and glanced at Papín. *How strange to be standing here with him.*

He leaned against the fence rail. "Last night, you are sad, no? You can tell Papín, if you wish."

She hesitated only a moment. "My daughter, she is not happy in that far-off school. Her heart is here, with the horse riding, with that new filly to train, over there." She pointed to a run where Shy Bird's four month old foal, Otter, darted to and fro, peering into the barn where Lena was brushing Shy Bird. "You are seeing for yourself, when she comes out riding that filly's mama."

"But last night, she seemed happy enough."

"A big show for her father. To me she is sad."

"Did you not agree that she go? Medina said you did."

"Last winter, yes." But she had not really agreed, "relented" was the better word. She'd agreed because Lena would be separated from the Alexander boy, who was now no longer a threat.

"It is turning out bad."

"Medina does not think so."

"He is blind. He is never forgetting the big shame put on him by school people here."

"Yes, he told me about that. Said he ran one of them off."

"A big, ugly mole-face named Henry Howard. Big like bear. But Medina beating him bloody with tomahawk." She felt a curious pride in this, despite her aversion to his bouts of violence.

Papín put on a rueful smile. "Medina's temper, I know it well."

"He is like those hissing waters in the land of yellow stones." She remembered how he had raged after the school play was cancelled, scalding her when she tried to calm him. There was no reasoning with him in the time of anger.

"Mole-face is leaving his pretty wife alone in her lodge, and running away after my husband is fighting him. Medina is taking her supplies every week."

Papín arched his eyebrows. "Pretty, she is?"

It was an invitation to share her suspicion that her husband's attention to the abandoned Mrs. Howard was more than kindness.

But she only said, "The visits are not worrying me." And that was true.

Papín gazed at her, expecting more.

"My worrying is for Lena. She is what matters." Takansy seized his arm. "My people, SoChee and Snow-cave Man, they are still encamped on the Bitterroot?"

Papín eyed her hand. "Yes. The reservation move, it is not for another year or two."

"I want to be going there again."

Startled, Papín turned. "You said you are never going back."

"I am thinking ,yes, now, to the going." A picture came to her of horses on the rich grassy bottomland at the base of Shining Mountain, of Lena racing Shy Bird in front of a cheering crowd of her people. The idea gladdened her heart as it blossomed in her mind.

"Papín," she said. "Please no telling my husband. It is surprise."

His eyebrows arched into question marks.

"Please. You must be promising."

He nodded. "Whatever you wish, no?" He patted her hand and looked into her eyes for a disconcertingly long moment until Lena led Shy Bird out of the barn and into the pasture. The little black filly danced about, snorting at the gate post.

That evening, Takansy took Lena aside. She patted the otter pouch tucked inside Lena's blouse.

"You still wearing it. Good. Otter Woman helped me find the Horse Spirit, and I was able to ride like you. Do you remember, my flower, when you were small, about seven winters old, your dream about the horse?"

"Yes, the black horse. I was on its back, flying through the clouds."

"You coming to me in the night, big eyed, like this." Takansy widened her eyes and got a nodding smile from Lena. "The Horse Spirit, it is visiting you. A powerful visit. It is telling you to become a horse woman, to do marvels with horses with your special gift, and to become a horse healer." She paused a moment to emphasize the next point. "To train that beautiful new filly of yours."

Lena's face softened. "I would like that."

"Then we must be finding a talking way to turn around your father, to not taking you back to that school."

The uplifted parts of Lena's face—her brows, mouth, eyes— all drooped at once, as if pulled by strings. "I cannot, Mami. He is counting on me."

Takansy sighed and drew her daughter close. "It is against God's will to ignore your Spirit Path. You come from a proud people, wise in the way of the horse. Your grandfather, Iron Hand..." She stopped herself, suddenly remembering her father's cruelty. Strange, she thought, how the Spirit strives to remember only the good. "Your grandfather, Iron Hand, would be proud of you. He is gone to the Great Beyond, but my sister and friends still live in the land of the Bitterroot. They have many beautiful horses."

"I would like to see that land."

"Yes, some day, perhaps. But better not speaking of it to your father. Unless we are turning him from the school."

The next morning, Takansy looked out of the kitchen window and saw, for the first time in many moons—the first time since before last winter—John Alexander riding into the Crossing.

57

John Alexander
September 1871

The first thing John Alexander saw when he rode his Illiff pinto up to Medina's trading post was Lena. She was standing on tiptoes, her back to him, hanging clusters of red peppers on the trading post porch's front wall. She wore a mid-length Spanish skirt, red with blue and gold trim, that lifted each time she stretched to reveal curves in her lower legs. A short-sleeved white blouse hugged her slender waist, made thinner by swells above and below. Her glossy hair, gathered on each side by bows, hung past her shoulders in two glorious waterfalls. They swayed as she moved from nail to nail.

When she finally turned at the sound of John's approach, he nearly fell off his horse. She'd gone from pretty to beautiful. A faint rosy color suffused her cheeks, accenting them under long-lashed dark eyes. Her now-full mouth was slightly open, showing a ridge of white teeth between lips redder than he remembered.

The inner fort he'd built around his feelings for her crumbled away. He felt himself staring, slack-jawed foolish.

"Lena. How are you?" he finally managed to say.

Her eyes registered her surprise. "Why, John Alexander," she said. "You have changed."

It was true. In the year he'd been at Iliff's, he'd sprouted a moustache, which so far had refused to take on the handlebar shape he admired. He wore a brown felt cowboy hat and a new, bright yellow shirt he'd bought just before his trip. It wouldn't hurt to look a mite dashing, he'd told himself, in case he ran into Julie Barthol. One look at Lena forced him to admit that Julie wasn't the real reason he'd spruced up.

Lena gave him an uncertain smile, a slight upturn at the corners of her mouth. But it was enough to make him feel like jumping out of the saddle. He couldn't stop a big, out-of-control grin spreading all over his face. He dismounted and looped the reins around the tie rail, conscious of her gaze. He tried his best to mimic the confident swagger of the Illiff hands he'd been bunking with.

"I'm a cowhand now," he said.

"Yes. And you have a horse." Her eye roved over the black and white pinto.

"Not mine, really. One of the Illiff string. Not the best I've ridden, but he'll do."

"Are you riding herd yet?"

"Yup. For about a year. Been riding point." That wasn't quite true, but he wanted her to picture him that way.

"Those Texas cows are mean," he added, to change the subject. "You don't watch them, they'll hook you, sure."

"You don't look hooked," she said, her eyes doing a little dance.

He laughed out loud. Hooked was the way he felt, but not on a cow horn. He raised his arms and turned around in front of her.

"I'm still in one piece." Then he looked at her square on, suddenly bold. "And you, Lena, how you been?"

A little flicker passed across her face, as if she were searching for an answer, then she brightened and said, "Shy Bird's new foal is beautiful. Muscled little rump, long legs, and straight. Pure black, no socks, no blaze. A filly. Oh, John Alexander! Would you like to see?"

Yes, indeed, he wanted to see.

She skipped down the steps and caught his hand as he stepped from behind the tie rail. Her eyes, he was startled to discover, were nearly level with his own. She pulled him into a trot toward the barn, his boots wobbling in the sand. Then she slowed, let go of his hand and hugged her arms to her body.

John's hand tingled. "You excited about that school down in Denver City?"

She turned her gaze toward the ground. "Yes. Yes, it is a good thing, and I'm learning to write, like you. Papi says the nuns are the best, the school is best. I share a fine room, looking out on the mountains, and I am learning to play the mandolin." Her words didn't match the expression on her face, which had turned glum.

"You sound more excited about your new filly than going back to school," he pointed out.

"She needs to be trained. She can be something if I train her. But school starts again next week."

"You're going back?"

She sighed. "Papi says it is time, you know, for me to grow up, to become a lady."

"What do you think?"

"He is right. I'll go." She squared her shoulders.

They reached the corral. She unlatched the gate.

"Wait here."

She glided over to the barn to open a stall door. Shy Bird stepped out into the run and turned sideways, eyeing John, her body between him and the foal. Four gray-black legs danced on the other side of the mare, visible beneath her belly. Lena stroked the mare, then slipped back through the gate and stood beside John.

She said something in her mama's tongue, then translated, "The little one's name. Otter."

"Where'd you get that?"

"Mami. It's a word from her people. The name of a medicine woman when my mother was a girl. A very powerful name."

At the sound of Lena's voice, the filly stepped from behind her mother's rump and turned to point her ears at them.

"She just turned four months," Lena said. "We will wean her soon."

Otter stepped toward them with a little buck, then twisted back around and darted away. Lena laughed and pushed her hand gently against John's arm.

"She likes you."

John leaned closer until his shoulder touched hers. He held his breath and tried to stay focused on the filly. Then, of a sudden, he felt watched. He turned. Mrs. Medina stood a few steps behind, having come up without a sound on her moccasined feet. He pulled away from Lena.

"Good day, Ma'am," he said, tipping his hat. His face felt hot.

Mrs. Medina's expression didn't change. She studied him with those strange gray eyes.

Lena said, "Mami, John Alexander has come to visit."

She reached out a hand to her mother and pulled her to the fence. John backed away to make room.

Lena said, "Otter is feeling brave today. And look, Mami, her front legs." She pointed as the filly took a few steps away from Shy Bird, braced her legs and snorted.

"Straight. Good." Mrs. Medina nodded with the hint of a smile. Her hair had a couple of gray streaks John hadn't seen before. Turning to him, she said, "You are coming back?"

"Just for a bit. Two days. I owe your husband. I aim to work it off." He sensed it would be good to reassure her about the shortness of his visit. The spark that had jumped from his shoulder to Lena's a moment ago was still hot on his sleeve.

Mrs. Medina nodded. "You staying where?"

"Mami," Lena said, touching her Mother's buckskin sleeve. "John Alexander can stay in the bunkhouse. There's room. With Miguel and…"

"No need," John said. "I have a place to stay nearby."

Lena gave him a look and didn't persist.

She knows I mean the hideout. He had thought about going home, seeing Mama and Mattie and the rest, even Pa, to show them he was doing fine as a ranch hand. But the hideout was a lot closer, and two days didn't allow time for being with his family.

The limits of his visit being set, Mrs. Medina turned to Lena and said, "Otter training now."

Lena backed away from John. "I'll go change clothes." She gave him a little wave, turned and hurried toward the house.

John tipped his hat toward Mrs. Medina, "Ma'am. I'm going to hunt up Mr. Medina now." He smiled at her, but got a stone face in return.

He walked to the trading post and found Mr. Medina inside. The trader hadn't changed much that John could see. He stepped from behind the counter, plucked the ivory pipe from his mouth, smiled with all his teeth and clapped John on both shoulders. Tobacco smoke curled past John's face, drawn to the open door.

"Johnnie," he said, "Welcome! My house is your house."

John couldn't tell if his heartiness was a habit he put on, like a shirt, or real.

"Good to see you again, sir. They call me John now. Just John."

Mr. Medina stepped back and eyed him up and down. "John. You are *vaquero* now, yes?"

"Yup. And I'm hoping to help you with some cattle work. Still got that ten dollars to work off."

"Yes, but, a problem. All my herd is up to the mountains, with Louie Papa until first frost." He thought for a moment. "But come, there are chores."

He guided John out of the store and put him to work repairing some rails on the holding pens, harvesting the last of some corn stalks for winter fodder, and cutting and stacking a supply of fireplace wood.

John worked on the corral repair first, so he could keep an eye on Lena and her mama and watch the horse training. A striking pair, mother and daughter. So much alike. He watched them ease in through the gate and stand sideways as first Shy Bird, then Otter, approached, ready for the training magic to begin.

As they worked with the filly, Lena would glance over now and then to give John that hint of smile that deepened the little creases beside her mouth. After an hour they turned Otter and Shy Bird out to pasture. Lena headed for the house.

Mrs. Medina floated over to where John was stripping the bark off another corral pole with a skinning blade.

"Supper...you are eating with us?"

An invitation of sorts. John sensed the suspicion in her gray eyes, the same wariness he'd felt when she had come up behind him and Lena at the corral rail. He decided not to press his luck.

"No thank you, Ma'am, much appreciated, but I'll need to be finishing up here."

She didn't insist.

He nailed on the last rail around dusk, mounted up and headed for his hideout, munching some biscuits and salt pork along the way.

The fall air was cool, perfect for sleeping, but he lay awake on his bedroll a long while, conjuring up the last time Lena visited his hideout. Now, she was no longer a young girl. The stars sparkled with promise.

The next day John chopped corn stalks in the morning and started on the woodpile in the afternoon. The chopping block stood between Medina's home and the travelers' guest houses. The woodshed, a lean-to attached to the Medina home, was about twelve feet long and four feet deep. It took until late afternoon to fill it halfway. Tired and thirsty, he sat down next to the home's log wall and rested his back against the stacked wood.

After a long swig on his canteen, a gap in the chinking caught his eye. Through it he could see inside. He scrunched down to get a better look. Mrs. Medina's altar stood against the opposite wall, the fine looking china cupboard on the left, the big, polished table and chairs in the middle.

The door swung violently open and thumped into the wall. In walked Mr. Medina, followed by Lena and her mama. Something about the way they held themselves set John on edge.

Mr. Medina started waving his arms and shouting. He pointed his finger right in Mrs. Medina's face. He spoke Spanish, staccato, like hail on a roof. Twice John caught the words "St. Mary's," and several times, "Lena."

Mrs. Medina stayed still as a post. Most of the time she faced in the direction of the spy hole, so John could see her eyes, unwavering and fiercely calm. Every so often, she would say something that set Mr. Medina to raging again.

The ruckus flew back and forth as Lena sat stiffly in a chair off to the side. Her eyes, shiny with tears, shifted from one to the other. Her hands hugged her shoulders then moved to cover her ears. Medina raised his hand.

Lena jumped up, riding skirt flaring over her leggings, and shouted, "No! No!" as Mr. Medina leaped toward his wife and slapped her hard across her face.

John stopped breathing. Mr. Medina froze as if shocked at his own action. Mrs. Medina didn't flinch. It was as if the blow had hit a rock. The room went silent, a frozen tumult.

Lena jerked the door open and fled. Several moments later, Mrs. Medina followed her. Mr. Medina stalked into another room.

John jumped up, ran back to the chopping block and started swinging the ax. Chips flew from the logs. Something crashed inside the house. He saw Mrs. Medina follow Lena into the barn, but she was too late. Lena galloped out on Shy Bird, thumped across the bridge and disappeared upriver, a flash of brown and black through the cottonwoods.

John dropped the ax, ran to the pinto and flung on the saddle and bridle. Just as he swung up and pulled the horse around, Mr. Medina walked up, face red and drawn. He tried to look affable. John tried to seem unhurried. Neither succeeded.

"You are leaving?" Mr. Medina said.

"Reckon I need to be getting on. I got to leave for Iliff's tomorrow early."

"You are welcome to stay here." He didn't look very welcoming.

"I'll be back to do more soon as I can get some time off."

"Yes, yes. Until then." Medina continued quickly toward the barn, absent-mindedly rubbing his face.

John set off at what he hoped was a normal pace. Once out of sight he took off on a dead run, the pinto laboring west along the river trail. Lena had disappeared.

58

Medina
September 1871

The morning following their ugly quarrel, Medina seethed at the cunning way Takansy had used Shy Bird's new filly to lure Lena back home. He should have caught on earlier to what was happening. Over the summer he had indulged Lena her time with Takansy, watched them spend hours together grooming and training the filly, riding and inventing new tricks for Shy Bird. He had thought nothing of it, even encouraged it, never imagining Takansy would forge the black foal into a weapon to get her way. Keeping Lena at home, ruining her best chance to make a good place in this new world. It was maddening.

Still, he was beginning to feel some regret about hitting Takansy. She had certainly provoked him, defied him, connived to undermine what was best for their daughter. She deserved the blow. But still…

He was glad Papín had gone off to be with Louie Papa, still

tending cattle in the back country. Medina had never struck his wife before, not once, in the twenty-seven years since he had won her away from Papín, and he didn't want his old friend to know about it, even though giving one's woman a good thumping wasn't that uncommon. Papín would find out soon enough, Medina supposed, when he returned with Louie Papa in a week or so.

Feeling the need to get away for a while, he hitched up his buggy, tossed in some potatoes, beets and a small slab of bacon, and set off for Susan Howard's place about three miles downstream. Since her oaf of a husband had left, Medina had been supplying her with a few things from time to time to ease her struggle to stay on and prove up on her homestead. A difficult thing for a woman to do without a man.

He drew the wagon to a stop as Susan Howard came out of her cabin to greet him. She smiled her usual pretty smile. Medina felt his sense of well-being returning, as it always did on these visits. Her dress, he noticed, had a new patch on the front. Perhaps next time he would bring her some fabric for a new dress.

"Mr. Medina. How nice of you to visit." She stepped away from the porch to greet him. Her gait had a nice spring to it with Henry Howard gone.

He climbed down from the wagon, and she extended her hand to his in that formal way she had. Her hand felt warm.

"Mrs. Howard. I bring a few things for you."

"Thank you. How much?"

"You don't have to pay."

"Some fresh eggs, then. To take back to your family."

Medina nodded.

"You look worried. Was there trouble?"

She had a way of reading his mood right off. Strangely enough, with her, he didn't mind. Susan Howard had a calming effect on him. He needed calming right now.

She said, "How about some coffee?"

Medina glanced around. He was glad Susan Howard's cabin was invisible from the road, screened from rumor and gossip by a low ridge. He followed her onto the porch and sat on a bench while she ducked inside and came back out with a steaming can and two tin cups. She poured out the thick brew and sat on another bench facing him, their knees inches apart. She was about forty, he guessed. Her dark hair was pulled back in a knot, but short curls framed her triangular face, full lips and wide, inviting eyes—a *simpática* face.

To his surprise, he began talking of his fight with Takansy over Lena, words avalanching out until the whole story was told. He felt his anger growing again with the telling.

"You were wrong to hit your wife," she told him afterward. "I know, from experience. But you are not a man to hit a woman every day. You can apologize." She gave him an understanding smile, as if she knew he would.

But he didn't feel apologetic, just then.

She added, "You are right to send your daughter to school. It is a thing some girls balk at when they are young, but later thank the one who made them go. You are the father. Your wife—it's wrong for her to try to block you."

Riding home, Susan Howard's eggs packed in straw beside him, Medina thought about how to break Takansy's stubborn resistance and persuade Lena to return to St. Mary's. He decided what he must do, then headed over to Hiram Tadder's place to do it.

59

John Alexander
September 1871

John Alexander rode up river looking for Lena until it got dark, then pushed the pinto up the steep slope to his hideout. His mind swam with questions about the fight and where Lena had gone. He started a feeble campfire. A soft, scraping sound caught his ear. He looked at the ledge above. There stood Lena, hair mussed, cheeks streaked by tears.

He jumped up to help her down. He lost his balance and they ended up in an awkward embrace. It started a little stampede in his chest. She pulled away. They stared at each other.

He finally managed to ask, "What happened?"

"Oh, John Alexander. My father. My mother. He hit her. He has never done that." She looked as if she might cry some more, but no tears spilled out.

Except for a little twitch in her cheek, she held her face still, like her mama. That twitch nearly broke his heart.

He didn't want to let on he'd seen the whole thing.

He said, "Tell me. Come sit and tell me." They settled down beside the campfire, not touching, but so close he had to work some to avoid staring at the soft skin of her brown ankles that peeked out between her moccasin tops and leggings.

As he'd guessed, the fight was about Lena going back to school. Lena, sitting cross-legged beside him, her chin resting in the palms of her hands, sounded tired. Hollows darkened her eyes.

"Papi says it is for my own good. Without the Academy, he says, I'll just be like any other half-breed. No chance to...well, have fine things, be treated like a fine lady." She poked the fire with a stick into a burst of little sparks. "Mami goes on about the horse spirit, says I cannot push it aside, that I must honor it, raise horses, become a horse healer, ride in parades."

Lena seemed to be giving both points of view equal weight, almost like a judge.

"But Lena, what do you want?"

She looked startled and gazed toward the darkening sky. Her knotted fists rolled back and forth under her chin.

"I want to train Otter. Oh, John Alexander, I want them both to leave me alone. But they cannot."

"Why?"

"They want what they think is best for me. They cannot stop themselves."

"But they can't both be right. So, you have to decide."

"Decide. Yes, I decide. Over and over. When I am with my father I decide to go to St. Mary's. When I am with my mother I decide to stay here." She let out a grim little laugh.

He poked a stick into the fire, touching the one Lena held.

"At least your folks both dote on you, Lena. That's something."

"But it is not. It's not good the way they fight. I am the cause of it."

"You're not the cause. There's nothing you can do, one way or the other. Except maybe leave." *Leave with me!* The thought rushed through him like a warm wind.

She nodded but didn't speak. The light was nearly gone. A little current of colder air raised the soft hairs on her forearm. She shivered.

He moved closer and wrapped her in his arms to warm her.

A little shudder ran through her shoulders, and he realized she was crying, her breath catching in tiny smothered sobs. After a while they subsided. He pressed his lips against the side of her head and then her cheek and then down to that little crease above her mouth, and then on to her mouth, and…glory be, she responded! His hands began to explore the smooth coolness of her arms and neck and he began to whisper her name over and over.

Then she pushed away and said in a husky voice, "No, we cannot! Please stop, John Alexander. Stop!" He immediately released her and she stood up.

He sat there, feeling both alarmed and thrilled, and said—more to break the silence than anything else, "What's that hanging under your shirt?"

She moved the silver cross aside and placed her hand over the small bulge between her breasts. She drew out a leather pouch.

"A gift made by my mother. These red beads stand for an otter." Her slender finger stroked the glistening rectangular pattern with four zigzag corners. "She knew a medicine woman once. When she was a girl. It's a medicine pouch, to keep me safe." She paused, her lips lifting into a sad smile. "It is good I had it today."

She pulled herself onto the low ledge, turned back to face him and said, "I must go now."

Then with a smile he knew he'd never forget, she said, "Thank you, John Alexander." Then she was gone.

A moment later it came to him in a rush. He scrambled up the ledge and shouted after her, "Lena, there's another way! Lena, come back!"

But she didn't hear. The sound of her horse's hooves knocking against rocks came from down the slope. He ran to where his pinto was picketed, but knew that by the time he saddled up to chase after her, she would be back at the Crossing. He stroked the pinto, moved the picket to a new patch of grass, and returned to the hideout. His mind scrambled to flesh out the details of a plan that kept him awake the rest of the night.

Homesteading. That was key. The idea of it bloomed as he rode back to the Illiff place, into the next day's early morning sun. He would get himself a piece of land. Get a couple of cows, a bull, start

David M. Jessup

a herd. He and Lena would get married. She would have fine horses she could train and sell. He imagined the look on her face, that glorious smile. He imagined her lying contented in his arms while he stroked her, stretched out warm in the sun, tracing every inch of skin.

At first they would be poor. Maybe they could sell things to settlers who kept pouring in, even now, twelve years after the gold rush. Potatoes. Corn. They could grow things. Maybe set up a store, if they could find some land in the right location. He could do a little lumbering if he had to make ends meet.

Would it be enough for her? She was used to pretty clothes, china, linen. Whatever it took. He Wouldn't allow her to live hardscrabble, like his own family. Maybe he could find some gold. Rumors of a strike on Redstone Creek were bandied about at the post office. He would take a tin plate and sift some creek gravel.

And what of her ma and pa? Would Mr. Medina accept his request for Lena's hand? Would her mama? He couldn't imagine it. They both had a powerful hold on her. Would she break free and run off with him, poor as dirt, who could offer little more than escape? Even if she did, could he betray two people who had been good to him, who trusted him and treated him near as close as one of their own?

In the books he read, love always won out. It could happen with Lena. She liked him. No question. But love? She was only fourteen. Fifteen in April, seven months from now. But others married at fifteen. It could work. It *would* work.

Back on the Illiff spread, the idea of a new life with Lena swelled into a certain thing. It took up all his waking moments, distracting him from work. He even started enjoying mucking manure, a job he could do without thinking, allowing more time for daydreaming.

Leather Bill noticed the change.

"Some gal got a ring in your nose?" he said the next day.

John denied it, but Leather Bill just grinned. He grinned even more when John asked him about homesteading.

"You got to fill out a piece of paper. Give it over to the little bald man down in Golden at the Land Office. Then you got to prove up on the land. Build a house. Plow some ground, run some cows. Then the bald man—Allen's the name—will get around to giving you title some day. After five years. Then comes the hard part."

"What's that?"

"Talking that little gal of yours to stick with you on a hundred sixty acres that ain't enough to make a living on." More wrinkles appeared on Bill's brown face as he grinned. Then he turned serious. "The thing is, John, a lot of the good land is already claimed. The pieces with water. If you don't get water, you can't do a thing on those acres, cattle-wise. And even with it, you'll need more than a hundred and sixty acres to make out. You'll need some of them sisters and brothers of yours to stake some more claims. That's how Mr. Illiff done it. I ought to know."

"What do you mean?"

"I homesteaded out there on Fox Hollow Spring for Mr. Illiff. Proved up by building a line shack for him, then sold it to him for a dollar. Can't complain. He pays me good. Every month, regular."

John felt himself get a little hot under the collar. "There's plenty other places to file a claim besides here."

"And you look love-struck enough to find one." Leather Bill winked, then turned serious again. "I heard tell of some open land along Owl Creek to the north. Some good bottom land along there, narrow, but plenty of grass." He stuck out a calloused hand. "Good luck, John. I'll give you a couple of days now and then to scout things out, but make sure you're back on time. Boss don't cotton to slackers."

John squeezed his hand hard.

"Yes, sir. How about just one day, this Sunday? Not for Owl Creek. It's...something else." John wanted to tell Lena his plan before she returned to school. She said she'd leave for Denver City in a week. He calculated it would be a week, come Sunday.

Leather Bill raised an eyebrow, hesitated, and finally nodded yes.

By Sunday, the weather had turned cold. A nasty September wind blustered the leaves off the cottonwoods as John rode into the Crossing. His pinto was lathered with foam.

"You're in a flat big hurry." Louie Papa frowned as John tied up at the rail in front of the barn. "Best get that horse inside and dried off."

"I came to do some more chores. Mr. Medina around?" John didn't want to come right out and ask for Lena.

Louie Papa tilted his head toward the store.

John took it in. New blankets livened the porch walls. Two

buggies waited outside. Customers. No sign of Lena.

As if reading his mind, Louie Papa said, "Lena ain't here. Saint Mary's."

John felt his face go hangdog. One of these days he'd learn to control his face like Louie Papa did, or Lena's mama. But at that moment he knew he looked about as droopy as his old dog Mac did when he'd left for the Illiff job.

Louie Papa noticed, of course, but his expression didn't change a bit.

"Best come with me," he said, his lips barely moving under his graying moustache. "Got to move the carry-over heifers to winter pasture, down the creek."

John looked toward the store.

"Best not to bother him just now."

"Why not?"

"Had another row. Him and my ma."

"About Lena?"

Louie Papa narrowed his eyes, reluctant to say more, but John persisted.

"She didn't want to go, did she? Lena, I mean."

"She'll do whatever the last person she talks to wants." Louie Papa paused, then added, "I reckon she'll do well enough down there, once she gets used to it again."

"But what about her horses? Shy Bird and Otter."

"He done sold that filly."

"What?"

"Otter. Sold to Tadder across the way." He nodded toward the post office north of the river.

Alarm rose in John like spring runoff. "But he can't just...Otter's hers! He can't sell her!"

Louie Papa patted John's arm to calm him like a weaned calf.

"That's what Mama said. That's what the row was about. But he done it anyway."

"Dammit!" John kicked at a stone in the road. It flew up and clacked against the barn side, bringing a startled snort from the horse inside. "Does Lena know?"

"Yup. That was the whole point. One more reason for her to stay at school and not here."

John turned to fetch the tired pinto.

"Where you going?"

It was one of the few times John had seen Louie Papa look worried. But he mounted up, keeping his lips pressed together.

"John, stop! Don't go off half-cocked." He reached out to grab the reins.

John skirted around him and headed south, toward Denver City. As he passed the store, Mr. Medina came out on the porch. The trader lifted his hand in greeting. When he took in John's stony look, his mouth froze in mid-smile. John kicked the pinto into a trot. Just across the road stood Mrs. Medina, arms across her chest, stock still. As he rode between them, their gaze shifted to each other.

The look on their faces sent a little shiver down John's back, a chill colder than the late September wind that bullied the cottonwood leaves overhead. The rope that bound him to them frayed and pulled apart.

At the Crossing's entry gate on the Denver City road, John pulled up short. A thought suddenly seized him, something he had to do before heading to St. Mary's. He turned around, rode between the Medinas and headed toward the toll bridge and the post office beyond. He needed to find Hiram Tadder in the worst way.

60

Takansy
September 1871

With relief, Takansy watched John Alexander turn his horse away from the road to Denver City and back toward the bridge. From the look on his face she guessed he had just learned about Otter. Lena, hurt by her filly's loss, would be open to the sympathy of young Alexander. Better for her not to see him now. Better for her to settle back into life at St. Mary's until Takansy had time to plan.

She cast one last glare at her husband, turned her back and stalked off through the fallen leaves toward the cemetery. She picked up a stick and whacked it against the ground as she moved up the hill.

She touched her cheek, the memory of Medina's blow still burning after a week. He had apologized, but now had done something far worse. His sale of Otter to Hiram Tadder was a betrayal that ended any chance of coming back together. They were like two caterpillars spinning separate cocoons. He with his grand schemes, the big man of the Big Thompson, using their daughter to bolster his pride.

She had gone along for many years, supplying his store with her beadwork, giving him her body, doing his cooking, cleaning, sewing. Raising his children. Her children. Everything else could be his, but the children were hers. Lena was hers.

From that moment on there would be no more arguing. *It is time for the war way. Not on his terms. On mine. Silent and calculating, like the fox.* She would appear to go along. Then she would spirit Lena away where he could not find them. Back to the Bitterroot. Back to her people. He could stay here with Susan Howard.

She knelt at the graves of Martín and Rosita. Unable to calm herself with prayer, she rose and walked back down the hill to find Papín. He had spent days with their son Louie and was now back at the Crossing, preparing to return to St. Louis. She found him loading his travel bag onto the back of his buckboard.

"*Ma cherie*, come to see an old man on his way?" He bowed and winked. "Maybe a kiss, for the sake of the old times?"

"Only if you go back north, and take me with you."

He took it as a joke, which she supposed it was.

"Your crazy husband will cut out my liver." He laughed and leaned against the wagon, looking tired.

"Tell me, Papín, some things I am needing to know. But you must promise it being our secret."

He turned grave. "What is it, my dove?"

She proceeded to ask him about the most hidden way to travel north, the places to avoid being seen, the best stops for rest and supplies.

He pulled a piece of paper out of his bag and drew a map on it, explaining the route.

"Why a secret?" He questioned her with his eyes.

"I cannot say."

He flashed his rakish smile and made a last bow. "To the Bitterroot, then. Perhaps our paths will cross there."

She gave him an impulsive hug, then stepped away.

"Perhaps."

61

John Alexander
November 1871

Despite John's eagerness to see Lena, it was almost two months before he managed to get himself down to St. Mary's to tell her of his plans. The problem was Leather Bill. The Illiff foreman had punished him for showing up a half-day late to work, and refused to allow him any more time off until Thanksgiving. But being late couldn't be helped. Hiram Tadder had been away deer hunting that Sunday afternoon back in September when John clattered across the bridge to find Otter. When Tadder finally returned to his cabin around midnight, it took John another hour to persuade him to sell the filly, and long into the morning before he could lead the balky young horse back to the Illiff ranch.

Leather Bill had given him the eye when he rode in late.

"Let it happen again, it'll be the last." There was not even a hint of the usual smile in his hard eyes. But he did allow John to build a small holding corral for Otter and let her graze with a couple of old mares in the mare-foal pasture.

Hiram Tadder had promised not to tell a soul about the sale. The last thing John wanted was for Mr. Medina to find out about it. That would cook his goose, for sure. Together, he and Tadder had made up a cock and bull story about selling Otter to a man headed to Missouri. But John worried about how much Hiram Tadder loved to talk, and even though he didn't run the Post Office anymore, he visited there a lot. The Post Office came a close second to Mr. Medina's store as the place for gossip. And Tadder, like lots of folks along the Big Thompson, owed Mr. Medina plenty for favors of one kind or another even though he didn't much take to being beholden to anyone, much less a "Mexican."

Leather Bill finally softened and allowed John two days off the weekend after Thanksgiving. John set out after supper and rode until he got to Tim Goodale's place on Boulder Creek, where he stopped to sleep for a couple of hours and rest his played-out pinto. He told the old mountain man he was going to the land office in Golden to file a homestead claim on Owl Creek.

"Iffen I was young again, I'd grab it myself," he said, winking and wagging his beard. His description of a valley and a trickling stream grew in John's mind to a vast, grassy ranch with hundreds of cattle and scores of Lena's fine horses drinking from miles of flowing river. For the rest of the ride into Denver City he let his mind imagine Lena's smile when he described it to her and asked her to marry him. He imagined her flinging herself into his arms and saying yes. Everything would be grand.

It was late on Saturday afternoon when he arrived at St. Mary's. The Academy compound hulked over California Street like a prison, surrounded by a black iron fence. Beyond it stood a two-story white house, almost as tall as the Catholic church a block away. To each side sat smaller brick buildings, one with soot on one side, as if burned by fire. In between the buildings stretched grassy areas tinged brown by early frost. In the center of the compound he could see an ample garden awaiting final harvesting. Pumpkins hung orange on drying vines. Corn stalks glowed like sentinels in the setting sun. A chill shadow thrown by the mountains to the west crept to the top of the white house's steps.

How, for glory's sake, was he going to get in there and find her? If he didn't make it back to Iliff's Ranch by the following night, he was likely to lose his job.

The church bell tolled, bringing a momentary hush to the barking dogs and clanging blacksmith noises along the street. Then the tall doors on the big white house swung open. Two nuns emerged. They floated down the steps like giant magpies, toward the gate where John stood. He looked down at his cowboy duds covered with two day's worth of road dust. He fled to a small haberdashery across the street where he pretended to eye the clothes in the window while watching the nuns. They unlocked the gate. As it creaked open, a platoon of girls filed, two-by-two, down the steps and out through the gate toward the church. Thirty-seven in all. Two nuns rode drag, while two others flanked the girls on either side. The two gate-openers led the way.

Dressed alike in dark blue skirts and shawls covering white blouses, the girls moved along like a giant caterpillar, bunching and stretching in little waves of black stockings and black shoes. Occasional titters of conversation passed among them, quickly stifled by nuns' sharp looks.

John spotted Lena walking alone at the end of the line. Taller than the others, she stared straight ahead without so much as a side glance. She also walked funny. Not the graceful, easy stride he remembered. Those shoes, he reckoned, must hurt her feet.

John fell in behind them at a safe distance, trying to mingle with other churchgoers. Many were well-dressed gentlemen and frilly fine ladies, but there were some Mexicans, too, and enough plain folk to help him blend in. A couple of cowboys sauntered along, as well. He sidled up behind one of them, a broad-shouldered hulk with matted beard reeking of beer, barnyard, and a hint of vomit.

The girls bunched up at the church doors. From the other direction about twenty boys approached wearing creased gray pants, blue coats over white shirts and red neckties. Students from the boy's school, he reckoned.

Then he saw Red-top.

What was his name? Robert? No, Richard. Richard Castillo. The one at the parade who was interested in the Medina family. The young man sidled up to Lena and began talking. Her face came alive, eager with talking. Red-top leaned close and said something in her ear.

Instead of pulling away, she leaned toward him. A little laugh shook her shoulders.

Stunned, John shrank back into the shadow of the big-shouldered cowboy's backside. The little speech he'd been practicing began to dissolve like sugar in coffee.

The church doors swung open and the crowd filed in. John slipped in behind Big Shoulders. They doffed their hats. The boys sat on the right, girls on the left. John spotted Lena sitting toward the rear on the narrow center aisle. Across the aisle, Red-top leaned toward her and whispered something. She shook her head, a shushing motion, and kept her gaze on the altar.

A white-robed priest with a sing-song voice launched into a chant. Droning on in a language John guessed was Latin, he swung a smoking ball on a chain as he circled the table below the altar. The smell of it floated back to do battle with the odor coming from Big Shoulders. An image of Pa came to mind, scowly and red-faced, beard a-quiver, finger shaking at John for being there. John felt sweat pooling under his arms, despite the chill in the air.

Every once in a while people read things out loud, and now and then they knelt on rails before the pews. Lena moved with them, back and forth, all wrapped up in the ceremony. Castillo kept looking her way. He didn't seem the least bit interested in the priest's doings.

With no warning, the big-shouldered cowboy sank down on his knees and started moaning, "Forgive me, Lord. Forgive me. I have sinned!" He repeated this several more times, his voice rising to an alarming shout. His big body began to twist and shake as if he were on the receiving end of some invisible bullwhip.

John edged away. Nothing like this ever happened among Presbyterians. Maybe not Catholics either, judging from the way heads turned in the crowd. A robed priest slid off a nearby side bench, knelt down and laid an arm across the big fellow's heaving shoulders. His words were lost in the hubbub of scraping boots and shifting noises as more people turned around to look.

John felt the urge to hightail it out of there, but seeing Lena turn, he held his ground. Her eyes, like everyone else's, were glued to the cowboy. John risked a little wave. She didn't notice. Finally, heart pounding, he squatted down right behind the pair huddled on the floor and waved his big hat in her direction.

Her eyes widened, and her brows twisted into question marks.

John mouthed, "I'll see you outside," and pointed to the door.

She looked puzzled at first, then nodded ever so slightly.

John couldn't tell if she was glad to see him. Maybe she was just too surprised. He backed toward the exit. Big Shoulders tuned down to a low whimper. Everyone turned back to the priest as John stepped out through the door.

For the next half-hour he wore a circular path in the grass. Doubt ate at him. Red-top seemed so cock-sure of himself. So lean and well-hewn. Regal, almost.

He stopped pacing for a moment to wipe the dust from his boots and brush the trail dirt from his pants. They looked wrinkled and dirty in the fading light.

The church doors finally creaked open. Big Shoulders came out first, a toothless smile announcing his redemption, at least for a day or two. Then Lena walked out, Red-top at her side.

John forced a smile and walked right up to them, trying to look sure of himself.

"Hello, Lena." He had a frog in his throat.

"Hello, John Alexander." A nod was all she gave. No leap of joy on her face, no rush forward, not even a handshake. The nuns were watching, John told himself. Plenty of reason to show restraint. But why was she standing so close to Richard Castillo? Weren't the nuns supposed to guard against this sort of thing?

"Meet Richard Castillo," she said. "Richard, this is John Alexander. Mr. Castillo is a student at Regis. John Alexander is a friend from home. A former teacher at Big Thompson school." Her voice was clipped, refined.

"Mister" Richard Castillo, crisp in his white shirt and ironed trousers, bowed slightly at the waist and extended a hand. Even from this position John felt looked down on, being as he was a good three inches shorter than Red-top.

"Pleasure," Castillo said. His dark eyes, set on either side of a narrow nose, showed no recollection of their earlier meeting. The smile on his thin lips widened in practiced charm. His hand felt smooth against John's calluses. Smooth, but firm.

"Howdy," John said, feeling idiotic. "I…we met before. At the parade."

Red-top's eyes flickered as they surveyed John from his hat down to his boots, searching for a scrap of memory.

"Yes, the parade." His voice was polished. His nose twitched into a little sniff.

"I work for John Wesley Illiff now," John said. Then, suddenly needing to puff himself up a bit, he added, "He asked me to come pick out some new tack. From Colorado Saddlery." He hoped Richard Castillo wouldn't ask where Colorado Saddlery was.

"Hmmmm," was all he said.

John turned back to Lena. "I've got something, some news. Could we…?"

She stood there long enough to force him to add, "It's private."

She turned to Red-top with a little nod.

"Could you please excuse us for a moment?" Her manners were perfect. Red-top, no less polite, bowed and walked away.

"Lena, what's it like for you here?" John tried to use his tutor's voice, but it sounded more like pleading. He wanted to know if she missed him.

She looked to both sides. None of the nuns seemed to be watching her.

"Oh, John Alexander, I do miss being outside. But there are good things here." Her words seemed carefully chosen.

The nuns started forming the students into a line.

"Lena, I have something I want to ask you, but not here. Can you…you know, meet me outside the Academy? In private, I mean. It's important."

More sidelong glances. The girl students took their places in line for the walk back to the school. The boys clotted in little knots, talking among themselves and glancing sideways at the girls. The nuns glided around, herding. Red-top looked Lena's way, as if trying to read her lips.

Lena leaned closer and said almost in a whisper, "The livery. The Elephant Corral. Tomorrow after lunch."

A nun with fat cheeks and a droopy left eyelid gave them a look.

"Sooner? I'm due at Iliff's tomorrow night."

She shook her head no. The nun started toward them and Lena turned to go.

"Lena. I have Otter. Bought him from Hiram Tadder. She's yours. Waiting for you."

This finally got the reaction John had hoped for. Her polish dissolved, her face went from shock to stunning smile. But it only lasted a moment. The droopy-eyed nun grabbed her and shoved her into line while giving John a stern look.

As Lena filed out to the street, she turned back with a little wave. The nuns didn't notice, but Red-top did. He caught John's eye and a smile, more like a sneer, formed on his thin lips. He mimicked her wave, as if to say, *you have no chance, you clumsy fool.*

He may be right, John thought. Lena's delight was all about her filly, not him.

That night John paced around and cussed himself for being so timid. When they were in school together, Lena had looked up to him. The nuns had changed her, given her airs. Could she be falling for Mister Richard Castillo's high-falutin' charm? He tried to see Red-top and himself through Lena's eyes. The comparison didn't give him comfort. St. Mary's prison-like fence was a good thing, he decided.

His jaw began to ache. He realized he was grinding his teeth as he paced around the tenting ground in time with the chirping crickets. The Big Dipper circled a quarter of its way around the North Star before he finally crawled into his bedroll. November cold snaked around the corners of his blanket. Curled into a tight ball, he finally drifted off, thinking of Lena and Red-top slumbering in warm beds. He wondered how linen sheets felt on the skin.

By the time he woke, the sun had climbed high in the sky. He rushed over to the Elephant Corral. The livery had a washroom for customers. He dashed around trying to make himself presentable. It cost him a dime to get his face washed, hair combed, and mouth cleared of sleep breath. Chewing on mint leaves helped, a trick he'd learned from Mr. Medina.

His clothes were another problem. He brushed them off with a damp towel and stretched and patted them into shape as best he could. The same towel served to dust off his boots. The Elephant Corral earned its dime. He squared his shoulders, donned his hat, mustered a confident smile and strode out to the corral rail to wait.

His hopes sank with the westering sun. He rode his horse over to St. Mary's. Nothing stirred. He felt low as a snake.

Heading north, he pushed hard all night. But daybreak beat him to the Illiff bunkhouse by several hours. He unsaddled the jaded pinto and slipped into the bunkhouse to change clothes. Before he could pull on his work boots there was a tap on his shoulder. Leather Bill. The foreman motioned him outside onto the porch.

"Where ya been?" His grizzled face was hard.

"I had to go to Denver City," John couldn't think of a reason, leastways not one he cared to tell, so he just shut up and looked down.

"Sorry, son. Boss got no use for slackers. After lunch, pack up and git. You're fired."

62

Medina
November 1871

On his next trip to Denver City, just after Thanksgiving, Medina rode with a divided heart. After dropping off a load of pumpkins at Jones Mercantile and picking up some supplies to haul back to the Crossing, including some doodads Jones pushed on him as being sure-fire sellers in the upcoming Christmas season, Medina headed to St. Mary's. It would be his first encounter with Lena since taking her back to school after the fight with Takansy, after he'd sold the confounded filly.

He stood up when Lena entered the Academy waiting room and held out the basket of dried fruit and cake that Takansy had sent with him.

Lena's face was guarded, like her mother's. She didn't look angry with him, to his relief. But she didn't look especially glad to see him, either.

"How you are, my daughter?" he said.

"Fine, Papi." Lena took the basket and peeked under the cloth cover. "Hmmm," she said.

"Your studies? Music lessons?"

"They are going well, thank you."

"Any sickness? Jones says there is scarlet fever in Denver City."

"No, Papi."

The stiffness of their exchange was beginning to wear.

"Come, sit down." He ushered her to a chair. He closed the door of the waiting room to shut out the bespectacled watchfulness of the Sister sitting at the reception desk just outside, and sat down facing her. "I just came from Jones. He says you are liking the riding, yes?"

Lena nodded. She perched on the edge of the chair like a bird about to take flight.

"Thank you for arranging it," she said.

"Lena, my daughter, I have something to say. It is difficult…"

She set the basket on a small table and folded her hands in her lap.

"About your filly, Otter. I am sorry I sell her. Sometimes I get the anger and I do things. Then I wish to take them back."

Lena waited, her expression unchanged.

"But it is done. Hiram Tadder sells your Otter already. To some man who passes through, to somewhere in Missouri. We must make the best of it."

He expected more of a reaction, even tears. But to his surprise and relief, Lena said, "It's all right, Papi."

Encouraged, he plunged ahead. "There will be more Otters. A new stallion, a fine animal, I am to buy. Jones helps me to find one. Shy Bird will produce fine colts, many of them."

This got a twitch of a smile from Lena.

"When you finish school, you are to have plenty of time for horses, for training, for the riding shows. You fond of the horse work, I know that, but school comes first, yes?"

Lena stood and reached for his hands. She pulled him out of his chair and squeezed. He was startled to see how tall she had grown, then realized the heels of those school shoes must add to her height. She said, "It is all right, Papi. I will stay here and study. And make you proud. Thank you for coming."

They walked together to the door. Lena kissed his cheek and bade him goodbye.

David M. Jessup

"Tell Mami thank you for the basket of treats."

On the way back to the Crossing, Medina puzzled over Lena's acceptance of the loss of Otter. He had expected more coldness and tears, like the ones she shed on first learning of the filly's sale. Now, his daughter seemed settled back into school life. Young ones, he mused, are less fixed in their ways than us old ones.

He turned his thoughts to the upcoming sales season, the sorting of cattle to take to market, and the question of whether to replace his bartender. But Lena's calm, coupled with what he sensed was a new coolness toward him, continued to nibble at the edges of his mind like a fish that never fully takes the bait and remains hidden beneath the surface.

63

John Alexander
December 1871

Back with his family, tail between his legs, John Alexander's mood was even bleaker than the weather. More snow than anyone could remember piled up during the winter of 1871-1872. Wind screeched out of the northwest, creating drifts the size of hogbacks. Roads were blocked for days at a time. Just before Christmas, the river froze near solid. It took a half-hour of ax-swinging each morning to hack through the ice so the livestock could drink. He had to haul water and grass hay to Otter.

Jennie still lorded it over everyone, heavier and unhappier on her way to old-maidhood. Pa looked more worn out, and was even more surly. Robert and Anna were older and quarreling, cooped up as they were by the cold.

Ma had taken to wandering off by herself, from time to time.

David M. Jessup

Once John had to fetch her back from the barn loft where he found her sitting and staring at nothing. When he climbed up the ladder to call her back, she looked at him in some sort of daze. Then her face softened and she cooed, "Johnnie," in a child's voice. She crawled over, bits of hay hanging from her hair, and snuggled against him.

"Johnnie, it's so good...you being here again," she said.

He put his arm around her and felt bony shoulders. She let out a soft, backward-in-time sort of laugh.

"It's all right, Mama," he said. But he couldn't bring himself to say the words she wanted to hear, that he would be staying on.

Part of him—the part that cared about Mama and Mattie and the younger ones—said *stay, help, they need you.* Another part said, *leave or go crazy.* The idea of homesteading up on Owl Creek kept pulling at him, with or without Lena. He hadn't completely given up on the notion of marrying her, but he had to admit that trail felt pretty cold after seeing her and Richard Castillo at St. Mary's. Problem was, he had no one to talk to about his plans. Not even cheery Mattie, the only one he felt close to. She might not keep his secret, good-hearted though she was.

He only visited the hideout once that winter, what with the snow and all, not to mention he now owned a weaned filly that needed hay. He had lied about Otter, telling his family he'd bought the filly from Illiff.

Pa was unsympathetic about the hay.

"We barely have enough hay for our own animals," he would say.

Jennie would chime in something about wasting money that should have come to support the family. So on many a day John would tromp out to cut dried grass on the south-facing slopes and haul it back to Otter. Despite his efforts, the filly's sides were turning into washboards.

One day, just before Christmas, he decided to visit the Crossing and ask Mrs. Medina for help with feeding. He figured Mrs. Medina might be sympathetic to the idea of Lena getting Otter back. Maybe she would loan some hay until he could pay her back. It would have to be on the sly, of course. He didn't cotton to Mr. Medina getting wind of what he'd done. With him, the visit would be explained as another work day to square the ten dollar debt he owed him.

It took John the whole morning and several bouts of shoveling snow from the road to get Old Dun and the wagon to the Crossing. As he drew near, he marveled at how the Medina store, unlike their own sorry homestead, glowed with cheer against the winter gloom. Glass jars with candles inside were set along the porch. A fir tree hung with strings of berries and other doodads stood tall in the courtyard. The light from the big fireplace inside framed the doorway and spilled out through the window glass. Wood smoke plumed up from the chimney and scented the air. The smell of something baking set his mouth to watering. It was enough to make him want to spend the rest of the winter there. The only thing missing was Lena. Could she possibly be coming home for the holiday?

He climbed to the porch and paused there, suddenly worried. Did Mr. Medina already know about Otter? But the trader came out smiling, quick-stepping over to greet him with his usual shoulder pats. *He doesn't know.* For a moment John felt like a betrayer, until he remembered how Mr. Medina had betrayed Lena.

"I'm here to square up that ten dollars," he said, trying to sound friendly.

"Ah, yes." Mr. Medina looked around the courtyard. A half a dozen Mexicans were shoveling snow, hauling this and that in and out of the barn, repairing a wagon. He scratched his head, thinking. "Wood chopping. We always to have that."

"I'll get right to it, thanks." John paused, then took a chance. "How's Lena doing?" He tried to sound casual.

"She is very well." Mr. Medina's face got the kind of proud look he'd seen on people when all they've worked for is coming true. "She is fond of the mandolin. Her teachers say she is a good student. She is very happy. *Muy contento.*"

John hoped he was wrong.

Just then the sound of harness bells announced the arrival of a sleigh pulled by two fine black draft horses snorting puffs of steam. Juniper branches tied with red ribbons hung from the sides. The Bartholf family climbed out led by Mr. Bartholf, who turned to give a hand to Mrs. Bartholf, handkerchief pressed against her nose, followed by Bisam, Eugene and Julie.

Julie looked grand. Yellow curls poked out from under a red hat with white fur trim. She was even prettier than John remembered. Her face lit up in a big smile when she saw him, and he felt himself grinning in return. Girls like her hadn't been a common sight on the Illiff Ranch.

"Happy Christmas!" Mr. Medina stepped up to greet them, arms reaching out in welcome.

Mr. Bartholf stepped forward with a formal handshake.

"So, Mr. Medina, what new surprises have you brought up from Denver City for the holiday?"

"Ah, come see the treasures I have! You will want the latest hat for Mrs. Bartholf, no?"

Mrs. Bartholf looked as if she could use a new hat, her own being drab as dust. Mr. Medina wheeled them around into the store. Mr. Bartholf nodded to John. Mrs. Bartholf marched straight past. Bisam and Eugene grinned and elbowed each other to be next through the door. Julie paused, then walked over to the side of the porch and stopped dead in front of him, still smiling.

"Johnnie, what a surprise to see you. You look different."

Her blue eyes roved over him, and he felt a flare in his face at her boldness. He fought hard to hold her gaze, and was pleased as punch when he succeeded.

"You look the same, Julie. Just as pretty." His own daring surprised him.

She laughed, a pleased-sounding giggle that fell nice on the ears. "Merry Christmas."

Quick as a cat she stepped up close and kissed him on the cheek, then, just as quickly, pulled away, her hand flying up to cover her rosy lips. Color flared in her cheeks, and her eyes looked shocked at what she'd done, but not sorry for it. Not a bit.

For a change John didn't feel like there was something wrong with her for liking him. His mind raced for something clever to say that would show him to be a fellow with a charming way with girls. But there wasn't time. The twinkle went out of Julie's eyes as her gaze shifted to someone behind him.

He whirled around to find Mrs. Medina staring at them. Startled, he stepped back too quick and tripped, barely catching himself on a porch post. Julie scurried into the store, head down. Mrs. Medina kept her eyes fixed on John. His first impulse was to get away, but he remembered why he'd come.

He pushed away from the post. "Mrs. Medina, could I talk with you a bit, I mean, over yonder, by the barn?" She held her ground for a moment, then joined him in what he hoped looked like an innocent trip across the snowy courtyard. Along the way, still blushing, he asked her how Lena was doing.

"She very unhappy. Nuns very hard. No horses."

They arrived at the south-facing entrance to the barn, bathed in pale winter sunlight. John tossed some hay into an open manger.

"Mr. Medina says Lena likes it there."

Something between a snort and a huff exploded from her nose, sending a little cloud of steam into the wintry air.

"I am telling you something." Her tone was angry. "Lena not happy. Her Spirit Partner is Horse. Very strong. She is born to it. At seven snows old, it is visiting her. Not waiting for twelve or thirteen. Strong medicine. Lena only happy when training, riding. It is her Spirit Path. You understand?"

He nodded, although he had only a vague notion of what she was talking about.

She continued, "My husband, he not understanding. But I know. It was same for me, in the long ago."

She turned on him with such a fierce glare that he would have stepped back if she hadn't grabbed his arm.

"Nothing must be coming between my daughter and her Spirit Path. No one! No thing! What happen to me must not happen to Lena. I am not allowing it! You understanding?"

"Yes, Ma'am." He felt uncomfortable in her grasp, so he played his ace. "Mrs. Medina, I have Otter. For Lena."

Now, it was her turn to pull back.

"The filly's at my place. She's there for Lena when she comes back. But there's a problem."

He quickly explained the feed situation, and just as quickly she agreed to a bargain. She pulled out a leather pouch and handed over some greenbacks, around ten dollars.

She said, "Go to Blackhurst. Plenty hay." She added, "We are not telling anyone about this."

"No. My folks think I brought her from Iliff's ranch." Their eyes locked in silent conspiracy. He thanked her and turned to go and start chopping wood.

She caught his arm. "Why you doing this?" Her voice was thick with suspicion.

"Just, well, I thought it was a shame, that's all, that Lena's filly...I mean she doted on her, and it just seemed wrong to, you know, take her away."

She gave him a hunting dog look. His cheeks burned.

To throw her off the scent, he said, "Julie Bartholf and me, we're...well, you saw us there, on the porch. We're sort of thinking about...marriage."

The lie amazed him, how he just blurted it out. But it had the right effect. Mrs. Medina seemed to soften up. He rushed on, trying to change the subject again.

"Did Lena say anything about a boy named Richard Castillo?"

The question dangled between them for a long moment.

"No," she finally said. "Plenty people name Castillo. How is he looking like?"

"My age. Tall. Thin nose. Hair, at least the top of it, as red as those rocks up there."

That got her attention. Her stone face cracked a bit in what looked like recognition.

"How you are knowing about this Castillo?

"I saw them together. At the Academy. Outside a church, I mean. I was down there buying tack. He seemed too interested, in Lena, I mean. Kept trying to stand next to her."

"You visited my Lena?"

"No, no, I just saw her from a distance, just before the students went into the church." John felt sweat beading on his forehead. He didn't tell her that Red-top's attraction to Lena might go both ways.

"Lena is knowing you have Otter?"

"No, Ma'am." His lies were stacking up like bricks, ready to fall. "But I plan to tell her, soon as she comes home again. Will she be here for Christmas?"

Mrs. Medina shook her head no. "Thanking you for Otter. We having a pact." She squeezed his arm, to seal it. Then she turned and walked away toward the store.

John watched her go. He wasn't the only one lying. He could see she knew more about Richard Castillo than she was saying.

64

Takansy
December 1871

Takansy crunched across the crusted snow, staying well off the river road. She didn't want to encounter anyone, especially Blue-eye. Or his son. It made for slow going. She pushed herself harder, impatient to return before Medina noticed her absence. Clouds of steam puffed from her open mouth. At the ford she stepped across the river on round gray stones exposed by the winter's low water. The walking was easier on the sun-baked side, and she made better progress toward the great canyon's mouth, where Otter was being held.

John Alexander had not spoken truth. He would not rescue Otter unless he had intentions toward Lena. The young lightface was no good at hiding his thoughts. Marry the yellow hair girl? If only it were true! But when Julie and John were on the store porch together, it was plain that any thoughts of marriage were hers, not his. His sights were on Lena.

John Alexander said he had not spoken with Lena in Denver. But why, then, had he not asked Takansy to tell Lena he had saved Otter? Did Lena already know? Why would she hide that knowledge from her mother?

She wished young Alexander were suitable for her daughter. Perhaps in time, if he became rich enough to raise fine horses. But not now. Lena was only fourteen, barely a woman. Having babies would destroy the Horse Spirit path.

When she reached the spot where the wagon track left the river and cut through the sandstone ridge into Alexander's valley, Takansy left the road and headed up the ridge to her right. From there, crouching behind some mountain mahogany bushes, she looked down on Blue-eye's homestead.

What she saw appalled her. The dugout had a hole in the roof. Pale smoke rose from a broken chimney and hazed over the riverbank and ragged garden. Broken branches littered the ground. Chickens, goats and pigs had the run of the place. *No, John Alexander is not fit for my Lena.*

Across a flimsy bridge to the south, a small mound of freshly stacked hay drew her eye. Beside it stood a lean-to attached to a rough-hewn corral. Otter walked out of the lean-to, looked at the hay piled on the other side of the corral rail and pawed the snow. So this was where the filly was kept. From that distance, Otter looked to be in good health, but she couldn't be sure.

Takansy scouted the approaches to the corral. A low ridge between the road and the mountains provided cover to a bare patch of ground. If she could get across that without being seen, she could follow a line of grass and brush that edged what looked like an irrigation ditch running directly past the corral. By spring the grass would be tall enough, and the bushes filled out enough, to hide her approach. Otter would follow her mother, Shy Bird, away to the tall ridge of the resting place. From there, she and Lena could escape to the north country.

She pictured Lena racing across one of the meadows along the Bitterroot while her people cheered. She banished the thought of riding beside her. *God let me ride north with her and I will never break my vow.* She made the crossing sign.

A barking sound caught her ear. A floppy-eared red dog snuffled through the snow toward the corral. Behind it trudged John Alexander. She watched him heft a pitchfork beside the lean-to and toss hay over the corral rail to Otter. He climbed over the fence and began stroking the filly's neck. Otter turned, mouth full of hay, and nuzzled the young man's arm.

A pang knifed through her. *If only I had been the one to rescue Otter!* Lena's attraction to the young lightface would be increased by him doing it. Did she know? Takansy hoped not. She wanted to be the news-bearer to her daughter.

The dog crouched in front of a hole between some rocks and stared, head tilted and ears perked, as if expecting a rabbit to run out. A small piece of meat should keep it quiet when the time came.

The dog's color reminded her of young Alexander's story of Richard Castillo. Could that red-haired youth be related to her husband's enemy in Taos? His son, perhaps? Should she share this news with her husband? No, not for the time being. Medina's outbursts were too unpredictable. But the information could be useful, if managed carefully. It might be used to persuade her husband to allow Lena to leave the nuns' school and come home long enough for her to arrange their escape.

Takansy edged back from the ridge top. She had seen enough to refine her plans. On the way back to the Crossing, she knelt beside the river and tickled two trout out from under a rock where they'd holed up during winter. The icy water numbed her hands. She reached home just as the short winter day faded.

As she opened the door, Medina raised his black bead eyes at her and she held up the trout, impaled through the gills on two of her fingers, and said, "Tonight we are eating the trout."

She hurried past him into the kitchen. He didn't ask where she had been.

65

John Alexander
April 1872

With the secret help of Mrs. Medina, John brought Otter through the bitter winter into a blustery spring. The filly's ribs filled out under her long-haired winter coat, her legs stretched to lanky yearling length. She would stamp out a greeting when John brought her hay, and push his arm with her nose. At such times John would drift into fancy, his mind hovering over a grassy meadow full of cattle on Owl Creek, a winding stream, a corral with horses, a fine log home, a big barn, and Lena stepping out of the house, graceful as a doe, smiling her brilliant smile.

At other times doubt would elbow in, especially in the dark of early-morning wakefulness, when he would torment himself with visions of Lena gliding through a hotel lobby on the arm of Richard Castillo, elegantly dressed, polished boots clacking on the marble floor, while John stood watching in his patched overalls and worn out boots. How could he possibly win her, accustomed as she was to a life of fine things, admiring crowds, doting family, good education, and mandolins, for glory sake? How could Mr. and Mrs. Medina accept him, even if they had no truck with Richard Castillo?

Then he would remember their last time together in the hideout, feel the touch of her hand, conjure up the silky shape of her perfect arm, remember holding her.

His mood shifted between warm April days sprouting with promise and raging snow squalls. He felt jumpy as a rabbit. He had to see Lena again. Maybe her attraction to Red-top had waned after five months. He tried to convince himself that he might still have a certain influence over her, as he did during the Posse days.

As soon as the weather warmed, he got word to Leather Bill that he wanted to buy the pinto with the money he'd saved, and the Illiff foreman agreed. He hitched a wagon ride east with Hiram Tadder to retrieve his mount, and from Iliff's, rode the pinto up to Owl Creek.

The land was still unclaimed. It wasn't quite the homestead of his imagination, but it would do. The creek meandered through one stretch of valley that ran from north to south for over a mile. A one hundred sixty acre claim would capture most of it. The grass grew lush along the bottomland. With some irrigation ditches, the green area could be enlarged.

On the east side of the valley was a red cliff that rose into a beautiful butte of the same color. It reminded him a little of his hideout. The cliff had a vertical cleft in it spanned by another horizontal one, a cross of sorts, when looked at just so. He stared at it, and suddenly it came to him. If Lena would have him, their marriage would have to be Catholic. And to do that, he would have to become Catholic. It was the only way that Lena's pa and ma could possibly accept it. A little voice inside his head said, no chance, but he argued it down.

He rushed back to the homestead, rested the pinto for a day, then set out for Boulder. There he looked up a priest Goodale had told him about, a Father Frank. Thin and tall, the priest's big nose was laced with tiny, red veins that proved up Goodale's claim that he loved whiskey a little more than was good for him. Confirmation classes, the priest told him, would begin on July first.

"I'll be there." *What a jolt it will be if Pa finds out!*

He rode on to the Land Office in Golden and filled out the homestead application form. Allen, the bald clerk, snapped his suspenders and gave him a weary look that signaled he'd seen a hundred like him and didn't expect he'd have the gumption to stick to a claim.

After a short and sleepless night camping on Clear Creek, John washed up, slicked back his hair, saddled up and headed downstream to Denver City. The weather turned cold and blowy. The iron gate at St. Mary's Academy stood black and imposing in the morning sun. He pulled the bell rope. He had a story all worked out to get through the nuns' defenses. An envelope addressed to Lena, supposedly from her parents, which had to be delivered in person by him, her former tutor. Could he please come into the office, and could they please bring Lena in to receive it?

The nun who came down the steps was not the droopy-eyed one who had sized him up at the church, but a pleasant, smiling young woman. He waved the envelope at her and spun his tale. She nodded sympathetically. Then her eyebrows bunched up into a little frown.

"Miss Lena is not here. She wasn't in her room at bedtime last night. We are worried she has run away."

"Run away?" John's gut twisted. "Do you know where she might have gone? I thought she was... did anything unusual happen?"

"Not that we know. We have talked with all her teachers. With her friends, although she has few. She is always dutiful, studies well, loves her music. No sign of anything wrong. You say you are her tutor?"

"Was. At the Big Thompson Crossing. I'm a friend of Lena's folks." He turned to go. "I'll let you know if I find out anything."

He headed straight for the Elephant Corral. As he suspected, one of Jones's horses had gone missing. Joe, the manager, was not upset.

"Someone borrowed it, again. Mr. Jones said he knew who it was and it was good by him." He shrugged.

It had to be Lena. John lit out north. By mid-afternoon he reached Tim Goodale's place on Boulder Creek. The old mountain man ambled out, hair in wisps, tucking a shirt into his pants. Round-faced Jenny emerged a few minutes later.

John had no time for niceties. "You seen Lena?"

"Yup, we seen her. Spent last night with us. Curled up on the floor, just like a kitten."

"Not the floor," Jenny said. "A straw mattress. My best blanket."

Mr. Goodale grinned at her. "She come in after we was t'bed. Lathered up a bit."

"What did she say?" John said. "About where she was going, I mean. And why."

"Just a visit home was all she said. She's a quiet one, that girl."

"There was more to it than that," Jenny said with a quick frown. "Why, that girl's face was vexed, plain as day."

Mr. Goodale chuckled. "My Jenny, she's always seeing things in faces. A durned shaman, this woman."

Jenny humpfed and gave John the once-over. "Something is wrong?"

John tried to hide his growing alarm. "Don't think so. When did she leave?"

"Slipped out before dawn. Quiet as a mouse."

"I heard her," Jenny said.

John wheeled the pinto around.

"Won't stay awhile?" Goodale said. "Have some vittles with us?"

"Got to go," John said.

Jenny gave him a look. "You better give that horse a blow. And some grain. Else you won't be able to catch her."

John reined up and stroked the pinto's lathered neck.

"You're right." He dismounted and walked his horse in a circle until it cooled off. Then he led it to the water tank while Jenny fetched grain. The feeding only took a few minutes, but it felt like hours. He finally jerked the pinto away and mounted up.

Jenny handed him a small packet. "Cornbread."

"I'm beholden to you."

"Good luck," Mr. Goodale said. "Tell my old friend Mariano hello for me. That little cuss done better than most all of us mountain men put together. And him a durned Mexican… 'Spaniard,' I mean." He laughed and slapped his knee.

John reined around, but Goodale's next words caused him to turn back.

"Speaking of Medina, another fellow stopped in this morning asking about him. Young man, like you."

"He give a name.?"

"Nope. Fine looking. Tall, he was, thin-nosed, with a swatch of red in his topknot. Bit of an accent."

The hairs stood up on John's neck. "What'd he want?"

"Wouldn't say. Looking for directions to Mariano's Crossing. I reckoned he maybe knew Mariano in Taos—him or his family."

"How long ago?"

"Maybe two hours. Say, you know him?

But John was already off at a fast trot.

He caught up with Richard Castillo at the twin Ponderosa trunks marking the entry to Medina's property. Red-top turned when he heard the pinto clatter up. By that time the sun was about ready to drop behind the mountains, its glow reddening his face.

Looking down his long nose at the froth on John's horse, he said, "You seem to be in a great hurry."

"What are you doing here?" John was surprised by the strength of his own voice.

Red-top put on his charm-smile. "Might not it be more polite to say, 'Mr. Castillo, it's so good to see you. What brings you this way on such a fine afternoon?'"

"Answer my question!"

Castillo shook his head from side to side and shrugged, as if being sassed by a spoiled child.

"Let's just say I have some business with the Medina family. Private business." He turned away and trotted his horse to the tie rail in front of the trading post.

John nudged his tired pinto to catch up. He wanted to yank that weasel off his high horse and start punching. He was smaller than Castillo, but his anger crowded out any thought about the odds. What stopped him was doubt. He didn't know if Lena had feelings for the arrogant sonofabitch.

Red-top swung a long leg over his cantle and dismounted his big fine bay, smooth and confident. He slung the reins over the tie rail, ducked under it and climbed up the steps to the porch.

John scrambled to catch up and got as far as the stairs.

Red-top never made it inside. Mr. Medina stepped out of the door, his face red, his body tightened like a fist. Castillo stopped short. They stared at each other as if John weren't even there.

Castillo finally bowed at the waist and said, in a voice that attempted charm, "Don Mariano. We meet again. Eight years, has it been? In the plaza, in Taos. You remember, I am sure." He paused long enough to let this sink in, brush some dust off his pants and rise up again to full height.

"I have come to pay a visit to your daughter, and I wonder if..."

The next instant he was staggering back, hands groping behind him for support that wasn't there. Neither John nor Castillo saw the blow coming. One moment Mr. Medina was standing there, glaring, and then his hand flashed out from behind his back clutching the tomahawk that whapped sideways against Castillo's head, bringing him down. The porch floorboards let out a *whump*. Red-top rolled to one side and struggled up on all fours. Blood dripped from his ear onto the porch. Before he could stand, Medina's moccasined foot crashed into his side. Castillo let out a wheezy bellow as he hit the porch railing. Mr. Medina hauled him up and pushed him over the rail.

Castillo crumpled up in a heap at John's feet, close enough for John to see a dark stain spreading in his crotch. Castillo's face raged. Snot, tears and blood flew from his head as he shook it back and forth, gathering himself. Reaching behind his back, he pulled out a knife and lunged to his feet.

"Knife!" John shouted, but Mr. Medina had already seen. His Hawken rifle, snatched up from God knows where, pointed straight into Castillo's face.

For a long moment, Red-top stared up into the muzzle's black hole. He shook from head to toe. Blood oozed onto his shoulder and down the front of his white shirt. Dark hatred radiated from his eyes. He sheathed his knife, heaved a shuddering sigh and backed up to the tie rail. His big bay pulled back, rolling its eyes.

Castillo managed to climb into the saddle.

In a voice thick with rage, he said, "*Hijo de perra*," followed by more Spanish words John didn't understand.

Mr. Medina kept the Hawken pointed at him as Castillo loped away. He looked at John.

"You are travelling in bad company."

Speechless, John shook his head no.

Mr. Medina's lips formed a tight line.

"Good. Welcome. My house is your house, as always."

Stunned, John stayed rooted while Mr. Medina came down the steps and gave him one of his grab-your-shoulders greetings.

John's head scrambled to make sense of all this. Part of him was thrilled. Thrashing Red-top was something he imagined doing himself. Another part was mystified. Why this outburst?

As if reading his mind, Mr. Medina said, "That one is no good. I know his father. In Taos."

"What'd he do?"

"*Patrón*. He is *patrón*."

As if that explained anything. The word, John thought, meant landowner. Mr. Medina must have seen his confusion.

"He treat the people like slaves. His son is the same."

John nodded. He'd been on the receiving end of Red-top's scorn. But a beating? The violence seemed lopsided. There had to be more to the story.

"What'd he say when he left?" John asked.

" 'I curse you and your daughter. You will pay.' " Mr. Medina made a dismissive, brushing motion with his hand, but his eyes remained troubled. "And you, young John. How you to know him?"

John wondered whether Mrs. Medina had repeated any part of what he'd told her about Castillo's interest in Lena, or whether Lena had said anything.

"I saw him at the parade three years ago. Is Lena here? Did he bother her?"

"I am to find out. But he will never see her again. I have friends in Denver City. Jones, others. They will watch him. Like horses watching a rattlesnake."

John was incredulous. "Lena's going back?"

"Of course. She learns much there. Good teachers. My Lena must finish the schooling."

"But, sir, she ran away from there."

"Yes." His face, surprisingly, smiled with pride. "She comes home to see me. Borrows horse from my friend Jones to visit her papá. But she is to go back. She likes it there. I to take her back on Monday."

"But..."

He gave John a look that signaled the conversation had come to an end.

John felt desperate to talk to Lena, but he turned to go, figuring maybe he could come back the next day when things had settled down. Then Lena suddenly appeared in the doorway. Her face was pinched, worried. John managed to hold himself back until Mr. Medina turned away to climb the steps. Then he signaled to her, pointing toward the rimrock and mouthing the words "hideout, tomorrow." A nod was all she managed before her eyes locked on her father as he walked across the porch toward her, stuffing the tomahawk back into his belt. He spun her around and swept her back inside.

John rode to the hideout to wait.

66

Medina
April 1872

Medina led Lena to a chair and sat her down. Her brows bunched into little worry knots as he began grilling her in Spanish.

"*El Rojo*. The red-hair. He followed you here. Why?"

"I don't know, Papi."

"His name is Castillo. You know him? He is bothering you?"

"No, no, Papi. He is nothing. I have seen him a few times only…in Church, when the boys' school comes."

"Then why does he follow you here?"

"I told you, I don't know."

He watched her for signs of deception. "What is his name?

"Castillo, you said."

"Ricardo?"

"No, Richard."

"So, you do know his name?"

"Well, yes, because he is known, in school, I mean. I don't… "

"You must not lie to your father."

"I'm not lying, please, Papi… " Tears filled her eyes and threatened to spill over.

He softened his glare. "Lena, my child, I am only trying to protect you. I know that family. They are no good. *Patrones*."

"He said he knows you, too, Papi. On the store porch, before you hit him. He said something about eight years ago, in Taos. What did he mean?"

"I knew his father."

"But why did you hit him?"

Medina didn't want to answer this question. He grimaced at the recollection of Richard Castillo crashing over the stout porch rail and toppling to the ground. Normally he didn't punish sons for the sins of their fathers. But in this case, when he saw young Castillo approach, witnessed his arrogant exchange with John Alexander, heard his request to see Lena, took in the sneering eyes, the haughty nose, the red hair—so similar to the older Castillo's features that for a moment Medina was mentally transported back to his childhood—something had snapped. His tomahawk had leapt into action with a mind of its own.

The hatred on Castillo's face as he struggled up from his humiliating sprawl had given Medina pause. It triggered a memory of the same eyes on a young boy's face in the Taos Plaza eight years ago. He cursed himself for not reining in his temper.

"I hit him because I could tell he was up to no good. With no introduction, no notice, he shows up asking for you, following you here. This is not permissible. Not just a lack of manners. It is a threat."

"But Papi, there must be something more… ."

"Daughter, enough. The question is, why did you run away?"

"I told you, Papi. I got lonely, for you. I miss you. I miss springtime here. I was out riding one of Jones's horses, as you arranged, and I rode north a ways, then just decided to come the rest of the way, to see you." She rose from her chair and disarmed him with a hug and a smile.

The sound of tiny beads spilling onto the wood floor caused him turn around. Takansy sat in the corner chair, beadwork on her lap, staring up at them. He hadn't noticed her when he hustled Lena in from the porch. Suspicion flared again in his chest. He grasped Lena by the shoulders and held her at arms' length.

"Has your mother lured you back here?"

"No, no. It's as I said. A short visit, that is all. The school tests are over. I did well Papi, you will be proud, and there is only a week or so left anyway, before summer."

He eyed her, then Takansy.

"Did you tell Mother Superior that you were leaving?"

Lena's eyes dropped. "No. I was out riding. It wasn't planned."

"Then you must go back, apologize. They will be worried. And they might not let you finish your last year."

"Papi?"

"Yes?"

"The last year. I wonder, could I study here, perhaps? With a tutor, I mean. I can already read now, Papi. You can buy books, and I can… "

"A year, nine more months really, it is not long. You cannot throw away your future." As if remembering the importance of American learning, he switched to English. "After you finish at the Academy, you to have plenty of time for other things."

Lena sighed. Takansy stirred in her corner. He expected another argument, but she just sat there, looking down at her hands working the beads. He wondered why she didn't say anything.

He drew Lena close and beamed at her with what he hoped was a reassuring smile.

"My daughter, I am honored you come to visit me. But you must go back, make things right with the Academy. And with Jones, who must also be wondering about you…and his horse. Then you to come home for summer, and everything is fine, yes?"

"Yes, Papi."

"Tomorrow I have a meeting, Big Thompson Creek Association. I to send word on the stage to Jones and the nuns that you are safe. You to have a free day. Ride Shy Bird, enjoy the spring air. The day after, on Sunday, I take you back." He patted her hair. "Now we have dinner together. You tell me about your examinations. We to celebrate."

"Yes, Papi." She turned toward the kitchen.

Takansy set her beadwork aside, rose, and followed Lena through the door.

Medina followed them outside, thinking about how he would deal with Richard Castillo and the threat he felt the young man posed. *What was it he said as he rode away? Some kind of curse.*

67

John Alexander
April 1872

John Alexander watched Otter nibble newly-sprouted mountain mahogany leaves. She mouthed them for a while, then pulled her lips back and pushed the foamy chewing out onto the ground and snorted. With two patches of gray colt hair around her eyes, she had the look of a rabid raccoon. John might have laughed had he not been so worried about whether Lena would come. It was the morning after Castillo's beating, and he was counting on his hurried signal on the store porch to bring Lena to where he was waiting.

John's boot marks were mixed in with Otter's tracks in every corner of the hideout's sandy floor. John couldn't sit still. Only the pinto stood quiet, exhausted from days of hard riding. It hadn't moved from the scrubby pine he'd tied it to when they arrived four hours ago.

Otter had climbed up to the hideout willingly enough. Over the long winter John had gentled her, having learned from Lena and her mama how to earn a young horse's trust. He was careful not to do things that might spook the filly or force her to do something unnatural out of fear. After all, she wasn't his horse. By April he could toss a blanket on her, rub her rump, pick up all four feet. She was pretty much spook-proof. He hoped Lena would be pleased.

That morning he'd slipped away from the dugout without much notice. Eagle-eye Jennie saw him take Otter out of the lean-to, but he explained it was just a training session. She seemed to buy the notion.

Mattie, on the other hand, knew something was up.

"Where you going, Johnnie?" she said.

"Training."

Her eye roamed over him and the colt and came to rest on the saddlebag stuffed with provisions.

"I love you, Johnnie," she said, and gave him a hug.

"I'll be back after lunch," he told her. Now, here in the hideout, lunchtime was long past. He paced around, patted Otter, and paced some more.

Of a sudden, Otter's ears pointed on alert as they both heard a scraping sound.

Lena appeared at the low spot in the hideout wall. He said her name, in relief as much as in greeting. Without answering, she launched herself off her perch and in one willowy motion, alighted and stepped gravely up to him.

His legs went rubbery.

"You came," he said.

Her eyes found Otter.

"She's beautiful! John Alexander, thank you. So very, very much!" She moved toward the filly, turned sideways and stopped. Otter stretched her neck, sniffed, stepped forward and allowed herself to be stroked.

John wasn't sure if the filly remembered her from a year ago, but it sure seemed that way. Joy was the word that came to his mind as he watched Lena's face. He felt a little jealous.

"Otter belongs to you," he said. "Couldn't stand to see her at Tadder's. Just wasn't right."

"How did you do it?"

Pleased to be cast as the hero, he told her the story of how he'd talked Tadder into selling the filly and promising secrecy, snuck

David M. Jessup

Otter away to their homestead, pretended she came from the Illiff ranch, struggled to provide her with fodder, and worked day after day to gentle her.

"Hope she's all right," he said, fishing for more thanks.

Lena's eyes shone. "John Alexander, she is perfect. Sleek. No ribs showing after this winter, ready to start training. You have brought her to just where she is supposed to be."

His chest swelled. "Did your mama tell you how she helped with the hay? Moneywise, that is."

Lena laughed. "She made it sound like her idea."

"That's curious."

"John Alexander, I had to sneak away today. I cannot stay long. They think I am out riding Shy Bird. I have not told them about our hideout."

Our hideout. He liked the sound of that. It helped him get where he wanted to go. He swallowed hard to wet his dry throat.

"Lena. We have to talk. I have something to ask you."

Her face went grave, questioning. He guided her to a rock bench and sat her down facing him.

"First, there's something I need to know about. Richard Castillo."

She looked away.

"Richard. It is finished. He is a brute. A pig. He is why I ran away from school. I do not know why I ever thought different about him."

"You liked him?"

"Oh, John Alexander. It is hard for me to say this. But at first, when I started school in Denver, I was so alone. I missed being outdoors, missed horses. I felt all caged up. Missed my family."

Missed me?

"None of the girls would…you know, be friends. I mean, they were friends with each other. The older ones, they were together in school in years past, and the new ones, the ones in my same entry class, they all seemed to be of the same circle, all knowing each other before, and there I was, from Big Thompson, a place they'd scarcely heard of, and I knew no one." She looked at him hard. "John Alexander, I hated it there. They called me 'the Parade Indian.' I guess I was known, in a way, but not in the way that counts at St. Mary's. I was different. They shut me out."

He nodded, urging her to go on. She looked away as if uncertain of his approval.

"That is why I broke many rules. Running away sometimes. Usually, not for long. To the livery. The Elephant Corral. Mr. Jones had some horses there he would let me borrow. He likes me, and Papi arranged it with him to let me ride. And there was the music teacher, Miss Little. She was my only friend, the only one who had any sort of…well, sympathy, you might say…and she would cover for me at times, tell the nuns I was studying at her place or staying for extra practice, as long as I didn't leave for too long. She and I had an agreement. As long as I was back in two hours—that was the limit. It kept me going."

She looked at him again. "You know how a horse moves away from pressure? You put a knee to him and he moves away?"

He nodded.

"That school was pressure. I had to lie a lot. To Papi, to Mami, to the nuns. I have become quite good at lying." She smiled a rueful little smile.

"And Castillo?"

"Yes, yes. I am getting there." She looked away again, her hands twisting strips of the leather fringe of her leggings. "You have to know what it was like for me. Richard was the only person I could talk to. He had the same things, in his school, I mean. Lonely and all. Missed his family in Taos. He had been sent away to Denver because it has the best school. At least that's what he said. And I believed him. And when I found out Otter was sold, it just seemed…well, I had to get used to it—being at St. Marys—and forget about horses and going back home. Richard was good to talk to."

She sighed, a regretful sound to his hope-starved ears.

"I first met him at the Church. The one you came to that day. He paid attention to me, sought me out. It made the other girls jealous. He was handsome, so sure of himself! Admired for his skill at that new baseball game. And clever. He said things that made me laugh. Took my mind away from other things. Being with him was like running away on a good horse." Her eyes searched John's face.

He tried to appear sympathetic.

She untwisted the braided fringe on her leggings.

"Oh, that Rebecca Welty. She wanted to win Richard's attention in the worst way. She would practically throw herself at him. It was most unrefined." Lena let out a little laugh.

Despite his fears about Castillo, John found himself wanting her to get the best of Rebecca Welty, whoever she was.

"Sometimes he would meet me at the stable. I'm not sure how he found out I went there, but one day, he was there, too, and we talked some more, and he asked if he could ride with me, and I said, yes. So he rented a horse, and we rode and talked and rode and talked. He was a good rider. And a good talker."

"Did you ever…kiss him?" He asked the question, his eyes on the ground because he wasn't at all sure if he wanted to hear the answer.

More fussing with the fringe. "Yes," she finally said.

He wanted—and didn't want—to hear more. All the details. Had he…touched her?

"A mistake. Things changed after that. He pressed himself on me. Tried to… ." She looked away.

"Force you?" His voice sounded funny in his throat, high pitched.

She nodded, her cheeks coloring.

"Did he?"

"No, John Alexander. Nothing happened. He tried, is all. On a ride. Grabbed me. But I am strong. And fast."

He believed her—*needed* to believe her.

"After that, he started waiting for me. I couldn't go on my rides, anymore. My only escape was taken away. Even in church. He would always manage to get into a nearby seat. He would not do anything, of course. Too many eyes. But he would whisper things, or pass a slip of paper to me."

"What kind of things did he say?"

Another flush came over her face. "Nothing to repeat," she said. Then she got up from where she was sitting and began to pace around. "One time he waited in a doorway, the saddle company door, on the way to the livery. It is in a little box kind of opening. I didn't see him. He reached out and tried to pull me in." A little shudder passed through her shoulders.

He stood up and pulled her close. "I'll kill him."

She pushed away, her hands against his chest, and his hands moved to her arms. They were locked in a kind of standoff embrace.

"Do not say such a thing!" she said. Her eyes were fierce.

"All right, Lena. It's all right. I just feel like doing it, that's all. But I swear. If he follows you again…"

They let go of each other and sat back down.

"What happened next?"

"I kicked him. Hard. And ran back to school." Her eyes fired up at the memory. "But the thing is, I cannot go back. I would have to stay inside. All the time. No more escapes. No more riding." She was close to tears.

"But Lena, surely your pa won't make you go back. He knows about Castillo. He wouldn't put you in danger."

"Ha! He knows nothing about what Richard did."

"But he thrashed him. On your porch. I saw it."

"That had nothing to do with what happened between Richard and me. He doesn't know a thing about that. There is something else. Between them, I mean. Something about Richard's father. My mother does not know what it is."

Suddenly, she turned, eyes fierce, her hand clutching his arm.

"John Alexander, you must promise me something. Promise!"

He nodded.

"You must not tell Papi what I just told you. You must not! He will kill him!"

"I promise."

"My father. He loves me, I know. Wants what is best. But I cannot go back to St. Mary's. I am dying there."

"Does your mama know?" I asked.

"About Richard? No, she must not know, either. Already she suspects something. If she finds out, she will tell Papi, for her own reasons. She wants me back here. She loves me, too." Her voice trailed off. Her eyes got a hopeless look.

He took a deep breath.

"Lena, do you know who else loves you?"

Her eyebrows arched into question marks. He plunged off the cliff.

"I do. I have loved you ever since school. Our school. First as a student. Now, in a different way." He held his breath.

She sat there a moment, then—could it be?—her mouth lifted into the beginning of a smile.

He pulled her to him. He brushed the hair back from her face and touched his lips to hers. He was scared she would pull back, but glory be, she didn't! For once he wasn't clumsy. He had been practicing kissing the back of his hand, trying out different pressure, different ways of holding his lips, tight shut or slightly parted. But when he tasted the sweetness of her mouth, he forgot about all that and got lost in the astonishing feel of it.

His tongue traced the curve of her lips and as she parted them, the edge of her teeth. Her hands clutched his shoulders, but they seemed to stop short of pulling him closer. He pressed against her. Their bodies touched. Bright sparks went off in his head. It was all he could do to pull back. He held her slightly away from him and looked straight into her eyes.

"Lena, I want you to listen to me." He put on his tutor voice, the one that used to influence her. "You're near sixteen years old. You can't live your life for your mama and pa. You got to have your own life. Your pa, he's a good man. But it's not right for him to force you back to Denver City. It's too much."

He was afraid he'd gone too far. But she was rapt, her beautiful eyes taking him in.

"And your ma. She's set on you becoming a parade Indian. But it's not right to force that on you, either, if you don't want it."

Lena nodded. He swallowed hard and plunged ahead.

"Lena, I love you. I've loved you for a long time. I want you to live your own life. I'll do anything to make you happy. That's why I saved Otter for you. I see how your eyes shine when you're with her.

"I have a plan. I've been thinking about it for a long time. There's a beautiful place, on Owl Creek, up north a ways. Grass enough for a dozen horses. I've got a homestead claim on it. Even got a cabin started. It can be our place. Our new hideaway, all ours, together. All we need to do is…get married."

The words hung between them like a ripe apple. Would she pick it? She stood there for a long moment, mouth slightly parted, eyes searching his face. He couldn't stand the suspense.

He gave her shoulders a little shake, and said, "Lena, will you marry me?"

Heartbeats ticked by, way too many. But finally she nodded.

"Yes, John Alexander. Yes. I would like that."

He grabbed her and lifted her off her feet and swung her around in circles until, getting dizzy, he tripped and they sprawled into a heap on the sandy ground, and he started laughing, and pretty soon she was laughing too, and the relief of it led to a kind of helpless shaking that turned into sobs then back into laughter again, and before he knew it his hands started roaming over her body until she pushed them away.

They sat there on the sand, facing each other. He was grinning like a young fool, hungry for more touching. Otter walked over and poked her nose in between them, snorting. Laughing again, they pushed her away.

He told her of his plan for getting married, which he had mulled over for weeks. Right away, Lena saw the holes in it.

"Papi will never give permission," she said.

"Yes, you're right," I said. "That's why we won't ask."

"But he'll come after me."

He had thought plenty about that. He didn't think he'd get the tomahawk on the side of the head treatment. Mr. Medina liked him more than that. But Lena's father would never say yes to a marriage that would derail his plans for his daughter. Just running off together wasn't possible. He would find them. He would take her back. John wasn't sure he'd be able to stop him.

"That's why we've got to have a proper Catholic wedding," he said. "We'll have the blessing of the Church behind us. Your pa'll have to respect that. He won't like it, but he'll come to respect it." He said this with more certainty than he felt.

"But John Alexander, you are not Catholic."

"I have decided to become one."

Surprise washed over her face. "You are sure? You would do that for me?"

"For you, I'd sign up with the Devil himself."

Her frown told him it was the wrong thing to say.

"Just a joke," he said. "There is a parish in Boulder. I've already talked to a priest there. Old duffer, Father Frank. He gave me stuff to read. Two months. I can get confirmed in two months. To finish I have to attend some classes in July."

Lena smiled for a moment, then frowned again. "But John Alexander, your family…"

He laughed out loud. One of the side benefits of this plan would be the look on Pa's face when he heard of his son becoming a papist.

"Don't worry about that," he said. "There's nothing Pa can take away from me."

He moved over behind where she was sitting, sat down and wrapped his arms around her. Her body rested snugly against his. It felt like shelter in a storm. Then she suddenly stiffened and looked up.

"Permission," she said. "The priest will not marry us without my parents' permission."

"This one will."

"But a priest cannot..."

"You're right about most priests. But Father Frank's different. Goodale told me something about him. He's the same priest who married your parents, years ago."

Lena's eyebrows rose.

"He'll marry us. It's arranged." He didn't tell her about the twenty dollars it cost him. Twenty dollars and a bottle of whiskey.

"When?"

"July 13."

"Why then?"

"That's when he said he could do it. After confirmation class is over, in two months."

She thought for a moment. "What will we do until then?"

"You'll let your pa take you back to school. You'll tell him you're ready to finish. Tell him you want to stay down there, for summer school, so you can finish even faster. He'll be pleased. You carry on as usual. Tell the nuns you've stopped running away. Stay in St. Mary's. Don't go out. I don't trust that Castillo sonofa...."

He stopped himself just as Lena twisted around, reached back and placed a disapproving finger on his lips. She smiled. He kissed her finger.

"Then you make your last escape," he continued. "On July tenth, at night. You'll have to set it up the day before, with Jones. Just tell him you're going for a ride. Then head north. I'll ride down from here. We'll meet on Boulder Creek, at the road crossing just upstream from Goodale's place. We should both arrive before dawn on the eleventh. Then we can go on to Boulder from there."

"And you?"

"I'm fixing to head up to Owl Creek, to build the cabin. In a couple of months I should get the roof on, have it all ready for you. After we get hitched, we'll pick up Otter and head up there. Then our lives will begin."

"You have thought of everything." Lena turned and settled back against his chest, her hands resting on his knees.

"There's one thing worries me." He turned Lena to face him. "Lena, I'm plumb broke. I've spent all my money getting ready for this moment. I worry that I'll not be able to give you the things you're used to. The fine things. I'm afraid you'll... ."

She turned and shushed him again with a finger to his lips. That silent answer left him giddy with joy.

She rose to go. He kissed her again.

"I hate you leaving me. Do you remember that poem we read in school, *A Thing of Beauty is a Joy Forever*?"

"Yes, John Alexander, I do."

"You said it meant keeping something pretty in your mind. That's what I'm going to do, keep you in my mind."

"I hate going back to St. Mary's."

"It's only a couple more months. Then we'll be free. Nothing real bad can happen in two months."

68

Takansy
April 1872

From her hiding place in a clump of pine trees, Takansy watched Lena ride back toward the Crossing along the river road. Her daughter had been gone a long time. Too long. At first she thought Lena might have wandered away for a walk. Then she found Shy Bird gone, and suspicion grew that her daughter had stolen away to the Alexander homestead. She had disappeared after the sun passed high noon, and now here she was, hours later, returning from the direction of where Otter's rescuer lived.

What other secrets were hidden behind her daughter's innocent eyes? There was more to that Castillo boy's visit than Lena was willing to say. She remembered what John Alexander told her about Castillo talking to her daughter at the Denver church.

In time she would find the truth. At least now she could rest easier about young Castillo. He would not be back to claim her daughter. Her husband had seen to that. Now the threat was John Alexander.

Takansy held her breath as Lena rode by scarcely a stone's throw away. Head erect, mouth upturned, her daughter looked as if she were floating above Shy Bird's back. Takansy knew that feeling, had felt it herself. Lena was younger than she had been when she threw her life away over a young man. It must not happen again.

John Alexander had done a good thing in rescuing Otter. Perhaps he would not stand in the way of Lena's spirit path. But more likely, nature would intervene. They would have children. Lena must not have children so young. It would take her away from her path. As the keeper of Alexander's lodge, she would have little time for horses. John Alexander had nothing. Lena would have to work hard just to survive.

Takansy left her hiding place, walked back to the Crossing and slipped back into their house, unnoticed. She would have to act soon, before her husband forced their daughter back to St. Mary's.

The otter pouch lay on the floor beside Lena's cast off clothes. Steam billowed over the edge of the large metal tub in which she bathed. Lena's soft crooning mingled with the sounds of water being scooped onto skin. Sounds of contentment.

Takansy willed her joints not to pop as she hunkered down beside her daughter's moccasins. The small tin in her left hand felt hot. It held the mysterious white powder, coarse brown mineral grains and desiccated roots of the tiny yellow alpine flowers that Otter Woman had braided together in the long ago. "Spirit theft," the old medicine woman had called it. Powerful magic. It had worked its spell on Charges Ahead. The young brave had come courting not two days after Takansy had secretly dropped a pinch of the root-powder mixture into his moccasin.

Would the magic work again? Would it bind Lena to her? She pinched off a tiny strand of the twinned roots and placed it inside Lena's right-foot moccasin. Then she sprinkled a bit of powder and grainy mineral on top. She closed the tin, creaked to her feet and crept from the room.

Despite the chill, sweat beaded her forehead. She tried not to think about what had happened to Charges Ahead after she had stolen his spirit with the mysterious mixture, about the Blackrobe's calling it "The Devil's powder." She hid the tin in the back of the drawer next to the obsidian blade, made the crossing sign and knelt to work her way through the rosary.

The following afternoon, Takansy trailed Lena down to the river. The time of the New Grass Moon had come, the time of new things. Sunlight filtered through the emerging cottonwood leaves and dappled Lena's glowing face. She saw with dismay that Lena walked as if floating on mist.

She caught up with her daughter as she reached the river bank. Lena started, then covered her surprise with a smile.

"Hello, Mami."

Takansy tucked a stray strand of hair behind her daughter's ear, and let her fingers linger there, resting lightly against the soft skin of her daughter's cheek.

"My flower. So happy you seem. What is happening with you?"

Lena looked away.

"Mami, I hope you will understand. I want to go back to school. It's just one more year. A little less if I go to summer school in June. I want to do that. Then I can come home and Papi will let me have Otter back, and then we can train her. We can work with the horses together." Lena cast her mother a tentative glance and just as quickly looked away. "Then everything will be as it was."

Summer school! The announcement hit Takansy like Medina's slap. Why in the name of Jésu would Lena want to return to such a place? She fought to keep her face still. Something lay hidden beneath her daughter's nervous smile. She must dig it out.

"But my daughter, just yesterday you are saying no to going back. What is changing in you?"

Instead of responding, Lena looked at the river. It gurgled along, not yet swollen with the spring rise.

"My daughter, to the Alexander boy you are feeling close, is it not so?" The startled look on Lena's face told her the answer. "It is to be expected. Otter he is saving for you, and you are thankful. I, also, am full of thanks." She kept her voice soft, sympathetic. "To going with such a boy, it is a natural thing."

Lena poked at a rock with the toe of her moccasin.

"My daughter, there is something you must know. Telling you this makes my heart heavy, but it is best you are knowing. Before you are having the idea to going off with the Alexander boy."

Lena's foot halted in mid-poke, her body tensing. She made no protest, no denial.

"Just before Christmas, the Alexander boy is coming here. Here he is meeting the Bartholf girl. Miss Julie. They are touching lips. There, on the porch. I am seeing them with my two eyes. They are talking, laughing together. Making plans."

Lena's face drained of color. Takansy drew her close and stroked her hair.

"John Alexander's is good, he is doing a good thing for you. But, my daughter, you must understand, he is too old for you. He and Miss Julie, she is woman, he is man, same years. About you he is caring much, but not in the way of man and wife. That is what he is doing with Miss Julie. Her mother is telling me this, that they will marry." A lie, but a necessary one.

Tears filled in Lena's eyes. "No, that cannot be. He told me…" Her shoulders began to quiver.

Takansy pressed her daughter's face into her neck, the familiar place used through the years to comfort hurts.

"My daughter, along your woman's way you are just beginning. Too soon becoming a mother is tying you like a rope, keeping you from your spirit path. Your spirit goes to your babies, not to the horses. Not to Otter. You are too young for having babies."

Slowly she rocked Lena in her arms. She felt her daughter's body settle in closer.

"Young Alexander has nothing. He cannot take care of horses. Even Otter, he cannot. For that he is coming to me, for hay. What can he give your babies? Nothing. About such things you must think, for the good of your future children. To go with a man, it is a big thing. You must think. There is much beyond the first fire of your heart." She felt Lena's head, still buried in her neck, give a little nod.

"Tell me, my daughter, what John Alexander is telling you, what you are doing with him."

Like a log jam breaking in the river beside them, Lena's words spilled out. She told about John Alexander's conversion, the plan to get married, to run away to a homestead, to take Otter, to start a cattle and horse ranch on Owl Creek.

"Julie Bartholf, it cannot be. He just now asked me to marry him, an hour ago." Lena wiped her eyes, which turned defiant.

Takansy's head swirled. Things had progressed much further than she had feared. Her mind thrashed around for a new talking way. She gently tilted Lena's face to look directly into her glistening eyes.

"My daughter, life with a man, one you care for, it is a good thing. And marrying your Alexander, it is possible. Listen to me well. Time is needed. Time for him to become strong for you. Time to make a special wedding ceremony. Time to find different land where your father cannot come for you. Owl Creek, it is too close by."

"But Mami, John Alexander is becoming Catholic, he is arranging a Catholic wedding, and Papi, he will have to accept it. He must…"

"Oh, my flower…my flower. Your father, he is not agreeing to marrying the Alexander boy, Catholic or no Catholic. In your heart you are knowing this is true, yes?"

Lena's face crumpled again.

Takansy clasped her close, and, like a sprinkle of magic powder, the talking way revealed itself.

"Shush, my daughter. In time all things are possible. You must trust me. Here is what we are doing. To school of summer, you go as planning. Your father is suspecting nothing. Then I am sending for you. We are going away together, mother and daughter, Shy Bird and Otter, to visit the land of my childhood, the Bitterroot. I am speaking with the Alexander boy, looking into his heart. Making sure he is turning away from Miss Julie. Helping him get horses, and cows. Then we are sending for him, and you and he are wedding, when the time is right."

Lena's eyes rounded. "Oh, Mami, that would be so wonderful! But, I have already…John Alexander is…"

"I am speaking with your young man. It is only for a short time, the waiting. You are meeting my people, learning from them. We are finding land to live on, plenty horses for you and John Alexander. Then we are sending for him. He is coming north and marrying you. Everything is being as you wish."

Lena nodded, but Takansy felt tenseness in her shoulders.

"What about Papi? I don't know if I can just leave him. He will be so sad."

"He will be angry. Remember him selling Otter! But in time,

even he is softening his heart. We can be telling him where we are when the anger is passed. After you and John Alexander are safely together."

Doubt lingered on Lena's face. Takansy gripped her shoulders.

"My daughter, I am old woman. My time is coming to enter the next world. I am having one last hope. To seeing my daughter walking her Spirit Path, to seeing her with good husband, and to seeing the land of my people one last time. And later, with her father once again. All this can be happening. You must be trusting me."

Lena's shoulders finally relaxed. "Yes. Yes. That is the best way." She smiled and gave Takansy a hug.

The magic had worked. They would ride north, covering their tracks with all the cunning Takansy possessed. Ride to freedom and a new life. For a while, Lena would pine for Alexander. But she would recover, and they would get on with their lives together. Her daughter would bloom and fulfill her destiny. Takansy would die content.

Takansy broke their embrace to look her daughter in the eye.

"It is decided, then. Listen well. A message you are to be receiving. Look for it inside the next food basket I am sending you. At the bottom, hidden. Hidden under the cloth. A secret, two moons from now. It is taking me two moons, the preparing. Then we are meeting and leaving. The rendezvous place, in the message you are finding it. You are coming then." She gripped Lena's head in her hands and forced their eyes to meet. "A secret. Not telling anyone. Not young Alexander. You are promising?"

Lena nodded.

"Thank you Mami. Thank you." Her arms reached around to pull her mother close. "I love you Mami."

"Two moons more in the school. But there is one more thing you must be promising me." She held Lena away so she could fix her with her eyes. "About the red-top boy, I know you are not telling all. He is danger, like the rattlesnake. You are staying inside that school, promising me you are not going out. Not seeing him."

Lena nodded.

"Say it, you promising."

"I promise, Mami."

Takansy pulled her close again.

"Stay safe, my flower. Stay safe."

69

Medina
April 1872

Medina breathed in the scent of Lena's hair. It matched the freshness of the spring day. She had fallen asleep as they entered Denver City and now slumped into the cradle of his arm and shoulder which he used to cushion her against the jounce of the wagon. The bluish pasqueflowers she had pinned into her hair were still fresh.

She had surprised him with the summer school idea, her telling him how eager she was to go back to St. Mary's, to continue learning, playing the mandolin, how splendid it all was, and what a lucky girl she was to have a father who would pay to send her to such a place.

Perhaps now his wife would stop her vexing attempts to lure Lena back home. Strangely, Takansy had not objected to summer school. The look on her face, never easy to read, seemed resigned, yet more than that. Medina had the uneasy feeling something lurked beneath the surface of this too-easy outcome.

The chill of early spring had vanished. Late-afternoon sunshine warmed his shoulders. It had showered in Denver City the day before, and the streets were free of dust. Energized by the change of season, the team of grays kept up a brisk trot as they neared the end of their journey.

He bent his head and brushed his lips against Lena's hair. She snuggled closer. An almost embarrassing wave of feeling passed through him, a strange mix of pleasure, satisfaction, nostalgia and sadness. Lena had touched something in him, something he couldn't name. A kind of joy, perhaps.

His daughter had just tuned fifteen, the year of her *quinceñera.* To celebrate her coming of age, he would orchestrate the grandest *fiesta* anyone had ever seen at the Crossing. Instead of its traditional timing on her birthday, which had already passed while she was in school, the celebration would take place in the fall, his favorite time of year. He imagined her in a pink gown, being applauded by the crowd he would assemble. He imagined escorting her to the dance floor for the first waltz.

What he couldn't imagine was who he would choose for her *Chambelan.* He was fond of John Alexander, but the boy's poverty ruled him out. Lena's escort would need to be the son of a community leader, someone like Bisam Bartholf, although he was a little young. Medina would think about it more when he returned. Plenty of time to decide.

When he reached Jones Mercantile, he pulled the team to a halt. Next door, the Elephant Corral pulsed with visitors, new arrivals from the east packing mining gear, their faces full of glittery hope. The city was growing, new stone buildings replacing the rough wooden ones that had sprung up during the stampede for gold.

Lena stirred, stretched and smiled up at him. He brushed a speck of sleep crust from the corner of her eye. He wondered if she was coming down with a cold. Sometimes he felt like a fussy old woman the way he worried about Lena's health.

"Jones," he said. "I will speak with him a moment."

Lena came alive when she saw where they were.

"There's Salty Joe," she said, pointing to one of the horses in the Corral. "And Sparky." She jumped down and ran to the horses.

Medina marveled at how lovely she had become. His eyes swept the street and found several men looking her way. He glowered at them, but they didn't seem to notice.

He found Jones at the back of the store.

"*Hola*, Jones!" he said, giving the merchant his Spanish greeting embrace. "How many innocents are you to cheat today?"

Jones pushed away with a gap-toothed smile.

"You'll be my first. I see you have your runaway daughter with you. Is she going for another horse ride?"

"No, my friend, I am to take her back to the Academy."

"Why did she run away? I was worried, sent word to you on the next stage as soon as I found out what happened. But I figured that girl knows her horses."

"She rode home. She say she miss her father. Comes to visit."

"She is beautiful. You must be proud of her."

Medina nodded as he watched Lena stroking a small sorrel mare.

"Jones, I to ask you a favor."

"Sure."

"There is a young man here. A student at the boy's school. Tall, thin. Easy to spot by red hair that grows here to here." Medina used his hand to trace the location of Castillo's strange topknot. "Same color of that mare, only redder."

"I seen a lad like that. Hangs around here sometime. Handsome, in a starched shirt sort of way."

"Yes, but no good. I know his family before." Medina lowered his voice. "Ever he try to be with my Lena?"

"You mean has he been sniffing around your daughter? Not that I've seen. When she rides, she goes out alone." Jones grinned. "You ain't ready to marry her off, is that it?"

"To him, never. He is poison. He follows my Lena all the way to the Crossing. I teach him manners and he goes away mad. Very mad."

"You beat him up pretty good?"

"Well, yes. Sonofbitch files a lawsuit against me next day, in district court at Fort Collins."

"A lawsuit! We never settled things like that in the old days."

Jones was right, and paradoxically, Medina had relaxed a little after the filing. If that was Castillo's revenge, he could perhaps stop worrying. But he wanted to make sure.

"Jones, I ask you as friend. That boy comes around my Lena, you run him off, yes? You see them together, you let me know *pronto*."

Jones's smile faded. "Why sure, *amigo*. I'll give him the evil Irish eye."

"And Jones, please to help me pass the word along. The bars, stores, everyone, yes?"

"Sure, Mariano. Sounds important."

"A thousand thanks. And one thing more. Not to let her to take horses again. No more riding out from here, yes?"

Jones nodded.

"I to take her to school now, tell the nuns the same warning, then I come back and buy from you. The barbed wire, I need."

Jones smiled again.

"Got a new shipment. For you, my friend, a special price."

Medina put on a mock glare. "Special high price, I think." Then with a grin, he returned to Lena.

When they arrived at the Academy, Lena jumped down and rang the bell. Medina tied up the grays, walked over and turned her to face him.

"Lena, *mi hija*, there is something you must promise me." He made his voice stern. "No more horse riding in the countryside. I have spoken to Jones about it. And no more walking about Denver City. I to speak to the nuns about it. You to stay here behind the fence unless you are going somewhere with your teachers."

Lena's face wrinkled into a frown. "Papi, I…"

"Promise me."

"Papi, please. Let me at least visit the corral. Just once in a while. I will not ride, but at least let me visit the horses. Please, Papi. ."

Medina felt himself soften. He looked toward the Elephant Corral two blocks away.

"Well, perhaps a few times, maybe, if you tell the nuns where you are going. I will tell them and Jones that much is all right."

She flung her arms around him. "Thank you, oh thank you, Papi." Then she pulled back, hands still clasping his shoulders. "I love you, Papi." Then tears spilled from her eyes and she turned away.

Embarrassed, he turned to see a nun approaching. He patted Lena's shoulder.

"Just stay safe, my daughter," he said. "Stay safe."

70

Takansy
June 1872

Takansy pulled the small metal trap from under her shirt and placed it inside a leather bag she had cached beneath a red sandstone boulder. The trap would help feed them on their way north. Cottontail rabbits, muskrats, even birds. She tightened the drawstring and replaced the flat stone that hid the cache from view. Her preparations were nearly complete.

To keep the trap from clanking when she walked out of the trading post, she had strapped it to her waist with a strip of leather. She needn't have bothered. Medina scarcely noticed her anymore. At the start of her secret trips to the cache, he had asked her where she was going. "Walking," she had replied. "Breathing the spring air. And where you are going when you leave in the buckboard?"

Medina had looked away.

"Deliveries," he had said. He hadn't asked her again.

She rose and glanced at the red cliff above, the ridge she had explored when the dreams came, the one with the hidden valley and secret "resting place" the gray jay had shown her. Their escape route would be up there, where they would not be seen.

She made her way back along the river trail toward the Crossing. A smile tugged at her mouth as she recalled how Lena had convinced Medina she wanted to return for the school of summer. How he had preened when hearing those lies! How he gathered them, like powder and ball, to shoot at her if she ever again dared to argue that Lena was miserable in that place. He suspected nothing.

One more task needed doing, and it posed a risk. A secret note to Lena, to hide in the bread basket—a note she could not write. It would have to be ready in time for Medina's next trip to Denver City. She would need the help of Lucas Brandt.

She found him in the tavern tipping the usual late afternoon whiskey with Louie Papa.

"Louie, my son, I am needing your help. Two stacks of shirts and pants, my beadwork, they are in our house on the table. You are please carrying them for me to the store?" To Lucas Brandt she said, by way of explanation, "My bones, they are aching, from the age."

Lucas Brandt raised his glass to her.

"Ma'am, I hope I'm always as fit as you are. My bones already ache, and I'm still a frisky cowboy." He laughed as Louie Papa left to do her bidding.

When he was gone, Takansy seized Lucas Brandt's arm.

"Your help I am needing, for the writing way. For a surprise, a secret. You are helping me, yes?"

"Why sure, Ma'am. Happy to."

She pulled him to a back table and handed him a pencil and paper. She huddled close, keeping her voice low.

"My Lena is coming to visit, but no one must know. We are surprising my husband. You are not telling anyone, not Louie, yes?"

"A surprise!" Lucas Brandt's face burst into a smile. "I know how your husband dotes on that girl."

"Be quick." She glanced toward the bar. The bartender had his back to them. "Here are the words: All is arranged. Meeting at Dry Creek and Big Thompson. July 12, at midnight. Otter waiting."

"Who's Otter?"

"Part of the secret. Hurry."

Lucas Brandt's writing was slow. Takansy felt sweat trickling in front of her ears. When he finally finished, she snatched up the paper and slipped it inside her sleeve.

"Thank you," she whispered.

They got seated back at the bar just as Louie Papa returned.

A week later she tucked the paper between two pieces of cloth at the bottom of a basket of sweet cakes. Medina took the basket without comment and set off for Denver City.

Two days after that, Medina handed her the empty basket along with a folded paper. Her heart nearly fell out of her chest.

"Lena says thank you for the cakes. She says to tell you she is happy. She sends for you a picture, a horse."

Takansy resumed breathing. She opened the paper. The drawing was an exact likeness of Otter.

71

John Alexander
June 1872

It took John Alexander two months of hard labor to build their cabin on Owl Creek. Logging was the easy part, he was used to that. Ponderosas were close at hand, and after he trimmed and skinned the logs, it wasn't too much of a haul for his Illiff pinto to drag them to the site. There were plenty of flat foundation stones nearby next to the red sandstone outcrop he'd chosen for the cabin. It gave nice shelter from north wind, and was real pretty, like the hideout. There was some good ground sloping gently down to the creek from where the front door would be, space for a garden and a nice corral and barn. He built the corral under a big cottonwood, shade for Otter. He kept picturing Lena coming out of the door, stretching in the morning sun, and walking down to feed her horse with a smile on her face.

By the end of June he managed to create a pretty little cabin, not as nice as Mr. Medina's, but a whole lot nicer than the dugout. He felt proud of himself. He imagined Lena looking out the window to see him ride up with a wave and a holler. He liked imagining her face there.

For the floor and roof he needed some saw-cut boards. He persuaded Pa to let him take a load in return for working at the sawmill. He told him it was for a cabin he was building for a fellow down near Boulder City.

Pa had changed a bit. He was still sour as vinegar, but there was more man-to-man talk since John had stood up for himself and shown he could get by on his own. With the extra income from summer tenters, Pa had gotten himself another hired man by the name of Rufus McSwain, who Pa bossed around instead of John. Rufus McSwain was a red cheeked Irish fellow who liked to play the fiddle of an evening. And Jennie had cottoned to him, so she wasn't paying much attention to John's doings.

Mattie, on the other hand, was curious as all get out.

"Can I go with ye, Johnnie?" she asked when he got the boards loaded up.

"Can't do it, Mattie. I'm headed all the way to Boulder City and will have to stay a month or more."

She had turned fourteen and was perfecting the pout, which she turned on with full force. He winked and chucked her under the chin, and the pout dissolved in a giggle.

"Besides, I need you to stay here and take care of Otter while I'm gone. You'll do it, won't you?

She nodded yes and gave him a hug.

Robert helped him with the boards. He had just turned twelve and had taken to wearing a shirt with no sleeves so he could watch his arm muscles grow. John gave him some pointers on how to keep a head of steam in the boiler and run the boards through without binding. Robert took it all in, real serious.

"You're becoming a good man," John told him.

Robert tried not to smile.

Anna, now thirteen, had turned pretty, real blond, a little like Julie Bartholf. She stuck close to Mama, who seemed to need her. Mama had given up on trying to get John to stay. She'd look at him all wistful now and then, but didn't say anything.

Now that he was going to be shut of them for good, he started missing them. Strange. Of course he couldn't tell them he would soon be a married Catholic with a homestead of his own.

He told his family he'd be back around July tenth, and set off with a wagonload of boards. Mac wagged him over the bridge but stopped on the other side. His roaming days looked to be about over. John hoped he'd still be alive when he got back.

In Ft. Collins he stopped long enough to purchase two bed sheets in exchange for three days labor. They were real linen, a wedding present for his new bride. The thought of crawling between those sheets with her kept him awake nights.

On July first, he swept out the cabin, locked the door and headed to Boulder City for his confirmation class. He was the only one there. The lessons weren't what he'd expected after years of Pa ranting about papists. There was nothing about the Inquisition or idol worship. It wasn't all that different, in fact, from what he'd learned in Presbyterian Sunday school.

Father Frank would squint up his bony face and fire questions about the seven sacraments, the seven gifts of the Holy Spirit, the four cardinal virtues, and the beatitudes. John fired the answers right back. The old priest didn't try to trip him up. He already had his twenty dollars and from the looks of him, he'd spent it all on whiskey.

On the final day, he laid his hand on John's cheek and anointed him with the Holy Sprit and his whiskey breath.

"Don't forget," John said. "I'll be back in three days to get married. July twelfth, like we arranged."

Father Frank gave him a snaggle-toothed grin. "Just be here before noon. My afternoons are taken up with other business."

"We'll be here."

John rode back to the dugout to finish packing and wait for midnight, July eleventh. He practically had to tie himself down to keep everyone from seeing how excited he was. The night of his secret leaving, Mama fixed a nice supper, a rare stew with onions and fresh greens. She fussed over him like he was the king of Siam, while Pa asked him about the house in Boulder. The grouch was gone out of Pa, at least for that meal, and even Jennie seemed pleasant. Robert studied how John spooned his stew, and Anna padded around helping Mama.

By the time John stretched out to sleep on the pallet next to Mattie's, he felt almost sad about leaving them, about how upset they might feel when they woke up and found him gone for good. The pang lasted only a moment. In less than six hours, he would meet Lena at their secret rendezvous on Boulder Creek, and his new life would begin.

72

Takansy
July 1872

Awakened by a strange unease, Takansy rose from her pallet and crept through the doorway into the main room of their house. Her knees hurt, but they were not the cause of her restlessness. Voices had spoken to her. Low, hushed voices, the kind that come from rocks. Not red sandstone spirits, but darker voices.

River, they said. *River what? River*, they repeated. Was the strain of waiting for Lena's escape causing her to hear things? She shook her head to clear it. But the voices still murmured like the sound of water swirling over rocks.

The past two moons had not been easy. The secret preparations. The pretense of normal life. Allaying her husband's watchfulness. *One more day to go.* Tomorrow she would take Shy Bird, steal Otter back, meet Lena at their secret rendezvous and ride away. *Yes, ride.* She would have to break her long-held vow. There was no other way. She hoped God would forgive her.

Her husband snored away, undisturbed, in the bed they used to share. Her eyes wandered the walls. His Hawken hung in its place of honor, draped with his pouch, belt and powder horn. Moonlight gleamed off its polished barrel.

She tiptoed to her altar. Her fingers traced the silver crucifix's familiar lines and touched the carved statue of Jésu. These things she would leave behind to confuse Medina into thinking her upcoming disappearance would be temporary.

She knelt on the cushion and crossed herself. "Lord Jésu," she whispered, "all praise be unto you, giver of life. Bring my Lena safely to me. Keep her in your loving arms. Help her to live her life in the way of the Horse Spirit. Use me to help her on her path."

The feeling of well-being that usually enfolded her in such moments did not come. Opening her eyes, she focused on the wooden face before her. Softly lit in the diffused moonlight, it stared back, unblinking. *Am I doing something wrong? Have I sinned by just deciding to break my vow, even before actually doing it?*

She repeated her prayer to the Creator Spirit of her people. Not so long ago she would have thought that blasphemy—now, an extra precaution.

For herself, she added, "Chase away the bad spirits that speak to me in the night."

No response. She tried to brush away the cold feeling of abandonment. It probably came from the hard waiting, a foolish woman's fears.

She pulled herself to her feet. The Jésu figure wobbled dangerously. She grabbed it and glanced toward the inner room where Medina slept. She slipped on her moccasins and stole out the door. It protested with a rusty creak. *I must grease that before tomorrow's escape.* Outside on the porch, the river smell floated to her.

River. The troubling voices again. She set out for the toll bridge. The sound of crickets stilled as she walked past, then rose again behind her. A horned owl flew across her path on silent wings. The hairs on her neck rose. She quickened her pace.

Moonlight filtered through the canopy of cottonwood leaves and spotted the ground with shifting shapes. A chill ribbon of night air curled around her as she neared the bridge and heard the river's rushing hiss. Halfway across, she leaned against the bridge railing and peered into the swirling current, still running high with the last of the snow melt. The water writhed in the moonlight. A branch swept by, caught in its grasp.

A click of hoof on rock caught her attention. Her eyes probed the shadowy thickets of chokecherry and willow along the river bank. There it was again. Suddenly chilled, she ran downstream along the riverbank trail, her chest laboring. The first ford below the bridge was empty—two worn tracks leading down to the dark river. As she neared the second ford, a gray horse thrashed its way out of the underbrush. She froze. The horse snorted, then stumbled toward her, tripping on the single rein that dangled underfoot. On its back was a cinched-on blanket and a dark object with a long neck and pear-shaped body that Takansy recognized. *Lena's mandolin.*

"Lena?" Then louder, "Lena!"

She ran past the startled horse and turned toward the river. A crumpled form lay partially submerged, rocking gently in the river's lapping grip. Even before she pulled it from the water, she saw the matted dark hair, the parted lips, the neck and face splotches, the staring eyes.

Lena!

She staggered back and sat with a *whump* on the river stones. A sound unlike any she had ever made shrieked out of her and echoed along the river through the trees, shattering the still night air.

David M. Jessup

73

Medina
July 1872

Medina rolled to his side, swung his feet over the edge of the bed, pulled out the chamber pot and let fly with an acrid-smelling stream of urine. The confounded need to piss interrupted his sleep more and more, it seemed. He knew it would be useless to try to doze off again. His finger stub hurt. He rubbed it back to tingling life, then stretched his arms over his head to pop the kinks out of his back. It was taking longer these days to get his body going.

He began a mental check of the day's doings. A horse buyer from the east would arrive that morning, a *medico* named Dr. Hutchinson who planned to settle next to Lord Ogelvie. A good time to sell, early July, when his horses were groomed clean of their winter hair and fattened up, sleek and well-muscled. Later, he would meet a Larimer County delegation who proposed to buy his toll bridge for two hundred dollars, probably a bargain considering that two new bridges being constructed downstream would undercut his prices anyway.

In the afternoon he would pack for tomorrow's trip to Denver. He made a mental note to pick up more books about Billy Cody from Jones. People were buzzing about "Buffalo Bill" guiding some foreign archduke on a buffalo hunt. Maybe he could finagle a Cody visit to the store. That would pack them in.

He stretched and reached for the familiar form of his wife, then remembered her separate pallet on the floor. Sighing, he groped his way to the armoire and pulled on his fancy blue pants with the sharp crease and the gold side-stripes. Newcomers like Dr. Hutchinson never quite knew what to make of a so-called "Mexican" dressed like a Spanish *patrón*. It kept them off balance, more willing to buy.

In the filtered moonlight he noticed his wife's pallet was empty. Strange. He was usually the first one up. He moved on into the kitchen to draw some water with the indoor pump handle and splashed it on his face. He lit a fire in the stove, tossed a handful of ground coffee into the pot and set it on the stove to boil. He lit his morning pipe and walked out onto the porch.

The night air was warm, unusually still. Not a leaf stirred. The river's rush was the only sound.

Across the courtyard, his trading post gleamed white in the moonlight. He could make out the *ristras* of last year's dried peppers Lena had hung on the porch posts before returning to summer school. He would visit her in Denver, perhaps hear her play the mandolin.

He tapped last night's ashes from his pipe. At that moment his wife's scream rose out of the riverbottom and lanced through the silent trees. He dropped the pipe, sprang from the porch and dashed toward the river.

Doctor Hutchinson stepped away from Lena and pointed to the reddish patches on her face, neck and chest.

"Scarlet fever."

Her body lay on the dining table, partly covered with a linen cloth. Lena's eyelids were half open, lips slightly parted. Her long hair, cleansed of river debris and combed by Takansy, spilled over the table's edge like a black veil.

The doctor lifted the cloth and drew it over Lena's face. As it fluttered down with terrible finality, Medina glimpsed her budding breasts, the small mound of dark hair sprouting between her legs. He turned away, unable to look any longer.

"It can be terribly quick and lethal, for some people," Doctor Hutchinson said. "Of course with proper care, staying in bed, drinking plenty of hot tea…the young can sometimes survive. I'm terribly sorry." He opened the black bag at his feet and dropped in the shiny instrument he had used to pry open Lena's mouth. "You say she was in Denver City, at school? Why did she leave to come here…when she was so sick, I mean?"

Medina jumped from his chair, knocking it backward. Without quite knowing how, he reached Takansy sitting in the other corner of the room and slapped her hard across the face.

"Why did she leave?" His voice came out strangled. "Why!?"

It was like speaking to stone. The ghost eyes stared through him, her expression no different from when he had found her on the river bank with Lena a few hours ago. The answer would have to wait until he could get to Denver City.

The doctor edged toward the door, eyebrows raised. "Can I help? Send for a priest, perhaps?"

"One of my men is to go, already. We are to bury her in the cemetery, there." He pointed toward the low stone wall guarding the graves of Rosita and Martín.

Medina suddenly remembered why the doctor had come.

"A thousand thanks, Doctor. Please see Valdez. At the barn. He will show the horses."

Medina closed the door behind the doctor and walked back to the table where Lena lay. A small silver crucifix on the mantle caught his eye. He placed it on the linen covering Lena's body and turned toward his wife.

"She needs to be dressed. I cannot… ."

Takansy bounded from her chair, eyes wild. With a push she sent him staggering back from the corpse. She grabbed the crucifix and heaved it at the log wall. Whirling, she rushed into the adjoining room. By the time Medina got to the door, candles were flying off her altar. She smashed the heavy silver cross onto the floor until the arms broke away, then heaved the base through the doorway, narrowly missing his head. She grabbed the wooden Jésu statue and pounded its face to a featureless mangle. Strange grunting sounds came from her.

Her braids unraveled. She snatched her rosary and flung it at him. Beads peppered the walls and his face.

He reached for her flying hands and managed to catch a wrist. Her other fist smacked into his cheek just under his eye. He twisted her around, trapped her arms against her body and held on until she finally went limp. He lowered her to the floor.

"What is it you know?" he shouted. "You know why she left school. Tell me!"

No response. She lay spent on the floor.

He released her and stepped away. "Dress her," he said, and walked out the door.

Grabbing a shovel from the shed, he climbed the hill to the cemetery, shoved through the gate and started digging. Visions of Lena wandering through Purgatory's fiery landscape flooded his mind. He'd never thought much about such things, but now the stories he heard from his childhood priests came back to him, stories of lost souls suffering throughout eternity. His mother's face, last seen when he was fifteen, appeared before him, warning about the fate of those who leave life without a priest's blessing. Worst of all was the fear of never seeing Lena again in the afterlife. A *padre* was what he needed. A priest would know what to do.

He drove the shovel into the hard ground. Dirt and rocks piled up beside the hole as he dug. Spent, he cast the shovel aside, slumped against the mound and began to sob.

74

Takansy
July 1872

Inside the house, Takansy opened the armoire and pulled out Lena's beaded white doeskin parade dress. She wrestled the garment over her daughter's head and shoulders by rolling the body to one side, then the other. When she forced a stiff arm into a sleeve, the elbow made a sickening pop. I am hurting her, she thought, before realizing its absurdity. She gritted her teeth and forced herself to finish.

Lena's eyelids were half open, her mouth parted unnaturally. Try as she might, Takansy couldn't get them closed. With a little shudder she finally gave up and began lacing together the beautiful white deer hides, originally intended for a magnificent new dress for her daughter. Now they were becoming her shroud. The last garment she would ever sew for Lena.

Her use of the spirit magic weighed on her like a stone. It had convinced Lena to run away to the Bitterroot when she was too sick to travel. She bit her lip, fought to concentrate on her work.

The broken Jésu lay in the corner. The Blackrobe religion had betrayed her. Destroyed what she loved most.

She glanced out the window to where Medina shoveled. The irony of it struck her. He was now the fervent Catholic insisting on a priest and full rites, she, Jésu's denier. She looked at the growing mound of earth in the cemetery and spat.

With sudden clarity, she saw what she must do. In this life she was unable to save Lena. In the next, she must help Lena travel to the Great Beyond where her ancestors' spirits roamed, where she, herself, would soon go.

The hidden cave on the sandstone ridge was meant to be Lena's final resting place. That's what the gray jay—Otter Woman—had been trying to tell her. She must steal her daughter's body and carry her to the hidden valley where Medina would never find it. *Tonight when he sleeps.*

She tied off the last stitch and opened a window. To the west, a towering thunderhead boiled up over the mountains. It would soon blot out the setting sun. She closed the window, and with a new sense of resolve, began her preparations.

David M. Jessup

PART 3

NOW

July 12, 1872

David M. Jessup

75

John Alexander

John Alexander has waited since midnight for Lena to appear at their secret rendezvous on Boulder Creek. Now it is dawn, and he is at Goodale's place. His head reels from what Tim Goodale has just told him: A week ago Lena had a "horse accident." Her dress torn, her arms scratched, she returned to St. Mary's and fell ill with fever. Then she went missing.

He wheels around in front of Goodale and urges his pinto into a ground-eating lope toward Denver City. A dark suspicion grows in his mind that whatever happened to Lena was no accident. His hands, gripping the reins, ball into fists.

Four hours later he arrives at St. Mary's. She also tells him Lena has not returned after her disappearance two nights ago. But she does tell him where to find Richard Castillo. She points down the street to a single-story brick building.

"In the hospital. Scarlet fever." Her nose wrinkles as if she could smell the disease.

He rushes to the hospital, dismounts, and hurries from window to window. When he finds the room he is seeking, he raises the sash and climbs through. A strange mix of tincturous odors assails his nostrils. He listens for footfalls in the hallway, but the only sound is Ricardo Castillo's raspy breathing.

He gapes at the figure in the hospital bed. Burning eyes stare back at him, hollow fever holes in a gray face, skin splotched with darker patches, reddish islands in a pale sea. His lips have lost their arrogant smile. They hang slack, quivering with each labored breath. Even the mop of red hair looks diseased, plastered against Castillo's sweaty skull. Four scratch marks darken his skin from cheek to neck.

"What do you want?" Castillo's voice croaks.

"When did you last see Lena?"

The fevered eyes narrow. "Why do you want to know?"

"Tell me, goddam you."

Castillo manages a weak smile. "Why should I? What will you do if I don't? Kill me?" He hacks out a wheezy laugh.

"Lena is missing. Run away. And she's bad sick with the fever."

The laughter stops. Eyebrows arch over eyes glittery with sudden interest. "Sick? What of?"

"Maybe the same thing you got."

"The scarlet fever?" A smile stretches the pallid skin tight over Castillo's protruding cheek bones. "The scarlet fever." He seems to savor the phrase. A laugh starts deep within and shakes his body into another wracking wheeze. He wipes his lips.

John stares at the patches on Castillo's face and imagines them on Lena's skin. He shakes off his rising panic.

"When did you last see her?" It is all he can do to keep from smashing that leering face. He advances a step despite his fear of the disease. "When!?"

Richard Castillo swivels his eyes back to Alexander's. "I will tell you on one condition. You tell that little shit *peón*, Medina, my exact words. You agree?"

"Yes. Yes, go on."

"Ten days ago, on her way to the livery. Our usual meeting place—the clothing store with the doors sunk back from the street. Where Medina's spies can't see us."

John's stomach heaves. "Did you touch her?"

"Of course. She was very passionate that day. Covered me with so many kisses I had to hold her back. I was feeling weak. The beginning of the sickness, you know."

Alexander's guts spasm. "You lying dog! She hated you!"

"Is that what she told you? You are such a romantic. You believe anything a girl... "

"She ran away from you!"

"Shush! You will bring the nurse." He lowers his voice, forcing John to lean closer.

"A lover's quarrel. We argued about our escape together. She wanted to go sooner. I wanted to wait until after school was out."

"She wouldn't. That's not... ."

"Not possible? You live in dreams." The sneer is back on Castillo's lips. "Tell Medina his precious daughter was planning to run away with me. Instead, the fever has taken her. Either way, I'm responsible. Tell him that. Then he will know that justice is done."

"Justice? What are you talking about?"

"Justice!" Castillo spits out the word so hard it brings on a coughing fit. His eyes glitter.

Comprehension suddenly dawns on John Alexander. To Castillo, Lena is nothing but a means of revenge.

"She scratched your face pretty good. I hope she kicked you in the nuts, too, you lying sonofabitch."

Castillo's eyes betray the truth of what John has said.

John steps over the window sill. He must find Lena, get her to a doctor. But he has one last question.

"Why do you hate Medina so much."

Castillo's reply hisses, snakelike. "Because he killed my father."

The words hang in the air as John drops to the ground. A church bell tolls. It is ten o'clock in the morning, July 12, 1872. He trades his tired pinto for a fresh horse at the Elephant Corral and lopes back toward Boulder Creek. When he reaches their meeting place, three hours later, he scans the circle of trees. Halfway around, pegged to a tree trunk, he sees it. A small leather bag with a red ribbon, a dangle of hope. He must have overlooked it in last night's stormy darkness. He yanks it down and extracts a folded piece of paper. On it are the words, *I am sick. Going home. Meet me there.*

The note is dated July tenth, two nights ago, right after her escape from St. Mary's. Why did she had run away earlier than planned, he wondered. The fever? Castillo's threats? At least she hadn't changed her mind. But she was sick, dangerously sick.

Thirty more miles to the Crossing. He digs his heels hard into the sides of the borrowed horse.

76

Takansy

Takansy dismounts, tethers Shy Bird to a juniper and unties the ropes that bind her daughter's body. Dawn lightens the edges of the great cloud that sparks and rumbles east of the Crossing. She hefts the leather-wrapped bundle onto her shoulder and staggers into the cave between the leaning sandstone slabs. She has forgotten to bring a shovel. A piece of sandstone will have to do. She finds one the size of a shovel blade and scrapes out a shallow hole. Into this opening she drags Lena's body.

With a rope she forces her daughter's knees close to her chest into a fetal position so Lena can leave the world as she entered it. Joints make cracking sounds as the rope tightens. She grits her teeth to quell rising nausea.

She scoops sand over the body and piles flat sandstone slabs on the mound. By the time she is finished, her hands are pin-pointed with blood. She is close to collapsing.

From her bag she draws Lena's otter pouch, a strand of crimson hair ribbon and a string of tiny bells. She kisses each in turn before placing them on the grave and covering them with one last stone to hold them in place.

Kneeling, she searches for the ancient words of a death song. It quavers out of her and echoes from the sheltering rocks until it dissolves into sobs. She collapses onto the grave and pulls her head to her knees. It crosses her mind that the death chant may be her own.

Shy Bird's whinny jolts her. *Someone's approach?* Panicked, she backs out of the tomb and eyes the mare. She must hurry. She wrestles a tall, thin sandstone slab over the cave opening. With a juniper branch she brushes out her footprints as she retreats toward the horse. She unties Shy Bird and continues back-trailing about twenty paces, brushing as she goes.

Takansy drags herself onto the mare and rides north along the cliff edge toward a second rock cut that connects with the river trail far upstream from where she left it. If her husband is on her trail, she wants him to find her far away from this hiding place. Shy Bird picks her way down, slipping on the still-wet rocks. They arrive at the river trail just as sun rays lance above the great storm cloud. She is spent, a dead woman riding.

She turns toward the Crossing where Medina's rage awaits. The thought of him kindles her own heat. Blaming him is better than dwelling on her own actions.

77

John Alexander

John arrives at the Crossing late in the day, his borrowed horse nearly spent. Hail rims the shadows north of buildings. In the courtyard the Medinas face each other, crouching like wrestlers, mud spotting their clothes.

John dismounts and rushes toward them. Only then do they tear their eyes from each other and look at him. Their expressions send a cascade of dread down his spine.

"Where's Lena?" He fights for calm.

They stare. He shouts the question a second time.

Together they answer—as if rehearsed. "Lena is dead."

John Alexander grabs the saddlehorn to keep himself upright. "Dead?" Denial wells in him, but their haggard faces force it into withering retreat.

Medina advances on him, eyes suddenly hard. "What do you know?" He seizes John's shirt front with both hands, knuckles grinding into John's chest. "You come riding hard, shouting for Lena. What you know about her?"

"Stop! I don't know. Let me go. What happened?"

"For why you look for her?" Medina's eyes are slits.

"I was in Denver City. They said she was gone. I came looking."

John is not a good liar. Medina gives him another shake.

"When you see her last?"

"For God's sake! What's happened to her?" He wrenches free, ripping his shirt, and turns toward Takansy. "Tell me please!"

"The scarlet fever." Takansy's face is dead. She looks through him toward the river.

The finality in her voice is a railroad spike in his head.

He feels Medina grab his shoulder, trying to spin him around. Suddenly enraged, he strikes out with both fists held together like a hammer.

Medina staggers back.

"Where is she, goddammit?"

"Ask her mother." Medina steps toward Takansy, arms swinging at his sides. "Where you have taken her?"

The slap of his hand on her face sounds like a bullet hitting a fence post. Her head snaps back, hair flying. She catches herself, drills him with eyes gone hard.

"My daughter safe from you. You no longer are forcing her where she is not meant to go."

"You help her to run away. If she still at St. Mary's she would be alive. They have good *medicos* there. But you lure her back here. For why? Say it!"

Her face goes white. "The sickness is in that school, not here. You forcing her back where she is unhappy, getting sick. She is dying because of you!" Takansy spits the last word out like a piece of rotten meat.

"You dare to accuse me? You *hija de perra*." Medina's second slap leaves a red mark on her cheek.

The blow barely registers on her wooden face. Her eyes go vacant again.

John steps between them. "You both killed her! Like two dogs pulling on a rag."

Takansy's eyes bore into him. "And you? You, too, are a pulling dog, taking her away."

She knows! John stumbles back. *God save me, I have killed Lena!*

To banish this unbearable thought, he whirls on Medina. "I know how Lena caught the fever."

Everything goes quiet.

"Richard Castillo. Red-top. He tried to...violate Lena. Ten days ago. Grabbed her and pressed himself on her. She fought back, scratched his face. He's in the hospital with scarlet fever. He gave it to her. On purpose."

The shock on their faces changes to relief at finding a new target for their rage.

Medina reaches for his tomahawk. "He is a dead man."

Takansy grabs John's arm. "What you meaning, 'on purpose?'"

John turns to Medina. "Castillo says you killed his father."

Medina goes white.

"Did you? Did you kill his father?"

78

Medina

Medina's knees quiver as the words hit home. An image of Castillo polluting his daughter flashes into his mind. He gropes for something to lean against, and, finding nothing, sinks to the ground.

Silence crowds the courtyard. He must answer, say something to deflect the accusing stares.

"I did not kill him."

His voice quavers, lacking conviction even to his own ears. How does he know for sure? He had meant only to wound, leave a scar. His knife had not penetrated. But how certain could he be? Perhaps he had sliced deeper than intended. He had been angry. Anger, he knows with a terrible sinking feeling, sometimes has a will of its own.

He remembers the young boy rushing to embrace the bleeding patron, remembers the boy's swatch of red hair, his cries of "father, father!," the hatred in his face. Young eyes ablaze with it. Hatred that smoldered through the years and flared again when Medina thrashed him on the trading post porch. *Young Castillo has found his revenge.*

Medina shakes his head and struggles to his feet. John and Takansy are waiting to hear more. They stare at him, two statues. He cannot face them. He needs to saddle up and ride away into the mountains where he can be alone.

79

Takansy

Takansy stares at her husband. Her mind is numb, her body beyond feeling.

John Alexander speaks, his voice pleading. "Where was she when you found her?

She can scarcely concentrate on her answer. "At the river. In the water."

"I must see her. Maybe she's only unconscious. Such things happen...people seeming to be dead and coming back to life." He seizes her shoulder. "Where is she?"

"In the Spirit World."

Medina pushes John's hand away, his face suddenly close. "She must to have a proper burial. You cannot deny her that. Her soul... ."

"Her soul? You controlling her life. You not controlling her soul!" Numbness leaves her. She is angry again.

"Not me! Her soul belongs to Diós, not to Purgatory. Not my

Lena. She must have the last blessing. To rest here, with us." He points to the mound of earth in the hillside graveyard. "For why you take her away? You are the bead-toucher, the one who prays morning and night. How can you deny her the eternal peace?"

Takansy stares past her husband without answering. Jésu has betrayed her. She has no reason to live. The obsidian blade waits.

David M. Jessup

EPILOGUE

John Alexander
June 1946

Why does God allow an innocent young girl to die and keep an old sinner like me alive so long? I am now ninety-two years old, missing most of my teeth and hair, barely able to gimp around of late, and not giving much of a hoot, anyway.

I left Colorado Territory soon after Lena died. I searched everywhere for her, then finally gave up. Seeing the red ridge every morning, riding past the old school, going to the Crossing, all of it reminded me of Lena and my part in her passing. I abandoned my homestead, went back to Illinois and took up teaching for the rest of my working life. I married a gentle young woman, Heather McGill, raised three girls with her until she died ten years ago.

This year, in June of 1946, I talked my youngest daughter, Sally, into driving me back to Colorado in her new Dodge pickup. I wanted to get one more look at the place where joy flitted in and out of my life, leaving me dumbstruck with an ache I've never been able to shake off.

David M. Jessup

Our trip took three days. In 1872, it took over a month. We passed through the town of Loveland, which was a cornfield when I was a boy, and headed west on U.S. Highway 34. According to a young man at a gas station, the road now ran past our old dugout and through the box canyon all the way to Estes Park. Back in my day, you couldn't even hoof it through that canyon if the water was high. The young man looked blank as a post when I asked him about the Crossing.

"The old stage stop and post office," I prompted. "There was a fort there."

"Oh, you must mean Fort Namaqua. Yup, it's still there, pretty much a ruin, now, no roof." He pointed west with the gas nozzle and grinned an eager, buck-toothed grin, glad to help.

Sally spotted the Namaqua sign after five miles and turned left onto a dirt road leading down to the river. Cottonwoods had grown up around the fort. Its walls were blackened from fire, the roof gone. We crossed a new bridge a bit downstream from where I remembered Medina's toll bridge, and on the other side found the hunkered ruins of Medina's barn, trading post and home. The whitewash was gone, and the buildings, once grand to my young eye, seemed shrunk and decrepit.

"You want to stop, Papa?"

"Not here, hon. Maybe up farther."

Sally eased the Dodge up the low hill to the south.

"Stop. There it is." The cemetery was where I remembered it. The wall had gaps where stones had fallen away with trees growing around it. In fact, trees were everywhere, a near forest compared to the prairie I remembered.

I got the pickup door open eased out. Sally tried to hold my elbow.

"I can manage," I said. "I'm not a durned cripple, yet."

She grinned and walked beside me as I snail-paced my way toward the cemetery gate.

The first grave stones bore names I didn't recognize. Then I saw two small ones, side by side, for Martín and Rosita, and next to them a larger stone for *Mrs. Maria Modena, died 12 June, 1874.* Takansy's grave.

"Folks said she died of a broken heart," Mattie had reported in one of her letters. "Lucas Brandt visited her just before she died. She said she was 'going to Lena.'"

The biggest headstone said, *Marianna Modeno, Born 1812, died 28 June 1878.* They never could spell his name right, and Lena wasn't around to spell it for them.

According to Mattie, Medina died from Captain Jack's bullet, never removed, which finally worked its way into his kidney. On his deathbed, Mariano Medina asked Lucas Brandt to "bury me with my big freight wagon, my team of grays and a keg of whiskey." Brandt took it as a joke. I suppose it was.

Not long after Takansy's passing, Susan Howard moved into the Medina place, and in July of 1876, they had a child, Rafaelito.

"It caused quite a scandal," Mattie said. "They got hauled into court for adultery and had to pay a fine." But a year later they got married "all nice and proper in a Catholic wedding after she converted and got herself baptized."

I thought of my own conversion, something I never told anyone. I looked at the Medina graves and wondered if things might have turned out different if the three of us hadn't kept so many secrets.

I felt Sally's hand on my arm. "Papa, you're crying."

"This dry air always makes me tear up." I pulled away and looked among the weeds for Lena's marker. Nothing. Medina never found her secret burial place. "Come, let's go on."

I let Sally take my arm on the way back to the car.

Our next stop was the homestead, the last turnoff before the Big Thompson Canyon. A hand-painted sign said, *Sylvan Dale Guest Ranch.* We drove across a bridge built on new cement pillars. The sawmill was gone, and little white cabins had sprouted up where our garden used to be. For tenters, I guessed. Folks now called them "dudes." Where our dugout once roosted in the river bank stood a lodge with two river-rock chimneys. The upper story had what looked like sleeping rooms, the lower opened onto a big cement porch beside the river. Next to it was a kitchen, judging from the smell of fresh baking that set my mouth a-water as I knocked on the door.

"Come on in!" A woman's voice.

I pushed aside the screen door and found a woman who looked to be in her thirties, a shapely five foot two, with brown eyes, prematurely gray hair and a friendly smile.

"How can I help you?"

"I used to live here a long time ago. My name's John Alexander. That big mountain yonder is named after my Pa. I was hoping I might come in and see if this was the place we lived in."

"Why of course." She waved me in, wiped her floured hands on her apron and brushed back a wisp of hair with her forearm. "I'm Mayme Jessup. Come right in and have a look."

I peered around. "This doesn't seem quite right. Our homestead was dug into the riverbank a little further back than this."

"I think I know where it was." She led me into the next room. "We use this for a pantry. It's the oldest part of the building, built with wood pegs and those old-fashioned square nails. My husband found some old newspapers, 1870s I think, lining some of the shelves when we cleaned and painted this spring."

I took a long look around. It felt right. According to Mattie's letters, Mac died in this room after being mauled by a mama coon who dragged him into the river and held him under until he half-drowned. "He was too old and weak to fight," she said.

Pa sold the place in 1881 and moved to Wyoming. Jennie finally found a husband among the tenters and ended up in California, but divorced after two years. Mama died before the turn of the century, and Pa followed suit a year later. I never saw either of them again. Mattie was my last link to the family, and she died in 1902. I never knew where Robert and Anna got off to.

I took in a deep breath. The room still smelled like a dugout, all earth and must.

"Yes. Yes, this is the place. I wanted to see it one last time."

"Won't you stay and have some cinnamon rolls?" She bustled off behind the counter.

"No thanks. My daughter's waiting outside. We need to be on our way." I turned toward the door.

Quick as a rabbit she thrust a bag of fresh rolls into my hand. "Now you just take these. You and your daughter can enjoy them later."

I thanked her and got into the car. Her smile followed us down the road.

"There's one more stop," I told Sally as we headed back toward Loveland. "May be a little rough."

Sally gave me a look. "Better not put any dents in my Dodge."

When we passed my hideout ridge on the way in, I'd noticed a road angling up the east side past some quarries to the rock cut and hidden valley beyond. No one was in the little guard shack, so I told

Sally to drive on up. She shifted into first and held tight to the steering wheel as we bounced up the incline, crossed the hidden valley and stopped where I told her on the far side.

"Where are you going?" Sally said, as I pulled myself out of the pickup and retrieved my cane.

"Come with me, I may need your help."

It took near an hour to find the hideout, what with me having to stop often to catch my breath. Other than some new bushes and taller trees, the place hadn't changed much. The sandy floor, the rock bench, the protected feeling. Tucked into a rock shelf was a rusty tin, my bone collection. Sally didn't notice it. I let it be.

She touched a tuft of bluebells growing in a crevice. "Wow! This is neat. Why did you want to come back here?"

"It was a secret place I used to come as a boy to be alone. To hide books your grandpa didn't approve of."

She laughed. "I'd sure like the kids to see this. Did you ever show it to anyone?"

I looked at the low spot in the wall where Lena had come and gone. "No. It was just my private place."

We left the hideout and walked along the cliff edge to take in the view of the valley below. New houses sprouted along the river's edge. I breathed the pine-scented air.

"Hope no one ever builds a house up here," I said. "I guess we'd best head back."

As we passed through some jumbled rock slabs I heard a squawking sound. Sally spotted the bird first, a gray jay. It sat in a juniper tree growing over a triangle-shaped opening between two sandstone boulders. We walked closer. The jay squawked a protest and flew off. Sally pulled the tree branches aside.

My heart stood still. A string of tiny brass bells lay at the edge of a pile of flat stones. Next to it rested a scrap of leather with blue and red beads in the shape of an otter. I braced my cane against the tree to keep from falling.

Sally stepped into the cave-like opening. "Look, there are bones in here." She pointed to what looked like two leg bones folded against each other.

"Leave them be."

"But Papa, they almost look human."

"Deer bones. Leave them be."

"But... ."

"I said no!" I poked her with my cane.

She whirled around, eyes wide. "You know something about this. Tell me."

"When we get back to the Dodge. Let's go.

She reached for the bells.

"Leave them."

"Okay, okay. Don't have a conniption." She backed out of the opening and brushed her hands on her jeans.

"Leave me be a minute."

She gave me a frown and walked back down the slope, hidden from my view by a a boulder.

I used my cane to push a rock over the bells and otter pouch. I took off my hat.

Lena, we loved you too much, the three of us. Pulled you apart.

I tossed some juniper berries on Lena's grave and headed back to the pickup.

Historical Notes

The major characters in this book, and most of the minor ones, were real people. Mariano Medina's remarkable life is chronicled in a biography called *Mariano Medina—Colorado Mountain Man*, by Zethyl Gates, Loveland Colorado's historian and librarian for many years. This book is dedicated to her.

"Unrecognized" was the word Zethyl used to characterize Mariano Medina. He never achieved the fame of people like Kit Carson or Jim Bridger, but his life was in some ways even more remarkable. Medina's exploits against Ute raiders and his rescue of the Marcy expedition might have been the stuff of legend, but they apparently didn't capture the fancy of chroniclers who popularized the feats of people like Kit Carson.

Medina made the transition from mountain man to businessman more successfully than most other fur trappers. The tax assessments recounted in my chapter on the school meeting come from actual records. He became the richest man in the Big Thompson Valley during its first twenty years of settlement. That this occurred at a time of prejudice against Mexicans and Indians—the war with

Mexico had ended a scant fourteen years prior to Colorado's gold rush—is extraordinary.

According to Larimer County Court records, Richard Castillo was a real person who suffered a tomahawk attack by Medina in 1864, although my account of their relationship is entirely fictional. (I also took the liberty of changing the date of the assault to better fit my story.)

Captain Jack is fictional, although the Ute raid and the retrieval of Medina's stolen horses are not. According to Gates, Medina died of complications from old bullet wounds suffered in various encounters with Indians.

Little is known of Takansy, although her Catholicism was typical of the Flathead people who went to great lengths to bring Jesuit "Blackrobes" to their homeland on Montana's Bitterroot River in the 1840s.

William Alexander was one of a surprising number of pioneers who settled Colorado, not for gold or ranching opportunities, but for health reasons. His lungs were damaged by a sawmill boiler explosion in Illinois in 1862, after which he came west, discovered the Sylvan Dale Valley, floated down the Platte River on a row boat to retrieve his family, and brought them back the next year to set up a sawmill at the base of what is now Mount Alexander.

John Alexander's culpability in the boiler accident is my doing. His and Lena's attendance together at the Big Thompson School is documented in school district records, but their love story is fictional, as is John Alexander's life, about which little is known. He did visit my mother at Sylvan Dale Ranch in 1946 and ask to see his old homestead. In recounting his visit to me years later, my mother always lamented that she was unable to persuade him to stay and tell more of his story.

I apologize to the descendents of people I characterized as less than admirable in this book. Knowing nothing about them, I hijacked their personalities to serve my story's purpose. That is the fun of being a fiction writer rather than a historian.

Mystery still surrounds the burial of Lena Medina. A long-time resident of Loveland, Al Stevens, reported in a 1973 oral history that a friend of his father often told a story that on the evening of Lena's death, he saw her mother "put Lena's body on the back of a horse with her and ride off with her toward the mountains." This story captured my imagination and became the catalyst for this book as I asked myself: how could such a thing happen?

In the 1930s, an Indian burial site was discovered on a sandstone ridge west of Loveland, but it was unclear whether the bones were male or female. When Larimer County officials moved bodies from Medina's abandoned cemetery to Namaqua Park closer to the Big Thompson River on a cold January day in 1960, only one female body was identified, presumably that of "Indian John" (Takansy).

Efforts are now underway to restore Medina's old cemetery. The owner of the cemetery site has generously donated it to the Loveland Historical Society, and a dedicated group of preservationists are raising funds to create a small park there. They are convinced that Larimer County's excavation (some would say desecration) of the site in 1960 was incomplete, and that based on early photographs of the location of headstones, Mariano Medina's body may still be buried there.

David M. Jessup

About the author...

David M. Jessup co-owns Sylvan Dale Guest Ranch in Loveland, Colorado, where he introduces low-stress, grass-fed cattle raising methods to guests, and guests to the ways of both the old and the new West. A history buff, he is passionate about preserving open space, battling invasive weeds, catching wild river trout on a fly, singing cowboy songs, and telling stories about the American West—some of them true.

Before returning to his family ranch in 2000, David served with the Peace Corps in Peru, worked for human rights in Latin America with the AFL-CIO International Program in Washington, D.C., and collaborated with his wife, Linda, in raising four children and exploring fresh worlds with three grandchildren.

Mariano's Crossing, his first novel, won first place for mainstream, character-driven fiction in the Rocky Mountain Fiction Writers Contest and was selected as a finalist in the Pacific Northwest Writers Contest and the Santa Fe Writers Project.

The ranch website is www.sylvandale.com

Jessup's blog, *Beef, Books and Boots,* can be found at:

www.sylvandale.com/ranch_stories/

David M. Jessup

Book Discussion Questions

With which character do you most empathize, and why?

If you could meet any character in this book and ask him or her one question, who would it be and what would you ask?

What drives Medina, and what obstacles, external and internal, stand in his way? How do his character traits, both strengths and weaknesses, affect his choices?

How does John Alexander change during the course of the book? What motivates him, and how does this motivation affect his choices?

What priorities direct Takansy toward the choices she makes? How does her past influence her choices?

Medina, Takansy and John Alexander have different points of view when it comes to understanding Lena's needs. Whose view did you find most compelling? Least compelling?

Have you ever experienced a dilemma similar to Lena's, of wanting to please different people you care about? How were your choices different than hers?

The poem at the front of the book mentions "Joy's trick." What is Joy's trick, and how does it apply to each of the characters?

What role do landscape and setting play in the story? What did you learn about the period and setting that you didn't know before? Were you caught up in the story's time and place?

What is your favorite scene in the book, and why? What major emotion does the story evoke in you as a reader?

At what points in the book were you most curious to find out what happens next?

What do you think the book is about? What are some of the book's strongest themes?

CPSIA information can be obtained at www.ICGtesting.com
Printed in the USA
BVOW072212240912

301196BV00005B/2/P